THE HUM BUG

THE HUM BUG

a novel

Harold Schechter

POCKET BOOKS

New York • London • Toronto • Sydney • Singapore

This book is a work of fiction. Names, characters, places and incidents are products
of the author's imagination or are used fictitiously. Any resemblance to actual events
or locales or persons, living or dead, is entirely coincidental.

 POCKET BOOKS, a division of Simon & Schuster, Inc.
1230 Avenue of the Americas, New York, NY 10020

Library of Congress Cataloging-in-Publication Data

Schechter, Harold.
   The hum bug : a novel / Harold Schechter.
     p. cm.
   ISBN 0-671-04115-0
   I. Poe, Edgar Allan, 1809-1849—Fiction. 2. Barnum, P.T. (Phineas Taylor),
1810-1891—Fiction. 3. Barnum's American Museum—Fiction. 4. New York
(N.Y.)—Fiction. 5. Authors—Fiction. 6. Museums—Fiction. I. Title.

   PS3569.C4776 H86 2001
   813'.54—dc21

                                      2001133040

First Pocket Books hardcover printing November 2001

10 9 8 7 6 5 4 3 2 I

POCKET and colophon are registered trademarks of
Simon & Schuster, Inc.

For information regarding special discounts for bulk purchases, please
contact Simon & Schuster Special Sales at 1-800-456-6798 or
business@simonandschuster.com

Printed in the U.S.A.

For
THE AMAZING KIMIKO!

That Prince of Hum Bugs, BARNUM, so it appears
Some folks have designated me for several years—
Well, I don't murmur; indeed, when they embellish it,
To tell the truth, my friends, I rather relish it.

—P. T. Barnum

HISTORICAL NOTE

In 1841, after years of struggle as an itinerant showman, Phineas T. Barnum managed to wangle possession of a run-down natural history museum on the corner of Broadway and Ann Street in Manhattan. Within two years, he had transformed this musty taxidermical warehouse into America's premiere entertainment showplace—a four-story emporium of wonder, packed with a staggering array of exhibits, from human "curiosities" to mechanical marvels, opera singers to performing fleas, waxwork figurines to live jungle creatures. By the middle of the decade, Barnum's American Museum was the most popular attraction in the city—the direct forerunner of all the modern amusement complexes to follow, from Coney Island to the Magic Kingdom.

Whether Barnum actually delivered the famous saying attributed to him—"There's a sucker born every minute"—remains open to question. Still, there's no doubt that "America's greatest showman" had a large streak of the sideshow huckster in him. To excite attention and bring in the crowds, he concocted a never-ending string of publicity stunts, including a series of spectacular hoaxes, or "hum bugs" as he called them. Barnum, however, didn't mean to scam the public. "We study to please" was his lifelong motto. And indeed—though customers paid good money to view supposedly genuine mermaids that turned out to be blatant fakes and a "Great Model of Niagara Falls" that was really a dinky, eighteen-inch miniature operated by a trickle of recirculating water—they rarely came away feeling cheated.

Once inside the museum, they always got their money's worth of fun, thrills, and excitement.

Indeed, the kind of "hum bugs" Barnum relished were a staple of American popular culture in the mid-nineteenth century. One of the most famous hoaxes of the time was an ostensibly factual newspaper account of a trans-Atlantic balloon flight, reportedly accomplished in three days by a crew of intrepid "aëronauts." This story, which appeared in a special edition of the New York *Sun,* created a sensation among the public, who had no idea that it was a complete fabrication.

Though we don't often think of him as a practical joker, the author of this famous "balloon hoax" was none other than Edgar Allan Poe—who, in the spring of 1844, moved from Philadelphia to New York City, where he and his wife found temporary lodging in a boarding house on Greenwich Street, just a few blocks away from Barnum's American Museum.

Part One

THE PRINCE OF HUMBUGS

CHAPTER ONE

"True!—*vexed*—very dreadfully vexed am I. But why will you say that I am *mad?*"

"Because you *are* mad at something, Eddie darling," my young wife endearingly insisted, pausing in the task that had engaged both her energies and attention since our return from breakfast. This was the mending of a small but conspicuous tear in the seat of my trousers, sustained when—upon arising from the communal dining table—I had somehow managed to snag the fabric in a small splinter of rattan protruding from the caning of my chair.

"I can't imagine why you're being so sulky," Sissy observed in a gently reproving tone. "Particularly after dining on such heavenly food." Seated in the capacious armchair that occupied a corner of our room—my perforated garment spread across her lap—she reapplied herself to her needlework while continuing thusly: "I sincerely hope, however, that you haven't worked yourself into a state over this teensy little hole. Your pants will look as good as new once I've worked my magic upon them."

This remark—uttered in a spirit of such pure, such artless devotion—could not fail to lighten, if not entirely dissipate, the angry cloud of gloom that had settled so weightily upon my soul. Garbed in the dressing gown I had donned after divesting myself of my trousers, I gazed warmly at my seraphic soul-mate and whimsically declared: "I fear, darling Sissy, that even your unsurpassed skills as a seamstress cannot restore my attire to such a *pristine* condition—not indeed, unless the needle you wield with such consummate dexterity were the magic wand of the fairy enchantress in Perrault's immortal tale of 'Cendrillon,' who—with a single incantation—could transform a mere gourd of the variety *Cucurbita pepo* into a magnificent coach-and-four."

Though meant as a pleasant *riposte*, this latter remark bore more than a tincture of all-too-bitter truth; for—owing to my badly straitened circumstances—the garment upon which Sissy was "working her magic" was in a sadly deteriorated condition, even apart from the injury it had suffered that morning.

"Still," I continued, "it is not this unfortunate—and exceedingly inopportune—mishap that has so unsettled my tranquility."

"Then what in the world has?" Sissy exclaimed, her voice betraying the merest hint of impatience.

In his magisterial (if occasionally ponderous) *Philosophical Discourses on God, Man, and Destiny,* no less an authority than Gottfried von Büchner observes that the most significant occurrences in human history have often sprung from mundane, if not entirely trivial, causes. So it proved with the extraordinary sequence of events it is my present purpose to recount. In attempting to trace the origin of these wild—these *unparalleled*—adventures, I am led inexorably back to that seemingly unremarkable morning on which Sissy and I engaged in the foregoing talk. Before proceeding with my narrative, therefore, I must pause to acquaint the reader with the train of circumstances leading up to the above-cited exchange.

My name is Edgar Allan Poe. For several years prior to the commencement of my tale, I had been residing in Philadelphia with that heaven-sent pair to whom I owed whatever measure of felicity I have known in this life. I mean, of course, my darling wife and soul-mate, Virginia, and her mother, my Aunt Maria Clemm, toward whom I felt all the ardor—the gratitude—the sheer, overpowering *devotion*—of an adoring son. Completing our household was our handsome female tabby, Cattarina, a creature of such beguiling habits and preternatural intelligence that she was treated less as a mere pet than as a fourth and much-beloved member of the family.

Within the sacred sphere of my domestic circumstances, I enjoyed a nearly perfect contentment. The situation, however, was markedly different as regards my professional affairs. These, indeed, were of a most unsatisfying—a most *insupportable*—nature. In my capacity as editor of *Graham's Lady's and Gentleman's Magazine*, I had managed to increase the circulation of that publication more than fourfold in the two years of my employment. And yet, my accomplishments had received neither proper recognition nor adequate remuneration from the owner. On the contrary. While Mr. Graham had profited mightily from my unceasing labors on behalf of his enterprise, my own salary had remained fixed at the pitiable rate of $800 per annum—a sum entirely insufficient for the support of myself and my dependents.

Equally egregious was my employer's increasing interference in matters pertaining to the editorial *content* of the magazine. In particular, he had begun to offer vociferous complaints about the ostensibly insulting character of my critical views—especially my opinions on the deplorable state of American letters, as well as on the generally vulgar and unformed sensibilities of the public at large. That the occasional asperity of my tone resulted from a sincere desire to *elevate* the still-rudimentary tastes of my countrymen seemed to matter not a whit to Mr. Graham, whose only concern was to pander to the vanity of his subscribers by assuring them of their (supposed) cultural superiority. At length—perceiving that, despite my most determined efforts, the magazine was fated to degenerate into yet another namby-pamby assemblage of cloying illustrations, gaudy fashion-plates, treacly love stories, and other such sentimental clap-trap—I saw no choice but to resign my position.

As the home of the immortal Dr. Franklin—founder of the first lending library in America, great benefactor of our first public university, and himself the author of a classic (if, at times, overly pedantic) autobiography—Philadelphia held an illustrious position in the intellectual history of our nation. It had been many years, however, since it could claim preeminence as a center of literary production and publication. That distinction now belonged to the great, bustling metropolis that lay one hundred miles to the northeast. With few or no prospects of employment in the so-called (but, in my experience, sadly misdesignated) "City of Brotherly Love," I thus made the bold resolution to abandon Philadelphia altogether and seek my fortunes among the brash, ambitious literati of New York.

My plan—arrived at in consultation with my loved ones—was to depart at once in the company of my darling wife. Muddy* would remain behind with Cattarina, joining us as soon as Sissy and I had located—and established ourselves in—a suitable dwelling. Accordingly, late on the afternoon of April 5, 1844, Sissy and I—after bidding a fervent farewell to our dearest Muddy—took a hack to the Walnut Street railroad station. After a wait of approximately forty-five minutes—during which we sat in loving proximity on a hard wooden bench, perusing the most recent edition of the *Philadelphia Ledger*—we boarded a train to Perth Amboy, New Jersey. From thence, we set out by steamboat for Manhattan, arriving at our destination on the afternoon of April 6, during an exceedingly violent thunderstorm.

Owing to the severity of the weather—as well as to the somewhat fragile state of Sissy's health—I thought it best to leave my dear wife snugly ensconced on the boat, while I went off in search of a lodging house. After stowing our trunks in the Ladies Cabin, I embarked on my quest, stopping first to purchase a blue cotton umbrella from a sidewalk peddler for the somewhat exorbitant price of sixty-two cents. Thus shielded against the driving sheets of rain, I made my way along Greenwich Street and, within minutes, had come upon a somewhat weatherworn but perfectly respectable-looking lodging house, not far from Cedar Street. A room had just become vacant, which the landlady, Mrs. Morrison, was willing to rent at an exceptionally modest rate, considering the desirable location of the house as well as its abundant amenities. We quickly reached an agreement, whereupon I secured a hack and returned to the wharf for Sissy. Alto-

---

*Note: The affectionate sobriquets "Sissy" and "Muddy"—as applied respectively to my darling wife, Virginia, and devoted mother-in-law, Maria—reflected the singular bonds of tenderness—sympathy—and sheer, exalted *love*—I shared with these two angelic creatures, who occupied a place in my heart far surpassing that of mere *cousin* and *aunt*.

gether, I had not been gone for more than half-an-hour, and she was quite astonished to see me back so soon. With the help of the driver, I loaded our trunks into the carriage; then off we drove to the lodging house.

Settled into our new accommodations, we supped—slept—then arose much refreshed and descended to breakfast. While I would not—*contra* Sissy—have characterized our morning meal as heavenly (it being impossible to conceive of such substantial fare as pertaining to the incorporeal realm of the seraphim), it was unquestionably delicious. We had excellent-flavored coffee, hot and strong; elegant tea cakes; a great dish of ham and another of cold veal slices; eggs; cheese; bread-and-butter—and everything in the greatest profusion. I could not recall the last time I had dined so heartily at breakfast (or, indeed, at any other period of the day).

Had this feast been enjoyed solely in the company of our landlady and her husband—a fat, good-natured old soul with a remarkable growth of fleecy, gray whiskers—I would have felt utterly contented. Regrettably, there were a half-dozen other boarders at the table, among whom was a hollow-chested, anemic young clerk named Griswald, who conducted an unintermitting monologue during the course of the meal, despite the fact that his mouth was continuously stuffed with partially masticated food. Even more than the irritating timbre of his voice, the unsightliness of his appearance, and the deplorable quality of his table-manners, however, it was one particular subject of his conversation that had so upset me during that otherwise splendid repast.

Now, as I sat in our room beside Sissy—who had temporarily suspended her sewing while awaiting my reply to her somewhat exasperated query—I recalled her attention to that singularly irritating personage. "The blame for my present, disgruntled mood," I observed, "may be laid to the individual who was seated directly across from us at breakfast."

"Mr. Griswald?" Sissy asked, her expression, no less than her tone, conveying genuine surprise. "He did go on a bit. But on the whole, he seemed like a pleasant enough young gentleman."

"I cannot concur with your opinion, dearest Sissy, having found his incessant chatter, no less than his etiquette, intensely disagreeable."

Casting me a mischievous look, my darling wife replied: "Are you sure that you aren't just jealous of all the attention he was giving me?"

"I do not fault him for that," I answered with an indulgent smile. "For such are your charms, dear Sissy, that no man—not even the most boorish—could fail to fall under their spell." This observation was no less than simple truth, for—at twenty-three years of age—my Virginia had ripened into a surpassingly radiant specimen of womanhood, whose hyacinthine hair—flawless complexion—brilliant brown eyes—harmoniously curved nostrils—and sweet, dimpled mouth—combined to create a vision of loveliness more wildly divine than the fantasies which hovered about the slumbering souls of the daughters of Delos.

Flushing with pleasure, Sissy returned to her needlework while stating: "Well, then, I am at a complete loss to explain your crabby mood."

"Do you recall the main subject of young Griswald's conversation?" I inquired.

"Of course," Sissy answered. "He was talking about his recent visit to Mr. Barnum's American Museum. I must say, it sounds like fun."

"If by fun," I replied somewhat caustically, "you intend to signify all that is most vulgar, sensational, and unredeemed by the merest whit of aesthetic value, then I cannot take issue with your statement."

"But you seemed interested in hearing about it, too," Sissy protested. "Didn't you ask to borrow that handbill he was showing around?"

"Very true. The item to which you refer can be found in the right front pocket of my trousers. And if you consult it, you will discover the source of my present distress."

"There!" Sissy exclaimed at that moment, biting off the excess length of thread with her small—remarkably white—and perfectly regular—front incisors. "Now let's see what has made you so grumpy."

Reaching into the pocket I had specified, she extracted a folded sheet of paper, then handed me my trousers. I saw at once that these had been repaired with a skill that would have drawn envious sighs from the swift-fingered spinners of the Kingdom of Han, whose silken cloth—according to legend—was woven with such exquisite art that the Emperor Wang-Fo himself felt unworthy to wear a robe fashioned from it.

In consideration of Sissy's maidenly sensibilities, I had, throughout the course of our marriage, maintained the highest standards of modesty and decorum in my relations with her. Now—in keeping with this practice—I stepped into a far corner of the room, outside my dear wife's line of vision, before divesting myself of my dressing gown and donning my newly mended pants. I then reseated myself on the edge of our bedstead.

Sissy, in the meantime, continued to peruse the handbill, an expression of intense, childlike pleasure suffusing her face. All at once, she looked at me with wide, scintillant eyes. "What fun!" she exclaimed. "Just listen."

Redirecting her gaze to the handbill, she began to read aloud in a voice that trilled with excitement: *"Come see P. T. Barnum's American Museum! The largest amusement enterprise on the face of the globe! A palace of marvel, mystery, and wonder! Novel and astounding exhibitions comprising more than 50,000 curiosities from every portion of the globe, among which are—the Amazing Murray Midgets, the most diminutive triplets in the world!—Minnie-Christine, the renowned two-headed lady!—Hoomie and Iola, the wild Australian children!—Big Hannah and Big John, the two heaviest people ever known to exist!—Crowley the Man-Horse, Nature's most astounding freak!—Waino and Plutano, the Wild Men of Borneo!—Signor Giovanni and his remarkable troupe of bird actors!—Dr. Hall's Eskimo dog!—A living, three-horned bull!—The Grand Aquarium!—Miss Zobeide Luti, the Circassian Beauty!—Count Borulawski's Bohemian glass-blowers!—"*

Interrupting her recitation, she glanced up at me again and said, somewhat breathlessly: "Doesn't it sound *grand?*"

By way of reply, I screwed my features into an expression of extreme distaste.

"So far as I can see, Eddie," Sissy declared in a gently chiding tone, "there's nothing here that should have upset you in the least. Do you know what I think? I think you just have trouble taking pleasure in things."

"You are wrong, Sissy," I replied. "There are many things from which I derive the deepest—the most intense—pleasure, not the least being your own dear self. What I do not appreciate, however," I continued, "is having the sacred memory of a beloved friend exploited for the most crass, pecuniary reasons by a self-confessed charlatan."

"Why, whatever do you mean?" my darling wife cried, her alabaster brow furrowing in confusion.

"If you examine the bottom portion of Mr. Barnum's advertisement," I stated, "you will find out."

Obeying my directive, she turned her gaze to the designated place and, after examining the page silently for a moment, read: *"Among the numerous exhibitions of unique educational, historical, and scientific interest, visitors will find such singular attractions as a splendid specimen of a living Ourang Outang from Borneo!—A child with one body, two arms, two heads, and four legs!—More than one hundred wax figures of noted personages, including one of Lieutenant-General Scott!—A curious mortuary memorial to William Henry Harrison, ten feet high and composed of over two million sea shells!—The head and right arm of Anton Probst, murderer of the Deering family, amputated after execution!—Phrenological examinations and charts by Prof. Livingston!—A diorama of the heroic death of Colonel David Crockett, including his actual 'buckskin' clothing, his celebrated rifle 'Ol' Betsy,' and his final farewell letter from the Ala—"*

At that instant, she broke off her recitation with a sharp intake of breath—raised her head—and, in a voice barely louder than a whisper, gasped: "Oh, dear." That the dismaying truth had finally dawned upon her awareness was sufficiently plain from her expression.

"So, dear Sissy," I said with a mirthless smile, "there at last is the answer to your question. *Now* do you see why I am mad?"

CHAPTER TWO

Nearly a decade had elapsed since Colonel David Crockett perished among the martyrs for American freedom at the Alamo mission in San Antonio, Texas. Even prior to that tragic event, the frontiersman had attained a nearly legendary status in the hearts of his countrymen. His heroic demise upon the battlements of the tiny, desperately besieged fortress—where, according to the most authoritative accounts, he had been one of the last defenders to die while wielding his rifle as a battle-club—had resulted in his virtual *apotheosis*. In the pantheon of American demigods, the name of Crockett now shone with no less a radiance than those of Washington, Jefferson, and other of our nation's immortals.

That Crockett had met his end in such a glorious way I could well believe, having witnessed at firsthand his capacity for dauntless courage—martial prowess—and sheer, physical audacity.* Though more than cognizant of his all-too-human frailties—his relentless self-aggrandizement, his frequently uncouth deportment, and his astonishing verbosity (which could, on occasion, render his company tiresome in the extreme)—I had, in the brief but memorable course of our acquaintanceship, come to regard him with a warmth of feeling that surpassed mere *affection*. Indeed, within the precincts of my heart, Crockett commanded a place only slightly less exalted than those enjoyed by my dearest relations.

---

*As recounted in my earlier chronicle, *Nevermore*.

It was for this reason that I possessed an intense, if not overpowering, aversion to everything that threatened to debase his memory. In the years since his demise, the marketplace had been flooded with a veritable torrent of tawdry merchandise relating to the celebrated frontiersman. These products included shoddy publications, often issued under Crockett's own name, which purported to recount his previously undisclosed exploits; crudely rendered lithographic images, depicting Crockett in various situations of Indian warfare and wilderness adventure; and even, in some cases, small, hand-painted, wooden figurines of the frontiersman arranged in assorted, wildly dramatic poses. To be sure, I recognized that Crockett himself—whose sensibilities, as regards cultural matters, were vulgar in the extreme—would most probably have perceived these cheaply manufactured articles as "splendiferous" tributes to his memory (to employ one of his own favorite honorifics).

Even Crockett, however—whose virtues included a manly and unwavering moral integrity—would undoubtedly have bridled at the imposition upon his adoring public of a shameless fraud involving his heroic sacrifice at the Alamo. And it was for this reason that I found myself exercised to the point of outrage at the brazen deception which—as I had just discovered—Mr. P. T. Barnum was even then carrying out at his wildly popular establishment.

My knowledge of this remarkable individual was based entirely on what I had read about him in the newspapers. This, however, was a considerable amount. For Barnum's great success derived not merely from his tireless acquisition of all that was most wondrous—strange—and sensational in the world, but from his genius (if I may employ the term so loosely) at exciting public notice. Barely a week went by without some item about "The King of Showmen" appearing in the press. Indeed, in comparison to his unceasing self-promotion, the extravagant boasting of my late companion, Colonel Crockett, seemed positively restrained.

Barnum had first achieved prominence—or, more correctly, *notoriety*—as the exhibitor of an exceedingly wizened female named Joice Heth, whose age, according to his claims, was estimated at 161 years! Even more than her longevity, however, it was her purported life-history that made this shriveled, nearly mummified, crone so extraordinary; for, if Barnum was to be believed, Joice Heth had been the devoted nursemaid of no less an eminence than George Washington himself! For the price of a mere twenty-five cents, visitors to Barnum's gallery could not only view this ancient prodigy, but hear her perform—in a voice still vibrant and melodious—the very lullabies she had crooned to the future president at bedtime. So utterly convincing were her fond reminiscences of her "dear little Georgie" that even the most inveterate skeptics found themselves persuaded of her authenticity. It came as a shock, therefore, when—following her death in Bethel, Connecticut, after a prolonged illness—a postmortem examination established beyond question that she could not have been older than eighty years of age.

The ensuing scandal would have put an abrupt and mortifying end to the public career of any other man. In Barnum's psychological constitution, however, the elementary capacity for *shame* appeared to have been replaced by a gift for unbounded *audacity*. Far from causing him the slightest personal qualm or embarrassment, the extensive publicity he received from the Heth affair only emboldened him to perpetrate an even more outlandish deception upon the ever-credulous public. This was the grotesque—the flagrant—the utterly infamous—hoax known as the "Feejee Mermaid."

For a period of several weeks during the summer of 1842, papers throughout New York City carried feverishly excited stories announcing the forthcoming exhibition of a genuine mermaid that had been captured by a whaling captain in the South Pacific waters. These articles were invariably accompanied by highly detailed engravings depicting a voluptuous female with the lower half of a fish and the upper torso of a singularly well-endowed (and fully unclothed!) young woman. It need scarcely be said that the prospect of viewing this prodigy at firsthand elicited the greatest and most intense excitement among the residents of the city (particularly its male population).

When the wildly eager throngs turned up at the exhibition hall to ogle this wonder, however, they were startled to discover—not the living, resplendent siren that had been so extensively advertised—but a blackened, dessicated, hideously malformed taxidermical specimen that had evidently been fabricated by sewing the tail of a large ocean fish onto the upper body of a mummified baboon. Once again, however, the uproar over Barnum's latest "humbug" only served to bring him to the forefront of the public's attention and bolster his reputation as a personage of extraordinary "gumption" (a quality much prized by my countrymen).

Now—as Sissy continued to regard me with a look of intense *perturbation*—the fingertips of her delicate right hand pressed to her half-parted lips—I reminded her of these and other equally brazen frauds associated with the notorious Barnum.

"The fellow is incorrigible," I cried, leaping to my feet and beginning to pace about the floor. "In this instance, however, he has carried his chicanery too far!"

"But, Eddie," Sissy replied, "from all that I've read about Mr. Barnum, he spares neither effort nor expense in securing the most wonderful rarities for his museum. Perhaps the items he has advertised really *did* belong to dear Colonel Crockett."

"Even if that were so," I declared, "my sense of indignation would be no less extreme. For in that case, Mr. Barnum would be guilty, not of simple fraud, but of outright *desecration*. Just think of it! Should those garments be the actual clothing worn by my late comrade at the time of his death, they could only have been obtained by stripping them from his sadly mutilated body—in much the same, ignominious manner that the battle armor of the noble Hector was removed from his corpse by the vaunting Achilles during the final siege of Ilium!"

At this, perhaps overly vivid analogy, Sissy's lily-white complexion grew, if possible, even paler.

"Moreover," I continued, gesturing with my chin toward the circular clutched in Sissy's hand, "I possess incontrovertible proof that the document described in that handbill as Crockett's 'final farewell letter from the Alamo' cannot possibly be as advertised."

"And what proof is that?" Sissy inquired.

By way of reply, I crossed the room, knelt before my trunk, and—after rummaging briefly through my belongings—removed a small, casket-shaped box of antique mahogany that lay carefully wrapped among my garments. This object had served for many years as a kind of "treasure chest," containing an assortment of mementos which—though of no *intrinsic* worth—were priceless in respect to their sentimental value.

Carrying this receptacle to the bedstead, I set it down upon the mattress, raised its burnished lid, and took from its interior a small, folded, exceedingly wrinkled piece of paper. I then turned back toward Sissy and, opening this item, held it up so that she could see what it was: a single-page letter, written in a strong (if somewhat clumsy) hand with a stubby lead pencil.

"What's that?" Sissy asked, her face registering extreme perplexity.

"Do you not recognize it?" I said. "It is the letter which Colonel Crockett sent to me from Texas, shortly after his arrival in the village of San Antonio de Béxar." Here, I paused and emitted a melancholy sigh. "By the time it made its way into my hands, its author had already suffered the awful pangs of brutal, violent death."

"Of course," Sissy exclaimed. "I'd forgotten all about it." Clasping her hands together and pressing them to her bosom, she said in a beseeching tone: "Oh, Eddie, it's been so long since I heard it. Please read it to me."

With an acquiescent nod, I positioned myself so that the table lamp cast its glow directly upon the somewhat faded print of the letter. I then moistened my lips and began to read:

"Dear Eddie—I expect you will be almighty surprised to get this letter, but I'll be shot if you ain't been on my mind lately. I am down here in Texas. Blamed if it ain't the garden spot of the world, with prime land and heaps of timber and the clearest springs and the splendidest range and game aplenty. I have thrown in my lot with a passel of patriotic Americans who have made up their mind that there ain't nothing more worth dying for than liberty and independence. Colonel Travis is our leader, and I'll be kicked to death by grasshoppers if he ain't a regular rip-snorter. I have also made the acquaintance of Colonel Bowie of Louisiana whose name has been given to a slam-whanger of a knife that is now in general use throughout the southwest. We are shoving off at daybreak tomorrow for the Alamo mission, which we have vowed to defend with the very last drop of our life's blood. I know just what you are thinking. You

are thinking—'Why, Davy, what kind of thundering hornets nest of trouble have you gotten yourself into now? Why don't you just skedaddle out of there before them Mexican hellhounds come down upon you like a hurricane in a cornfield?' Well, Eddie, there is no use in preaching to me. You might just as well sing psalms to a dead horse as try to persuade me to cut and run. For if there is anything that would render death pleasant to a brave man, it is his country's freedom. Just let them pestiferous varmints try to drive us out of here. We'll tame them! Well, old hoss, it is time for me to go. I trust you are well. Send my respects to your purty wife, Miz Virginny, and your dear Aunty Maria. Your pard—Davy Crockett."

Having arrived at the conclusion of the letter, I glanced up at Sissy and saw that her eyes were moist with tears.

"Poor Colonel Crockett," she said in a tremulous voice. "He was such a brave, exceptional man."

"Indeed," I said, my own voice husky with emotion. "It is unlikely that the world shall ever witness his like again." After pausing for a moment to regain my composure, I cleared my throat and continued thusly: "Here, then, is the incontrovertible proof to which I alluded moments earlier. For there can be no doubt whatsoever that *this*, and no other document, is Colonel Crockett's final letter from Texas."

"But isn't it at least *possible*," Sissy replied, "that he wrote another, even later, message before he perished?"

"The likelihood of such an occurrence is so minuscule as to be nonexistent," I asserted. "For between the time this note was composed and the final fall of the Alamo, the mission was under constant, ferocious siege by the merciless forces of General Antonio López de Santa Anna. To imagine that any man—even one as insouciant in the face of imminent destruction as Colonel Crockett—would have devoted himself to letter-writing under such dire circumstances strains the very bounds of credulity."

"It *does* seem unlikely," Sissy conceded. *"Still—"*

"Well," I said, perceiving that a particle of doubt remained entrenched in my dear wife's mind, "there is only one way to find out. We must pay a visit to Mr. Barnum's establishment."

CHAPTER THREE

Nearly a week elapsed before we were able to put our plan into effect. This delay was occasioned by Sissy's poor health. To the undiscerning eye of the casual observer, my darling wife was the very image of youthful bloom and vivacity. And yet, her glowing appearance was deeply deceptive. Hers was a most delicate—a most fragile—constitution. Always vulnerable to illness, she had been rendered even more so by the physical demands of our journey, as well as by the emotional strains of our enforced separation from Muddy. These enfeebling circumstances—added to the deleterious effects of the damp, unseasonably raw weather to which she had been exposed—caused her to be seized by a sudden, violent *grippe*, whose onset occurred only hours after our foregoing talk regarding Colonel Crockett.

For the next several days, Sissy remained entirely prostrate, while I passed many long, wearying hours seated at her bedside, ministering as best as I could to her needs. I applied cool, moist compresses to her feverish brow—fed her spoonfuls of the fragrant tea and savory chicken *consommé* prepared by our exceedingly solicitous landlady—and beguiled the time by reading to her from Thomas Crofton Tyler's collection, *Traditional Faerie Legends of the English and Scottish Peasantry*, a work which had come into my possession the previous October, when I had been asked to review it for Mr. Graham's magazine. Knowing Sissy's fondness for old wives' tales concerning goblins, faeries, and other such colorful beings, I had—after completing my assignment—given her Tyler's entertaining (if somewhat carelessly assembled) volume, and it had quickly become one of her favorites.

Late in the afternoon on the third day of her illness, I was seated in the rocking chair, reading aloud from Tyler's book. The tale, as I distinctly remember, was "The Stolen Child," about an infant boy abducted by evil faeries who leave a grotesque, changeling baby in his place. As I reached the part of the narrative where Tyler describes this uncanny being—a deformed, dwarfish creature with "black, shaggy hair, greenish-yellow skin, and hands like the claws of a barn-owl"—Sissy (whose symptoms, until that moment, had been limited to a moderate fever, a sick headache, and severe nasal congestion) broke into a violent cough.

Alarmed by this development, I waited until the paroxysm subsided, then threw on my cloak and hurried out onto the still-rainswept streets. Proceeding along Greenwich Street, I almost immediately came upon a small but exceedingly well-provisioned pharmacy, where, after a brief consultation with the proprietor, I purchased a bottle of Mayhew's Miracle Cold Remedy—"a pleasantly flavored tonic" (according to the information printed on its label) "certain to drive all the poison germs of illness from the bloodstream!—bring buoyancy of spirit in place of lassitude and despondency!—procure the sleep so necessary to the brain and nervous centers!—and allow the overtaxed system to start fairly on the road to health!"

With this medication in hand, I hastened back to our lodging-place and—after borrowing the appropriate utensil from our landlady—went upstairs and gave Sissy the prescribed dosage of four tablespoons. Her features wrinkled in extreme distaste as she swallowed the bright, chartreuse-colored fluid. Its effect was nearly instantaneous. Within minutes of imbibing it, Sissy's eyelids grew heavy—her respiration assumed a placid regularity—and she fell into a deep and peaceful slumber.

Curious as to the chemical composition of this remarkably efficacious potion, I poured a small quantity into a tumbler and took a sip. What was my surprise at discovering that Dr. Mayhew's elixir was little more than potent, spiritous alcohol, blended with an admixture of chemical ingredients that endowed it with a singularly repellent, medicinal flavor. Small wonder, I thought dryly, that such an ardent brew would have an intensely soporific effect on Sissy, a creature of such sheer, angelic purity that she has never so much as *tasted* inebriative liquor.

My own nerves having been badly overtaxed by my worries over Sissy's health, I replenished the tumbler with another portion of Dr. Mayhew's medicament and quaffed it in a single gulp. Though unspeakably foul-tasting, the concoction had an intensely pleasurable effect, producing a sensation of voluptuous warmth that coursed through every fiber of my being. After helping myself to one final measure of the liquid, I retired for the night and, within minutes, subsided into a profound—though not entirely untroubled—sleep.

In my dreams, I found myself wandering through a dark, dense, singularly dreary forest. At length, I came upon a little clearing, at the the center of which stood an ancient and moss-shrouded tomb. Pausing to examine this grim, timeworn monument, I saw—to my inexpressible horror—that the letters engraved in the crumbling stone spelled: VIRGINIA CLEMM POE.

A groan of the uttermost despair arose in my throat. At that instant, something clutched at my shoulder—I felt a violent shaking—and, opening my eyes, I found myself gazing directly up at Sissy, whose pale, lovely countenance was arranged into an expression of the deepest concern.

"Wake up, Eddie," she gently urged. "You've been having another nightmare."

Overwhelmed with relief at the realization that the ghastly sepulcher I had beheld was nothing but a mere, mental *phantasm* (born, no doubt, of my anxiety over Sissy's health), I struggled into an upright posture and inquired as to her condition. Words can scarcely convey my delight when I discovered that (owing less to its supposed medicinal properties than to the long, unbroken slumber induced by its inordinately strong alcoholic content), Dr. Mayhew's cure-all had indeed produced a most beneficial effect on my wife. Like the heroine of the well-known wonder tale, "Sleeping Beauty," Sissy had awakened from her protracted repose with a feeling of nearly complete refreshment and renewal.

We spent the rest of that day indoors, the weather outside remaining overcast and chilly. The following morning, however—Friday, April 12—the heavens were clear, the sun glowed with a singular brightness, and Sissy felt sufficiently recuperated to desire an outing.

"I feel as if I've been trapped inside *forever*," she declared. "Let's go and have some fun!" And so, donning our street clothes, we descended onto the teeming pavements of the city and proceeded to make our long-deferred visit to Barnum's American Museum.

Gotham—as New York had been denominated almost from the time of its inception—was, in the view of its most ardent admirers, the foremost municipality in existence: a place of unparalleled excitement, dynamism, and variety. To others, however, it possessed all the defects of a vast, sprawling metropolis without any of the redeeming graces that characterize such ancient cities as London, Paris, and Rome. It was to this latter, deprecatory class of individual that I myself belonged. Though professional considerations had necessitated my current move to New York, I counted myself among its harsher critics. I had long viewed Manhattan as little more than a noisome hive of vulgar ambition and raw commercial activity, inimical in almost every way to the physical—moral—and spiritual well-being of its inhabitants.

Now—as Sissy and I strolled along Broadway on our way to Barnum's establishment—all of my prejudices were confirmed by the countless noxious *stimuli* that assaulted us from every quarter: the throng and rush of the traffic—the deafening clatter of carts, carriages, and coal-wagons—the intolerable din of iron horseshoes striking the cobblestones—the coarse profanities of the teamsters and omnibus-drivers—the cacophonous shouts of clam-vendors, newsboys, and street-merchants—the hordes of pedestrians, hurrying along in inexplicable confusion—the roving herds of scavenging pigs—the insufferably dirty sidewalks—the malodorous aroma of garbage, human effluvia, and horse-manure that pervaded the atmosphere.

Even the handsome conveyances of the city's mercantile elite—with their escutcheoned panels and liveried coachmen—smote harshly upon my nerves; for these flagrant displays of ostentatious wealth only served to remind me of my own, pitiably straitened circumstances. Owing to Sissy's illness—which had kept me at her side since our arrival from Philadelphia—I had been unable to commence my search for remunerative work, and I was only too painfully aware that my wallet contained our entire fund of monetary resources: a sum amounting to slightly less than ten dollars, barely enough to support us for another fortnight.

In spite of these vexations, however, I could not help but feel a large measure of contentment in my present circumstances. After all, the sky was a pure, pellucid blue—the sun beat down with a beneficent warmth—and (save for a slight, vestigial sniffle) my darling wife appeared to be completely recovered. Glancing over at Sissy as we promenaded along the great, bustling thoroughfare, I felt my bosom expand with an unaccustomed surge of happiness. I was embarked on a new, exhilarating phase of life. Unprecedented opportunities for literary success and recognition awaited me. And—though Broadway was full of striking young ladies, garbed in the most fashionable attire—the radiant being walking at my side was, by far, the loveliest of them all.

CHAPTER FOUR

Unhappily, my buoyant mood was not destined to last. Indeed, I could feel it begin to evaporate the moment we came in sight of our destination.

Occupying the corner of Ann Street and Broadway, the American Museum stood directly opposite the hallowed precincts of St. Paul's church and diagonal to the celebrated Astor Hotel. Both of these edifices—the venerable house of worship and the elegant hostelry—exuded an air of perfect dignity and stateliness: an effect which only served to underscore the exceptional vulgarity of Barnum's establishment.

The building was five stories high. Its rooftop sported scores of colorful international flags that floated and flapped in the breeze. Looming over these brightly variegated banners was a gigantic lighthouse lamp whose powerful beam swept the city every evening, illuminating Broadway from the Bowery to Niblo's Garden. Enormous letters—painted in a particularly vivid hue of cherry-red—blazoned the name of the proprietor across the upper expanse of the façade; while the entire exterior was bedecked with literally hundreds of oval paintings of every imaginable species of bird, beast, and reptile: lions and gnus, pelicans and polar bears, ostriches and rattlesnakes, elephants and hippopotami, peacocks, ant-eaters, alligators, and giraffes.

From the balcony that encircled the entire third floor, a four-piece brass band—consisting of an E-flat bugle and three mismatched trombones—sent a cascade of surpassingly inharmonious music down upon the street. To judge from the unholy discord produced by these instrumentalists, Barnum's purpose in employing them was not to *lure* customers into his establishment, but rather to *drive* them inside in order to escape the deafening cacophony.

Standing before this exceedingly garish structure, I was plunged into a mood of bitter reverie. So this, I grimly reflected, is the celebrated American Museum. What a grotesque—an *outrageous*—misnomer! By rights, the word "museum" should be reserved for such glorious institutions as the Uffizi or the Louvre: great palaces of art housing a nation's most sublime cultural treasures. But here, among my own, hopelessly boorish countrymen, the term is used to signify a place of crude sensationalism, crass entertainment, and carnival excess. Why, this monument to American philistinism bears as much relation to the Louvre as the brazen frippery of a harlot does to the coronation gown of an empress! Is it any wonder that, in a nation of such vulgar—such *debased*—sensibilities, the true artist finds himself in a condition of near-total obscurity and extreme material privation?

At that instant, I felt a gentle tug on my coat sleeve and, glancing over at Sissy, saw that her face was aglow with a look of pure, childlike pleasure. "Oh, Eddie," she exclaimed. "Isn't it splendid?"

Though somewhat disconcerted to find that my own precious wife had thus succumbed to the tawdry allure of the flamboyantly embellished building, I had no wish to dampen her excitement. Imbuing my voice with all the enthusiasm I could muster, I replied: "Indeed, it is a most singular edifice."

"Hurry," she cried, pulling me by the arm. "I can't *wait* to get inside."

A buzzing crowd of visitors—men, women, and children, their faces, like Sissy's, infused with a look of delighted anticipation—stood in line before the building. Taking our place at the rear of this formation, we slowly made our way toward the entrance. At length, we arrived at the ticket booth; whereupon, I discovered, to my great consternation, that the cost of admission was twenty-five cents per adult—a shockingly exorbitant sum in my present circumstances.

Still, I reminded myself, it was a small enough price to pay for my beloved wife's happiness. Indeed, to purchase even a few hours of pleasure for my darling Sissy, I would gladly have spent ten—nay, a *hundred!*—times the amount. Extracting my wallet from my pocket, I counted out the requisite fee. Then, tickets in hand, we passed through the curtained entrance and crossed the threshold into Barnum's vast emporium of curiosities.

Once inside, we found ourselves within a long, narrow, brightly illuminated hallway. Stationed at the far end of this corridor was a tall, middle-aged gentleman with a bulbous nose and receding brown hair, who was cradling an armful of octavo pamphlets bound in paper covers of bright peacock blue. To reach the exhibition space proper, visitors were required to make their way past this individual, in much the same way that the traveler to ancient Thebes could only enter the city by first getting beyond the sinister, chimerical creature that guarded its gateway.

"Programs for sale!" he cried, waving one of the blue-colored publications in the air like a newsboy brandishing an "extra." "A complete guide to the grandest museum ever conceived by mortal man! Indispensable facts on more than 5,000 objects of wonder! Fully illustrated with hundreds of lifelike engravings! Only fifteen cents today, reduced from twenty-five!"

I was somewhat astonished to see how many of these slender and (to judge by their outward appearance) cheaply manufactured booklets were bought by the happily chattering patrons as they filed past the bulbous-nosed fellow. In many cases, the purchaser was a family man, accompanied by a wife and several children. This meant that— before he had so much as set foot inside the exhibition halls—he had already expended a considerable sum.

Intending to draw Sissy's attention to this remarkable fact, I turned in her direction. I immediately perceived that she was gazing toward the middle-aged "hawker" with an exceedingly *wistful* expression. Such was the intense—profound—and long-established—bond of mental and spiritual intimacy that existed between Sissy and myself that I had no difficulty in construing the meaning of this expression.

"Shall I buy you one of those souvenir programs, dear Sissy?" I gently inquired.

Looking up at me eagerly, she exclaimed: "Do you really think we can afford one, Eddie?"

The dictates of absolute honesty would have compelled me to reply in the negative. But to deny such a simple gift to my darling wife—a person who asked for so little, endured so much, and gave so unstintingly of her love—was unthinkable.

"The cost is a mere pittance," I said, "when measured against the pleasure you will undoubtedly derive from the purchase."

Subduing the spasm of anxiety that seized me as I made the transaction, I extracted a dime and five pennies from the rapidly dwindling sum in my wallet, exchanged the coins for one of the gaily colored pamphlets, and handed the latter to Sissy, who beamed with pleasure as she took it in her hands.

"Just look at how happy you've made her, my friend," the middle-aged vendor remarked jovially. "And that's just for starters! Welcome to the greatest amusement enterprise on the face of the earth!"

As it happened, the purchase proved to be an exceedingly practical one—for, without it, many of the museum's wildly eclectic contents would have remained utterly bewildering to us. Only with the information provided in the guidebook could we know that the battered wooden object on display in the Natural History Salon was (supposedly) the actual aboriginal war-club used to slay Captain Cook. Or that the large oaken splinter exhibited inside a jar in the Room of Heroes was (presumably) a piece of the door from Christopher Columbus's birthplace. Or that the length of badly twisted metal standing in a corner of the Hall of Scientific Knowledge was (ostensibly) one of Dr. Franklin's original lightning rods. Even so, we often found ourselves entirely overwhelmed by the sheer, chaotic *profusion* of the myriad attractions, curiosities, and artifacts we encountered as, for the next several hours, we wandered from one exhibition hall to the next.

There were Roman statues, Grecian urns, and Egyptian mummies in their elaborate sarcophagi. Medieval suits of armor were displayed alongside Indian totem poles and ivory carvings fashioned by Alaskan Esquimo. There was a cavernous natural science room, containing a vast collection of preserved insects and butterflies, minerals and crystals, seashells and corals, mounted skeletons, anatomical specimens, and stuffed birds and beasts of every imaginable variety. There was a dizzying array of optical, scientific, and mechanical implements, many of surpassing ingenuity—telescopes and microscopes, kaleidoscopes and thaumatascopes, camera obscuras, dissolving views, galvanic batteries, and a knitting machine powered by steam. There were dioramas, panoramas, cycloramas, and cosmoramas. The world's greatest cities—Paris and Dublin, London and Rome, Jerusalem and Istanbul—were re-created in miniature in astonishing detail. Waxwork figures of celebrated historical personages—Julius Caesar, Napoleon, Thomas Jefferson, Moses, Daniel Boone—were arranged in dramatic tableaux. And then there were the countless, unclassifiable novelties, curiosities, and relics—a great ball of hair removed from the belly of a sow, a top hat made of broom splints by a lunatic, the bedroom curtains of Mary, Queen of Scots, George Washington's shaving brush, a troupe of performing fleas, the skeleton of a chicken with four legs and three wings, and infinitely more.

Barnum's celebrated menagerie contained a formidable assemblage of exotic beasts—from armadillos and anacondas to wombats, yaks, and zebras. Although much impressed by their sheer number and variety, I had reason to doubt the absolute authenticity of several of these creatures—in particular, a large, rather docile-looking primate identified in the guidebook as "The Ferocious Mountain Gorilla of Equatorial Africa! Captured at fearful risk to life and limb and transported to America at enormous cost! The only living specimen ever exhibited in this country!" To my own eyes, the beast appeared to be a singularly lethargic member of the species *Papio anubis,* or common baboon. The menagerie also featured the exceedingly popular attraction known as "The Happy Family"—a collection of living cats and rats, owls and mice, hawks and sparrows, and other natural enemies that had somehow been trained to coexist with one another within the confines of a single cage.

The furred and feathered denizens of the menagerie were not the only living attractions in Barnum's museum. Far from it. Human performers and concessionaires could be found throughout the establishment: ventriloquists and contortionists, phrenologists and mesmerists, fortune-tellers and clairvoyants, magicians and jugglers. Professor Rosco Pym, "taxidermist extraordinaire," had a booth on the museum's second floor, where he conducted a brisk business among the owners of recently deceased dogs, cats, parrots, and other household pets. Upon their arrival, the bereaved could drop off the remains of the dearly departed and, after spending several diverting hours touring the museum, pick up the freshly mounted specimens, "restored" (so the guidebook promised) "to an uncannily lifelike state." There was Mme. Rockwell, the "world-famous petrologist," who—by gazing into a small, polished gemstone—was "capable of foretelling events with astonishing accuracy." Visitors could marvel at the lightning-fast computations of Dr. Elmo Hutchins "the human calculator"—thrill to the lively vocalizations of "Uncle Frank" Brower and his Virginia Minstrels—delight in the melodious tintinnabulation of Mr. Johann Flieck and his Swiss Bell Ringers—gape at the extraordinary pantomimes of Signor Antonio Blitzo, the "living statue"—and purchase any one of dozens of delicately wrought *objets,* fresh from the kilns of Count Josef Borulawski and his Bohemian Glass Blowers.

And then, of course, there was Barnum's Hall of Human Oddities, containing his world-renowned collection of giants, dwarfs, living skeletons, bearded ladies, Siamese twins, and other freaks of nature. These remarkable specimens of human malformation were undoubtedly the single most popular attraction at the museum. Deterred partly by the sheer number of people awaiting on line outside the hall—and partly by the exceedingly tender-hearted sensibilities of my darling wife, who felt equally torn between curiosity and repugnance at the prospect of viewing these grotesque anomalies—Sissy and I decided to forgo this experience, at least for the present.

For myself, the most intriguing attractions of all were those uncanny figures that managed to render indistinct the normally well-defined boundary between the living and the inanimate. I refer, of course, to Barnum's unparalleled assemblage of rare *automata*—machines so cunningly contrived as to simulate, with almost preternatural accuracy, the motions and appearance of actual life. These astonishing inventions included the surpassingly realistic "Duck of Vaucanson." When wound by a key, this life-sized mechanical fowl ate and drank with avidity, performed all the quick movements of the head and neck which are peculiar to the duck, and even produced the sound of quacking in the most natural manner.

Even more remarkable was the miniature coach invented by Monsieur Pierre Bourdieu for the amusement of Louis XIV when a child. This exquisitely crafted little vehicle, measuring no more than six inches, was drawn by two wooden horses. One window being down, a lady was seen in the backseat. A coachman held the reins, and a footman and page were in their places behind. Upon the activation of a small switch, the coachman cracked his whip, and the horses proceeded in a perfectly natural manner, drawing after them the carriage. Having reached the uttermost limit of the tabletop upon which it was displayed, the vehicle drew to a halt, the page descended and opened the door, the lady alighted and curtsied politely to the audience. She then reentered. The page put up the steps, closed the door, and resumed his station. The coachman whipped his horses, and the carriage was driven back to its original position.

As remarkable as these automata were, however, they could not compare to the world-famous Chess-Player of Baron Maelzel, a device of such seemingly fantastic ingenuity that it had been declared by men of great general acuteness and discriminative understanding as the most astonishing mechanism ever contrived by the human mind. I had read much about this wonderful invention, and now—as Sissy and I stood among a large gathering of spectators, watching a display of its apparently miraculous powers—I studied its operations with a singular intensity.

For those who have never witnessed Maelzel's Chess-Player at firsthand, a brief description of this marvel will be appropriate. The automaton itself is in the shape of a Turkish sultan, garbed in a loose-fitting robe of multicolored silk and wearing a plumed turban. This exceedingly realistic mannequin is seated behind a large maplewood cabinet which is mounted on brass castors. The front of the cabinet is hung with a single door equipped with a silver lock plate. An ordinary chessboard, conventionally arranged with the usual pieces, sits atop the cabinet directly in front of the mannequin.

Maelzel himself—a portly little fellow with remarkably fat, florid cheeks and an abundant growth of chin-whiskers—begins the exhibition by displaying the inside of the mechanism to the audience. With a great flourish, he takes from his pocket a small, silver key, unlocks the cabinet, and throws it open to the inspection of all present. Its whole interior is apparently filled with wheels, pinions, cogs, springs, and levers—all crowded so densely together that the thought of any person being concealed inside seems utterly preposterous.

Leaving the compartment door open, he then swivels the apparatus entirely around and exposes the rear of the Turkish figure by lifting up its robe. A small metallic hatch, about ten inches square, can be seen in the middle of the mannequin's back. Pulling open this hatch, Maelzel exposes the inside of the mannequin, which—like the cabinet—appears to be completely full of machinery.

Returning the apparatus to its original position, Maelzel then announces that "Sultan Osmani" (as the Turkish figure is denominated) will play a game of chess with anyone disposed to encounter him. The challenge being accepted by an audience-member, a chair is set up at the table across from the mannequin, and the volunteer takes his place. Maelzel then winds up a large brass key protruding from the back of the figure, activates a switch in the rear of the cabinet, and the contest commences.

The game proceeds as follows. After the human challenger has made his move, "Sultan Osmani" appears to consider his options. At length, it raises its left hand (which is gloved and bent in a natural way) and brings it directly above the selected chess-piece. After a momentary pause, the hand slowly descends upon the piece, the fingers receiving it without difficulty. The automaton then slides the piece to the desired position on the board. At every movement of the automaton, the *clack* and *whir* of the interior machinery can be heard distinctly by the spectators.

In the particular match witnessed by Sissy and myself, "Sultan Osmani's" human challenger was a young, rather cadaverous-looking fellow with pince-nez eyeglasses, who plucked nervously at his lower lip as he studied the board intently between each of his moves. Sissy and I had been observing this contest for nearly fifteen minutes when she turned to me and exclaimed: "How marvelous! Have you ever seen anything like it, Eddie? What a genius the baron must be!"

Not wishing to say anything that would diminish my dear wife's delightfully ingenuous pleasure, I merely pursed my lips and uttered a noncommittal sound. Then, taking her by the elbow, I said: "Come, Sissy. Judging from its current pace, this game is likely to continue for a considerable period of time. Its outcome, moreover, is virtually pre-determined, since—from all that I have read about Maelzel's device, the Chess-Player rarely, if ever, loses a match. There are numerous ex-hibits we have yet to see, including the one that constitutes the pri-mary goal of my visit."

By this time, we had been at the museum for nearly three hours and had thus far seen all but the fifth and topmost floor. Now, arm in arm, Sissy and I ascended the handsome marble staircase. As we reached the landing, I saw that the salon directly facing us was packed with another sizable crowd, nearly as dense as the one we had wit-nessed at the Hall of Human Oddities. Curious as to the nature of this exhibition, I asked Sissy to consult her guidebook.

"It's the Hall of Crime and Punishment," she replied after briefly perusing the pamphlet. "Here's what it says in the book: *This exception-ally interesting display contains more than thirty-five waxworks tableaux, represent-ing in minutest detail some of the most ghastly acts of murder, bloodshed, and atrocity in recorded history. Also on view is an unparalleled collection of torture implements and execution devices, including a rack, thumbscrew, ducking stool, strappado, gibbet, branding iron, and working guillotine. The proprietor wishes to emphasize that this exhibition is presented solely in the interest of public enlightenment and moral edifica-tion, the object being to impress upon the viewer the awful consequences of crime, and the swift retribution certain to befall all those who violate the Lord's stern command-ment:* Thou Shalt Not Kill!"

Though intensely eager by this point to view the relics pur-portedly belonging to Colonel Crockett, I found my curiosity piqued to an extreme degree by this description. I therefore pro-posed to Sissy that, before proceeding to our ultimate objective, we take several moments to examine the contents of this grimly in-triguing gallery.

"I *knew* you'd be interested in seeing it," Sissy remarked in a gently chaffing tone. "If I live to be a hundred, Eddie, I'll never understand how someone so sweet can be enamored of such horrible things."

"Indeed, it is a most paradoxical phenomenon," I replied, taking my wife by the hand. "For while it is indisputably true that the ghastly—the morbid—and the *fearful*—exert an irresistible enchantment upon my soul, the contemplation of Ideal Beauty—such as you yourself embody in the highest degree, darling Sissy—is the source of my deepest pleasure."

"Oh, Eddie, you say such nice things," my wife exclaimed, squeezing my hand affectionately. "Come, then. Let's see this highly educational show. I must warn you, however, that—when it comes to torture and bloodshed—my stomach is considerably more sensitive than your own."

"Rest assured, dear wife," I said, leading her by the hand toward the gallery entranceway, "that, should anything cause you the slightest unease, we shall exit at once."

Unlike the rest of the museum, which was brilliantly lit by countless wall-mounted gas jets, the cavernous hall we now entered was shrouded in gloom. A half-dozen elaborately wrought *torchéres*, bearing four-branched candelabra and stationed at wide intervals around the periphery of the floor, provided the sole illumination. Their feeble gleams served to render sufficiently distinct the waxworks tableaux, punishment devices, and other items on display, while investing the room as a whole with a suitably *dismal* atmosphere.

The mood of the visitors seemed equally somber. Up until this point, I had been struck by the pervasive sounds of gaiety—the excited chatter, merry laughter, and exclamations of delight—that echoed through the museum. Here, in this shadowy chamber, a funereal hush prevailed, broken only by an occasional horrified ejaculation, gasp of dismay, or startled intake of breath.

As Sissy and I moved around the hall, pausing before each of the displays, she clutched my arm nervously. On several occasions, she was compelled to avert her eyes from the grisly scenes of horror depicted so realistically in wax. Here—sculpted with startling anatomical accuracy—were exceedingly lifelike effigies of the world's most inhuman fiends, committing deeds of appalling cruelty: the Roman madman Nero, disemboweling his own mother, the Empress Agrippina—Countess Elizabeth Bathory of Hungary, performing her ghastly ablutions with the blood of a sacrificed virgin—Gilles de Rais, Marshal of France, applying a branding iron to the naked flesh of an agonized child—Peter Stubbe, the German lycanthrope, gnawing on the forearm of a freshly butchered victim.

More recent atrocities were also represented. One diorama portrayed the notorious murderess, Hortensia Howard, who had killed no less than sixteen husbands by pouring molten lead into their ears as they slept. Another depicted the infamous "river pirate," William Burckhardt, responsible for shooting, stabbing, bludgeoning, and otherwise disposing of an estimated one hundred unwary travelers along the Mississippi. Yet a third showed the horrible butchery of the two Adams children who had been savagely attacked by a vagrant named Ludlow while disporting themselves in a forest meadow outside Bedford, Massachusetts.

I have already stated that this gallery was *thronged* with visitors. For this reason, we rarely had a completely unimpeded view of the displays—a circumstance somewhat irritating to me, though of little consequence to Sissy, who (even when her vantage point was relatively unobstructed) cast only a few fleeting glances at the lurid tableaux. As we approached the far end of the exhibition hall, I observed a crowd of even greater magnitude than usual congregated around the final diorama.

"Mr. Barnum has evidently put something of particular interest on display over there," I remarked to Sissy. "I wonder what it can be."

"I shudder to think," she answered.

Something in her voice caused me to regard her closely. Even in that dismal light I perceived that her face looked decidedly *wan.*

"Are you feeling ill, Sissy?" I inquired solicitously.

"I just find this gallery very disturbing, that's all," she replied somewhat wearily.

"Then we shall leave it at once!" I declared. "Though the sheer number of people gathered about that display—no less than their air of rapt fascination—has excited my curiosity to an exceptionally high pitch, your own happiness and well-being are, as ever, my paramount concern."

Elevating herself on tip-toe, Sissy applied a gentle osculation to my left cheek—an act of such flagrantly public affection that I instantly felt a flush of embarrassment suffuse my countenance.

"Dear Eddie," she exclaimed, "you are always so good to me." Then taking me by the arm, she said: "If you really wish to see it, we can stay."

"Are you certain?" I asked.

"Absolutely," she replied with an emphatic nod. "I'll be fine."

With my dear wife's hand looped through the crook of my arm, we crossed the floor and took our place on the periphery of the crowd. At length—the intervening spectators gradually dispersing—we arrived at a position of close enough proximity to observe the diorama clearly. I saw at once why *this*—of all the waxen displays in the room—had attracted such intense and wholesale interest.

The scene before us was indeed a most arresting—a most *appalling*—sight. Sprawled across a blood-soaked bedstead in the center of a lavishly appointed boudoir was the fearfully mutilated corpse of a singularly beautiful young woman whose rich, reddish-brown tresses bore a striking similarity to my own darling Sissy's. She was scantily garbed in a silken *peignoir.* From her careless state of *dishabille*—which exposed to the viewer's gaze a shockingly frank glimpse of her snowy-white bosom—it seemed evident that the victim was a woman of questionable virtue. It was impossible, however, to conceive of any sin she had committed that would have merited the dreadful fate she had suffered.

She had been attacked in the most fiendish way imaginable by a hatchet-wielding assailant. Her throat had been *hacked* with such savage ferocity that she was very nearly decapitated, her head retaining its connection to her body by the merest thread of flesh. Both of her forearms had been similarly—though even more completely—mutilated, the hands having been utterly severed from the wrists. Her arms—which terminated in gore-imbrued stumps—were extended at her sides. As horrific as these injuries were, however, they were exceeded in sheer *grotesquerie* by one final, ghastly detail: a single, long-stemmed rose inserted between the tightly clamped teeth of the victim, whose lips were drawn back in a rictus of agony.

The perpetrator of this atrocity—a dark-haired youth, wrapped in a voluminous cloak—could be seen in the rear of the room, effecting his escape through the wide-flung bedroom window. In one hand, he clutched the dripping murder implement; in the other, a blood-stained canvas sack which bore the victim's hacked-off extremites—the gruesome mementos of his crime. His otherwise handsome face—turned so that he could take one final look at his awful handi-work—was contorted into an expression of sheer, infernal triumph. The anonymous sculptor of this scene had outdone himself in regard to both the exceptionally lifelike appearance of the figures and the astonishing verisimilitude he had achieved in his simulation of the victim's unspeakably grisly wounds.

It was unnecessary for me to consult either Sissy's guidebook or the explanatory placard resting on a wooden tripod beside this diorama to recognize it as a singularly lurid re-creation of the infamous Ellen Jennings murder. This crime had taken place slightly more than a year earlier, in late January 1843. So sensational was the story of the beautiful young prostitute, slain by an insanely jealous paramour named Lemuel Thompson, that—although it occurred in Manhattan—it had been extensively reported in newspapers throughout the country. I myself had kept abreast of the case—from the discovery of the horribly butchered body to the arrest, trial, and conviction of the perpetrator—by perusing the nearly daily accounts printed in the *Philadelphia Inquirer.*

Only weeks before Sissy and I embarked on our journey to New York City, Thompson had gone to the gallows, albeit not without many protestations of innocence. On the scaffold—moments before the hangman drew the bolt that sent the hooded prisoner plummeting to oblivion—Thompson had called down a bitter curse upon the people of Manhattan, who had cried so vociferously for his blood. He would return from the grave and haunt the city, he vowed, becoming in death the monster he was falsely accused of having been while alive.

So engrossed was I in my contemplation of the gruesome tableaux before me that I had temporarily become oblivious of Sissy's presence. All at once, I became cognizant of an insistent tugging on my arm. Turning in my dear wife's direction, I was startled to perceive that her countenance was wrought into an expression of extreme distress.

"Sissy, what is the matter?" I asked in alarm.

"I was wrong when I said I'd be fine," she said in a weak, tremulous voice. "This is all just too, too awful for words. Oh, Eddie, get me away from this dreadful sight at once, or I fear that I shall faint!"

CHAPTER FIVE

Prominently posted throughout the museum were garish signs, inviting patrons to visit the "aerial garden"—"an oasis of pleasure"—according to these placards—"where customers may enjoy a splendid rooftop view of the city while refreshing themselves with a delicious glass of lemonade or dish of ice cream."

It was to this ostensible garden of earthly delights that—after hastening her away from the offending display—I ushered my darling Sissy. Climbing a narrow flight of stairs, we emerged into the late afternoon sunlight, where—in place of the promised "oasis"—there stretched before us a tar-papered expanse of rooftop, outfitted with a dozen tables, a few earthen pots filled with wilted geraniums, and a rickety refreshment stand manned by a dyspeptic-looking fellow perched on a wooden stool.

Under ordinary circumstances, this latest evidence of Barnum's boundless capacity for shameless misrepresentation would have filled me with the utmost outrage and indignation. At present, however, my only concern was for my dear wife's well-being. Leading her to one of the vacant tables, I helped her into a chair, then immediately repaired to the refreshment stand, where I purchased (for the predictably exorbitant price of ten cents) a large glass of chilled lemonade.

Carrying this back to Sissy, I placed it in her slender, slightly tremulous hands, then seated myself beside her and fixed her with a worried gaze as she slowly imbibed the revivifying beverage.

"How do you feel, Sissy dear?" I anxiously inquired after a few moments.

Setting the partially drained tumbler down upon the table, she looked at me and sighed: "Much better now. I felt really dizzy for a moment."

"I hold myself entirely to blame," I exclaimed. "It was exceedingly thoughtless of me to have subjected you to such a gruesome display, particularly in your still-recuperative condition."

"It *was* awfully upsetting," she said after taking another sip of her lemonade. "I remember reading about that poor, fallen creature in the papers." Here she shuddered visibly, as though the ghastly spectacle of the horribly butchered woman were once again present before her eyes. "I don't know which was worse—that horrid wax figure with its throat all mangled and its hands chopped off, or the sight of all those people taking such enjoyment from it."

"Tender-hearted as you are, darling Sissy, the dread fascination exerted by such gruesome displays must forever remain a mystery to you," I replied. "Suffice it to say that the great majority of men have always taken a morbid pleasure in grisly scenes of violence. This is by no means to imply that the human soul is, in essence, hopelessly depraved. For it is a paradox of our nature that the bestial and the sublime are mysteriously interwoven within us. Thus, the most highly advanced civilizations have often been among the most brutal. Within the soaring architectural splendors of the Roman Colosseum, savage gladiatorial combats and other unspeakable entertainments were staged for the delectation of the masses; while a gentleman of Shakespeare's day might attend, on the same afternoon, a performance of *The Tempest* and the public dismemberment of a condemned criminal. Indeed, if there is any consolation to be derived from the exhibit we have just viewed, it is in the recognition that our modern society has advanced to the point where we are satisfied with simulated representations of sensational violence, and no longer insist on seeing the real thing."

"I suppose you're right," Sissy said, albeit with a distinctly dubious note in her voice. "But if you don't mind, Eddie, I'd just as soon not even *think* about that awful exhibit anymore." Closing her eyes and tilting her face to the sun, she added: "Mmmm. The fresh air feels so *nice*."

And indeed—though Barnum's "aerial garden" had all the grace of a Bowery oyster-saloon; though the "splendid view of the city" was largely obscured by the looming bulk of the rooftop Drummond lamp; and though the overall tranquility of the setting was severely marred by the hideous din wafting up from the brass band on the balcony several floors below us—a sense of the deepest contentment welled up within me as I sat there in the sunlight, observing the beatific expression on the face of my darling Sissy.

At length, she opened her eyes, picked up the lemonade glass, quaffed its remaining contents, and smacked her lips with pleasure. "Anyway, I don't want you to fret about me," she said brightly, her spirits now fully recovered. "I can't remember the last time I've had so much fun. There are just so many wonderful things to see here."

"Indeed," I said in a tone not entirely devoid of irony, "in regard to sheer *quantity* at least, Mr. Barnum cannot be accused of defrauding his patrons."

Picking up the guidebook which she had set down on the table, Sissy began to leaf through its pages. All at once, she paused in her perusal and exclaimed: "My goodness! It says here that there's a real, live changeling on display in the Hall of Human Oddities! Listen: *This remarkable being, no bigger than an infant of six months of age—though with a thatch of coarse, coal-black hair, a mouth full of abnormally large teeth, and eyes that seem to burn with a preternatural intelligence—was reputedly discovered one morning by an Irish peasant-couple named O'Malley in the simple oaken cradle where, on the previous evening, their angelic newborn son had lain. Its insatiable appetite, incessant crying, refusal to sleep, and generally abominable behavior persuaded the heartsick parents that, sometime in the middle of the night, their beloved baby boy had been stolen by evil goblins and replaced with this monstrous homunculus. Overwhelmed with grief and repugnance, they resolved to destroy the evil creature by burning it in the hearth fire. The village constable getting wind of their plan, however, the strange child was removed from their custody. Eventually, Mr. Barnum, having learned of its existence, acquired it at enormous expense. It is now on permanent display in the Hall of Human Oddities where visitors may decide for themselves if, as has been claimed, it is truly a member of the goblin tribe!*"

Gazing up wide-eyed at me from the guidebook, Sissy exclaimed: "Isn't that strange, Eddie? You were just reading me that faerie story about a changeling baby. Do you think this one could be *real?*"

Smiling indulgently, I replied thusly: "While the belief in goblins, faeries, and other such strange and secret people continues to hold sway in certain portions of the world, no convincing evidence of their existence has ever been adduced. It is far more likely that this anomalous being is some poor, singularly malformed child whose unfeeling parents could not tolerate his presence and—rather than be burdened by its upbringing—sought to dispose of it by any means possible."

Glancing upward, I took note of the sun's position, then rose from my chair and continued thusly: "I perceive that it is growing late. If we intend to view the articles that constitute the main reason for our visit, I suggest we do so at once. Would you care to accompany me, Sissy dear, or would you prefer to remain here and rest a bit longer?"

"I am much too curious," Sissy said, getting to her feet. "Anyway, I feel one hundred percent refreshed."

Crossing the rooftop to the staircase, we returned once more to the fifth floor, where, with the aid of the guidebook, we quickly located Colonel Crockett's ostensible belongings in a glass-fronted cabinet situated in a remote corner of the main hallway.

My suspicions were confirmed in an instant—for I needed but a glance to see that the exhibited garments could not possibly have been those of the fabled frontiersman. Though Crockett's raw physical power and colorful personality had endowed him with a larger-than-life aura, he was, in truth, a man of only average height. By contrast, the clothes before me, though resembling in their general *style* the buckskins I had seen Crockett wear on several occasions, were nearly large enough to fit one of Barnum's giants—an accurate reflection, perhaps, of the epic stature Crockett had assumed in the minds of his countrymen in the years since his death, but in no wise corresponding to his actual, physical dimensions while alive.

The fraudulence of the accompanying letter—presumably composed by Crockett in the days immediately prior to his martyrdom—

was equally flagrant. While its deeply patriotic sentiments were ones to which the frontiersman would undoubtedly have subscribed, its exceedingly ornate and perfectly grammatical language bore no resemblance whatsoever to the crude, if colorful, diction of the semi-literate backwoodsman.

"It is as I suspected," I said in a voice that quivered audibly with indignation.

"Those clothes *do* look awfully big for Colonel Crockett," Sissy mused aloud.

"And this letter!" I exclaimed with a derisive snort. "It is nothing but another of Barnum's blatantly fabricated 'humbugs'! To think that this elegant missive could have been written by the meagerly educated backwoodsman. Why, these phrases about *'the indefeasible, hereditary rights of man'* and *'the demonstrable superiority of the representative system of government'* might have flown from the pen of Thomas Paine!"

"What will you do, Eddie?" Sissy inquired.

"My sense of outrage is such that I cannot forebear to take immediate action. I intend to seek out Mr. Barnum and demand that he remove this forgery from public view."

"Right now? But where will you find him?"

Taking the booklet from Sissy's hands, I rapidly leafed through its pages until I came upon the information I was seeking. "Here," I said pointing to the relevant passage. "According to this guide, the proprietor's office is located in the basement." Returning the publication to Sissy, I added: "Will you come with me, Sissy?"

After a moment's reflection, she shook her head and said: "I don't think I want to be there in case you two have an argument. It will get me too upset. Maybe I'll return to the menagerie for a bit. We went through it so fast that I didn't really have a chance to see everything."

"Very good," I said. "Let us say, then, that we will meet in front of the lion's cage thirty minutes from now."

Having agreed upon this arrangement, Sissy and I descended the grand staircase together as far as the second floor, at which point, she took her leave and went off in the direction of the menagerie—while I continued my journey into the deepest reaches of the building.

Having arrived at the foot of the descent, I paused to get my bearings. Before me stretched a wide, dimly illuminated corridor, lined with barrels, crates, and a heterogeneous assortment of Barnum's surplus curiosities, from a stuffed African ostrich to a mummified Egyptian crocodile to a plaster-of-Paris replica of Michelangelo Buonarotti's world-famous statue of David, complete in every detail (albeit with the addition of a discreetly placed fig leaf).

At first, the basement seemed devoid of any human presence but my own. All at once, however, my finely attuned auditory faculties detected the muffled but unmistakable noise of human vocalization, emanating from a source only a short distance away. Following this sound, I soon arrived at a paneled wooden door standing partly ajar. Through the opening, I could make out with perfect clarity two male voices engaged in an animated exchange. One of these voices—which rang with a singular self-assurance and vivacity—had a strangely familiar ring to it, though I could not for the life of me recall where I might have heard it before. There was nothing particularly remarkable about the other fellow's manner of speech, apart from a slight linguistic defect that caused him to articulate the letter *r* as though it were a *w*. It was this second, far less impressive-sounding personage who spoke as I halted before the doorway.

"But can it possibly be real?" he inquired, his tone a perfect admixture of skepticism and credulity.

"I have seen it with my own eyes, Parmalee!" answered the sonorous voice of the other. "It is a marvel, I tell you! One of Mother Nature's inexplicable wonders!"

"And you say it comes from *where?*" the man named Parmalee eagerly inquired.

"Direct from the river Nile, m'boy. Colonel Bancroft, the gent who procured it, is—or rather *was*—a famous world-traveler. Gave no more thought to circumnavigating the globe than you or I think about taking an omnibus down Broadway. It was during his last trip to El Gizeh that he purchased the creature from an old A-rab fisherman. Paid a pretty penny for it, too. Not a doubt in his mind, you see, that he'd make all his money back—plus a thousand times *more*—by exhibiting the creature once he returned to the good old U.S. of A. Unfortunately for him—though not necessarily for *you*—he was stricken with a rare, semi-paralytic disorder upon his return from Egypt. Poor fellow can barely stagger across the room. Terrible thing to witness. He is desperate for money, you see—needs it to pay his physicians—and is willing to let the creature go for a song."

"And this Bancroft can be trusted?"

"The man's word is his bond!" replied the other somewhat indignantly, as though the honor of a friend had been impugned. "His handshake is more secure than a notarized contract. You can rest assured, m'boy, that the little fish is of a most astonishing formation. Within six weeks from the time of your purchase, it is absolutely guaranteed to pass through an amazing alteration by which its tail will disappear, and it will then have *legs!*"

"But such a thing is guaranteed to cause a sensation," Parmalee exclaimed. "It will startle the naturalists—wake up the whole scientific world—and draw in the masses! It cannot help but make its exhibitor a fortune."

"Fortune! Lord bless you, Parmalee, the word is too puny for the wealth that can be realized from it."

"Then why," asked Parmalee, a sudden note of suspicion creeping into his voice, "are you favoring me with this most remarkable opportunity? Why not purchase the creature yourself?"

A deep, protracted sigh emanated from his unseen interlocutor. "Hard times, Parmalee. My monetary situation, in spite of what you might believe, is almost as desperate as poor Bancroft's. Can't afford to part with the funds right now—simple as that. So I thought I'd do a friend a turn."

"I'm flattered that you continue to think of me in such terms," Parmalee said. "Particularly since I have been under the impression that you were still angry at me for that small misunderstanding."

"Misunderstanding?" said the other in a tone of perplexity. "You can't mean that unfortunate business about the dwarf hippopotamus you sold me last fall? How could you have known that the poor beast was suffering from a scrofulous disorder and would perish within days of my purchase?"

"Why, I *couldn't*—that's just the point," Parmalee exclaimed. "Or else I never would have proposed the transaction."

"And after all, what did I lose?" scoffed the sonorous-voiced fellow. "Two hundred dollars? A pittance to me in those halcyon days, my good fellow—a mere bagatelle."

"Well," said Parmalee in the tone of a man arriving at a decision. "I don't see how I can possibly turn my back on a chance like this one. How do I go about securing this marvel from its owner?"

"Tell you what," replied the other. "Why don't you leave me your personal cheque as a deposit. Make it out for, say, two hundred and fifty dollars. Might as well put it in my name—that'll be easiest. I'm on my way to the bank right now. I'll exchange it for cash and hand the deposit over to poor, crippled Bancroft when I visit him tonight. I'll take possession of the fish. You can return tomorrow with the balance, and I'll put the fascinating little creature into your hands."

"Fine, fine," said Parmalee eagerly. A brief period of near-total silence passed, during which the only sound emanating from the office was the scratching of a quill-point against paper.

"There," Parmalee said.

"Allow me to congratulate you, m'boy. Let me shake your hand. And I can only hope that, in the future, as you contemplate the wonder you have just purchased, you will remember the man who arranged its acquisition for you."

These words were followed by the scraping of two chairs against the floorboards. A moment later, the door flew open and out burst a stout, middle-aged fellow, garbed in the respectable habiliment of a successful businessman. His eyes were aglint with excitement, his somewhat porcine countenance infused with a look of the fullest satisfaction. Donning his hat, he strode past me without so much as a glance in my direction and disappeared down the hallway.

Straightening my cravat, I rapped on the doorjamb, threw back my shoulders, and passed into the office.

The center of the room was occupied by a massive, claw-footed desk behind which sat a personage whose features I could not, at that moment, clearly discern. He was in the process of igniting the largest cigar I had ever seen, and the dense puffs emanating from his mouth effectively obscured his features. When, by slow degrees, the smoke began to dissipate, I was startled to perceive that he was none other than the same, bulbous-nosed individual from whom I had purchased Sissy's guidebook upon entering the museum!

At that moment, he became aware of my presence. Removing the big cigar from his lips, he looked at me narrowly and said: "Yes, my good man? What can I do you for?"

"I am seeking Mr. Barnum," I answered.

"Then seek no more!" he jovially replied. "Your quest is at an end!"

"You?" I ejaculated. "Forgive me for seeming so amazed, but I momentarily mistook you for a vendor I saw earlier in the day."

"Your eyes didn't deceive you, friend. That was me. Not a task I normally assume, of course. Usually, it's handled by Slim Jim McCormack—the World's Skinniest Living Man. Forty-three years old, five-feet-ten-inches tall, and weighs only sixty-three pounds fully clothed! Hasn't gained or lost an ounce since he was stricken with scarlet fever at the tender age of eight! Gives the customers a thrill, you see, to buy something from one of the *stars*."

Yes, I thought dryly, and no doubt beguiles them into parting more readily with their cash.

"Unfortunately," Barnum said, "Slim Jim was a tad—ah—*indisposed* this morning. If you take my meaning." Here, he favored me with an exaggerated wink, while simulating the motion of a man tipping a bottle to his lips.

"But you have me at a disadvantage, sir," continued Barnum. "To whom do I have the great, the immense pleasure of speaking?"

Bowing slightly, I replied: "My name is Poe. Edgar Allan Poe."

Barnum took a deep draw on his cigar, puckered his lips, and blew out the smoke in a slow, steady stream. "Poe . . . Poe . . . Poe," he repeated meditatively. All at once, his eyes grew wide with recognition. "Lord bless me!" he exclaimed. "Poe the writer?"

Leaping to his feet, he strode around the desk, his right hand extended. "Let me shake you by the hand, m'boy. That balloon hoax of yours was a corker. Magnificent humbug, absolutely first rate. Haven't seen such a stir among the public since I first brought the Feejee Mermaid to town."

This effusive outburst was in reference to a newspaper story I had

written several months earlier which purported to be the actual account of a successful transatlantic crossing by the noted balloonists,
Messrs. Osborne, Mason, and Holland. Owing to the inordinate
pains I had taken to endow it with an air of authenticity, this composition had been accepted as absolute truth, occasioning a great deal of
excitement upon its publication. Indeed, it had proven to be nothing
less than a *sensation*.

Barnum's immediate recognition of me as the author of this
piece could not fail, in some measure, to gratify my vanity. His characterization of it as a "humbug," however, was objectionable in the
extreme. Drawing myself up to my full height, I coolly replied:

"I am pleased that you found my balloon story so enjoyable. It
can scarcely be termed a 'humbug,' however, for—though written as a
jeu d'esprit—there was nothing meretricious about it. On the contrary,
it was created with the same painstaking artistry that I have lavished
on every one of my compositions, whether in poetry or prose."

"I see, I see," Barnum replied with a slight smirk as he cast an appraising look at my coat sleeves. "So you're an *artist*, eh? Well, that
would account for the frayed cuffs, I guess." Here, he clamped his
cigar into a corner of his mouth, clutched the lapels of his own handsomely tailored jacket, and rocked back and forth on his heels. "As
for me, I'm just a humble entertainer."

Stung to the quick by his unfeeling (if all-too-accurate) allusion
to the threadbare condition of my garment, I indignantly retorted:
"It is true that I cannot afford to flaunt, as you do, a costly new suit
of clothing—a circumstance owing entirely to the shameful neglect
inevitably suffered by the serious *litterateur* in a country dominated by
the crude taste of the masses. But my apparel, however humble, has
not, at least, been purchased at the price of my own integrity—nor
through the perpetration, upon a credulous public, of an unmitigated
and brazen fraud."

"Fraud?" sputtered Barnum, plucking the cigar from his mouth.
"*Fraud?* Why, I have never committed a fraud in my life!" Pausing
briefly, he carelessly waved one hand in the air. "Well, all right, maybe
a time or two in the old days, before I knew better. Youthful indiscre-
tion and all that. But as for your insinuation that I have cheated the

public in any serious way—why, there's not the smallest jot of truth to it."

After taking another quick pull on his cigar and exhaling the smoke through the side of his mouth, he continued thusly: "Do you know how many people have tramped through these hallways in the past three years? I'd tell you, but you wouldn't believe it. Let's just say it's a figure that would have staggered the mind of Archimedes and made Sir Isaac Newton's brain spin. And of that immense—that *stupendous*—number of paying customers who've made Barnum's American Museum the greatest showplace of its kind in all of Christendom, do you know how many have ever asked for their money back?"

By way of answering this obviously rhetorical question, he raised his free hand and curled the thumb and forefinger into a circle. "Zero!" he announced in a tone of extreme self-satisfaction. "I ask you, sir, does that sound as if my customers have felt themselves cheated?"

"Nevertheless," I insisted, "certain of your displays are not what they purport to be."

"I challenge you to name a single one!" he demanded.

"Very well," I said. "The buckskin costume supposedly belonging to the late Davy Crockett cannot possibly be real. I base this assertion on my personal acquaintanceship with Colonel Crockett, with whom I shared a most memorable adventure shortly before his tragic demise at the Alamo."

"Why, I have a sworn affidavit certifying to the absolute, one-hundred-percent authenticity of that apparel," Barnum said. "Bought it from a fellow who had served under Santa Anna himself. Paid a pretty penny for it, too."

"In that case, Mr. Barnum," I said, "it is *you* who have been defrauded. But those blatantly spurious items are not the only fakes I have detected during my tour of your establishment. The so-called 'Mountain Gorilla' exhibited in your menagerie, for example, is nothing but a common baboon."

"Rubbish!" Barnum cried. "That creature is a unique—a wholly remarkable—specimen of a gorilla!"

"But gorillas have no tails," I calmly retorted, "whereas the primate in question very clearly *does*."

"I know perfectly well that *ordinary* gorillas have no tails," Barnum said. "But that's what makes *mine* such a remarkable specimen!"

The fellow was not merely shameless but absolutely incorrigible. To expect that he would freely confess to his deceptions was, I now realized, a consequence of my own naïveté—akin to believing that a man-eating tiger might succumb to the entreaties of a subjugated victim and renounce its taste for blood. To extract an admission from him would require something more emphatic on my part than a mere accusation of dishonesty. I therefore fixed him with a penetrating look and said:

"There was another hoax that I encountered during my tour of your exhibition halls—one that I can prove, to the absolute satisfaction of all but the most biased of arbiters, is utterly, *egregiously* false."

He regarded me with narrowed eyes. "Is that so? And what, pray tell, might that be?"

"I refer to Baron Maelzel's purported chess-playing automaton. Far from being a pure machine, as you so boldly claim, the apparatus is little more than a cunningly contrived *puppet*, guided by a concealed human operator."

Barnum's response to this declaration was dramatic in the extreme. Just prior to my statement, he had taken another protracted draw on his cigar. Now, his jaw literally fell open, and the smoke—which he had been accustomed to expelling in either a thin, steady stream or a succession of perfectly formed circles—emerged from his mouth in a great, amorphous cloud.

"That's the most amazing thing I've ever heard, and, believe me, I've heard some dillies!" he cried. "Why, the baron's Chess-Player has been universally proclaimed as the greatest mechanical marvel ever devised by man! Explain yourself, sir—for this isn't just a matter of false accusation, but of active and *actionable* libel!"

"I shall be happy to comply with your request," I calmly replied. "While observing a demonstration of the Chess-Player not more than one hour ago, I made note of several anomalous circumstances.

"First, when Baron Maelzel unlocked the cabinet to permit an examination of its interior, I perceived that it was densely crowded with machinery—wheels, cogs, gears, springs, and so forth. He then turned the entire apparatus around to exhibit the rear of the figure. Now, in scrutinizing the interior workings while the automaton was in motion—that is to say, while Maelzel was swiveling it on its castors—it appeared to me that certain portions of the machinery changed their shape and position in a degree too great to be accounted for by the simple laws of perspective. Only one explanation for this phenomenon seemed plausible—to wit, that these undue alterations were attributable to *mirrors* in the interior of the cabinet. Common sense dictates that the introduction of mirrors among the machinery could not possibly have been intended to influence, in any degree, the machinery itself. I at once concluded that these mirrors were so placed as to deceive the eye of the spectator—that is, to give the cabinet the *illusion of being crowded with machinery.*

"Moreover, when Maelzel, immediately prior to the commencement of the game, wound up the automaton by means of the large key protruding from the figure's back, I discerned at once from the peculiar sound made by this operation that the axis turned by the key in the box of the Chess-Player could not possibly be connected to either a weight, spring, or any system of machinery whatever. The inference here is the same as in my last observation. The winding up was inessential to the operation of the automaton, and was performed solely with the design of exciting in the spectator the false idea of mechanism.

"Third, while your guidebook describes the automaton as 'life-sized,' I perceived at once that the Turkish figure is, in truth, considerably above normal size. When Maelzel stood alongside the figure, I was struck by the fact that his head was at least eighteen inches below the head of the Turk, although the latter was in a sitting position. This clearly suggested to me that the Turk was so constructed as to permit a human operator to hide comfortably within its body."

There was other evidence I might have adduced to support my case. This, however, proved to be unnecessary; for at this point in my explanation, Barnum—whose facial expression had undergone a notable alteration as I spoke, changing from frank hostility to grudging admiration—broke into a wide grin and delightedly exclaimed:

"By Jove, but you're a pip, m'boy. I'm not saying you're right—don't misunderstand me. But I *do* say that you have a rare talent for both precise observation and logical deduction. And, believe me, if there's one thing P. T. Barnum has a keen eye for, it's talent!"

All at once, his eyes lit up as though he had been struck with a brilliant inspiration. "Why, here's a splendid notion—absolutely crackerjack. Why not write up a story for the papers?—an exposé, that sort of thing, denouncing Maelzel's Chess-Player as the greatest, most colossal humbug in the history of the world. Give all your reasons, just as you gave 'em to me, and throw in a few more for good measure. The papers'll snatch it up, I guarantee it. Why, it's sure to create a perfectly *blazing* controversy. Bring the public flocking in droves! They'll want to judge for themselves, you see, whether the thing is a true machine or not!"

Extracting a thick gold watch from the pocket of his vest, he snapped open the lid and quickly consulted the time before exclaiming: "Drat it all, I'm late for my appointment. Supposed to see a gent downtown. Claims he owns a dog that can smoke a corncob pipe, tell the time of day, and perform complex mathematical calculations."

Grabbing my right hand in both his own, he shook it vigorously and said: "Pleasure to meet you, Poe, m'boy. Consider my proposition. Benefit us both. Here take this—"

Hurrying around to the opposite side of his desk, he reseated himself in his chair, slid open a drawer, and removed a slip of paper, upon which he quickly scrawled his signature,

"Complimentary pass," he said, reaching the slip across the desk. "Come back any time."

By now, it was sufficiently plain that—in the matter of the spurious relics purportedly belonging to my late companion—I was utterly without recourse. Nothing I might do or say could compel Barnum to remove the offending items from display, or in any way confess to their fraudulence. Absently pocketing the paper he had just handed me, I strode toward the doorway. Before leaving, however, I turned back to Barnum and said:

"One thing more. While waiting to speak to you, I could not help overhearing your conversation with your previous visitor, the gentleman named Parmalee. Pardon me for appearing skeptical, but—having delved at some length into the literature of ichthyology—I am firmly convinced that no fish such as the one you described can possibly exist. True, there is an aquatic creature that does indeed undergo a comparable metamorphosis. It is not a member of the piscine species, however, but rather the early larval stage of an *amphibian.*"

"Well," Barnum said with a chuckle, "I just thank my lucky stars that Alexander Parmalee isn't as clever as you, m'boy—that's all *I* have to say. Otherwise, I wouldn't have the very great pleasure of bamboozling him the way he bamboozled *me.*"

Without another word, he bent down until his head disappeared below the level of the desktop. An instant later, he straightened back up in his chair. Clutched in his hands was a jar that had evidently been hidden on the floor behind the desk. As he set it down before him, I saw that it was filled with brackish water. A little, brownish-green creature was swimming around inside, propelled by a busily wiggling tail that would be all but gone within a matter of weeks.

"Imagine the gall of that fellow, selling me a diseased dwarf hippo for two hundred dollars!" Barnum exclaimed. "Well, sir, we'll see who has the last laugh. Oh, it'll be sweet, all right—seeing the look on old Parmalee's face when he realizes that he has just bought himself a *two hundred and fifty* dollar tadpole!"

CHAPTER SIX

In the days immediately following our visit to the American Museum, I began to ruminate on Barnum's suggestion that I write an exposé of Baron Maelzel's automaton. Given the universal renown of the Chess-Player, such an article would, I knew, create a sensation, bringing my name to the attention of the general reading public and securing my reputation as a writer to be reckoned with. Not incidentally, the fee I received for the publication of the article would provide a small but desperately needed infusion of cash.

That Barnum had actively urged me to produce such a piece I took for mere bravado—a crude stratagem to *discourage* me from writing it, akin to the time-tested method, known to every parent, of tricking a child into following a particular course of action by suggesting that he do the *reverse*. A newspaper piece proving beyond a reasonable doubt that the so-called "mechanical marvel" was merely an elaborate hoax would be sure to discomfit Barnum. *If I cannot compel him to remedy the rank imposture of his Crockett exhibit*, thought I, *I can at least occasion him some embarrassment.*

Accordingly, over the next several days, I devoted myself to the composition of a lengthy essay, in which I demonstrated by means of incisive, unassailable logic that Maelzel's Chess-Player could not possibly be a pure machine but must work through the agency of a concealed human operator. Published in the *Daily Courier*, this article—as I had anticipated—caused a great stir among the public and did

51

much to improve my pecuniary circumstances, not only by earning me a payment of ten dollars but by securing me a job as the New York correspondent for a gazette called the *Columbia Spy*, whose editor was much impressed with my exposé.

In only one regard did the piece fall short of my high expectations. It did not seem to cause Barnum any distress whatsoever. In making my calculations, I had failed to take into account one crucial factor—that Barnum's stock of human emotions did not include the elementary capacity for shame. Far from occasioning him the slightest twinge of embarrassment, the success of my piece seemed to please him mightily.

I knew this from a note I received in the post less than a week after the publication of my essay. Written in Barnum's strong, sweeping hand, the letter praised me for having heeded his advice and informed me that attendance at his museum had nearly doubled since my essay appeared, owing to the large number of visitors intent on judging for themselves whether the Chess-Player was genuine or not.

"Marvelous job, m'boy—absolutely tremendous!" his letter had ended. "Hope you made a few shekels from it, too. You've earned them. Don't fail to drop by soon and pay me a visit."

In spite of his concluding invitation, I doubted that I would ever set eyes on Barnum again—especially since, shortly after the publication of my article, Sissy and I moved a considerable distance away from the center of town. The various noxious stimuli of the city—its insufferable smells, noise, dirt, and congestion—had so wrought upon my nerves as to make sustained creative labor an impossibility. Seeking to escape to a more congenial environment, I had rented a small cottage on a two-hundred-acre dairy farm in the rural hinterland of Manhattan, just north of Eighty-fourth Street. This property, owned by a couple named Brennan, abounded in ponds, streams, meadows, and groves. No sooner had Sissy and I settled into these enchanting surroundings than we sent for Muddy and Cattarina, who arrived in high spirits and sound health during the first week of May.

Thus comfortably ensconced with my loved ones, I led a reclusive but deeply satisfying existence. Each morning after breakfast, I would take a long, exhilarating ramble through the fragrant fields and vernal nooks, ruminating on those subjects so stimulating to my imagination: premature burial, homicidal mania, and the death, by slow wasting disease, of lovely young maidens. Returning home, I would work furiously at my writing table until it was time to enjoy a leisurely dinner with my family. On the whole, it was a singularly pleasant, if uneventful, period in my life. And like all such idyllic interludes that occur in the course of one's existence, it proved to be exceptionally short-lived.

It was a brilliant, cloudless morning during the second week of June. Returning to my little abode after a long, invigorating stroll that had taken me to the very banks of the Hudson, I could discern my darling Muddy seated on the front porch of the cottage, busily engaged in her knitting. Beside her sat Sissy, drawing in a sketchbook that lay open in her lap. Even as they worked, they chatted merrily. Altogether, the scene that presented itself to my vision was picturesque in the extreme: the two-story cottage, surrounded by a stand of blossoming horse-chestnut trees; the gently undulating hills in the distance; the little flower garden, rampant with color, situated at the side of the house; and, seated on the rustic porch, the two angelic beings clad in gowns of summery white.

Crossing the luxuriant yard—where our beloved feline, Cattarina, was intently engaged in stalking some unseen quarry that lay hidden in the high grass—I stepped onto the porch and planted a fond osculation on the brow of each of my loved ones.

Muddy immediately looked up from her knitting. "Hello, dearest Eddie," she said, a loving smile upon her broad, somewhat coarse-featured, but (to my eyes) supremely endearing countenance. "How was your walk?"

"Exceptionally bracing," I replied. "You will remember that it was about eight in the morning when I left. I bent my steps immediately toward the west and, about ten, found myself upon a trail that was entirely new to me. The scenery which presented itself on all sides, though scarcely entitled to be called *grand*, had about it an indescribable and, to me, delicious aspect of desolation. The solitude seemed absolutely virginal.

"I continued along this path, which proved so exceedingly sinuous that, after a short while, I lost all idea of the direction in which I journeyed. My interest became focused with a singular intensity upon the minute, natural phenomena surrounding me. In the quivering of a leaf—in the hue of a blade of grass—in the gleaming of a dewdrop—in the humming of a bee—in the breathing of the wind—there came a whole universe of suggestion, a gay and motley train of rhapsodical thought.

"At length, I found myself on the very brink of the Hudson. For many minutes, I stood and contemplated the splendid vista before me: the vast and beautiful river, bounded on the opposite shore by the towering cliffs of the Palisades. Only then, did I turn around and make my way homeward."

"Well, that all sounds very nice," Muddy said. "I'm so glad that you're getting a little exercise. I worry about you, cooped up all day in your study."

"And how have my two darling girls been passing the time since my departure?" I inquired.

"I was telling Muddy about our trip to Mr. Barnum's museum," said Sissy, who continued to sketch as she spoke. Glancing down at her pad, I saw that she was at work on a most striking illustration, depicting the scene in Charles Perrault's well-known fairy story, "Le Barbe Bleu," in which the heroine, disobeying the strict injunction of her sinister husband, opens the door of the forbidden chamber and discovers therein the horribly butchered corpses of his previous brides.

"And did you describe the rather confusing denouement of our visit?" I asked.

Although this question was directed at Sissy, it was Muddy who replied. "I was just chuckling over it when you arrived," she said.

"I suppose it *does* sound pretty comical now," said Sissy, "though it didn't seem at all amusing at the time."

The foregoing remarks were in reference to an episode that occurred immediately after I had taken leave of Barnum in his office. Ascending to the menagerie, where—as the reader will recall—Sissy and I had agreed to rendezvous at a prearranged time, I was surprised to discover that she was nowhere in sight. Thinking that she had become so engrossed in the exhibit that she had lost track of the hour, I made a quick circuit of the cavernous hall, but could see no sign of her. I was immediately seized with concern. Perhaps, I thought, she had suffered a relapse and retreated to the so-called "aerial garden" for a revivifying breath of fresh air.

Accordingly, I repaired to the rooftop—but again, my darling wife was nowhere in sight. By this point, my anxiety had intensified into positive *alarm*. I was only too aware of the lurking perils of the city, where—on any given day—young, unescorted women fall victim to the blandishments of honey-tongued lotharios and other, even more detestable human predators who batten on female innocence. Hurrying from the rooftop, I rapidly—and fruitlessly—searched each of the exhibition salons in turn, growing more frantic by the moment.

Satisfied at last that Sissy was nowhere in the building, I resolved to waste no more time and notify the police at once of her disappearance. I had just emerged from the building, however, when—to my astonishment—I saw Sissy standing on the sidewalk directly in front of the museum, with a look of the most acute frustration on her countenance.

At her first glimpse of me, her expression turned into one of profound relief. After we exchanged a brief but heartfelt greeting, she proceeded to explain what had occurred in the interval since we had separated.

She had indeed passed a pleasant half-hour viewing Barnum's collection of exotic zoological specimens. Upon reaching the far end of the hall in which the menagerie was housed, she noticed a large, canvas banner hanging over the entrance to a stairwell. Painted upon this cloth were a downward-pointing arrow and the words: "This way to the Egress!" As she stood there puzzling over this sign, several other people sauntered over and began to discuss its meaning.

"Egress?" said one. "Why I've never heard of such a creature."

"I believe it is a species of giraffe," observed another.

"No, no," exclaimed a third, "it is a giant reptile."

"You are both wrong," exclaimed the fourth, "for I am certain it is nothing other than a breed of wild boar."

Caught up in the excitement of this little group, Sissy had followed them down the stairwell—whereupon, to her great dismay and confusion, she found herself outside on the street!

Only after speaking to the ticket-seller—with whom she pleaded fruitlessly for readmission, and who seemed much amused by her predicament—did Sissy realize what had occurred. She and the others had fallen victim to one of P. T. Barnum's most audacious ploys, a stratagem designed to trick his customers into believing that a rare and marvelous creature was on display at the bottom of the staircase. In reality, of course, all that awaited at the foot of the descent was the museum *exit*. In this way, Barnum was able to alleviate the overcrowding in his establishment by luring a certain portion of his customers out of the building and onto the street.

"Well," Muddy now commented as she returned to her knitting. "At least Mr. Barnum gave you a free return pass."

In reply to this exceedingly ingenuous comment, I emitted a loud, ironical snort. "I am afraid, dearest Muddy, that Mr. Barnum's ostensible 'gift' turned out to be, like so many of his offerings, entirely specious. For—scrutinizing this certificate upon our return to the boardinghouse—I discovered that, printed on the bottom in letters so small as to be nearly indecipherable, was a string of stipulations. It was not valid on weekends, holidays, or evenings after six P.M. Moreover, it was due to expire on the fifteenth of April. Our visit, as Sissy has perhaps informed you, took place on Friday, April twelve. Since the intervening days were a Saturday and Sunday, the pass proved totally worthless!"

"I must say," Muddy remarked with a shake of her head, "Mr. Barnum sounds like quite a 'character.' "

"Unhappily, it is a type of character that is entirely too emblematic of American society."

"What do you mean, Eddie?" Sissy inquired.

"I mean that Mr. Barnum epitomizes a desire for coarse, uncultivated amusement that, more and more, is beginning to dominate in our culture. His so-called museum—which is, in fact, little more than a carnival of novelties—represents, I believe, an exceedingly crass but increasingly popular form of entertainment, one that appeals to the most infantile tastes for thrills, sensationalism, and wonder. Such low pastimes, I fear, threaten to overwhelm, if not entirely supplant, the more refined and elevating pleasures of the past—not least the sublime gratifications to be derived from the reading of great literature."

"Oh, Eddie, I don't mean to sound harsh, but there are times when you can be such a fuddy-duddy!" Sissy exclaimed. "Great literature is one thing. But Mr. Barnum's museum is a place to have *fun*. I don't see anything wrong with *that*."

Somewhat stung by Sissy's unflattering characterization of me as a "fuddy-duddy," I opened my lips with the intention of delivering a spirited reply. Before I could utter a word, however, I was distracted by the clatter of wheels and the clopping of hooves: the unmistakable sound of an approaching vehicle.

"Who can *that* be?" Muddy said.

Her question was entirely apt—for the arrival of a visitor at our outlying abode was a phenomenon so rare as to be virtually unprecedented. Since moving to the countryside, I had led a life of extreme isolation. Apart from Muddy and Sissy, my human contacts were limited to our landlords, Mr. and Mrs. Brennan, and the editor of the *Columbia Spy*, with whom I met once each fortnight when I hiked the five miles into town to deliver my latest manuscripts.

Now, as I gazed intently at the rutted dirt road leading up to our cottage, a coach came jouncing into view, its rapidly spinning wheels churning up a thick cloud of dust. With a tug of his reins and a commanding "Whoa!" the driver drew the vehicle to a halt directly before the front porch. A moment later, the door swung open and out climbed the sole passenger. The reader may easily imagine the intensity of my astonishment when I perceived the identity of this unforeseen caller.

It was none other than Mr. P. T. Barnum himself!

CHAPTER SEVEN

The near-simultaneous occurrence of two disparate but interrelated events can strike us, on occasion, with the force of the uncanny. As we stroll along the city streets, the face of someone we once knew in the long-ago past suddenly enters our mind; moments later, we round a corner and run into the very person. Or perhaps, as we sit at the breakfast table, we find ourselves thinking about a former acquaintance from whom we have received no communication in many years. Later that day, the post arrives bearing a letter from that same individual.

There are few persons, even among the calmest thinkers, who have not occasionally been startled into a vague yet thrilling half-credence in the supernatural by such occurrences—coincidences of so seemingly marvelous a character that, as *mere* coincidences, the intellect has been unable to receive them. Thus it proved with me. Under any circumstances at all, the unannounced appearance of P. T. Barnum at my home would have occasioned me the most inordinate surprise. But to have him materialize at that very instant—when Muddy, Sissy, and I were conversing on the very subject of his museum—seemed so improbable as to render me virtually speechless. As I watched him approach our cottage, I was seized with a spasm of premonitory dread—with the wholly unnerving sensation that the tall, imposing figure striding in my direction was not the world-famous showman but rather the living incarnation of my own inescapable *fate*.

Stepping onto the porch, he thrust his right hand toward me and exclaimed: "Poe, m'boy. Bless me, but you're looking fit. Healthy living, I suppose, out here in the sticks." Here, he inhaled deeply and slapped his expanded chest with both hands. "Ahh, the fresh country air. Marvelous stuff! Wish I could figure out a way to bottle it. Make a fortune."

Having suspended their occupations, my dear ones gazed up curiously at this unexpected and—to them—wholly unfamiliar visitor.

"Muddy, Sissy," I said. "Allow me to introduce Mr. Phineas T. Barnum."

Doffing his hat, Barnum gave a little bow. "Delighted to make your acquaintance, ladies," said he.

"Why, we were just talking about you!" Sissy exclaimed in amazement.

"Speak of the devil and he'll appear, eh?" Barnum said with a chortle.

"So they say," Muddy piped up pleasantly. "Though surely you are no devil, Mr. Barnum."

"Oh, but I *am*, my dear woman, I *am*. Evil incarnate. Beelzebub himself! Lucifer risen from the fiery pit!" His voice having mounted to a resounding pitch, he now lowered it again to a more conventional level. "At least according to some people," he added dryly.

By this point, my amazement at Barnum's wholly unforeseen arrival had been supplanted by a distinct feeling of indignation at the bizarre familiarity he had assumed with me. Our acquaintanceship having been limited to a single—and, to my mind, decidedly unsatisfactory—previous encounter, I found the inordinate cordiality with which he had greeted me peculiarly offensive.

I therefore made little effort to affect a hospitable manner in addressing him. "To what do we owe the great pleasure of this visit?" I said in a tone replete with irony. "For I confess that, had someone asked me this morning—'Of all the occurrences that might conceivably transpire today, which would you deem the least likely?'—I should have answered without hesitation: 'The sudden advent on my doorstep of Mr. P. T. Barnum.'"

"Well, I won't pretend I'm here on a social call, Poe, m'boy—

59

delightful as it is to see you again. No, no. Wouldn't do at all to try pulling the wool over *your* eyes. They're much too sharp for that. Fact is, I'm here on a matter of business—most urgent business." Pausing briefly, he motioned toward the little slatted bench that stood on the porch beside the chairs occupied by Sissy and Muddy. "May I?" he inquired.

"As you wish," I replied somewhat coolly.

"Can I offer you something to drink, Mr. Barnum?" asked my ever-thoughtful Muddy as our visitor lowered himself onto his seat. "A nice glass of buttermilk, perhaps?"

"Nothing for me, my good woman, thank you kindly."

"Your driver perhaps—?"

Cupping one hand to the side of his mouth, Barnum called out: "Willie! Care for something to drink?"

Following the direction of Barnum's shouted query, I cast my gaze across the yard, where the driver of the coach remained seated on his perch, gazing serenely about at the countryside. Until this point, I had taken little notice of this personage. Now—as I scrutinized him more closely—I was struck by certain anomalous aspects of his physical appearance. He was an exceedingly stout fellow with a great bushy growth of whiskers that extended halfway down his bosom. His countenance, however, possessed a strangely delicate, even feminine cast, while his remarkably luxuriant hair hung all the way down to his shoulders. Equally peculiar was his attire, which appeared to consist of a shapeless, flower-patterned smock!

"No thanks, Mr. B.," this individual called back in a lilting, high-pitched voice that—emanating from such a large and hirsute individual—seemed incongruous to the point of *grotesquerie*. "I'm happy as can be, just drinking in the scenery."

"She's fine," Barnum said to Muddy.

"*She?*" Muddy, Sissy, and I cried out in unison.

"Why, yes," Barnum said in a somewhat puzzled tone, as though surprised that we had not been aware of this astonishing fact before. "Wilhelmina Schnitzler, my bearded lady. Farm gal from Ohio, Willie is. Born and bred on the banks of the Wabash. Seemed a mite down-at-the-mouth lately, so I invited her along for the ride. Loves to handle the reins every now and again."

"Well, I *never*," Muddy exclaimed, gawking in undisguised wonderment at this remarkable being.

"Muddy, dearest," said Sissy, leaning close to her parent and speaking in a soft, confidential voice, "it isn't polite to stare."

"Bless you, child," Barnum said with a guffaw. "Willie won't mind! Why, it's her bread and butter." Addressing Muddy, he continued thusly: "You go ahead and ogle her all you like, my good woman. In the meantime, I'll tell Poe why I'm here."

"In truth," said I—forcing my gaze away from the anomalous being (who did indeed appear utterly unfazed by our attention) and fixing it on Barnum—"my curiosity in that regard has risen to a most acute pitch."

Assuming an expression of the utmost gravity, Barnum declared: "To get down to business, then—it's about yesterday's murder."

So unexpected—if not *startling*—was this announcement that even the sight of the bizarre bearded female, perched atop the carriage only several yards away, could not retain the interest of my loved ones. Swiveling their heads in Barnum's direction, they looked at him in dumbstruck silence, while I declared: "I fear that we have heard nothing about the crime to which you allude."

"Can it be possible?" Barnum exclaimed. "Why, it's the talk of the town. Biggest sensation in years—absolutely stupendous. Whole city's abuzz with excitement."

"I do not doubt it," I replied. "As you see, however, our home is sufficiently remote from the metropolitan center that news—even of the most notable events—requires several days to reach us. What precisely are the particulars of this exceptional crime?"

Heaving a sigh, Barnum answered: "Damnedest thing in the world—if you'll excuse my language, ladies. You recall that grisly Jennings business a few years back?"

It was Sissy who replied to this query, in a voice tinged with consternation: "Eddie and I saw that ghastly tableau in your museum. Is that the one you mean?"

"That's it. Horrible crime—absolutely appalling. Magnificent specimen of waxworks, though. Sculpted by no less an artist than Monsieur Joseph Dorfeuille, protégé of Madame Marie Tussaud herself. Paid a fortune for it. Worth every penny, too. Draws like a dog-fight!"

"But what in the world has that infamous atrocity to do with this recent homicide?" I asked.

"Why, everything!" cried Barnum. "It's the Jennings horror all over again. Different woman, same dreadful butchery. Head nearly severed. Hands completely gone—hacked off and taken by the fiend, Heaven knows for what unholy reason. And do you know what was found in her mouth?"

"From what you have already indicated, I can only surmise that it was the same, incongruously fair and delicate object inserted between the teeth of the earlier victim."

"Exactly so," Barnum said, nodding vigorously. "A single, long-stemmed rose."

"But how can this be?" I asked. "The perpetrator of the Jennings murder is no more, having been sentenced to a swift and richly merited death."

"*Swift?*" Barnum cried. "The word is a gross understatement. Never saw a man convicted so quickly. Why, it takes longer to judge my annual beauty contest—Barnum's Grand International Pageant of Pulchritude, the most spectacular display of female charms ever assembled under one roof! Young Thompson wouldn't agree with you about the 'merited' part, though, Poe, m'boy. Insisted he was framed right to the bitter end."

"But such professions of innocence are not at all uncommon, even among malefactors whose guilt is beyond reasonable dispute," I observed. "And the evidence against him, as I recall from the journalistic accounts, was conclusive. Were not the poor victim's missing extremities, their stumps still caked with blood, found on Thompson's premises?"

"Indeed they were," said Barnum. "Caught him red-handed, so to speak."

At that moment, our attention was distracted by Sissy, who uttered something in a voice so soft and ruminative that her remark was unintelligible.

"Did you say something, Sissy?" I inquired.

"I was just thinking aloud," she replied. "Perhaps the curse has come true."

"Curse?" Muddy asked, her brow deeply furrowed in perplexity.

"The condemned man, Lemuel Thompson," Sissy replied. "Just before he went to his death, he swore he'd come back and do all the terrible things he'd been accused of. I read all about it in Mr. Barnum's guidebook."

"Now *there's* a story for you!" Barnum cried, delivering a resounding smack to one thigh with the flat of his hand. " 'Killer Ghost Returns from the Grave!' You'd think Bennett and his ilk would leap at it. Why, their papers would sell in the millions! Wear out the printing presses, trying to keep up with the demand! But *no*—they'd rather blame *me!*"

"*You?*" I exclaimed. "Why, whatever do you mean?"

By way of reply, Barnum reached into the side pocket of his jacket and extracted a folded sheet of newsprint, which he thrust into my hands.

Opening it, I saw that it was a page torn from that morning's edition of James Gordon Bennett's exceedingly popular "penny paper," *The New York Herald.* Occupying the center of the page—and boldly set off from the surrounding columns by a heavy black border—was an editorial essay headlined, BARNUM'S AMERICAN MUSEUM: HARMLESS ENTERTAINMENT OR PROVOCATION TO MURDER?

"Let the ladies hear it, Poe," said Barnum. "Wouldn't want them to miss such a perfectly wondrous specimen of outright and damnable *slander!*"

"Very well," I said. Then—in the cadenced voice I employed for public recitations—I began to read aloud:

"The gruesome particulars of the murder of the beautiful Paphian, Ellen Jennings, are too well-known to require recapitulation. The hideous barbarities inflicted on that poor, doomed member of the frail sisterhood were such as to inspire the utmost revulsion and horror in the soul of every citizen.

"Now, a second, equally abominable murder has come to light. Summoned to the Thomas Street apartment of a lovely maiden named Isabel Somers, police officers yesterday discovered a scene of the most awful butchery. There, upon a blood-clotted mattress, lay what had only recently been the most bewitching of all God's creations, a

beautiful and blooming damsel—now transformed into a fearfully mangled corpse! Her white, slender throat was so dreadfully gashed that her head was nearly severed from her body. Her mutilated arms terminated in two gore-imbrued stumps from which the hands had been violently removed. Her face—which wore the expression of someone who had perished in the throes of unbearable agony—was rendered even more grotesque by the presence of a macabre token left by her killer: a crimson rose protruding from between her tightly clenched teeth. Altogether, the shocking spectacle which presented itself was a chillingly precise replication of the Ellen Jennings murder.

"The fiendish perpetrator of that prior atrocity, the inhuman monster Lemuel Thompson, has long been consigned to a fiery perdition. How, then, can we account for the appalling crime which occurred only yesterday and which bore all the ghastly hallmarks of the earlier case? Even now, the police are energetically pursuing the solution to that mystery. One answer, however, immediately suggests itself as a distinct possibility.

"At this very moment, there exists in our city an exhibit of the most shockingly irresponsible variety. We refer to the ghoulish tableau that forms the culminating display in Mr. Phineas T. Barnum's 'Hall of Crime and Punishment' at his exceedingly popular American Museum. This uncannily realistic specimen of the waxwork-sculptor's art depicts, in all its gruesome detail, the dreadful slaughter of Ellen Jennings in her boudoir on the night of January 29, 1843. Each and every day, men, women, and (we shudder to think it!) children of the most tender sensibilities flock to Mr. Barnum's museum to view this ghastly spectacle of murder and depravity. May we not reasonably assume that this exceedingly graphic display—designed for no other purpose than to stimulate the morbid passions of the public—has inflamed the mind of one especially impressionable viewer and inspired him to emulate the unspeakable deed it portrays?

"While there is much to enjoy in Mr. Barnum's establishment, we must question his judgment in pandering to the vulgar craving for rank sensationalism. Other, similar institutions in our city manage to attract customers without depending on such lurid fare. We particularly have in mind the Gotham Museum on Lafayette Street. Within the many galleries and exhibition salons of this praiseworthy establishment visitors are treated exclusively to wholesome and uplifting entertainments suitable for the entire family.

"We certainly do not mean to suggest that Mr. Barnum is wholly or even primarily accountable for yesterday's tragedy. But should the perpetrator, when apprehended, turn out to be one of the countless individuals who have stood rapt before the many shocking exhibitions on view at the American Museum, should not Mr. Barnum be held at least partly to blame?"

No sooner had the final sentence of this article issued from my lips than Barnum leapt from the bench, exclaiming: "I ask you, my friends—have you ever heard a more scandalous pack of lies? Why, you'd think I wielded the murder weapon myself! Oh yes, I know what you're thinking—a man of my extraordinary prominence can't expect anything else. Sooner or later, the pygmies are sure to come after you with their poisonous blow-darts. Best thing to do is ignore them. But I'm not made of stone. Prick me and I bleed, like the rest of humankind. Besides, it isn't solely a matter of outraged feelings. It's not just P. T. Barnum that's under attack—it's my *business!*"

While our visitor continued with his tirade, I attempted to analyze my own, deeply equivocal feelings about the essay I had just completed. On the one hand, any denunciation of Barnum—whose devious practices I myself found so intensely deplorable—was a source of the keenest satisfaction to me. At the same time, I was forced to concede that this assault by James Gordon Bennett's newspaper was exceedingly hypocritical. The *Herald*, after all, was notorious for exploiting stories of sensational crime for its own commercial purposes. Indeed, it had covered the Ellen Jennings affair with an almost feverish intensity—an avid attention to each gruesome detail that bordered on the *salacious.*

Moreover, as a writer whose own fiction frequently dealt with the morbid—the fearful—the wildly *outré*—I bridled at the notion that the mere *portrayal* of even the most appalling acts of violence would inevitably lead to their actual commission. Such a view, I believed, betrayed a nearly complete ignorance of one of the most important rôles of artistic representation: i.e., to permit the ordinary individual to gratify—*in the imagination*—dark, even criminal, impulses that, in his daily life, he would never dream of indulging. For an artist who, by temperament, was irresistibly drawn to grotesque themes and macabre subjects, the censorial implications of Bennett's editorial were nothing less than chilling.

Handing the sheet of newsprint back to Barnum—whose countenance was suffused with an indignant flush from his dimpled chin to his bald, extensive brow—I therefore remarked: "Your outraged sentiments seem perfectly justified, Mr. Barnum—particularly in view of Bennett's own shameless and habitual reliance on grisly violence as a means of increasing the circulation of his newspaper. Indeed—to resort to a timeworn, though still colorful, cliché—this essay strikes me as a singularly *glaring* instance of 'the pot calling the kettle black.' "

"Bennett's a rascal, all right," Barnum declared. "Not a scrupulous bone in his carcass. Always admired him, though. First-rate businessman—absolutely tip-top. No. Bennett's not the one I blame."

Elevating my eyebrows in surprise, I inquired: "Then who, in your view, *is* the culprit?"

"That infernal knave Parmalee, blast him!" Barnum angrily replied. "He put Bennett up to this."

Though the person thus denominated sounded somewhat familiar to me, I could not immediately recall him. Only after the lapse of several moments did the realization come to me.

"Was not 'Parmalee' the name of the gentleman who was in your office on the day I came to speak with you?" I asked.

"That's the scoundrel, all right," Barnum said with a growl.

"But on what basis do you hold Mr. Parmalee responsible for this editorial?" I inquired.

"Why, it's plain as day. All that hogwash about the Gotham Museum—how much nicer, more wholesome it is than my own establishment. Well, it so happens that Alexander Parmalee is the *proprietor* of the Gotham. Hates my guts, too, ever since that little transaction involving the two-hundred-fifty-dollar polliwog. And he's known to be chummy with Bennett. Mark my words, Poe—Parmalee's behind this. I'd wager anything on it—my vast collection of rare conchological specimens—my actual gold doubloons retrieved from the sunken vessel of Blackbeard the Pirate—my one-of-a-kind, living, two-headed Leghorn rooster! Anything!"

Though Barnum belonged to that species of inveterate charlatan whose veracity is always open to doubt, there was no mistaking the sincerity of his feelings on this occasion. His reason for having sought me out, however, remained as obscure as ever. I therefore looked at him narrowly and said: "I must confess, Mr. Barnum, that—while the information you have thus far imparted is of a most intriguing nature—it has failed to shed adequate light on the motive for your visit."

"Why, you surprise me, Poe," he replied. "A man of your immense perspicacity. Thought you'd have figured it out by now." Pausing for a moment, he fixed me with a solemn look and said: "I want you to help me find poor Isabel Somers's killer."

The reader may easily imagine the reactions provoked by this announcement. Sissy gasped aloud—Muddy emitted a startled, "Oh my!"—while I stood there absolutely thunderstricken, looking at him in mute astonishment. At length, having recovered myself in some measure, I exclaimed: "So extraordinary is your statement that I cannot tell which part of it has left me more amazed: your expressed determination to discover the killer yourself, or your desire to have me assist you in this remarkable enterprise. Are not the duly delegated officers of the law, even now, conducting a diligent investigation into the case?"

"Why, that's just the trouble!" Barnum cried. "That's the problem in a nutshell! Take my word for it, Poe—I know whereof I speak. I've seen something of the world in my day. Been invited to Buckingham Palace. Shook hands with King Louis-Phillipe of France. Hobnobbed with the Crown Prince of Bavaria. And I can tell you that every great city in Europe can boast a constabulary to be proud of—manned by seasoned professionals and furnished with the best, most advanced crime-fighting equipment that modern science can contrive. And what've we got here in New York? Not even a real police force! Just a handful of full-time officers, plus a ragtag bunch of stevedores, porters, cartmen, and laborers of every stripe who pick up a few extra shekels by hiring themselves out as watchmen. It's more than a travesty—it's an absolute disaster! Mark my words, Poe, m'boy—if something isn't done about it soon, you'll see a breakdown of civic law and order that'll make the fall of Rome look like a Sunday-school picnic.

"No sir," he continued after pausing momentarily to catch his breath. "Why, Poe, do you imagine that I've risen to the immense heights of success I've attained by leaving things in the hands of amateurs? 'If you want a job done right, do it yourself'—that's P. T. Barnum's motto. And I want this crime solved *now*. The public will see that there's no connection at all between this heinous deed and the splendid host of attractions available at the world-famous American Museum. They'll see that Phineas Taylor Barnum—someone who has dedicated his entire adult life to bringing the most thrilling, delightful, and morally elevating amusements to the common man—is now the target of a vicious and unbridled campaign of character assassination, mounted by envious rivals who are bent on his utter ruination!

"Besides," he added with a wink. "Just think of all the free publicity it'll bring."

Perceiving at last an opportunity to interject a word, I somewhat mordantly remarked: "Your personal motives for undertaking this venture are now sufficiently plain. Thus far, however, you have failed to explain your reasons for soliciting my help."

Grinning slyly, Barnum tapped his nose with an index finger and declared: "This proboscis of mine may not be much to look at—no, no, ladies, no need to protest—vanity, thank the Lord, isn't one of P. T. Barnum's failings! But plain as it may be, there isn't a better apparatus in the world for sniffing out talent. And *you*, Poe m'boy, have a rare gift for putting two and two together. Realized it the first time we met. And that article about the Chess-Player only proved it. Magnificent example of logical thinking—absolutely stupendous. Not that I'm admitting you were *right*, of course. Still, I was mightily impressed. Mark my words, Poe, you've got the makings of a first-rate detective."

"Well," Muddy exclaimed, her voice imbued with maternal pride, "Eddie *did* solve those dreadful murders in Baltimore ten years ago."

"What did I tell you?" Barnum cried out in delight. "When it comes to talent, I'm a regular bloodhound—smell it a mile away."

For the first time since our visitor's arrival, I began to regard him in a somewhat more favorable light. Though not in the least susceptible to anything that smacked of mere *flattery*, I could not help but feel gratified by his recognition of my superior ratiocinative abilities. Accordingly—in a tone far less caustic than the one I had hitherto employed—I addressed him thusly:

"While modesty dictates a self-deprecatory response to your

words, Mr. Barnum, honesty compels me to acknowledge their accuracy. Indeed, as I have already demonstrated in the matter to which my dear Auntie Maria has just alluded, my skill at both precise observation and deductive reasoning are ideally suited for a mystery such as this. Moreover, I concur with your assessment of the typical American police officer, who is, by and large, a functionary of the most plodding and unimaginative sort. For both of these reasons, I am sympathetic to your proposal. There are, however, a number of problems with it, not the least of which is the amount of time such an undertaking would detract from my own livelihood."

"Why, bless you, Poe, if that's all you're worried about, put the matter out of your head. You can work for *me!*"

Once again, Barnum had succeeded in rendering me speechless. For some moments, I merely looked at him incredulously. Before I could fully regain my composure, he continued thusly:

"There's always plenty of stuff that needs writing—souvenir pamphlets, guidebooks, and the like. Do a bit of scribbling myself from time to time—Barnum's life story, struggles and triumphs, rules for success, that sort of thing. But there's always more to do. Take Madame Cleo Ben Dib, my Egyptian snake-lady. Ever witnessed her act, Poe, m'boy? Performs an exotic dance with no fewer than twenty mammoth serpents wrapped around her body. Exceeds in novelty and wonder anything ever seen in this country! Fine figure of a woman, too, with a form surpassing the Venus de Medicis. Can't write worth a damn, though. I had to hire a two-bit hack to dash off her autobiography. Makes more sense to have a splendid writer like you on the payroll. And I'd give you a regular salary, too—none of that penny-per-word nonsense the magazines offer. What do you say?"

Here was a most unexpected turn. To be in the employ of P. T. Barnum—a person who epitomized all that I most deplored about the vulgar tastes and crass, commercial values of my countrymen—would constitute an utter violation of every principle I held most dear. At the same time, I perceived that distinct advantages—even apart from the obvious, pecuniary ones—would accrue to me from such an arrangement. By working for Barnum, I would be able to imbue his publications with a tincture of literary excellence, thereby adding a degree of refinement to his otherwise tawdry enterprise. In this way, instead of merely raging in impotent protest against the showman's degrading influence on America's cultural life, I would be helping, in some measure, to offset it.

Moreover, the search for the madman would afford me an opportunity to utilize those ratiocinative faculties I possessed in such abundance but rarely had a chance to exercise. Finally, there was the issue of basic, civic responsibility—my duty, as a citizen no less than as a *man,* to do everything possible to help bring the killer to justice before he could perpetrate yet another atrocity.

With these considerations in mind, I addressed our visitor in the following terms: "Though beset by certain qualms in regard to your proposition, I cannot, in good conscience, decline an opportunity to assist in the resolution of so foul and savage a crime. I have therefore decided to accept your offer in its entirety."

"Spoken like a man, sir, spoken like a man!" Barnum exclaimed, enveloping my right hand with his own and pumping it up and down vigorously. "Let me congratulate you!"

"I do hope you will be careful, Eddie," Sissy said, gazing up at me worriedly.

"Oh, I'm certain Mr. Barnum will watch over him, won't you, Mr. Barnum?" said Muddy, reaching out a hand to give her daughter a reassuring pat on the lap.

"Like a mother hen," Barnum asserted with a chuckle.

"And when shall we commence this undertaking?" I inquired of the latter.

Consulting his pocket watch, Barnum replied: "Let's pile into the coach, Poe, m'boy, and head back right now. Willie has a noon performance to make. She can leave us off at the museum, and we can foot it from there."

" 'Foot it?' " I exclaimed. "To where?'

"Why, to Number 14 Thomas Street," said Barnum. "Isabel Somers's living quarters. The scene of the crime. Might as well get started straight away. After all, there's no time like the present—that's P. T. Barnum's motto!"

Part Two

BOOGEYMAN

CHAPTER EIGHT

Perhaps it was true, as Barnum claimed, that he had invited Wilhelmina Schnitzler to drive his carriage for entirely generous reasons: i.e., so that the hirsute performer—who had grown up in rustic surroundings but now spent her days confined within the walls of the American Museum—could enjoy a refreshing jaunt in the countryside. But as our vehicle drew closer to the metropolitan center, another, more characteristically self-interested motive became apparent.

Even in a city like New York—whose inhabitants typically assumed a *blasé* demeanor as a badge of their sophistication—the spectacle of an immense, brightly garbed, heavily bewhiskered female at the reins of a carriage could not fail to cause a stir. Peering through my open window, I was much amused to observe the reactions of the crowd as our vehicle proceeded down Broadway. Dignified men in black frock coats and stovepipe hats halted in midstride and gaped in amazement. Fashionable women raised their hands to their mouths and grew wide-eyed beneath their colorful bonnets. Young children of both sexes leapt up and down and emitted high-pitched exclamations of astonishment and delight. Even the operators of other vehicles— the coachmen, carters, wagoners, and omnibus-drivers—were seized with wonder as they caught sight of the anomalous being seated atop our carriage.

It need hardly be said that my companion was in no way displeased with the inordinate degree of attention directed at his singular employee. Indeed, as our carriage approached the heart of the city, Barnum thrust his head through the window nearest to himself and, directing his remarks at the tide of humanity on the pavement, called out: "That's right, folks! She's big!—she's beautiful!—and she's hairy as a lumberjack! She's Madame Wilhelmina Schnitzler—just one of the countless rare attractions, wonderful curiosities, and instructive entertainments to be found at Barnum's American Museum, Ann Street and Broadway—the greatest amusement enterprise in existence!"

By this means did the ever-canny showman transform our conveyance from a simple mode of transportation into a rolling advertisement for his establishment.

Arrived at length at our destination, we quickly disembarked from the coach. No sooner had he set foot on the pavement than Barnum raised his right hand and snapped his fingers sharply, as though struck with a sudden recollection.

"My walking stick," he said aloud.

Reaching back into the vehicle, he removed from the floor the item in question—a highly polished, ebony cane with a heavy brass head wrought into the shape of a trumpeting elephant.

In the meanwhile, Wilhelmina Schnitzler, having clambered down from the driver's box with surprising agility for a person of her magnitude, made her way toward the museum, provoking a burst of delighted cries and amazed ejaculations from the visitors awaiting entrance. For several moments, Barnum merely stood at the edge of the sidewalk and ran his eyes over the line of customers, as though rapidly calculating their number. Then, after emitting a self-satisfied chuckle, he took me by the arm and led me away in the direction of Isabel Somers's abode.

The walk to our ultimate destination was a matter of minutes. As we rounded the corner of Thomas Street, I perceived a small crowd of people milling on the sidewalk before a four-storied edifice. Several were pointing toward the shuttered upper windows. Others were engaged in animated talk. Still others were merely gazing at the building with a kind of objectless curiosity.

"Look there, Poe," said Barnum in a voice tinged with bitterness.

"Come to gawk at the murder scene. And the newspapers accuse *me* of corrupting public morals. Why, I'm just giving folks what they want. And in a tasteful way, too."

"Indeed," I replied, "there can be no doubt that the sites of ghastly carnage have always exerted a grim fascination upon our fellow creatures."

"Can't help it. Human nature," said Barnum. "People love a mystery. And there's no bigger mystery than death, Poe, m'boy. The final summons. The last muster. 'The undiscovered country from whose bourn no traveler returns,' as the Immortal Bard says." Emitting a sigh that seemed expressive of both admiration and regret, he continued thusly: "Now *there* was a showman for you. Knew how to give the public what it wants. Blood-and-thunder, with a smattering of poetry thrown in for good measure. Wish he were alive today. Make a mint off the fellow."

As we advanced toward the entrance of the handsome brick dwelling, an excited murmur arose from the little congregation of bystanders.

"Look," exclaimed one. "Isn't that P. T. Barnum?"

"So it is," said another. "But who's that gloomy-looking fellow with him?"

"Must be the coroner," ventured a third.

Pausing at the front stoop, Barnum turned to the assemblage and—assuming a solemn mien—said: "Greetings, friends. Delighted to see you. Wish I could stay here and shake each and every one of you by the hand. Duty calls, however. Most urgent business to attend to."

Reaching into his coat pocket, he then extracted a small packet of coupons, and—undoing the band that secured them—proceeded to distribute them to the crowd that was now pressing close about us. "Here you are, friends. Take one for yourself and pass the others around. Good for a complimentary bag of peanuts with every paid, weekday admission to the American Museum. Hope to see you there soon!"

Then, tipping his hat to the crowd, he took me by the elbow and ushered me into the building.

Traversing a narrow foyer, we ascended the dimly lit staircase with Barnum in the lead. As we made our way upward, I observed that each of the floors was divided into three separate apartments. Arrived at length at the topmost landing, Barnum tried the knob on the heavy oak door directly facing the stairwell—only to find that it was locked. Nothing daunted, he reached into the right hip pocket of his trousers, removed a key, inserted it into the corresponding hole in the brass plate, and gave a decisive, counterclockwise twist—whereupon the bolt slid back with a resounding click!

That Barnum possessed the means to open the door to the murder scene was a source of some astonishment to me, as my expression must have conveyed; for—gazing in my direction—he gave me a conspiratorial wink and explained: "Paid a little visit to the landlord this morning, before heading up to your neck of the woods. Mr. Schuyler Colfax. Very reasonable old gent—most accommodating. Happy to provide me with the use of the key. Of course, he expected a small show of gratitude in return. But that's just human nature. All of us like to be appreciated."

"I see," said I. "And what precisely did this appreciation amount to?"

"Oh, we haggled over that for a bit," Barnum said with a chuckle. "Drives a hard bargain does old Mr. Colfax. Oh yes. Wouldn't settle for a penny less than twenty-five dollars—*half* of what I was prepared to pay him!"

Tossing the key upward, he snatched it in midair with a flourish, and returned it to his pocket—then threw open the door and waved me inside.

During the initial portion of our coach-ride from the country to the city, Barnum had imparted to me what little he knew about the murder victim's background. According to the accounts published in that morning's newspapers, Isabel Somers was an unmarried woman of twenty-one who had moved to Manhattan from her birthplace in upstate New York less than a year prior to her violent demise. Her Thomas Street neighbors recalled her as a pleasant young woman— handsome rather than beautiful—with a decidedly reclusive bent.

Of her origins, very little was known, though rumors suggested that (like my own long-deceased progenitors) her parents had, at some earlier point in their marriage, been itinerant play-actors. Having failed to distinguish themselves at this calling, they had abandoned the stage and settled in the area around Schenectady, where they had purchased some land and taken up dairy farming. Unfortunately, they had proven as ill-suited for the *agrarian* way of life as they had for the *thespian*. When Isabel was eighteen years of age, the farm had failed, plunging the family into penury. Shortly afterward, both of her parents died (reportedly within a few months of each other), leaving their only child both orphaned and indigent.

Of Isabel Somers's existence between that period and the time of her arrival in New York City nearly three years later, nothing was known. Nor had the newspapers provided any details about her current situation, beyond reporting that she lived by herself in the Thomas Street apartment.

In light of these facts, the scene that now presented itself to my view as I stood beside Barnum in the parlor of the dead woman's residence was surprising in the extreme; for the sheer luxury, if not *opulence*, of the room was wildly at odds with her reportedly humble circumstances.

There were two windows in the parlor. Their curtains were of an exceedingly rich crimson silk, fringed with golden tassels and held open with a thick rope, also of gold. These same colors—crimson and gold—appeared everywhere in profusion and determined the *character* of the room. The carpet—of Saxony material—was quite half-an-inch thick and of the same crimson hue, relieved simply by a border of finespun gold cord, like that festooning the draperies.

The walls were covered with a glossy paper of a silver-gray tint, spotted with small arabesque devices of a fainter shade of the prevalent crimson. Numerous paintings relieved the expanse of the paper. These were chiefly landscapes of an imaginative cast, reminiscent of the fairy grottoes of Stanfield and the Lake of the Dismal Swamp of Chapman. There were also three or four female heads of an ethereal beauty—portraits in the manner of Sully. The frames were richly carved without being filigreed, and had the luster of burnished gold.

The furnishings, though somewhat sparse, were of the most exquisite workmanship. There was a single easy-chair, upholstered in crimson silk with a speckling of delicate gold florets. Beside it stood an octagonal table, its top formed of the richest, gold-threaded marble. A cut-glass decanter, half-filled with amber liquid, sat upon the table, along with a goblet, also of the finest crystal.

Positioned against one wall was a handsome pianoforte, without cover, and thrown open. A Sheraton writing desk, or *escritoire*—made of bird's-eye maple with trimming of mahogany veneer and a row of ebony and holly inlaying below the drawers—stood against the opposite wall. A light and graceful hanging shelf sustained a dozen or so richly bound volumes. Beyond these things there was no furniture, except for an Argand lamp with a plain, crimson-tinted, ground-glass shade that depended from the ceiling by a single, slender gold chain.

"Great Scot!" my companion exclaimed. "Mighty grand diggings for a penniless farm girl!"

"Indeed, I have just been marveling at the same incongruity." Casting my gaze about the parlor once again, I noted that—except for the *escritoire,* whose drawers were hanging open in a haphazard fashion—the order of the room seemed largely undisturbed.

Catercorner to where I stood was a wide-flung door, opening into another chamber. Crossing the parlor with Barnum at my heels, I stepped over the threshold and found myself in the slain woman's boudoir. The scene that here offered itself to my contemplation was intensely gruesome. The victim's body had, of course, been removed from the premises—transported, I surmised, to the quarters of the coroner's physician, where, as was usual in such cases, it would undergo an extensive postmortem examination. Even without the material presence of the mutilated corpse, however, a palpable air of catastrophic horror pervaded the chamber.

The room was dominated by a mahogany four-poster whose wildly disheveled bedclothes were encrusted with thick gouts of dried blood—the all-too-vivid evidence of the atrocity that had transpired within the precincts of the young woman's sanctum. The unspeakable savagery of the murder was equally apparent in the clotted, reddish-brown stains that discolored the floor and bespattered the wall above the bedstead. Adding to the intensely unsavory atmosphere of the room was an unusually large congregation of houseflies that had evidently been attracted to the scene by the faint but unmistakable *fœtor* of decay emanating from the dark and stiffened bedclothes.

"Lord bless me, what a sight!" Barnum exclaimed. "Never seen anything like it. Why, the room's as bloody as an abattoir."

"Your choice of simile is entirely apt," I replied, "for the inordinately sanguinary condition of the chamber only confirms what the newspapers reported: that the crime perpetrated upon these premises was nothing less than an act of the most cruel—ferocious—and appalling—*butchery!*"

Withdrawing my attention from the bedstead, I quickly surveyed the rest of the chamber, taking particular note of three of its furnishings: a small oblong chest of highly varnished cedar that sat at the foot of the bed, a mahogany wardrobe or armoire, and a matching bureau whose drawers (like those of the writing desk in the parlor) had been pulled out to their fullest extent. Various items of apparel—including (I could not help but observe) assorted, delicate pieces of female underlinen—hung from the drawers in the greatest disarray; others lay strewn on the floor at the foot of the ransacked dresser.

Following the direction of my gaze, Barnum bitterly remarked: "Looks like the vile miscreant had plunder on his mind as well as murder."

"Only if we suppose that it was the *killer* who rummaged through Isabel Somers's possessions," I replied, "a hypothesis that the evidence by no means supports."

"How do you mean?" Barnum asked in surprise.

"To begin with," I said, "the sheer, overwhelming savagery of the murder indicates that its perpetrator was impelled not by greed but by passion—that *bloodlust*, not robbery, was the motive for this crime.

"Second, according to the newspaper accounts—as you related them to me during our journey earlier this morning—several of Isabel Somers's neighbors testified to hearing a single agonized shriek issuing from her apartment in the middle of the night. In light of this circumstance, it is difficult to believe that the killer would have lingered on the scene to rummage through her belongings. Once having committed his ghastly deed, he surely would have fled without delay, under the assumption that the other residents of the building—alarmed by the poor victim's cries—would hurry to investigate.

"Finally, if you will direct your gaze to the top of the bureau, you will notice several items that remain undisturbed. These include a woman's silver-handled grooming set, including a hairbrush, matching comb, and hand-mirror, all eminently transportable and clearly of substantial value—in short, precisely the sort of objects that the malefactor would have made off with, had robbery been his intent."

"By God, Poe, you're right! The police must have done this. Leave it to those blunderheads to make such a mess while looking for clues."

"If clues were, indeed, the object of their search," I said in a musing tone.

For a moment, Barnum merely stared at me narrowly. "You're a great one for riddles, Poe, I'll say that for you," he remarked at length. "Not that I'm criticizing, mind you. I'm fond of them myself. Nothing like a good riddle to whet the public's curiosity. 'Come see Zip, the amazing What-Is-It? Is he man or monkey, human or beast? You decide for yourself!' Always leave 'em guessing—that's P. T. Barnum's motto. Still and all, Poe, I'd be a happier man if your comments didn't leave me in the dark *quite* so often."

"I apologize for the somewhat cryptic nature of my remark," I replied, "but I was merely thinking aloud. Before elucidating my meaning, however, I would prefer to conduct a more thorough investigation of the premises. The hypothesis that I have begun to consider remains, at present, merely *that*—a strong, though still largely unsubstantiated, *possibility*."

"All right, then, Poe, m'boy. You go right ahead. That's what you're here for, after all. I'll just poke around a bit while you attend to your investigating."

Leaving Barnum in the bedchamber, I returned to the parlor, where, for the following thirty-five or forty minutes, I carefully examined the contents of the room. I began by checking the front door leading into the apartment, paying special attention to the lock plate and surrounding wood. I then crossed to the opposite side of the room, where I spent several minutes studying the open writing surface of the drop-front *escritoire*. Next, I examined each of the volumes on the hanging bookshelf, closely scrutinizing the corner edges of their covers. A short distance away from where the bookshelf depended, I noticed a nail jutting from the wall. It had been driven into the plaster at approximately eye level and was angled upward, as though it had originally been used to hold a small mirror or framed picture that had since been removed.

Proceeding to the easy-chair, I inspected its soft, overstuffed cushion. Then I peered into the crystal goblet that sat on the marble-topped table directly to the right of the chair. As I was replacing this receptacle beside its matching, half-emptied decanter, I was struck with a sudden suspicion. Kneeling at the foot of the armchair, I bent low to the floor and peered closely at the carpet.

I was on my hands and knees with my face only inches from the thick, though exceedingly supple, pile, when I heard a bitter imprecation issuing from the other room. Rising to my feet, I strode into the bedchamber and saw Barnum standing beside the open cedar chest. A pamphlet of some sort was clutched in his hand, and his countenance wore an expression of the most extreme displeasure.

"What in heaven's name is the matter?" I asked. "From the look on your face, you appear to have discovered something disturbing."

"*Damned* disturbing," Barnum confirmed with a scowl. "To *me*, at any rate. I just thank my lucky stars that the bunglers who rummaged through this place overlooked it. Why," he continued, waving the pamphlet before my face, "if this had fallen into the wrong hands, the newspapers would've had a field day." So saying, he thrust the slender publications into my hands.

Frowning, I began to peruse it, and saw at once that it was a souvenir booklet from Barnum's establishment, containing brief descriptions—accompanied by remarkably detailed engravings—of the various performers featured in his Hall of Human Oddities. These included John Hanson Craig, the twelve-year-old, four-hundred-pound youth known as "The Carolina Fat Boy"; Colonel Routh Goshen, the seven-feet-eight-inch tall "Arabian Giant"; Raddo Schauf, the eighteen-inch German midget billed as "The Lilliputian King"; the sixty-three-pound "Living Skeleton," Slim Jim McCormack; Signor Bruno Saltarino, "The Armless Wonder"; our erstwhile coach-woman, the hirsute Wilhelmina Schnitzler; Charley Dockery, "The Man with Two Bodies"; and more. There was also a passage devoted to the creature that Sissy had remarked upon with such awed fascination during our visit to the American Museum: the so-called living "changeling baby" reputedly left by malicious goblins in exchange for the abducted infant son of an Irish farming couple.

"Here I am, trying to prove that this heinous murder had no connection at all to my museum," Barnum declared after a brief interval of silence, "and *this* turns up! Of course, it proves nothing—only that the poor woman paid a visit to my Hall of Human Oddities, like countless other people who've made Barnum's American Museum the most popular showplace in existence. Still, if my enemies ever got wind of this, it would be an infernal nuisance. They'd find *some* way to use it against me, you can be sure of it. Especially Bennett. Oh, he's a sly devil, Bennett is."

"And where precisely did this come from?" I asked, looking up from the booklet.

"In there," said Barnum, pointing his walking stick at the open cedar chest.

Handing the booklet back to Barnum—who quickly folded it in half and thrust it into the side pocket of his coat—I stepped over to the chest, squatted on my haunches, and peered inside. Strewn about the bottom was a disorganized heap of printed matter, including a dozen or so issues of popular monthly magazines, along with numerous pieces of sheet-music. Several of the magazines had been so carelessly handled that their covers had become partially detached; others had pages torn from their bindings. From the exceedingly chaotic condition of this material, I surmised that it had been rummaged through in a most precipitous—if not *violent*—manner.

Glancing up at the showman, I asked: "When you first examined this chest, were its contents in a state of such extreme disarray?"

"My word, yes," he replied. "I sifted through it, of course—shoved things around a bit. But it was an unholy mess to start out with."

Removing one of the magazines that lay at the top of the heap, I perceived that it was a recent issue of *The Ladies' Companion*, containing the usual collection of cloyingly sentimental stories, treacly ballads, and articles on such subjects as "The Follies of Intemperance" and "Poetical Happiness"—along with fashion-plates, hand-colored floral prints, and steel engravings of domestic scenes and romantic situations with titles like "First Love," "The Widowed Bride," and "My Childhood's Happy Home." Opening its pages at random, I came upon a typical offering—a mercifully brief piece of doggerel by a female poetaster named Miss C. Godfrey:

FLOWERS

I love the little simple flowers,
Altho' they perish fast,
And in their dying moments tell
No earthly sweet can last.
They're types of brighter things above,
Breathings of hopes divine;
Emblems of innocence and truth,
Where gems immortal shine!

Grimacing at this deplorable—though all-too-typical—example of the sort of *tripe* that filled the pages of America's literary magazines (even while men of true poetic genius struggled fruitlessly for recognition), I dropped the journal onto the floor—reached back into the chest—and extracted several loose sheets of music. Upon closer inspection, these proved to be songs of the most saccharine nature conceivable—"She Lives Within My Heart," "Dry Up Your Tears," "Bright Morn of Life," "Oh! Do Not Bid Me Cease to Love"—arranged for pianoforte, harp, and guitar.

"What do you think, Poe?" Barnum asked as I set the sheet-music on the floor beside the discarded magazine. "Can you tell anything from that stuff?"

"Nothing more than the obvious," I replied. "Evidently, Miss Somers employed this chest as a repository for those pieces of printed matter to which she attached a particular value. That most, if not all, of these items possess little or no *intrinsic* merit merely indicates that—as is true of the vast majority of Americans—her aesthetic sensibilities were of the most rudimentary sort."

Even as I voiced this opinion, a thought occurred to me. Bending nearer to the chest, I reached both hands inside it and began to remove the remainder of the material. Having emptied the chest entirely of its contents, I carefully scrutinized its interior. As I did, my gaze fell upon a small, roughly triangular scrap of fine-textured paper, wedged in the crack formed by the juncture of the bottom and rear panels. I carefully extracted this fragment, and—raising it to my eyes—saw that it constituted the torn-off corner of a piece of stationery. Only one word—written in strong, distinctly masculine hand—was visible upon its surface: "horn."

Pocketing this item, I got to my feet and asked my companion whether—in his exploration of the room—he had discovered anything noteworthy, apart from the brochure that had occasioned him so much dismay.

"Can't say that I did," Barnum replied. "Unless you count *that*," he added, pointing his walking stick at the wardrobe.

This handsome and commodious piece of furniture was of bright red mahogany with golden markings in the grain. Its double doors were thrown wide open, exposing the interior cabinet. This was divided into two adjacent compartments, the left-hand side serving as a closet in which a dozen or more sumptuous female garments hung suspended from a rod; the right consisting of a series of six, vertically stacked drawers with milky, cast-glass knobs.

The anomaly that had attracted Barnum's notice was apparent at a glance. While the closet appeared to be completely untouched, someone had thoroughly rifled through the drawers, most of whose contents lay scattered about the floor at the foot of the wardrobe.

"See what I mean?" said Barnum. "One side looks as though it's been struck by a tropical hurricane. The other's neat as a pin. Strange, wouldn't you say?"

"Yes and no," I replied. "Considered in isolation, the incongruity to which you refer does indeed seem highly peculiar. It is, however, entirely consistent with certain other circumstances which I have noted and which may provide us with an important clue in our search for the solution to this dark and troubling mystery."

"You don't say? Why, that's wonderful! Absolutely marvelous! What a head you have on you, Poe, m'boy! Of course, I have no idea what you mean—but I assume that you won't keep me waiting for an explanation."

"Indeed, I will satisfy your curiosity at once," I replied. "If you will just follow me into the parlor."

CHAPTER NINE

Leading the showman back into the parlor, I began by asking him if his own examination of the apartment had led him to form any opinion respecting its slain occupant.

Barnum's visage assumed a look of intense concentration—brow deeply furrowed, mouth arranged into a meditative frown. "Well, she certainly had a taste for the finer things in life, I'll say that for her," he remarked at length. "That armchair you're standing beside—genuine Hepplewhite, unless my eyes deceive me. Purchased one very much like it for Mrs. Barnum on our fourteenth wedding anniversary last November. Paid a pretty penny for it, too. But why not buy the best if you can afford it? That's *my* feeling."

"But that is precisely the point," I said. "Or rather, the *question*. How was Isabel Somers—a young, unmarried woman from an impoverished background and with no visible means of support—able to afford such luxurious surroundings?"

"I've been wondering the same," Barnum said. All at once, his eyes grew wide. "Bless my soul!" he exclaimed. "Of course! The woman was a Cyprian—a common harlot—just like Ellen Jennings. Why didn't I see it before?" He shook his head slowly. "Didn't want to think ill of the dead, I suppose."

Crossing my arms over my chest, I responded to Barnum thusly: "While the conclusion at which you have arrived is not wholly unreasonable, it is not *entirely* supported by the evidence at hand. As you well know, the great metropolis of New York is as infamous for its countless inducements to vice, sin, and debauchery as it is renowned for the unparalleled richness and variety of its cultural institutions. Females of licentious character abound. Virtually all of these wicked creatures, however, ply their trade in the many houses of ill-fame that operate so flagrantly throughout the city. This was the case with Ellen Jennings, whose murder was perpetrated in the den of iniquity in which she resided.

"That Isabel Somers might have pursued such a calling here, in this very apartment, seems so unlikely as to be inconceivable. The building itself is, to all appearances, an eminently respectable dwelling place, inhabited by law-abiding families who, it must be assumed, would scarcely have tolerated the presence of a known and active prostitute in their midst. Nor is it likely that any woman, even of the most degraded character, would be inclined to conduct her immoral trade in surroundings where she—as well as her customers—would be subjected to the constant, close, and embarrassing scrutiny of outraged and censorious neighbors.

"Moreover—and this is a point of the highest importance—in the newspaper accounts of the murder, Isabel Somers is at no time identified as a prostitute. In the case of the unfortunate Ellen Jennings, the daily gazettes—and the *Herald* in particular—placed extraordinary emphasis on the victim's disreputable profession, for the obvious reasons. That Jennings was not merely a young woman of surpassing beauty but a notorious *fille de joie* added an exceptionally *titillating* element to the story, thus ensuring that the vast and vulgar reading public—whose appetite for lurid sensationalism is nothing less than boundless—would clamor for every detail. Of one thing we may be certain—had Isabel Somers trodden the same iniquitous path as Ellen Jennings, the fact would have received equally prominent and salacious attention in the press."

"Makes perfect sense," Barnum conceded. "Yes, it's mighty sound reasoning—though I don't go along with *all* your views. Especially about the public's interest in these matters. Why, you make it sound downright *indecent*. But there are lessons of immense importance to be learned from these tragic cases, Poe, m'boy. That's what makes my

Hall of Crime and Punishment one of the most morally edifying exhibitions ever conceived by man. More than three dozen wax tableaux of the world's most grim, gruesome, and ghastly murders—all designed to show the dreadful fate that awaits the hardened sinner!

"But let's stick to the point," he continued with a careless wave of the hand. "The point is—if Isabel Somers was an innocent, then how did she afford all this luxury?"

"I merely meant to indicate that she did not derive her income from the trade of prostitution—not that she was an innocent," I replied. "On the contrary, my observations have led me to conclude the opposite: that Isabel Somers fell into that class of individuals belonging to what the French call the *demimonde*—in short, that she lived as a *kept mistress*. I am further convinced that her unknown benefactor is a man not merely of exceptional wealth but of extraordinary prominence and political influence—i.e., a member of the city's social and financial elite.

"Moreover," I added, "I have managed to ascertain that this personage visited Miss Somers at some time shortly before—if not immediately *prior* to—her murder. The discovery of this man's identity is thus of the utmost urgency; for—if not himself the perpetrator of this cold-blooded deed—his intimate knowledge of the victim might well afford important clues that will lead us to the culprit."

Barnum's response to my statement was dramatic in the extreme. His mouth fell open, and he regarded me with an expression of unconcealed wonder. "You never cease to surprise me, Poe, m'boy. Yessir, I don't hesitate to say that I am absolutely staggered with amazement. How in heaven's name did you arrive at this conclusion?"

"Permit me to explain," I said. "Upon our arrival at the apartment, I observed that you had no difficulty in opening the door with the key which you so cleverly obtained from the landlord, Mr. Colfax. This fact suggested that the lock had in no way been tampered with—a supposition I subsequently confirmed by a close examination of the door, which showed no signs of a forcible entry. Since there are no other means of ingress into the apartment—the windows being utterly inaccessible from the outside—only one conclusion presented itself: that the perpetrator of this atrocity either entered the apartment by means of his own key, or was freely admitted by Miss Somers herself.

"Let me now direct your attention to this armchair, which—as you so astutely observed—is an exceptionally fine specimen from the workshop of the master furniture-maker, George Hepplewhite. You will note that its cushion clearly retains the imprint of the last person to have been seated upon it. It is very evident that an indentation of this depth and dimension could only have been produced by a sitter of considerable weight.

"Now, as we know from the newspapers, Isabel Somers was a woman of slender, even maidenly, stature. We may therefore surmise that the impression on this cushion was left by a *visitor* to the apartment, almost certainly a male. This inference in itself means little or nothing, since it is conceivable that—at some point during the search of the apartment—one of the police officers seated himself upon the chair. There are other pieces of evidence, however, which argue against this possibility.

"Take this goblet, for example," I continued, raising the object in question from the marble-topped side table. "It contains a very small quantity of brandy—no more than a mere *thimbleful*, to be sure, but enough to indicate that someone has recently drunk from it. Moreover, when I bent to the floor and made a close inspection of the carpet, I noticed a tiny but detectable quantity of cigar-ash lying at the foot of the chair. That a police officer would have paused in the midst of an urgent investigation to indulge in a glass of brandy and a cigar is a notion that cannot be seriously entertained.

"There is another circumstance in regard to this armchair that I wish you to consider. You will note that it is the only piece of furniture in this room designed for leisurely repose, the parlor lacking a sofa. We are thus led to conclude that—while her caller relaxed in this chair—Miss Somers remained on her feet. Of course, it is also possible that he was alone at the time, having admitted himself with his key during her absence and making himself comfortable until her return. Either of these alternatives, however, is indicative of the same state of affairs: namely, a rare degree of familiarity between Isabel Somers and her male visitor.

"But on what basis can we so confidently assert that this mysterious gentleman is a personage of exceptional wealth, standing, and power in the city? The first of these attributes can scarcely be doubted, if we assume (as I believe we *must*, in light of the evidence) that the luxurious mode of living enjoyed by Isabel Somers was furnished by this unknown benefactor. The others can be inferred from the following considerations.

"There is, to begin with, what may be termed the *negative* evidence— i.e., the complete *absence*, in the newspaper accounts of the crime, of any allusion whatsoever to the victim's inordinately comfortable circumstances. As we have already agreed, the penny press—ordinarily so alert to even the merest *hint* of scandal—has displayed uncustomary discretion in regard to its treatment of Miss Somers's character, which has been presented as nothing less than immaculate. We are therefore justified in believing that a deliberate decision has been made to conceal the unsavory truth from the public. But *why?* Only one answer seems plausible: Bennett and his fellow publishers—either from a sense of their own self-interest, or from the application of outside pressure—are eager to suppress any information that might lead to the exposure of Miss Somers's keeper. We can only conclude from this deduction that the latter is a person to be reckoned with—if not, indeed, to be *feared.*

"But there are other, more tangible reasons for my suppositions in regard to this mysterious individual," I continued. "If you will step over to the writing table, I shall show you what I mean."

Wearing a look of the most intense curiosity, Barnum accompanied me across the room, where we paused before the *escritoire.* "In examining the writing surface of the desk," I explained, "I noticed *this.*" With my right index finger I traced the outline of a faint discoloration upon the open, drop-front lid. This mark was in the shape of a somewhat ragged right angle, each of its sides measuring approximately two inches in length. "Clearly, it is an ink stain. Judging from its size, shape, and location, we are justified in assuming that it was created when someone—most probably Isabel Somers—overturned her open ink pot, whose contents spilled onto the desk and pooled around the corner of a *book.* Miss Somers must have then blotted up the fluid, but not before it had produced this stain in the wood.

"Now, the most reasonable inference is that the book was one in which she was *writing* at the time of the mishap. This would account for the *unstoppered* ink pot. But what sort of book would this be? Clearly, a diary or journal. Certainly it was not one of the literary works to be found on her shelves—for when I examined these volumes, I found no trace of an ink stain on any of their covers.

"But where, then, *is* this journal? Here, I believe, lies the explanation for the incongruity you noticed in regard to her *armoire*. The fact that, in the entire apartment, the only places thoroughly searched were the drawers of this desk—the drawers of her bureau—the drawers of the wardrobe—and the trunk at the foot of her bed—leads us to the following deduction: whoever conducted the search was looking, not for clues to the crime (which might, after all, be equally derived from other items in the apartment that were left completely untouched), but for *specific articles that would be logically stored in these particular locations.*

"And what were these articles? The missing journal, for one. For another—personal letters that Isabel Somers deemed significant enough to save. This latter inference is based on my discovery of *this*—" Reaching into my pocket, I removed the small scrap of paper I had found wedged into the bottom of the trunk. "As you can see, it is a piece of stationery, evidently torn from the corner of a letter.

"That Isabel Somers employed the chest to preserve her most cherished documents," I continued, "we have already surmised. That the chest itself was violently ransacked is beyond dispute. Since, among the various items still remaining in the chest, not a single letter is to be found—including the one from which this fragment was detached—we may surmise that her personal correspondence has *vanished* from the chest. Indeed, I believe we may go farther and state that her personal correspondence, along with her missing journal, *constituted the very object of the search.*

"Taking all these circumstances into account, we are thus fully persuaded that a deliberate and concerted effort has been made to remove from the crime scene any evidence that would serve to identify—and possibly *incriminate*—the individual upon whose largess Miss Somers's luxurious mode of living depended. Whether this effort was undertaken by the police or by some minion acting on behalf of this unknown personage is immaterial, at least in regard to our immediate concerns; for in either case, it is clear that the latter must be a man of formidable power and influence."

For several moments, Barnum merely stared at me silently. At length, he raised his right hand to the level of his shoulder—delivered a resounding smack to the corresponding thigh—and, in a booming voice, exclaimed: "God bless my soul, but you're a bona fide wonder, Poe, m'boy! Why, it's a feat of cogitation worthy of my world-famous mental marvel, Professor Emil LeBeaux, the Human Encyclopedia!"

"Perhaps you have overestimated the complexity of my analysis," I replied, dismissing Barnum's characteristically *unbridled* effusion with a modest wave of the hand. "Indeed, my 'feat,' as you call it, represents the very *opposite* of the marvelous, depending as it does not on any strange or preternatural faculty of mind, but—*au contraire*—on the eminently *human* capacity to arrive at rigorously logical deductions, based upon the precise observation of fact.

"In any event," I continued, allowing a note of concern to enter into my voice, "my analysis will, I fear, avail us nothing unless we are able to discover the next piece of the puzzle. I mean, of course, the name of Isabel Somers's benefactor."

"Why, nothing could be easier," Barnum confidently declared. "We'll just ask around the building. I'll wager dollars to doughnuts that *someone* has caught sight of the fellow. Once we get a description, discovering who he is should be simplicity itself."

"I am afraid that I cannot entirely share in your optimism," I replied. "As the evidence suggests, the person we are seeking has gone to extraordinary pains to prevent the world from learning about his illicit relationship with Miss Somers. In light of this fact, it seems reasonable to assume that his visits were restricted to those times when he would be least likely to attract the notice of witnesses—most probably, during those nocturnal hours when the average person would already be abed.

"Let us assume, however, that one or more of the residents *did* get a glimpse of him. Persuading such a person to share this intelligence may well prove impossible, for the reasons already adduced. Miss Somers's benefactor—as our investigation suggests—has not scrupled to exert whatever pressure necessary to ensure his anonymity. This same pressure would almost certainly have been brought to bear on any potential witnesses. In short, it would not surprise me in the least to discover that Isabel Somers's neighbors have been either bribed or *coerced* into silence."

"We'll just see about that," Barnum proclaimed. "This fellow, whoever he is, may not be a man to be trifled with. But neither is P. T. Barnum! Just look at me, Poe—take a good long gander. What do you see? No need to answer—I can tell what you're thinking. You're thinking: *here stands a man who has climbed to the very peak—the very zenith!— of fame, success, and public adulation!* And how do you imagine that I've scaled those immense heights? By allowing other men to get the better of me? Hah! I don't care who this fellow is, or how much pressure he's put on the good, decent folks who live in this building. P. T. Barnum's powers of persuasion are second to no one's. And I say that with all modesty, Poe—with the full and humble recognition that it was the good Lord Himself who bestowed these amazing gifts upon me.

"Now, come along and let's have a talk with Miss Somers's neighbors," he said, heading for the front door and motioning for me to follow. "You mark my words, Poe. They'll open up like steamers at a New England clambake by the time I get through with them."

Emerging into the dimly lit hallway, we proceeded to the neighboring apartment; whereupon Barnum administered several sharp raps to the door with the heavy brass knob of his walking stick. This action being followed by a protracted silence, Barnum knocked once again—with equally negative results. Persuaded that the occupant was not at home, we were just turning away from the door when we became cognizant of the faint but unmistakable sound of shuffling footsteps, emanating from the interior of the apartment. A moment later, the latch was thrown—the door swung in upon its hinges—and we found ourselves gazing into the exceedingly wizened countenance of a small, stoop-shouldered old fellow who peered up at us with narrowed, rheumy eyes.

"Good day," Barnum declared, tipping his hat. "P. T. Barnum at your service."

Far from being impressed by this announcement, the old man showed no recognition at all of Barnum's name. "Yeah?" he brusquely replied, scrutinizing the latter with a look of the keenest suspicion.

Somewhat taken aback by the old man's exceedingly inhospitable response, Barnum cleared his throat and said: "Pardon the intrusion, my good fellow. We'll only take a minute of your time. My associate, Mr. Poe, and I wish to ask a few questions about your neighbor, the unfortunate Miss Somers."

"Don't know nothing about it," the old man declared—and, without another word, unceremoniously slammed the door in our faces!

For a moment Barnum appeared too startled to speak. At length, he regained his composure and, shaking his head, sadly remarked: "Poor old gent. Obviously suffering from the debilitating effects of advanced senescence. Hope it never happens to me. Rather be put out of my misery at once than spend my declining years as a doddering imbecile. Come along, Poe. There are plenty of other people in this building. Someone's bound to know something."

In this sanguine belief, however, Barnum proved to be thoroughly mistaken. The next apartment we tried was occupied by a middle-aged woman with the gaunt, hollow-eyed, intensely careworn appearance of a housewife who has been either widowed or abandoned. Huddled around her in the doorway was a brood of somewhat bedraggled-looking offspring, the youngest a toddler of approximately two years of age, the oldest a lad of twelve or thirteen.

On this occasion, Barnum's vanity could hardly fail to have been gratified by the response he received. At the mention of his name, the woman's sunken eyes expanded in amazement, while her children emitted gasps of awestruck delight (all excepting the two-year-old, who merely gazed up in mute incomprehension, noisily sucking his thumb). Impressed as she so obviously was by her illustrious caller, however, the woman proved to be no more cooperative than the surly old man. No sooner had Barnum explained the purpose of our visit than she squeezed her mouth so tight that her lips seemed to vanish—she shook her head emphatically—and, after shooing her children away from the threshold, she pushed the door closed and locked it.

Thus it proved with every tenant we questioned. However amazed and excited they were to find themselves face-to-face with the celebrated showman, they fell into an abrupt—absolute—and unyielding silence the moment they were questioned as to Isabel Somers's circumstances. Even the liberal distribution of his complimentary coupons—entitling the bearer to a gratis bag of peanuts—could not induce them to speak. By the time we had worked our way down to the ground floor and, finally, back out onto the street, Barnum's face was contorted into a look of the greatest exasperation.

"By George, that's annoying," he grumbled as we stood before the entrance of the building. "By George, that's frustrating. Never been more vexed in my life. You can be sure of it, Poe—those people knew more than they were letting on. I could see it in their eyes."

"Indeed," I said, "though by no means given to the odious practice of *gloating*, I cannot help but observe that they reacted in precisely the way I predicted."

"Yes, yes," Barnum said. "You were perfectly right. Right as rain. But what the devil are they so afraid of? Why, it doesn't make any—"

All at once, he broke off his statement and—with a deeply puzzled expression—swiveled his head and looked over his shoulder. Curious as to the cause of this sudden interruption, I likewise peered behind him, and observed a scrawny, tow-headed lad, dressed in somewhat threadbare garments, tugging on the hem of Barnum's coat. I recognized the boy at once as the oldest child of the harried, middle-aged woman who was the second of the tenants we had approached.

With several rapid, sideways jerks of the head, the underfed youth motioned for us to follow, then hurriedly led us into the alleyway adjoining the building. After casting a few nervous glances about him—as if to assure himself that we weren't being spied upon—he focused his gaze upon Barnum, while I took a moment to study his features more closely.

He was a lad of singularly unprepossessing appearance, with small, close-set eyes, a sharply upturned nose, and excessively protruding upper incisors of the sort commonly referred to as "buck teeth." His facial expression was inordinately *knowing* for someone so young, and served to heighten his resemblance to a particularly cunning member of the order *Rodentia.*

"Speak up, young man, speak up," said Barnum in a tone of mock severity. "I am not in the habit of following strangers into darkened alleyways. Explain yourself at once."

"You really P. T. Barnum?" the boy rather impudently demanded.

"In the flesh! The King of Showmen! The sun of the amusement world from which all lesser luminaries borrow their light! And this is my associate, Mr. Edgar Allan Poe."

"Never heard of him," said the churlish, surpassingly unattractive young boy.

"And what is *your* name, my lad?" asked Barnum.

"Frankie Plunkitt."

"Well, Master Plunkitt," said Barnum. "State your business. We have urgent matters to attend to."

After taking another quick look around him, the boy turned back to Barnum and—lowering his voice to a volume barely louder than a whisper—said: "That lady, the one that got her throat cut and her hands chopped off. I know something about her."

"You do, do you?" said Barnum with a frown. "And what exactly do you know?"

A look of the deepest *disdain*—peculiarly offensive in a child whose age (to judge from his stature) could not have been older than thirteen—spread across the boy's countenance. "I ain't saying nothing 'til I get something first," he declared with a sneer.

For a moment, Barnum seemed visibly taken aback at this brazen declaration. Quickly recovering himself, he said: "Fair enough. Business is business. 'If you want to dance, you must pay the fiddler'— that's P. T. Barnum's motto. Here—" Reaching into his coat pocket, he extracted one of his coupons and passed it to the boy. The latter held it close to his face and began to peruse it in silence, his lips laboriously forming each word as he read.

At length, he looked up from the coupon and, in a voice fraught with derision, said: "A bag of peanuts? That's *all?*"

"Why, what more could you desire?" cried Barnum, evidently astounded at the child's effrontery.

"I want to get into your museum for free and see them freaks."

So extreme—so absolute—so apparently *boundless*—was the temerity of the boy that, for a moment, Barnum appeared to have been deprived of the power of speech. All at once, he grinned broadly, emitted a hearty, appreciative chuckle, and exclaimed: "By George, you're a pip, Frankie Plunkitt! A lad after my own heart. I see a great future for you, m'boy—absolutely immense. Why, if you're not *swimming* in money before you attain your majority, I'll be mighty surprised. All right, then. I'll consider your terms. But first, I have to know what I'll be getting in return. 'Never buy a pig in a poke'— that's P. T. Barnum's motto."

Several moments elapsed while the boy warily regarded Barnum. "That lady," he said at length. "A man visited her. I seen him."

Barnum shot me a quick look, then turned back to the boy and— assuming a tone of casual indifference—said: "Is that all? Well, it isn't much, not really. . . . Oh, well, all right. I suppose I'm willing to go along, just for curiosity's sake. Here. Hand me back that coupon—"

Taking the latter from the boy's hand, Barnum extracted a stubby lead pencil from his inside coat pocket and rapidly inscribed some-thing on the back of the coupon. "There you are," he said, returning it to the boy. "Just show this to the gentleman at the ticket booth."

The boy took several moments to read what Barnum had written. Apparently satisfied, he folded the coupon in half and carefully in-serted it into the pocket of his threadbare trousers.

"Now, tell us what you saw, and *when*," said Barnum.

"*When* was a couple weeks ago," said the boy. "Tommy Watkins, my best chum, he bet me five cents that I was too big a scaredy-cat to walk through that big cemetery down on Second Avenue after mid-night. So I sneaked out of the house late at night when Ma was sleeping and run down there and climbed over the gate and done it. I wasn't even scared. So Tommy, who's waiting by the gate, gives me my money and I go home. That's when I seen him. He was coming out of her door. He didn't see me, though, 'cause I ducked into the shadows."

"And what did this person look like?" Barnum said eagerly.

At first, the boy made no reply. As I stood there and scrutinized him, awaiting his answer, his countenance underwent a remarkable transformation. His inordinately shrewd, precociously *canny* expression melted away, and—for the first time—Frankie Plunkitt looked like a frightened little child. When he finally spoke, there was a conspicuous quaver in his voice.

"He looked like the boogeyman," said the boy.

CHAPTER TEN

That the boy had observed an all-too-palpable horror emerging from Isabel Somers's apartment could scarcely be doubted. The terror on his face—no less than the tremor in his voice—vividly attested to the fright he had suffered. Barnum, however, appeared to be intensely skeptical of the lad's statement.

"The boogeyman?" he incredulously exclaimed. "Come, come, Frankie, m'boy. You're not out to bamboozle us, I hope. Why, I've played fair and square with you, haven't I? Gave you just what you wanted. I expect something more than a fairy story in return."

"It ain't no fairy story," the boy indignantly replied.

"But what, precisely, did this fearful apparition look like?" I interjected, directly addressing the boy for the first time.

"Apparition?" said the boy. "You mean what I saw?"

"Exactly so."

"Like somebody that was dead and buried and dug up again after the worms had ate away half his face," came the unsettling reply.

At this exceedingly colorful description, a startled gasp issued from Barnum's lips.

"Why, what is the matter?" I inquired, regarding the showman narrowly.

"Nothing, nothing," he hastily replied—albeit with a look that seemed to say: "Let us refrain from further conversation on this subject until we are alone!" Then, turning back to the boy, Barnum remarked: "All right, lad, all right. You've lived up to your end of the bargain. Run along now."

"That writing you give me—you swear it'll get me in to see the freaks?" asked the ever-wary youngster.

"Why, you wound me, Master Plunkitt—wound me to the quick. P. T. Barnum's word is his bond. Just show that paper at the door, and you'll be treated like visiting royalty. Like Prince Albert himself."

With a nod of satisfaction, the boy swiveled on his heels—darted from the alley—and disappeared around the corner of the building.

In obedience to Barnum's unspoken injunction, I waited until the lad was safely out of sight; then, turning to the showman, I addressed him thusly: "Pray share your thoughts with me at once, for I am greatly puzzled by your response to the intelligence we have just received. The loud gasp you uttered appeared to be one of surprised, if not *shocked*, recognition. And yet I cannot believe this to be the case. Surely, there is no *actual* being with a countenance so gruesome—so ghastly—so sheerly *grotesque*—as the one described by the Plunkitt lad."

His own countenance wrought into a deeply troubled look, Barnum replied: "Oh, but I'm afraid there *is*. I've run into him a time or two. Got a phiz that would throw a scare into Satan. Won't find anything like it outside my museum. Makes Señor Hermano, my Patagonian Cyclops, look like a Broadway swell. Matches every one of *your* deductions, too. Rich as Croesus. Lots of powerful friends. Or at least lots of powerful folks too scared to go against his wishes."

"And precisely who," I cried, "is this extraordinary individual?"

"Name's Vanderhorn," answered Barnum. "Morris Vanderhorn."

It was now *my* turn to emit an astonished gasp. Reaching into my pocket, I extracted the torn scrap of paper I had discovered at the bottom of Isabel Somers's storage chest. "Why, that explains *this*," I exclaimed.

"What is it?" Barnum asked.

Passing it to the showman, I said: "The fragment of stationery I retrieved from the cedar chest in which the slain woman apparently preserved her treasured pieces of *ephemera*. As you can see, it contains four letters that I initially took for a single word—'horn.' It now appears likely, however, that these letters constitute, not a discrete word, but rather the final syllable of this man's *cognomen*."

"Bless me, I believe you're right," Barnum said as he scrutinized the paper. "It's part of Vanderhorn's signature, I'd wager my soul on it. The Somers woman must have been saving his letters—just as you deduced!"

"But you must tell me more about this singular individual," I said, "for I confess that my curiosity has been raised to the highest imaginable pitch."

"All right," he said, consulting his pocket watch. "My Lord—it's nearly three. No wonder my belly's rumbling like Vesuvius. Tell you what, Poe. Why don't we repair to Bodé's and have a confab."

"Bodé's?"

"Henry Bodé's restaurant, over on Courtlandt. I'm a man of regular habits, Poe—part of the key to my enormous success. Let's take our dinner and figure out how to proceed. Can't think clearly on an empty stomach—and when you're dealing with a man like Morris Vanderhorn, you need your wits about you at all times. Come along now, Poe, m'boy, come along," he continued, taking me by the elbow. "Makes the most extraordinary mince pies in town, Henry does. Mouth waters just thinking about them."

Conducting me out of the alleyway, Barnum ushered me toward Broadway, then led me at a brisk pace in the direction of Courtlandt Street. Along the way, he maintained a steadfast silence. Whether his mind was dwelling on the course of our investigation, or on the mince pie he was so keenly anticipating, I could not say. Whatever the case, he was so deeply engrossed in his thoughts that he remained uncharacteristically oblivious to the excited reactions of various pedestrians, who—recognizing the celebrated showman—stopped, stared, and occasionally called out exuberant greetings as we passed.

At length, we arrived at our destination. The entrance to the restaurant was below street level. Following Barnum down several steps and through the door, I found myself in a dimly lit hall, exceedingly redolent of the most savory aromas imaginable. Though nothing short of cavernous, the place was so packed with humanity that every inch of space appeared to be occupied. So great was the din, moreover, that it smote painfully upon my auditory faculty. The chattering of the patrons—the bellowing of the waiters—the clattering of plates and utensils—the scraping of chairs against the wooden floors—all were commingled into a nearly deafening cacophony.

Along one entire wall stretched a zinc-topped counter, crowded with customers, some standing elbow to elbow, others perched on stools. None, so far as I could perceive, was enjoying his repast in a leisurely fashion. On the contrary, I had rarely witnessed a crowd of men dining in such an animated, if not *frenetic*, manner—brandishing knives and forks and spoons—conversing with their mouths full—gesticulating with their heads, arms, and bodies—and consuming their food as if they were on the eve of a journey around the globe and did not expect to partake of another meal this side of the antipodes.

Other diners sat at small wooden tables, vigorously laying into their dinners, or calling their orders to the waiters, who in turn transmitted them at the very top of their voices to the cooks. The latter, indeed, must have possessed miraculous powers of hearing to be able to comprehend the waiters' shouted commands, which blended into a single, strident, unbroken cry: "Ham'n'eggs-for-two-oyster-stew-coffee-apple-pie-for-three-pork'n'beans-ale-for-four-beefsteak'n'onions-porter-for-five-muttonchop-mincepie-black-tea-for-one!"

As we stood by the entrance way, contemplating this exceedingly chaotic scene, the crowd before us suddenly parted and a rotund figure came waddling toward us. His florid countenance beaming with pleasure, he seized the showman by the hand and—in a voice loud enough to be heard over the *hubbub*—exclaimed: "Mr. Barnum, delighted to see you again."

"Pleasure's all mine, Henry, m'boy. Business is booming, I see."

"Can't complain. Nothing like yours, of course. Still, it keeps the meat on my table."

"And in other places, too," Barnum chuckled, reaching out and giving the proprietor an amiable pat on his remarkably *protuberant* abdomen. "Better watch out, Henry, or you'll be replacing my fat boy one day."

"Ha, ha! That's what the missus says. Usual table?"

"That'd be outstanding, Henry, m'boy—absolutely ideal."

Making our way through the densely packed dining hall with our portly host in the lead, we arrived at length at a secluded area in the rear, separated from the main section of the restaurant by a shoulder-high wooden partition. Here—comfortably removed from the prevailing clamor—we were seated at a spacious round table. Barnum wasted no time in placing his order, then instructed me to do the same.

"Have whatever you please, Poe, m'boy—you must be famished. Nothing makes a man hungrier than cudgeling his brains all morning long. Believe me, I know. Why, it's harder work than blacksmithing."

Though perhaps somewhat overstated, there was more than a modicum of truth in Barnum's observation. For—as the brain is an infinitely more complex mechanism than the arm—it logically follows that the energy expended on sustained mental activity must equal or exceed that required by the performance of any merely *manual* task. (That this is especially true for those rare individuals whose intellectual endowments are far above the ordinary need hardly be stated.)

Complying, then, with the wishes of my companion (who hastened to assure me that my meal was "on him"), I tendered my request for a dinner of beefsteak, roasted potatoes, succotash, and coffee. As the proprietor bustled away to transmit our order to his cooks, Barnum settled back in his seat, avidly rubbing his palms together.

"Well, Poe," he declared, "might as well put our time to good use. Food won't arrive for a few minutes."

"Very well, then, " I replied. "Perhaps you may start by providing me with additional particulars as to this Vanderhorn fellow. To begin with, how old a man is he?"

"Can't say, exactly," Barnum answered with a frown. "He's no stripling, though—that's for sure. Not a day younger than fifty, I'd guess."

"And what of his facial disfigurement? In spite of your earlier assertion, I cannot conceive of a visage such as the one described by our juvenile informant. Like all children, the Plunkitt youth is undoubtedly equipped with an exceedingly colorful imagination. It is also the case that, just prior to his encounter with Vanderhorn, the boy had—on a dare—made a solitary sojourn in a completely deserted and night-shrouded graveyard. Is it not fair to assume that the grisly horror he saw was, to some extent, a mere figment of his overstimulated mind?"

"Not by a whit. Not by the merest *iota*. If anything, the lad was understating the case. I tell you, Poe, this Vanderhorn's got the damnedest mug you ever laid eyes on. Never come across anything like it in all my born days—and, believe me, I've seen some *pips*. Why, you wouldn't believe the gargoyles that come trooping into my office, hoping I'll hire them for my Hall of Oddities. But I've got my standards, Poe—I'm not running a cheap Bowery dime show. No sir! It takes more than just a hideous face to make it into the Barnum Museum!"

"But what precisely *is* it that renders his lineaments so unnerving?"

"Why, it's as if he's got *two* faces, split right down the middle. One side's as regular as can be—downright distinguished, in fact. See him in profile, and you'd take him for a Roman consul. Like a marble bust of Marcus Crassus, come to life. Then he turns his head and, by Jupiter, it's as if you're looking at the Grim Reaper himself! Picture it, Poe—a gaping socket where his right eye should be. Half his nose missing, as if a great big chunk of it just rotted right off. Ever see a leper, Poe? Well, neither have I—but I imagine they have noses like Vanderhorn's. And his mouth!" Here, Barnum gave an exaggerated shiver, as though struck with a sudden ague. "One side all twisted up, like the grin on a Hallowe'en jack-o'-lantern. I tell you, Poe, it's enough to give a grown man the fantods."

"I confess that, in respect to his facial appearance, the man sounds like a positive *monstrosity*. What in heaven's name caused this singular deformity? Was it a defect of birth, the result of a dreadful disease, or the consequence of some dire accident?"

"Wish I could tell you," Barnum said with a shrug. "Oh, there are all sorts of speculations. Wildest tales you ever heard. Some people say he came out of the womb looking like that. Claim his mother was walking past an undertaker's parlor while in a family way and caught a glimpse of a half-rotted corpse."

Arranging my features into an intensely *skeptical* look, I remarked: "Though endorsed in earlier times by such eminent figures as Ambroise Paré and Jan Swammerdam, the ancient and widespread belief in 'maternal impressions' has long since been discredited by modern science. Surely, no reasonable being can seriously entertain the notion that a child may be born with no legs—or with a scarlet birthmark on its brow—or with severely diminished eyesight—merely because its mother was startled by a limbless beggar, ate an excessive number of cherries, or squinted through a keyhole during her pregnancy."

"Oh, I don't know," Barnum said. "Take Waldo Toft, my frog-faced boy. Most astonishing sight you've ever laid eyes on. One of the greatest curiosities in existence. They say his pregnant mother fell asleep by the bank of a millpond one afternoon and woke up with the fattest bullfrog you ever saw squatting on her belly.

"Mind you," Barnum continued, "I'm not saying Vanderhorn *was* born that way. There are plenty of rumors to pick from—you pays your money and you takes your choice. I've heard it said he was captured by the Indians while fighting against that rascal Tenskwatawa in the battle of Tippecanoe. The redskins had just gone to work on him—gouged out one eye, burned off half his face—when Harrison's troops attacked their camp and rescued him. Other folks swear that it happened during the Battle of New Orleans, when his own rifle misfired and blew up in his face." Here, Barnum shrugged again, as if to say: "Which—if any—of these stories is correct, I am at a loss to state."

"Truly," I observed, "this man's physiognomy must be nothing less than *appalling*. I marvel that Isabel Somers—by all accounts, a vivacious and attractive young woman—could bring herself to entertain such a surpassingly repellent being, much less submit to his embraces."

"You know how it is, Poe," Barnum said, placing his forearms on the table and leaning closer to me. "Some women will do whatever they have to for money. Not to impugn the gentler sex, of course.

Why, compared to most men, they're angels, blessed angels, sent down from heaven to save us poor brutes from perdition. Who knows where I'd be today if it weren't for Mrs. Barnum?—still running a little country store in Bethel, most likely. And that lovely creature you're married to—"

"My darling Virginia," I interposed. "Indeed, in perfection of spirit, no less than of face, she is a being without compare. Her purity of soul is equaled only by that of the holy seraphim who dwell in perpetual beauty in God's *superlunary* realm."

"Took the words right out of my mouth," Barnum said. "Why, even Vanderhorn's wife is an unusually good-hearted creature, from what I hear."

"His wife?" I cried in astonishment. "Do you mean to say that a person so physically abhorrent is married?"

"Amazing but true," Barnum said. "Of course, once again, money figures into the matter. Wife comes from one of the oldest families in the city. Knickerbockers. Blood doesn't run any bluer. Not a penny to their fancy name, though. That's where Vanderhorn comes in. Got a face that would freeze the blood of a Gorgon—but he's filthy rich and burning with ambition, just *blazing* with it. Before you know it, a marriage is arranged, and everyone's happy. The family coffers are replenished. The groom buys instant respectability and social position."

"And precisely what benefit does the young lady derive from this transaction?" I inquired.

"The satisfaction of saving her family from the poorhouse, I suppose. They say she's an astonishingly sweet-tempered soul—devout and docile to a fault. Spends her time doing charity work and poring over Scripture. Who knows? Maybe she likes being a martyr. Some folks *do*, you know. Not me, of course. Never cared much for sacrifice and discomfort. Which reminds me—where the *deuce* is our food? Another few minutes and, by George, I'll be ready to turn cannibal. I'm not fooling, Poe—you're beginning to look mighty appetizing to me."

At that very moment—as if in response to the showman's complaint—a waiter materialized at our table, balancing in his hands two enormous, oval platters, each extravagantly piled with food. Setting these dishes down before us, he took a step backward and politely inquired if he could assist us in any other way. By then, however, Barnum had already thrust his napkin into his shirt-collar, snatched up his utensils, and begun to feed himself with a somewhat alarming voracity.

My own hunger having been whetted to the utmost—partly by the piquant aromas pervading the restaurant, partly by the inordinate length of time that had elapsed since I had consumed my abstemious breakfast—I followed the showman's example and applied myself to my own dinner, albeit in a manner far more consistent with the dictates of gastronomical etiquette. For the next fifteen minutes or thereabouts, Barnum and I ate in silence, my own thoughts being preoccupied with the intelligence he had just imparted to me about Morris Vanderhorn.

At length, having completed my meal—or at least, as much of it as I could manage, given the exorbitant size of the portions—I settled back in my chair with a barely suppressed groan. Barnum—who had consumed every morsel from his own platter—now fixed his gaze avidly upon mine and asked if I had any intention of "polishing off the remains of that perfectly *splendid*-looking beefsteak." Receiving a negative reply, he proceeded to help himself to my leftovers, while I reverted to our former subject.

"What is the source of Vanderhorn's wealth?" I inquired. "Since, as you have just related, he found it necessary to marry into polite society, it is clear that he himself was not—to quote the immortal Cervantes—'born with a silver spoon in his mouth.' "

"Heavens no," Barnum said, his own mouth full of half-masticated beefsteak. "Vanderhorn's a businessman. Always has been, from what I gather."

"And what is the nature of his business?"

"Just what you'd expect from such a scoundrel. First made his fortune as a liquor merchant." All at once, Barnum looked at me narrowly and said: "Hope you're not a drinking man, Poe."

For a moment, I merely returned Barnum's gaze, while considering how best to reply to this query. At length, in a tone of the deepest sincerity, I addressed him thusly: "I will not deny that I have, at various points in my life, succumbed to the lure of alcoholic indulgence. At no time, however, have I ever been what men call *intemperate*—that is to say, I have never been in the *habit* of intoxication. For a very brief period, it is true, while residing in Richmond, Virginia, I did give way, at certain intervals, to the temptations held out on all sides by the spirit of Southern conviviality. My sensitive temperament could not resist an excitement which was an everyday matter to my companions. In short, on a few, rare occasions, it happened that I became somewhat inebriated.

"However," I continued, "it is now many years since anything stronger than water has passed my lips—with the exception, perhaps, of a single deviation which occurred shortly after my departure from Richmond, when I was induced to resort to the *very* occasional use of cider, with the hope of relieving a nervous condition. In general, my present habits are as far removed from intemperance as the day from the night."

"Delighted to hear it," Barnum exclaimed, reaching out and patting me on the forearm. "There's nothing that'll destroy a man quicker than drink. You know what Shakespeare says about liquor— it's like putting an enemy in your mouth to steal away your brains. By Jove, what a wordsmith that man was! I'll tell you a little secret, Poe. Used to be a bit of a tippler myself, until Mrs. Barnum, Lord bless her, broke me of the foul habit. Why, it's nothing but poison—and that's not just a figure of speech. You know how most liquor is manufactured in this country, don't you?"

"I cannot claim to possess any extraordinary knowledge on the subject."

"Why, it's the greatest scandal in the world. Here's how it's done. Say a wholesale liquor merchant in Buffalo imports some genuine brandy. More often then not, he'll 'rectify' it by adding eighty-five gallons of refined whiskey to fifteen gallons of brandy. Then he colors it, doctors it, and it's ready for sale. Now suppose an Albany wholesaler buys a hundred gallons of this 'pure brandy' from the Buffalo man. The Albany man immediately doubles *his* stock by adding an equal quantity of whiskey. By now you have just seven-and-a-half gallons of brandy in a hundred! Of course, to pass his stuff off as the real thing, the Albany man, too, mixes in a batch of villainous drugs for coloring and flavor. And on and on it goes. By the time a hundred-gallon cask of this 'fine imported brandy' reaches a New York City tavern, more than ninety-nine gallons of it is nothing but cheap whiskey! And you know what the stuff's been doctored with in the meantime? Why, everything from deadly nightshade and turpentine to sulphuric acid and opium! And *that's* the business our friend Vanderhorn was in for many years!"

"Indeed, it is a most scandalous affair," I exclaimed. "How is it possible for Vanderhorn to maintain his cherished façade of respectability when he is engaged in so deplorable an enterprise?"

"Oh, he's been out of that business for years. Once he'd made a bundle and married into the upper crust, he switched to a more legitimate operation. *Apparently* more legitimate, anyway."

"And what is that?"

"Manufacturing patent medicine. Something called Mayhew's Miracle Cold Remedy. Immense success—absolutely enormous. Sells it by the wagon load."

"Why," I cried, "that is the very medication I purchased for my darling wife, Virginia, shortly after our arrival in New York, when she was stricken with a sudden *grippe!*"

"Did it work?"

"It's main effect was to induce a profound and prolonged slumber—from which, however, she awoke much refreshed."

"Knocked her out, in other words," said Barnum. "And no wonder. Why, the stuff's nothing but hard liquor, mixed up with enough foul-tasting ingredients to make you think you're taking something that's good for you. That's all it is, Poe—a way for old maids and Methodists to get tipsy with a clean conscience!"

These remarks completely conformed to my own impression of Mayhew's Miracle Cold Remedy, a small quantity of which—as the reader may recall—I had imbibed at the time of Sissy's illness, in the interest of scientific curiosity. "It is very evident," I remarked, "that this Vanderhorn is a man seemingly without scruples. Whether he is capable of an atrocity such as the one visited upon the unfortunate Isabel Somers is another matter entirely."

"Well, we'll never find out by loafing around here," said Barnum. By this point, he had scraped my platter clean of every vestige of food. Plucking the napkin from his collar and dropping it onto the table, he rose to his feet and declared: "Come on, Poe. If you're done with your dinner, let's be off."

"Off?" I exclaimed. "To where?"

"Why, to talk to that blackguard Vanderhorn, of course."

CHAPTER ELEVEN

Like other members of the moneyed class—who had migrated
steadily northward as the lower portions of Manhattan became
increasingly usurped by commercial enterprises and immigrant en-
claves—Vanderhorn resided far uptown, on Fourteenth Street, adjacent to Union Square Park. Disinclined to walk (partly, no doubt,
because of the *prodigious* amount of food he had just consumed), Barnum proposed that we take a hack. During our ride up Broadway, we
passed the time discussing the best strategy to employ in our forthcoming meeting. It was decided that Barnum—who had been introduced to Vanderhorn on one or two previous occasions—would do
the greater part of the speaking, while I employed my superior powers of observation to make a discreet survey of the surroundings and
take note of anything that might be of significance to our investigation.

Having arrived at our destination, we disembarked from the cab
and paused for a moment on the sidewalk. Before us loomed a four-
story brownstone mansion with a handsome mansard roof. A wide,
marble stairway led from the sidewalk up to its massive front door,
which was surmounted by a pediment of fantastic, Baroque design.
After gazing for a moment at this imposing edifice, I turned to Barnum and said: "Are you quite certain that Vanderhorn will consent to
see us?"

This query caused the showman to bridle. "I'm surprised at you,

Poe," he said in an offended tone. "Rendered speechless, in fact. Look at me, m'boy—do I strike you as a man who is used to being turned away by mere upstarts like Morris Vanderhorn? Why, P. T. Barnum has been received by the crowned heads of Europe! To say nothing of the highest statesmen of our own great land! Do you know what the president said to me the last time I was in Washington? 'Phineas,' he says, 'just having you around to chat with is a tonic to my spirits. Drop by anytime you're in town. Door to the White House will always be open. Don't even bother to knock, just stroll right in.' And you wonder if a scalawag like Vanderhorn will admit me into his house? Well, we'll just see about that!"

And so saying, he strode up the stairway and—ignoring the gleaming brass knocker—rapped repeatedly on the door with the elephant-shaped head of his walking stick.

A moment later, the door swung open and we found ourselves face-to-face with one of the most singular beings I had ever laid eyes upon. Though only of average height, this personage possessed an upper torso of such enormous dimension that his shoulders and chest appeared to be in imminent danger of bursting through his garments. His neck was as thickly muscled as a bull's. As for his head, it was unusually large—entirely bald—and ovoid in shape, with a massive jaw and a crown so exceedingly narrow that it seemed nearly pointed. His features were exceptionally unprepossessing: tiny, black eyes—snub nose—thick, sensual lips beneath a drooping brown mustache. The bottom portion of his right ear, including the entire lobe, was missing, as though someone had bitten it off; while the opposite cheek was badly disfigured by an exceedingly jagged scar of the sort that might have been inflicted by a broken whiskey bottle during a savage tavern brawl.

Regarding us with an insolent, appraising stare in which curiosity and contempt seemed equally commingled, he gruffly inquired: "Yeah? What can I do for you gents?" In timbre, his voice was little more than a low-throated growl.

"Good afternoon," replied the showman. "I am P. T. Barnum, and this is my associate, Mr. Poe. We are here to speak to Mr. Vanderhorn."

"Barnum, eh? Been to your museum a couple of times."

"And I trust, my good man, that, like countless other visitors, you had a thoroughly edifying and enjoyable time."

"I've had better," said the other with a shrug of his massive shoulders. "Come on in." Turning his back on us, he ambled into the house, leaving us to follow at his heels and close the door behind us.

"Have a seat," he commanded, pointing his heavy chin to a pair of Chippendale chairs that sat in the foyer. With no further word, he proceeded to the sweeping marble stairway at the center of the entrance hall and made his way upward at an unhurried pace.

"Can't say I think much of the manservant," Barnum muttered as he watched the hulking figure recede up the stairway. "Nasty-looking brute—with the manners to match. You'd think Vanderhorn would hire someone with a little more *breeding,* given all this—" This latter comment was accompanied by a sweeping gesture that took in the opulent decor of the surroundings: the marble floor—the frescoed walls—the gilt-framed mirrors—the crystal chandelier—and the lofty ceiling adorned with a painting of the goddess Aurora disporting herself among the clouds.

"Perhaps he is employed in a capacity other than that of houseservant," I ventured. "That Vanderhorn's business dealings have been of a highly *dubious* nature seems incontestable. That he has incurred the bitter enmity of others in the course of these dealings seems likely, if not inevitable. Under the circumstances, he might well feel the need to employ a personal bodyguard—a job for which this singularly ferocious-looking individual appears eminently qualified."

"Maybe so, maybe so," Barnum replied. Seated before me—his knees widespread, his gloved hands resting atop the head of his walking stick—he gazed about the spacious foyer for a moment, then turned to me and said: "Now remember, Poe. Let me do the talking. You keep your eyes peeled for anything that might tie Vanderhorn to the Somers woman."

"I will, of course, endeavor to do so. If, however—as we suspect—Vanderhorn has taken such inordinate pains to conceal his relationship to the victim, even my most diligent efforts may prove fruitl—"

At that instant, my remark was interrupted by a booming cry from above: "Hey!"

Casting our eyes in the direction of the sound, we perceived Vanderhorn's formidable underling posed—arms akimbo—at the head of the curving stairway.

"Come on up," he brusquely declared. "Mr. Vanderhorn says he'll see you."

As we rose from our seats, Barnum gave me a triumphant look that seemed to say: *"There!* What did I tell you?" Together, we ascended the curving, marble staircase. No sooner had we reached the first-floor landing than our guide swiveled on his heels and led us down a thickly carpeted corridor, whose richly brocaded walls were hung with dozens of oil paintings in elaborately carved frames.

Glancing at these pictures as we passed, I was struck by the consistently unsettling nature of both their subject matter and style. Some depicted strange, monkish creatures whose ghastly complexions, grotesque postures, and painfully attenuated physiques were reminiscent of the wildly distorted figures characteristic of the Spanish master, El Greco. Some were lurid, infernal landscapes in the manner of the great medieval visionary, Bosch. Yet others were phantasmagoric conceptions which—in terms of sheer *bizarrerie*—exceeded even the glowing yet too-concrete reveries of Fuseli.

As we approached the far end of the hallway, I perceived an open door, flanked by two complete suits of medieval armor, each arranged in a posture of rigid attention and clutching in its gauntleted right hand a savage-looking halberd. Passing by these grim and lifeless sentinels, we crossed the threshold and entered the sanctum of Morris Vanderhorn.

The scene that now presented itself to me was peculiar in the extreme. The chamber itself was pentagonal in shape and of capacious size. The ceiling, of gloomy oak, was excessively lofty and vaulted. Depending from the central recess of this melancholy vaulting was a huge, golden censer, Saracenic in pattern, that emitted a dull and flickering glow.

Occupying one entire wall of the chamber was an immense pane of unbroken glass, tinted of a leaden hue, so that the daylight passing through it fell with a ghastly luster upon the objects within. This window was framed with heavy and massive-looking draperies, of a material that was also found as a carpet on the floor. The material was the richest cloth of gold. It was spotted all over with arabesque figures, about a foot in diameter and wrought upon the cloth in patterns of the most jetty black.

The walls were papered with the same brocaded material that covered those of the hallway through which we had just passed. Hanging everywhere about the room was a large and promiscuous assortment of exceedingly somber *objets:* the head of a wild boar, taxidermically preserved and mounted on an oaken plaque—a pair of crossed, somewhat rusty-looking broadswords—a stuffed member of the species *Vultur gryphus,* or great Andean condor, perched on a shelf that protruded from the wall above the mantel—a wax facsimile of the death mask of Napoleon Bonaparte—several specimens of the fiendish devices favored by the Inquisitors of Toledo, including a thumbscrew and pincers—and numerous other items of a surpassingly macabre and even *forbidding* nature. One object in particular arrested my attention. This was a traditional headsman's axe with a worn wooden handle and a great, sweeping blade, of the sort employed in countless executions from the Dark Ages to the present.

That the chamber served as Vanderhorn's office was evident from its furnishings, which consisted of several massive, glass-fronted bookcases—a number of comfortless-looking chairs—and an enormous desk heaped with papers, writing tablets, and ledger books. Seated behind this desk was a being I took to be Vanderhorn himself. His features, however, were not, at that moment, visible to me. Head bowed, quill in hand, he was busily affixing his signature to a series of papers that were being laid before him, one at a time, by a fellow of a most grotesque appearance.

This personage—who stood behind the desk at Vanderhorn's side—possessed an unusually narrow, utterly colorless face; a nose so excessively long, crooked, and tapered that it resembled a parsnip; and the most severe case I had ever witnessed of that unfortunate condition known as posterior spinal curvature, more commonly referred to as *humpback.* Despite (or perhaps in *consequence* of) his extreme physical deformity, he displayed a considerable degree of vanity in regard to his dress, being handsomely clad in a costly gray tailcoat, a black vest crossed by a golden watch-chain, and a white cravat that was wound about his throat in voluminous folds.

In addition to Vanderhorn and the somewhat foppishly attired hunchback (whose manner plainly indicated that he was employed in a secretarial capacity), another person was present in the room when we entered. This was an elderly gentleman of such exceedingly *wizened* mien that he appeared to be virtually mummified. He was seated in an elaborately carved chair of Flemish design that stood beside the desk. A few white, wispy strands of hair were brushed over his otherwise bald, age-mottled skull. His eyes—behind the lenses of his pince-nez glasses—were pale almost to the point of colorlessness. His gray lips were tightly pursed, and his expression was one of the purest ennui. He sat with his bony hands folded in his lap, rotating his thumbs about each other in a manner that conveyed the keenest boredom and impatience.

So richly carpeted was the floor that our footsteps had made no echo as we crossed into the room. Nevertheless—and in spite of being intent upon his own paperwork—Vanderhorn was clearly aware of our presence; for—as Barnum and I moved closer to the desk—he suddenly raised his head and, in a surpassingly deep and sonorous voice, said: "Be with you in a minute, gentlemen."

Had Barnum's description not prepared me for the sight, I might well have emitted an involuntary shriek of the purest terror. Even so, I could feel a shudder of absolute *dread* course through every fiber of my being. Bathed in the yellow glow of the desk lamp, the visage that now confronted me was appalling in the extreme.

Though Barnum's characteristic rhetorical mode was one of shameless hyperbole, I saw at once that—in this particular instance—he had not been guilty of the slightest exaggeration. If anything, his description of Vanderhorn's ghastly physiognomy had fallen short of the truth; for the living reality of that hideous countenance—the hollow eye-socket; the partially missing nose; the mouth half-twisted into a skeletal *rictus*—was infinitely more shocking than any merely *verbal* description could possibly convey. The impact of these deformities upon the viewer was somehow rendered even more intense by their extreme contrast to the undamaged half of his countenance, whose features were as cleanly cut and shapely as those on a Greek medallion.

Struggling to prevent my own countenance from betraying the revulsion I felt, I kept my gaze firmly fixed on Vanderhorn, who soon returned to his task. At length, his malformed assistant placed one final document upon the desk. After signing it with a flourish, Vanderhorn exclaimed, "There!" He then picked up the paper and handed it back to the hunchback. Before the latter could take it, however, Vanderhorn appeared to be struck by an afterthought; for—with a puzzled exclamation—he suddenly reached up and snatched the paper back.

Up until that point, it was evident that—like many powerful men who delegate the preparation of their routine correspondence to their trusted secretaries—Vanderhorn had simply been signing the papers without bothering to review them. Now, for the first time, he took several moments to carefully peruse the document. At length, he turned to look at his assistant, exposing his undeformed profile to my view. His features were wrought into an expression of the deepest outrage, and his previously pallid complexion was suffused with an angry red hue.

"Where the *hell* did this come from?" he shouted at the hunchback, whose own visage wore a deeply *stricken* look.

"Mrs. Vanderhorn, sir," replied the latter in a tremulous voice. "She told me to write it up for you to sign. Said you'd be happy to donate a hundred dollars to a cause as worthy as Reverend Frothingham's mission."

Leaping to his feet, Vanderhorn shouted: "She did, did she? Her and her damned charities! *I'll* decide who gets my money—not that pious old bitch! Now get the hell out—and don't you *ever* try to slip something by me again!"

Abjectly bowing his head, the mortified assistant stepped from behind the desk and quickly made his way toward the door. As he hurried across the room, Vanderhorn crumpled the offending letter into a ball and, drawing back his arm, hurled it at his retreating underling. With unerring accuracy, the paper struck the latter directly upon his upper back—bounced off the grotesquely bulging hump—and landed a few feet away from where Barnum and I stood. This disgraceful act was rendered even more odious by the reaction of Vanderhorn's hulking subordinate, who—leaning insouciantly against the marble mantel of the fireplace—emitted a loud chortle of contempt at the poor hunchback's public humiliation.

For several moments, Vanderhorn remained standing behind his desk, breathing heavily and holding his tightly clenched fists rigidly at his sides. At length, he regained a measure of composure. Opening the lid of an elaborately carved box of teakwood, he removed a panatela, inserted it into the unimpaired corner of his mouth and lit it with a phosphorous match. He then resumed his seat, positioning himself upon the chair in such a way that the illumination from his desk lamp fell directly upon the *presentable* side of his countenance, leaving the disfigured half partially shrouded in shadow. Viewed from that angle—and with his deformities further obscured by the exhalations from his cigar—his face appeared practically normal.

"So, Barnum," he said, expelling a great puff of smoke, "to what do I owe the pleasure?"

Before Barnum could reply, the dessicated gentleman seated beside the desk spoke up in a voice as dry and hollow-sounding as the scraping of a gravedigger's shovel upon the wooden lid of a disinterred coffin: "You are forgetting your manners, Morris."

"A thousand pardons," Vanderhorn said. "Dr. Mayhew, permit me to introduce America's greatest showman, Mr. P. T. Barnum. I have no idea who his gloomy-looking friend is."

"My associate, Mr. Poe," Barnum replied. That my companion—like myself—had been utterly incensed by the scene that had just transpired was very evident from the unusually *constricted* sound of his voice. Casting a rapid glance in his direction, I perceived a corresponding *tautness* in his expression, as though he were exerting every particle of his will-power to keep his indignation in check.

Indicating the wizened gentleman at his side, Vanderhorn addressed us thusly: "Gentlemen, allow me to present the eminent Dr. Archibald Mayhew. Dr. Mayhew is here to discuss our plans for his new miracle tonic, Mayhew's Revitalizing Vegetable Cordial. Guaranteed to cure everything from rheumatism to consumption."

"I see, I see," Barnum said in the same tone of barely suppressed outrage. "New miracle tonic, eh? Cures every ailment under the sun, eh? Now isn't that amazing? Isn't that simply incredible? Wouldn't be trying to put one over on the public by peddling them a cheap concoction of worthless chemicals and wood alcohol, now would you, Mayhew?"

Curling his thin upper lip into an expression of the deepest scorn, the old man raspingly replied: "Those are mighty funny words coming from *you*, Barnum. The Prince of Humbugs himself. The man who has so memorably proclaimed that there is a sucker born every minute."

"I resent your insinuation, sir!" the showman angrily declared. "P. T. Barnum has never duped the public in his life! Oh, all right— once or twice, perhaps, if you count my Feejee mermaid and prehistoric woolly horse. But those were mere *lures*, if you will, designed to draw in the crowds. Perfectly harmless—all in good fun. Why, I've always given my customers *double* their money's worth! At the very *least!*"

"Gentlemen, please," interjected Vanderhorn. "I'm sure Mr. Barnum didn't come here to argue." Drawing deeply on his panatela, he emitted the smoke in a long, unbroken stream from the working corner of his mouth. "Of course, now that I think of it, I have no idea why you *are* here, Barnum. Some sort of business proposition, I presume?"

"Vanderhorn," said Barnum, "I'm not the kind to beat around the bush. Don't believe in it. Speak your mind—that's P. T. Barnum's style. So I'll get straight to the point. Mr. Poe and I are pursuing the solution to a mystery. We have reason to think you might be able to help us out."

"Mystery?" said Vanderhorn. "What sort of mystery?"

"Murder most foul," said Barnum. "Young woman named Isabel Somers. Dreadful crime, absolutely appalling. Whole city's in an uproar about it."

For a moment, Vanderhorn said nothing. Then, leaning back casually in his seat and crossing one leg over the other, he airily replied:

"Yes, yes, of course. Read something about it in the *Morning Journal*. But what's all this got to do with me?"

"Poe and I have been doing a bit of investigating," Barnum declared. "Just come from her apartment building, in fact. Interviewing witnesses, that sort of thing. Someone said they saw you there."

For one, exceptionally fleeting moment, Vanderhorn cast a meaningful glance at his ferocious-looking subordinate, who continued to stand by the fireplace, one elbow resting on the mantelpiece. Then he fixed his single eye on Barnum again and said: "I don't know who the hell you've been talking to, Barnum. But they're wrong. Or *lying*. I never even heard of this Somers woman until I saw her name in the *Journal*."

Taking another long draw on his cigar, he added: "And anyway, what business is it of *yours?*"

"Have you read today's *Herald?*" answered Barnum. "No? Well, you'd know the answer if you had. I'm under attack, Vanderhorn. A vicious, cowardly attack from quarters unknown. And it's not just your everyday mudslinging, either. Someone's out to ruin me. Of course, it's only to be expected, I suppose. World's full of malcontents. Can't bear it when someone rises to the extraordinary heights I've achieved."

"Sorry to hear about your problems," said Vanderhorn. "But I'd leave this affair to the police, if I were you."

"You would, eh?" replied the showman. "Well, I guess that's just one of the many ways we differ, Vanderhorn. When P. T. Barnum sets out to do something, there's no stopping him. Might as well try to stop a herd of stampeding pachyderms with your bare hands!"

"Have it your way," said Vanderhorn, sitting upright in his chair. "But I'm afraid I can't be of help. And now, if you'll excuse us. Dr. Mayhew and I have important matters to discuss. Show them out, will you Croley?" This latter comment was addressed to the menacing-looking individual by the fireplace.

With an acquiescent grunt, Vanderhorn's hulking assistant pushed himself away from the mantel and proceeded toward the door.

"Come along, Poe," said Barnum. "Let's leave these gentlemen to their business." In making this pronouncement, he laid a subtle but decidedly ironic stress upon the word 'gentlemen.'

Barnum and I then turned to leave the room. As I swiveled about, I suddenly tripped and pitched forward, landing with a thud on the thickly carpeted floor.

"Are you all right, Poe, m'boy?" Barnum anxiously inquired.

"I am perfectly fine," I said, pushing myself to my knees. "The toe of my left boot apparently became caught in the inordinately *dense* pile of the carpet, causing me to lose my balance." Getting nimbly to my feet, I took a moment to straighten out my garments—which had become somewhat disarranged as a result of my fall—then quickly followed Barnum out of the room.

Trailing several feet behind Croley, we retraced our earlier route: along the gloomy corridor—past the wildly eccentric collection of paintings—down the curving, marble staircase—and into the spacious foyer. Then—without so much as a word of farewell—Croley spun around and strode away.

No sooner had he left us than Barnum and I walked toward the doorway to make our exit. All at once, we were brought to a halt by a somewhat startling circumstance; for, as we drew close to the massive oak door, it slowly began to swing in upon its hinges, as though opening *itself* in response to our approach. An instant later, this mystery was explained when the door opened to its fullest extent, and a pallid, black-clad woman stepped over the threshold. I surmised at once that she was none other than the mistress of the house—the exceedingly devout and heavenly minded Mrs. Vanderhorn.

In truth, there was something distinctly *unearthly* about her—a vague but palpable sense of being not *quite* of this world. Thin to the point of emaciation, with cadaverous skin and raven-black hair parted severely down the center, she seemed to float, rather than to walk, across the marble floor of the entranceway. Clutched to her narrow bosom in her exceedingly slender (if not *skeletal*) fingers was an enormous, morocco-bound bible, its pages edged in gold.

It was her eyes, however, that made the most forcible impression upon the observer. Far larger than ordinary, the protruding, black-hued orbs shone with a miraculous brilliancy. In that strange—that *unnatural*—luster, I fancied that I perceived a degree of religious zeal that bordered on the fanatical—perhaps, indeed, even the *maniacal.*

As this sable-clad, uncanny-seeming female drifted past us, she nodded her head slightly in greeting, while Barnum and I quickly tipped our hats and responded with a muttered "Good day." Then—as she glided off in the direction of the staircase—we hurried out of the still-open door, down the front steps, and onto the sidewalk.

Without speaking a word, Barnum took me by the arm and led me briskly across the street and deep into Union Square Park, where we paused beside the spiked iron fence surrounding Hablot K. Browne's imposing equestrian statue of Washington. By then, the sunlight was waning. It was that supremely bewitching hour of the day—perfectly poised between late afternoon and eventide—that the French, with their native genius for *le mot juste,* so poetically describe as *"l'heure bleue."* Only a short time earlier, at the height of the day, the park would have been filled with strolling pedestrians, luxuriating in its oasislike calm. Now, however, it was largely deserted, affording Barnum and me an opportunity to converse in near-privacy.

"Bless my soul, but I'm glad to be out of that vipers' den," Barnum said at length, inhaling a deep, grateful draught of the crepuscular air. "Made my skin crawl just to be there."

"Indeed," I said, "I, too, found the ambience of Vanderhorn's sanctum intensely unsettling. To say nothing of the man himself."

"Didn't I tell you?" Barnum exclaimed. "Great heavens—what a monster. Know your Scripture, Poe? Well, I don't claim to be a chapter-and-verse man myself. But I know what Satan's called—'the Father of Lies.' If that doesn't describe Vanderhorn, that two-faced devil, I'll be hanged!"

"A devil he may or may not be," I replied. "I concur, however, with your opinion of his honesty; for it appeared to me that—in his response to your queries concerning Isabel Somers—Vanderhorn was engaged in a deliberate act of evasion, if not outright *prevarication.*"

"*Appeared?*" Barnum exclaimed. "Why it was plain as a pikestaff. Plain as the way to parish church. Still," he continued, shaking his head in frustration, "it doesn't *prove* anything. Tell me, Poe, m'boy. Did those amazingly keen eyes of yours detect anything?"

"Apart from the generally forbidding, if not morbid, quality of his possessions, I saw nothing of a questionable nature."

"Blast!" my companion ejaculated. "I'm disappointed, Poe, I won't deny it. P. T. Barnum's not a man who hides his feelings. Wear my heart on my sleeve. Can't help it. It's just the way I'm made. And right now, I'm feeling mighty let down. Hate to go to all that trouble and come away empty-handed."

"I merely said that I saw nothing of an incriminating nature in Vanderhorn's dwelling—not that I came away empty-handed."

"Why, what do you mean?" asked Barnum.

By way of answer, I reached into the side pocket of my coat and removed an item that I held out for Barnum's perusal: a sheet of paper, crumpled into a ball.

For a moment, he merely stared at my outstretched hand in perplexity. All at once, his eyes grew wide with comprehension. "Why, isn't that the paper Vanderhorn threw at his hunchback?" he exclaimed.

"So it is," I replied. "It came to rest on the floor not far from where we stood. By the time of our departure, its existence had apparently been forgotten by everyone but myself. I therefore contrived to retrieve it by pretending to trip over my feet and falling to the ground—an ostensible accident that was, in fact, a carefully preconceived and cunning charade. As I knelt on the floor, I had no difficulty in taking hold of the paper without observation. I then rose to my feet and—while straightening out my disarranged clothing—discreetly slipped it into my pocket."

"Why, that was marvelously clever, Poe, m'boy. Had me completely fooled. Never seen such a convincing display of clumsiness in my life. There's just one thing—now that we have it, what *good* does it do us?"

"That is readily explained," I said, opening up the paper and uncreasing it as much as possible. "You will recall that Vanderhorn flung this document at his unfortunate underling *after* affixing his signature to it."

"Hadn't really noticed," Barnum said. "But I'll accept your word for it."

Reaching into the breast pocket of my coat, I extracted the fragment of stationery that I had discovered in Isabel Somers's storage chest. I then placed this scrap beside Vanderhorn's signature on the unfolded paper—compared the two for a moment—then handed them over to Barnum.

"Behold," I said. "It does not require an expert in the field of calligraphic analysis to perceive that the handwriting is identical in both cases. My earlier deduction is thereby confirmed. This fragment, torn from a letter stored in Isabel Somers's boudoir, is indisputably inscribed with the final syllable of Morris Vanderhorn's signature."

"Lord bless you, you're right!" Barnum cried, peering closely at the two pieces of paper. "This proves it beyond any *wisp* of a doubt! Vanderhorn was lying through his teeth! Didn't know Isabel Somers, eh? *Ha!* Knew her well enough to be sending her love notes!"

"I wonder if we are entirely justified in making that assumption," I said. "Thus far, we have merely established that Vanderhorn was corresponding with the Somers woman. The precise *content* of his letters, however, remains unknown. Indeed, to conclude that they were romantic *billets-doux* now strikes me as somewhat premature."

"And why is that?" Barnum demanded.

"Since the fragment of stationery found in Miss Somers's apartment contains the syllable 'horn,'" I answered, "it is clear that Vanderhorn inscribed the letter not merely with his *first* but with his *family* name as well."

"So?"

"Does it seem likely to you," I answered, "that any man would sign a love letter—the most personal, the most *intimate*, of all species of written communication—in so *formal* a manner?"

"Now that you mention it, it *does* seem a mite peculiar," Barnum musingly replied. "But then, Vanderhorn's no ordinary man. Besides, why the devil *would* he write to her? And why would she save his letters in her treasure box?"

"Those are among the many questions yet to be resolved in this case. As it will soon be nightfall, however, I propose that we suspend our efforts until the morrow."

"Yes, that makes good sense, all right," Barnum said. "Don't want to overtax that marvelous brain of yours. Come—let's hunt up a cab and send you back home. Back to the bosom of your family. Now, you make sure to get a good night's sleep, Poe, m'boy. You've earned it. Earned every *wink!*"

CHAPTER TWELVE

The wisdom of Barnum's parting injunction—that I "get a good night's sleep"—could scarcely be doubted. The manifold events of the day—beginning with the showman's unanticipated arrival at my dwelling and culminating in our interview with the devious Vanderhorn—had reduced me to a state of intense physical and mental fatigue. As I rode in the jouncing hack away from the city and back toward my country abode, I gazed numbly out the window, imagining how my darling Muddy and Sissy had passed the time since my departure.

The journey seemed nearly interminable. The night was well advanced by the time we reached our destination. Under the vast, starry heavens, my little cottage loomed in the darkness, its front windows aglow with the warm illumination of an oil lamp, left burning by loved ones. As the carriage drew to a halt, I looked out at this welcoming *beacon* with a feeling of unutterable gratitude.

Alighting from the cab with a groan, I staggered across the overgrown yard—up the porch—and into the cottage. The stillness suffusing our little dwelling informed me that my dear ones had already betaken themselves to bed. Making my way into my chamber, I quickly shed my garments—donned my nightclothes—and threw myself onto my mattress.

Much to my dismay, however, sleep proved exceedingly elusive; for I had arrived at that condition of extreme nervous exhaustion in which the brain, however weary, is unable to subside into inactivity. Try as I might, I could not seem to position myself comfortably on my bed. I turned myself this way and that. I made every adjustment imaginable to my pillow. I straightened the blankets and smoothed the sheets. All in vain! For the rest of that long, dreary night I remained in a state of agitated half-wakefulness, lapsing only occasionally into fitful periods of slumber. And even *then*, my overwrought mind continued to dwell on the unsettling events of the day, conjuring up phantasmagoric visions of sneering, grotesque creatures with bifurcated faces—of groveling, hunchbacked dwarves—and of horribly mutilated young women with bloody arm-stumps.

Thus did that wearisome night pass. When at length the first pale rays of daylight filtered through my window, I arose from my mattress, quickly performed my ablutions, threw on my clothing, and stole from the house.

For a full ten or fifteen minutes, I lingered on the porch, watching the coming of the "rosy-fingered dawn" (in the intensely lyrical phrase of the divine Homer). Having spent the previous day breathing in the noxious effluvia of the metropolis, I now eagerly imbibed the surpassingly pure and perfumed air of my bucolic surroundings. So revitalizing was this atmospheric elixir that I felt my strength returning with every respiration. All at once, I was filled with an overpowering urge to engage in my usual, daily exercise. Flinging wide my arms, as if to embrace the morning, I stepped from the porch and struck out in a westerly direction.

As I have already indicated, I had passed the entire night in that state of extreme mental (as well as physical) agitation characteristic of severe *overtiredness*. My brain had been in a continuous tumult—my thoughts chaotic to the highest degree. Now, as I strode through the dew-drenched meadows and mist-blanketed fields, I was finally able to contemplate the previous day's events in a composed and methodical fashion.

Barnum and I had already made considerable strides in our investigation. In the course of a single day, we had managed to link the corrupt and powerful Morris Vanderhorn to the victim. Whether Vanderhorn was implicated in the murder itself, however, remained unclear. Certainly—as Isabel Somers's likely benefactor—he would have had the *opportunity* to commit the crime. From what I had witnessed of his behavior, it also seemed clear that he possessed the requisite ruthlessness and cruelty. Indeed, the double-faced Vanderhorn seemed the very type and emblem of human duplicity—of the innate capacity for evil and depravity that lurks within the bosom of every mortal.

Still, the question remained: what possible *motive* could have driven him to perpetrate such a horror?

Moreover, if Vanderhorn *were* the culprit, did this mean that he was also responsible for the butchery, one year earlier, of Ellen Jennings—a killing identical in every appalling detail to that of Isabel Somers? Had Lemuel Thompson—the man who was hanged for the Jennings murder, despite his fervent protestations of innocence—been telling the truth after all? Or was this more recent crime a deliberate emulation of the earlier atrocity, as the newspapers were now claiming?

And what about the grotesque token left at each crime scene?—the long-stemmed rose clamped between the teeth of the horribly mangled victim. Surely, there must be some particular significance to so anomalous a clue. But what could it possibly be?

As I continued on my ramble, I kept my mind focused on these and other topics related to the case. By slow degrees, however, I became cognizant of a distracting sensation emanating from the pit of my stomach. Pausing in my stride, I quickly realized that I was feeling almost *ravenously* hungry—understandably so, since I had not consumed a morsel of food since my dinner with Barnum the previous afternoon. I immediately swiveled on my heels and bent my steps toward home.

Forty minutes later, the charming, two-story cottage that I shared with my loved ones came into view. Drawing nearer to this dear, domestic *haven*, I was greeted with a sight that caused my heart to swell with pleasure. There, seated on the front porch, was my darling Sissy, garbed in a dress of the purest white. Her rich, reddish-brown tresses shone in the sunlight. She was perusing a book; while—curled and dozing in her lap—lay our beloved tabby, Cattarina.

So deeply engrossed in her reading was my dear wife that she did not become aware of my presence until I stepped onto the porch and planted a fond osculation on the peak of her brow. Quickly glancing up from her book with a look of almost *supernal* happiness, she exclaimed: "Oh, good morning, Eddie dearest! Isn't it a glorious day?"

"Indeed, it is," I replied, "though its splendor pales beside that of your own radiant beauty. Tell me," I continued as Sissy beamed with pleasure at my affectionate tribute. "What reading matter has so thoroughly engaged your attention at this early hour?"

"The usual," she replied with a soft, somewhat apologetic laugh, holding the book aloft. I saw at once that it was the same volume with which I had beguiled my angelic wife during her illness immediately following our arrival in New York: Thomas Crofton Tyler's *Traditional Faerie Legends of the English and Scottish Peasantry.*

"I know you must think I'm terribly silly to spend so much time reading fairy tales," she continued. "But I just find them so *enchanting.*" All at once, a look of concern spread over her countenance. "Are you all right, Eddie? You have such dark, droopy bags under your eyes."

"Sleep came not near my bed last night," I answered with a sigh, "my mind being overly preoccupied with the perturbing events of the day."

"Well, I'm eager to hear everything that happened," said Sissy. "Muddy, too. She's fixing breakfast right now. Come," she continued, rising to her feet and taking me by the hand. "You can tell us all about it while we eat."

"I wholeheartedly endorse your proposal, dearest Sissy," I replied as she led me toward the front door. "For, at present, my sense of fatigue is surpassed only by my craving for sustenance."

Proceeding into the cottage, we repaired to the kitchen, where we found Muddy busily laying out plates and utensils on the table. After greeting me with a warm, maternal embrace—and clucking her tongue in dismay over my haggard appearance—she directed me to seat myself at once. With Sissy's help, she then completed the preparations for our breakfast; whereupon the three of us settled down to our simple but intensely satisfying repast of cheese, boiled eggs, toasted bread, butter, jam, and tea.

For many minutes, I ate without speaking a word, my hunger

being so acute that I could concentrate on nothing but my food. At length, having reached a point of satiety, I leaned back in my chair and began to regale my loved ones with an account of the previous day's events—omitting only those details (such as a too-vivid description of Vanderhorn's hideous deformities) that would have caused them unnecessary distress.

"Well, it's all very strange," Muddy ventured when I had finished. "This Vanderhorn seems perfectly dreadful, all right. And I must say, his wife sounds pretty peculiar, too. Goodness knows, *I* certainly wouldn't marry such a brute, no matter *how* rich he was. Still, if you ask me, whoever butchered that poor woman in such a horrible way was an out-and-out *madman.* And it doesn't sound to me as if Vanderhorn's *that.*"

"I agree, dear Muddy, that Vanderhorn does not appear to be hopelessly lost to sanity," I said. "On the contrary, as his inordinate success in the commercial realm attests, his judgment—at least in certain areas—must be of the most sound and sagacious variety. Still, such rational behavior is not, in itself, inconsistent with what might be termed *moral* insanity. For, as the annals of crime make abundantly clear, there are men whose *heads* can remain subject to the law of reason, even while their *hearts* riot in the complete exemption from that law. Toward the accomplishment of an aim which—in sheer atrocity—would seem to partake of the insane, these men direct a cool and methodical intelligence. I need scarcely add that such men are indeed madmen, and of the most dangerous sort—for their lunacy is not continuous but rather occasional, evoked by some special object or circumstance."

"Well, if you ask *me,*" Sissy interjected, "I *still* say it's Lemuel Thompson's vengeful ghost come back to fulfill his dying curse!"

"I am afraid, Sissy dearest," I jocularly replied, "that your imagination has been stimulated to an excessive degree by the tales of the uncanny in Mr. Tyler's volume."

"Well, that's a funny thing for *you* to say, Eddie," Sissy answered. "Someone who's written all those creepy stories about haunted houses and supernatural masquerade balls and people coming back from the dead!"

I was about to reply to this observation with a brief discourse on the fundamental differences between the ordinary *wondertale* and my own, far more subtle and artistic productions, whose effects depended less on the crude devices of Gothic fantasy than on the evocation of the deepest *spiritual* terrors. Before I could say a word on this subject, however, my attention was diverted by the sound of an approaching vehicle, clearly audible through the open kitchen window. This was a most unexpected development. I knew that Barnum planned to send a coach to pick me up, since he had informed me of this intention prior to our leave-taking the previous evening. He had stressed, however, that it would not arrive until shortly before noon (thus affording me ample opportunity to rest); whereas the time was now just shy of nine o'clock.

Casting a quizzical glance at my loved ones, I pushed myself away from the table and hurried out onto the porch, Muddy and Sissy following close behind. A coach, drawn by a handsome sorrel, was indeed driving up the rutted path leading from the main road to our cottage. Seated on the driver's box was a personage who—even from that distance—I recognized at once as Barnum's bearded female prodigy, Wilhelmina Schnitzler. In another minute or so, the carriage drew to a halt in our front yard, Miss Schnitzler pulling tight on the reins and crying, "Whoa, Molly!"

"Morning, folks," she said. Her visage was wrought into a grimace of distaste. Raising a fist to her mouth, she coughed several times into her hand before looking at Muddy and saying: "Ma'am, I'd sure appreciate some of that buttermilk you offered me yesterday. I was driving along, singing 'The Gypsy Rover,' and a bug flew into my throat."

"Why of course," Muddy exclaimed, then turned on her heels and bustled back into the house. Sissy and I remained standing on the porch, regarding the enormous, bearded female with a commiserating look as she was stricken with another fit of coughing.

A moment later, Muddy reappeared with a glassful of the requested beverage and handed it up to the driver, who drained it in a single gulp. "There, that's better!" she said with a sigh. With the fingertips of one hand, she then delicately patted away the droplets of buttermilk clinging to her hirsute upper lip.

"I confess, Miss Schnitzler, that I am somewhat surprised to see you at such an early hour," I remarked, "Mr. Barnum having indicated that my presence would not be required for another few hours."

"Mr. Barnum said to tell you that something important's come up, so he was hoping to see you right away," she replied. "And please call me Willie."

"I see," I answered. "In that case, Willie, I will be with you presently." Entering the cottage, I quickly repaired to my bedroom, seized my hat and traveling cloak, and returned to the porch. Bidding farewell to Muddy and Sissy (both of whom urged me to be careful), I then mounted the coach.

Just before I disappeared inside, the bearded woman turned around on her seat to look at me. "Oh, Mr. Poe," she said. "You'll find a newspaper in there. Mr. Barnum said for you to read it on the way."

"Thank you, Willie," I replied and took my place inside.

As the coach rolled away, I thrust my arm through the window and waved good-bye to my loved ones. I then settled back in my seat. Beside me lay a folded newspaper—obviously the one Barnum intended for my perusal. Opening it, I saw that it was that morning's edition of the *Herald*. Occupying the center of the front page was an engraved portrait of a handsome young woman with a lofty brow—large, if somewhat close-set, eyes—a nose of a prominent Roman model, and full, rather voluptuous lips. Her countenance was framed with luxuriant, dark, and naturally curling tresses. The caption beneath this picture read: "Portrait of the Murder Victim, Miss Isabel Somers, From an Oil Painting by Mr. Gilbert Opdyke."

As I studied this portrait, a sudden realization dawned on me. While examining Miss Somers's apartment, I had taken note of an exposed nail jutting from the parlor wall, where a picture had apparently hung. It now occurred to me that the missing artwork was none other than the very oil painting that had served as the basis for this engraving. Someone—perhaps an investigating officer, perhaps a reporter in the service of the newspaper publisher, James Gordon Bennett—had evidently removed the painting from the crime scene and supplied it to Bennett, no doubt in exchange for a hefty reward.

Next, I turned my attention to the stories accompanying this illustration. The main article dealt with the progress of the official investigation. According to this story, a number of suspicious individuals— including several "swarthy-skinned strangers" seen loitering in the vicinity of the Thomas Street building in the days leading up to the murder— had been taken into custody for questioning. Authorities were also going through the criminal records kept on file at police headquarters in search of any felons with a known history of criminal assaults upon women. Though no suspect had as yet been identified, officials assured the public that they were making "great strides" in the case, and expressed "absolute confidence" that an arrest would soon be made.

A second article focused on the many dangers to which unmarried young women were exposed in the great metropolis and attributed the shocking decline in civic morality to the growing influx of immigrants from Italy, Ireland, Russia, and other foreign countries less highly civilized than our own.

Yet a third article consisted of a detailed description of the Somers murder as it had been reconstructed by investigators. This exceptionally vivid—if not *lurid*—piece spared the reader no detail of the ghastly atrocities to which the poor victim had been subjected.

At the bottom of this last article there appeared a small notice indicating that further stories on the Somers case could be found on the third page. Accordingly, I opened to the designated place and continued my reading. All at once, an involuntary gasp of astonishment issued from my lips. Barnum's reason for sending me the newspaper was now abundantly clear; for occupying the bottom left-hand column of page three was a story that ran as follows:

BARNUM PLAYS DETECTIVE!
REMARKABLE DEVELOPMENT IN SOMERS CASE!
Showman Seeks Solution to Mystery!
Case "As Good as Solved," He Claims

The hunt for the fiendish killer of Miss Isabel Somers, whose horribly butchered remains were discovered in her boudoir on Wednesday afternoon, has taken

a most unexpected turn. In a printed statement delivered to the offices of the *Herald* and other newspapers
late yesterday, Mr. Phineas Taylor Barnum—proprietor
of the American Museum and self-styled "King of the
Amusement World"—announced that he has embarked
on his own private investigation, with the full expectation of solving the crime within days.

In his communiqué, Mr. Barnum provides several
reasons for this extraordinary undertaking: his overwhelming sense of civic responsibility; his doubts about
the competency of the New York City constabulary; and
his desire to lay to rest certain "outrageous insinua-
tions" (as he deems them) regarding the rôle played in
the affair by one of the numerous gruesome exhibitions
on display at his popular showplace.

"No offense intended, but the police in this great metropolis of ours are the rankest kind of amateurs. Not
that I'm a professional lawman myself, mind you. But I
know how to get the job done. Never failed at anything
in my life. Don't know the meaning of the word. Besides,
I have a personal, vested interest in the affair. I intend
to disprove the highly irresponsible and slanderous
proposition that this unspeakable atrocity has any connection whatsoever to my business. Why, the American
Museum offers the most wholesome, educational, and
morally uplifting entertainment in Christendom! Anyone
who doubts the truth of this statement is invited to visit
the museum at the corner of Ann Street and Broadway
and see for themselves. Open ten A.M. to midnight every
day of the week, except the Sabbath. Admission a mere
twenty-five cents for adults, fifteen cents for children.
Mention this notice and get an additional five cents off!"

According to his statement, Mr. Barnum is being assisted in this enterprise by a gentleman named Edgar A.
Poe, formerly of Richmond, Baltimore, and Philadelphia,
currently residing with his wife and mother-in-law at the

Brennan farm on Bloomingdale Road. Mr. Poe has had prior experience in the detective line, having assisted the legendary frontiersman, Colonel David Crockett, in solving a string of ghastly murders in Baltimore some years ago.

Mr. Barnum further wishes it to be known that he is making rapid headway in his search for the killer. "We're hot on his trail. Breathing down his neck. Can't reveal his identity yet—need a bit more evidence. But when the public finds out who it is, they'll be astounded, I tell you. Absolutely thunderstruck. Can't say any more about it at the present. Wish I could. But you won't have to wait much longer for the answer. Matter of a few days—maybe less. The case is as good as solved."

By the time I reached the end of this article, my sense of surprise had entirely dissipated. What, after all, could be more *predictable* than an act of such shameless self-advertisement by Barnum?—a man whose very name had become a byword for brazen hyperbole. Shaking my head at the showman's unsurpassed genius for garnering public attention, I refolded the paper and dropped it onto the seat.

With one part of Barnum's pronouncement, at least, I could not take issue: his disparaging remarks about the New York City constabulary. Their methods were clearly doomed to failure, in spite of the blithe optimism of their official statement. That a murder of such savage cunning had been committed by a common felon seemed wildly improbable. Equally remote was the likelihood of discovering the culprit through such clumsy and haphazard means as poring over old criminal records, or questioning strangers of supposedly sinister mien.

As we proceeded southward, the rhythmic, rocking motion of the coach began to have an intensely *lulling* effect upon me. By slow degrees, the weariness I had thus far managed to keep at bay reasserted itself with an irresistible force. My eyelids felt weighted with lead. My head sank lower on my bosom. Folding my arms, I leaned into a corner of the seat and fell into a profound slumber.

A moment later (or so it *seemed*, though the actual time which elapsed could not have been less than an hour), I awoke with a start. The coach had come to a complete halt. Through the open window, I could hear the unmistakable *hubbub* of the city—the clamor of the traffic, the shouts of the drivers, the cries of the street vendors hawking a variety of wares, from strawberries and sponge-cakes to puppies and gentlemen's neckties. Mingled among these other noises was a sound that I quickly recognized as the dreadful din produced by the brass band that played continuously from the balcony of Barnum's museum.

All at once, the door of the coach flew open. There stood the massive figure of Willie Schnitzler, a broad grin spread across her face, her dark, shaggy beard extending down to her voluminous bosom.

"Here we are, Mr. Poe!" she said.

Descending from the coach, I took a moment to straighten out my frock coat, which had become somewhat disheveled in the course of our journey. Directly before me loomed the garishly ornamented façade of the American Museum. Scores of patrons were lined up in front of this establishment, awaiting their turn to enter. A surprising number of them, I noticed, were perusing newspapers. The explanation for this fact readily became apparent; for—striding up and down the line—was a tow-headed newsboy brandishing a folded paper. "Extra! Extra!" he shouted. "Barnum Hunts Killer! Read all about it in this morning's *Tribune!*" Copies of this publication were being snapped up by the customers, as well as by passing pedestrians.

Walking (or rather *lumbering*) directly ahead of me, Willie led me toward the building entrance. It need hardly be stated that the sight of the enormous, bearded female caused a great deal of excitement among the people on line, who emitted a chorus of amazed ejaculations as we made our way past them. No less astonishing than Willie's appearance, however, was that of the being in charge of the ticket booth. Dressed in nothing but a tight-fitting suit of "long johns," this fellow was the single most emaciated being I had ever laid eyes upon. Indeed, he appeared to be little more than a skeleton with a thin overlay of flesh and a pair of twinkling blue eyes set into the sockets of his skull-like countenance. I immediately surmised that this singular being was none other than Slim Jim McCormack, the sideshow performer whose duties Barnum had been compelled to assume on the morning of my earlier visit.

My inference was quickly confirmed when, leading me past the ticket booth, Willie cheerfully called out to him: "Morning, Jim. This here is Mr. Poe."

"Go right on in, Willie," croaked the skeletal fellow, waving a long, bony hand in greeting. "Mr. B's waiting in his office."

Entering the building, we descended the main staircase, proceeded through the mazelike basement, and at length found ourselves by the closed door of Barnum's office, where Willie took her leave. I then rapped sharply on the door and—in response to Barnum's shouted directive—opened it and entered.

I found the showman seated behind his massive desk, a letter in his hand and a strangely troubled expression on his countenance. Beckoning to me with a wave of the hand, he said: "Have a seat, m'boy, have a seat. No need to stand on ceremony. Seen the papers?"

Stepping to the chair that faced his desk, I lowered myself onto the seat, and—crossing one leg over the other—replied: "I did indeed examine this morning's *Herald* in accordance with the instructions conveyed to me by Miss Schnitzler."

Barnum screwed his visage into a grimace of disdain. "Sorry to expose you to that rag, Poe, but I had no choice in the matter. It's the only paper out that early. I'll say one thing for Bennett—the man knows how to get a jump on the competition. He's a mighty sharp businessman, and no mistake. But did you ever see anything more outrageous? Imagine—banishing me to page three! I tell you, Poe, he's in cahoots with that rascal Parmalee. You can bank on it. Luckily for me, the *Herald*'s not the only paper in town. Here—take a gander at *these*."

Reaching down to the stack of newspapers lying before him, he proceeded to lift each one in turn and hold up the front page for my perusal. Extending across the top of each of these publications—the *Sun*, the *Tribune*, the *World*, the *Examiner*—was a headline with one or another variation of the same basic theme: "BARNUM TO THE RES-

CUE!" "BARNUM PURSUES KILLER!" "BARNUM JOINS MANHUNT!" "BARNUM VOWS TO SOLVE SOMERS CASE!"

Dropping the last of these newspapers back onto his desk, the showman reclined in his seat, laced his hands over his portly midsection, and—grinning broadly—declared: "Now *those* are what I call attention-getters! Why, they're sure to cause a sensation. Mark my words, Poe, those headlines will bring the customers *stampeding* to my museum—swarming like the Visigoths over Rome."

"Judging from the sheer number of people gathered outside your establishment this morning," I said, "your stratagem already appears to be having the desired effect."

Slapping his hands in delight, Barnum exclaimed: "What did I tell you? You can't buy that kind of publicity, Poe, m'boy. It's a hundred—wait, hold on, what am I saying?—it's a *thousand* times better than any paid advertisement!"

"I do not doubt that such flagrant 'attention-getting'—as you denominate it—will redound to the benefit of your business," I replied in a tone not entirely devoid of irony. "Whether it will be of equal value to our investigation, however, is an entirely different matter."

"Why, how do you mean?" Barnum asked in seemingly genuine perplexity.

"I merely mean to question the absolute wisdom of attracting so much notice to our activities. I cannot help but feel that our pursuit of the killer would proceed more smoothly were it not conducted under the intense and curious scrutiny of the entire city."

"Stuff and nonsense!" Barnum declared, sitting upright in his chair. "Why, just the opposite is true. In fact, that's why I sent Willie to fetch you so early. My strategy has already borne fruit!"

It was now my turn to express puzzlement. "How so?"

"Lend an ear, Poe—I've got immense news for you. Now, as you've probably guessed, I'm a man who doesn't fritter away his time. Early to bed, early to rise, as Dr. Franklin advises. Always followed that rule religiously—one of the keys to my extraordinary success. Up at the crack of dawn, in my office when your average man is just swinging his legs out of bed and rubbing the sleep from his eyes. This morning was no different. Well, here I am, seated at my desk, attending to business, when no less than three of my performers come strolling in. Well, perhaps 'strolling' isn't precisely the right word in the case of Sammy Wainwright, the Amazing Half-Man. No body below his waist—walks on his hands. But you get my drift. The point is that Sammy—along with my armless wonder, Signor Bruno Saltarino, and Gunther the Alligator Boy—suddenly shows up with something important to tell me."

"And what was that?" I eagerly inquired, my curiosity having been roused to an acute pitch.

Placing his forearms on the desk, Barnum leaned closer to me and said: "Each of them, separately, had already seen the morning *Herald.* And each of them had recognized Isabel Somers from her picture on page one."

"Why, what do you mean?" I exclaimed. "Recognized her from where?"

"Why, from *here!*" Barnum replied. "Remember that souvenir brochure I turned up in her bedroom? Well, it seems that Miss Somers wasn't just a one-time visitor to the American Museum. On the contrary. According to Sammy, Bruno, and Gunther, she was a regular customer. That's what made them notice her. As you well know, Poe, m'boy, Barnum's museum is the most popular attraction on the face of the globe. Makes the holy city of Mecca look like a ghost town. People flock here by the thousands. So the performers don't ordinarily pay much attention to any particular individual. But this Somers woman showed up so often they couldn't help but take note of her. Must've come two or three times a week, according to Sammy. And she apparently spent most of that time hanging around my human curiosities."

Here Barnum rubbed his chin and added in a ruminative tone: "Guess she had a fascination for human deformity. Must be what attracted her to Vanderhorn. That and the money, of course."

For a long moment, I merely looked at him in silence, absorbing this intelligence. "That the victim visited these premises frequently enough to be identified by your performers is certainly an *intriguing* fact," I said at length. "Its *significance*, however, remains to be determined. Did you question your trio of attractions any further?"

Barnum shook his head. "Thought I'd wait until Willie fetched you. No point in making them repeat it twice."

"Then we must go and speak to them at once."

Here Barnum's cheeks ballooned outward—he blew out a long sigh—and the same, worried expression he had been wearing upon my arrival returned to his face. "I'm afraid you'll have to handle it yourself, Poe, m'boy. Something big's come up that requires my immediate attention. Have to catch a ferry to New Jersey at once. Emergency situation. Can't delay another minute."

Deeply surprised at this development, I inquired as to the precise nature of the emergency. Holding up the letter he had been perusing when I entered, Barnum replied thusly:

"Found this waiting for me when I arrived this morning. Must've been delivered late yesterday, when you and I were out investigating. It's from a gentleman named Adams, owns a dairy farm in Hoboken. Claims that one of his cows has given birth to a living, two-headed, cyclops calf. That's right, Poe, m'boy. Your ears didn't deceive you. A newborn calf with two heads, each with a single eye smack in the middle. Damnedest thing I ever heard of. Oh yes, I know what you're thinking—two-headed animals are a dime a dozen. And you'd be right, Poe, you'd be right. Why, I've already got the finest taxidermical specimen of a two-headed collie dog in existence. Not to mention my stuffed cyclops pig. But this creature has *both* deformities at once. And even more remarkable—it's alive and breathing!"

"I concur that it sounds like a most unusual creature—a true *lusus naturae,* as Aristotle would have denominated it. The extreme urgency of the situation, however, remains somewhat unclear to me."

"This Adams is a shrewd customer," Barnum replied, giving the letter a little shake. "Wants to sell the beast to the highest bidder. Says he's already contacted another party who might be interested. Guess who? That's right—none other than Mr. Alexander Parmalee! I'll be doubly damned if I let that scoundrel get hold of this prize, Poe. Of course, P. T. Barnum's not the kind of man to buy a pig in a poke, either. Want to see the creature with my own eyes before I invest in it."

Removing his heavy gold watch from his vest pocket, he consulted the time, then snapped the lid shut and leapt to his feet. "Must be off, Poe, or I'll miss the ferry. I'll be back late this afternoon. In the meantime, you'd best go talk to Sammy, Bruno, and Gunther. They're expecting you."

"Very well," I said, rising from my chair. "Where will I find them?"

"Why, where else?" Barnum exclaimed. "Upstairs on the third floor. In the Hall of Oddities."

CHAPTER THIRTEEN

Of the innumerable attractions on display at the American Museum, none excited greater interest among the public than Barnum's unparalleled assemblage of human curiosities. This in itself was unsurprising. Throughout the ages, grotesquely malformed specimens of humanity—"freaks," in the common parlance—have exerted a profound fascination on the mind of the multitudes. During ancient times, dwarves, hermaphrodites, and other such anomalous beings were regarded as nothing less than supernatural prodigies, to be either venerated as divine or sacrificed as portents of evil. Thus, in the famous *tabulae anatomicae* of the early Chaldeo-Babylonians, we find these injunctions: "When a woman gives birth to an infant with no lower jaw, affliction will seize upon the country"; whereas "when a woman gives birth to an infant that has three feet, there will be great prosperity in the land."

In later ages, when pagan superstition had long been superseded by Christian belief, human monstrosities continued to inspire a potent mixture of awe, horror, and fascination—in short, a kind of sacred *dread*—in those who paid to view them. As early as the thirteenth century, "freak shows" were a common and exceedingly popular feature of English carnivals and fairs. By Shakespeare's day, such exhibitions had become so widespread that the demand for three-legged men, bearded women, giants, conjoined twins, and other anatomically deviant humans far outstripped the available supply. Indeed, in his final, intensely moving (if, perhaps, somewhat desultory) play, *The Tempest*, the Bard himself takes note of this phenomenon, having the clownish Trinculo observe that—if only he could succeed in transporting the bestial Caliban back home to England—he could grow rich by displaying this grotesque being at Bartholomew Fair. "There would this monster make a man," says Trinculo, remarking on the public's seemingly boundless appetite for the *outré* and the freakish. "Any strange beast there makes a man."

Even in our own intensely enlightened and scientific era, severely deformed members of our species retain the power to elicit a shudder of primal dread in spectators. That this is the case I can attest from my own personal experience. During my boyhood in Richmond, an itinerant showman named Vernon leased a vacant shop on Clay Street and installed an exhibition of human oddities. As I passed by the storefront one afternoon on my way home from school, my attention was riveted by the colorful sign suspended above the entranceway. This garishly painted banner depicted—in the crudest conceivable manner—the ostensible wonders within: a "caterpillar woman" with a voluptuous torso but no limbs, a "dog-faced boy" with the head of a canine, a "devil man" with a long, curving horn protruding from the center of his brow, and several other, equally prodigious specimens.

The cost of admission was ten cents—a seemingly modest sum, yet nearly prohibitive to a lad whose notoriously penurious guardian kept an inordinately tight hold on the family purse strings. Nevertheless, by dint of much cunning, cajolery, and resolve, I at length managed to accrue the requisite sum. Clutching my pennies in my fist, I therefore repaired to Clay Street one brilliant, autumn afternoon—handed over the payment to the somewhat disreputable-looking personage at the entrance—and, with racing heart, stepped into the dim, musty interior of the converted shop.

The sights that immediately assaulted me were unnerving in the extreme. Rather than the colorful, fantastic creatures advertised on the banner, I found myself face-to-face with an array of the most dreadfully deformed humans I had ever encountered. One of the curiosities in particular—a hydrocephalic boy with a head nearly as large as his body—elicited an instantaneous and violent response. My heart quailed—the blood congealed in my veins—dizziness overcame me. Stifling the involuntary shriek of terror that arose in my throat, I spun on my heels and fled from that chamber of horrors, while behind me I could hear the hideously malformed boy and his fellow monstrosities burst into a chorus of derisive laughter.

Although it had occurred a full three decades earlier, my childhood experience had made such a deep and enduring impression upon me that even now—as I reached the third-floor landing of Barnum's establishment and approached the door leading into the Hall of Oddities—I was seized with a sensation of intense, anticipatory dread. Pausing at the threshold, I steeled myself as best I could—took a deep breath—and entered the domain of the freaks.

A hushed and somber atmosphere prevailed in the cavernous chamber. I was instantly seized with an acute feeling of disorientation, as though I had crossed into a strange—an intensely *dreamlike*—world. This sensation was heightened by a most unusual circumstance. The clock had yet to strike ten—the time at which the museum doors would open to admit the gathered throng on the sidewalk. The Hall of Oddities being thus devoid of any outside visitor but myself, I could not help but feel like an alien presence. Within that realm of the monstrous—the grotesque—the wildly aberrant— *I* was the greatest anomaly of all.

For a moment, I remained rooted in place, taking stock of the scene that now presented itself to my view. Occupying the center of the gallery was a series of glass display cases containing Barnum's collection of stuffed and mounted teratological animals—six-legged cows, three-headed sheep, dogs with multiple tails and the like. The human attractions, two dozen in all, were arrayed around the periphery of the room, each displayed on a raised platform partitioned off from its neighbors by heavy, scarlet-hued draperies. At the moment, the performers were busying themselves in a variety of ways, preparatory to the beginning of their workday.

On the platform immediately to my right stood a family of albinos—father, mother, and little boy. Each was dressed in a costume that revealed as much of his utterly colorless flesh as the dictates of propriety permitted. Their hair was exceptionally long—bushy—and as white as the winter pelt of a Siberian ermine; while their eyes were of the brightest pink. They appeared to be engaged in some sort of family dispute, the parents angrily berating their child, who stood with his head bowed, his thin arms held rigidly at his sides.

The adjacent platform was occupied by a bizarre-looking creature garbed in the savage costume of a South Seas cannibal. He was fully six feet tall, with a well-developed physique and muscular limbs. His head, however, was as tiny as an infant's. Its shape was also exceedingly abnormal, the entirely bald, severely tapered cranium resembling the pointed crown of an egg. In short, he was a striking specimen of a congenital *microcephalic*—more commonly (and cruelly) referred to as a "pin-head." Since the singularly undersized skulls of such unfortunates can only accommodate a brain of commensurately diminutive size, these individuals are invariably characterized by extreme mental deficiency. This was clearly the case with the bizarre-looking being now on display, who stood on the platform mumbling happily to himself, his not-unpleasing features arranged into that look of childlike abstraction characteristic of the hopeless imbecile.

Willie Schnitzler was the next attraction in line. She had changed her clothing and was now formally attired in a gown of rich, crimson velvet, tailored to accommodate her enormous bulk. Both her luxuriant beard and her dark, wavy, shoulder-length tresses had apparently been treated with some sort of pomade, giving a distinct glow or patina to the hair of both her face and head.

Seated on an oversized stool, she was beguiling the time by reading from a book that was clutched in one hand. This volume—to judge by the ornate floral design embossed in gold on its emerald cover—was evidently one of the many cloyingly sentimental novels that had inundated the American marketplace in the wake of Miss Rowson's deplorable best-seller, *Charlotte Temple.* In her other hand, Willie held a thick sandwich of what appeared to be ham and cheese. As she read, she took occasional, exceedingly *dainty* nibbles of this snack. In spite of her fastidious mode of eating, however, I could not help but notice that her shiny beard had already become dotted with a sprinkling of wayward crumbs.

A baby's crib, fashioned of oak, stood on the platform immediately to the right of Willie's. Its legs had been carved to suggest the vine-covered limbs of an ancient tree; while rising from each corner was an elaborately wrought finial in the shape of a hovering faerie. Through the slender, widely spaced bars of the crib I could perceive a child-sized fig-ure, lying on its back. Its inordinately large, misshapen hands—whose fingers resembled the talons of a bird of prey—clutched at the air; while from its lips there issued an unutterably mournful sound—a kind of low, continuous *keening.* This creature, I immediately surmised, was none other than the ostensible "goblin child" that had exerted such a power-ful hold on Sissy's imagination when she came upon its description in the souvenir guidebook I had purchased for her during our visit to the museum several months earlier.

As I surveyed the rest of the great hall, I was struck by the excep-tionally wide and exotic assortment of teratological humans Barnum had managed to assemble under one roof. There was a bearded male giant, towering to a height of nearly eight feet and garbed as an Ara-bian sheikh. He was sharing his platform with an eighteen-inch-tall midget costumed as the King of Lilliput, who stood upon a tabletop, minuscule hands cupped to his mouth, shouting something up to his colossal companion. There was a man whose hands resembled the claws of a lobster and another with legs as massive and pendulous as the limbs of a pachyderm.

One of the most unnerving of all the curiosities was a fashion-ably attired, middle-aged gentleman of ordinary stature with a par-tially developed, parasitic twin protruding from his midsection. This second, rudimentary body—scarcely larger than a toddler's—was at-tached by its neck, as though its head were embedded in the abdomen of its host. A pretty young girl with arms resembling the flippers of a harbor seal was seated on the neighboring platform. Beside her stood a teenaged boy suffering from a grotesque dermatological condition that endowed his face, exposed upper torso, and bare arms with the scaly appearance of a reptile. This individual, I immediately surmised, was none other than Gunther the Alligator Boy—one of the three performers who had approached Barnum earlier that morning with information concerning Isabel Somers.

Casting my gaze around the hall for the other two members of this trio, I quickly spotted Bruno the Armless Wonder. An exceptionally fine-featured young fellow who could not have been much older than nineteen or twenty, he was seated in a high-backed chair upon the red-curtained platform, sipping from a teacup whose handle was gripped between the first and second toes of his naked right foot.

And then my gaze fell upon the third of the informants. This was Sammy Wainwright, the Amazing Half-Man—perhaps the single most remarkable of all of Barnum's human prodigies. Indeed, so astonishing was his appearance that, at my first glimpse of him, I actually raised my hands to my face and performed the instinctive gesture of one who doubts the reliability of his vision: I rubbed my eyes.

Having passed so much of my life residing in large cities—Richmond, Baltimore, Philadelphia, and, of course, New York—I had encountered more than my share of poor, legless beggars who propelled themselves along the streets on wheeled, wooden platforms. Sammy Wainwright, however, was no mere cripple or amputee. His physical deformity was of an entirely different—and infinitely more *disconcerting*—order. He was a young man still in his twenties, with piercing eyes, attractive features, and thick, naturally curling, black hair. His upper body was completely normal—his chest, shoulders, arms, and head all perfectly formed. Below his rib cage, however, his entire body was missing: not merely his lower extremities but his belly, buttocks, pelvis—*everything.* That he could survive at all seemed nothing short of miraculous, since—as far as could be determined from outward appearances—he seemed to possess no vital organs beyond those that are nestled within the pectoral cavity.

He was perched on a swing that depended from the ceiling. This arrangement was intended to prove to the spectator that there was no trickery involved—no cunningly concealed mirrors or hidden cabinets of the sort employed by professional magicians to produce their illusions. No. Here, at least, there was no taint of the "humbug" about one of Barnum's marvels. If anything, Wainwright's billing as the "Amazing Half-Man" was an understatement; for no less than *two-thirds* of his body appeared to be nonexistent.

So unsettling—so incomprehensible—so sheerly uncanny—

was the sight of this grotesquely *truncated* being that, as I contemplated him from across the hall, I was suddenly gripped by a spasm of vertigo. Closing my eyes, I waited until the dizzying sensation subsided. Then—under the curious gaze of the other performers—I crossed the floor and came to a halt before Wainwright's small wooden stage.

He was in the process of cleaning his fingernails with the point of an open penknife blade. As he carefully removed the dirt from beneath the nail of his left pinkie, he suddenly became aware of my presence and—regarding me with a look of the deepest vexation—said: "Hey, pal. The museum ain't open yet. Who the hell let *you* in?" Though Wainwright was no taller than a midget, his voice, like his entire upper body, was that of a normal, adult male.

Taken aback by the exceedingly *belligerent* tone of this remark, I somewhat stammeringly replied: "Please excuse the intrusion. My name is Poe—Edgar Poe. I am here at the behest of Mr. Barnum."

"So you're Poe, eh?" said Wainwright, snapping his penknife shut and slipping it into the side pocket of his jacket. This garment was of a specially tailored length. Unlike the ordinary jacket that extends to the level of the wearer's thighs, this one terminated at a point just below Wainwright's chest, thus affording the spectator a clear view of his deformity. "Why didn't you say so? C'mon."

Gripping the ropes that supported the swing, he slid from his perch and dropped onto the platform, landing on his open palms. He then scurried to the edge of the little stage, hopped onto the floor, and—balancing himself on his left hand—reached up with his right and shook mine with a surprisingly powerful, if not *crushing*, grip.

"Let's find somewheres more private to talk," he said, lowering his voice to a confidential level. "That giant A-rab over there ain't the only one with big ears."

Using one hand as a pivot, he quickly spun around and made his way across the hall. He moved with an astonishing celerity, head outthrust, body bouncing slightly as he propelled himself forward on the flats of his hands.

Pausing before the platform on which the Armless Wonder was seated, he looked up and said, "Hey, Bruno. This here is Mr. Poe. The one who's helping Barnum. C'mon. We're going out into the hallway to talk."

Setting his teacup down upon the little table before him, the armless young man arose from his chair and descended from the platform. Viewed from such close proximity, he was even handsomer than he had initially appeared. His face was perfectly oval in shape, with prominent cheekbones and a finely molded chin. His deep-set brown eyes were large, liquid, and luminous in the extreme; his nose handsomely formed with a scarcely perceptible tendency to the aquiline; his lips somewhat thin but of a surpassingly beautiful curve. His glossy brown hair was of a singularly *gossamer* texture; while his graceful upper lip was adorned with a thin, neatly trimmed mustache.

Standing before me, he smiled urbanely, revealing a set of strikingly regular, brilliantly white teeth. "Pleased to meet you, sir," he declared in a genial tone. "You will forgive me for not shaking hands."

Somewhat nonplussed by this self-satirizing witticism, I merely replied: "The pleasure is all mine."

"Hey, Bruno," exclaimed the truncated figure at my feet. Even balanced on his hands, Sammy Wainwright barely came up to the level of my thighs. "Go get lizard-boy and meet us out in the corridor."

"Right," the armless young fellow replied, then strode off across the exhibition hall toward the little stage shared by the half-naked Alligator Boy and the phocomelic Seal Girl, each of whom seemed deeply absorbed in his own thoughts, utterly ignoring the other.

Scuttling ahead of me by means of his singular style of manual locomotion, Wainwright then led me out into the corridor, where we came to a halt beside a tall glass case displaying the colossal tusks of a prehistoric mastodon. A moment later, Bruno emerged from the exhibition hall. Beside him was the Alligator Boy. He walked with a shuffling, stoop-shouldered gait, eyes downcast. Pausing before me, he extended his slender right hand and, in a barely audible voice, muttered, "Hullo."

Certain of Barnum's curiosities derived their colorful sobriquets from their *anatomical* resemblance to members of the animal kingdom. The stunted limbs of the Seal Girl, for example, did indeed bear an uncanny likeness to the flippers of the marine creature after which she was named. Such, however, was not the case with the extraordinary individual who now stood before me. *Structurally*, there was nothing about him suggestive of a *crocodillian*. His head, countenance, limbs, and torso were all well-formed and of normal development. His anomalous appearance was of an entirely *dermatological* order. He suffered from a uniquely exaggerated case of *ichthyosis*—a morbid hyper-development of the *papillæ*, accompanied by an extreme thickening of the epidermic *lamellæ*. As a result of this condition, his skin had hardened—cracked—and darkened to a greenish-black hue, creating the impression that he was covered from head to foot in the scaly hide of a Mississippi alligator.

So bizarre was his condition that—as he held out his hand in the time-honored gesture of introduction—I was seized with an instinctive reluctance to grasp it, as though I might be contaminated by such contact, and my own flesh transformed into the hideous integument of a reptile. This reaction, however, lasted but an instant, overcome by my deeply ingrained sense of Southern etiquette and civility. Reaching out, I firmly clasped his proffered right hand. Though my nape-hairs prickled slightly at the feel of its strange, utterly nonhuman texture, my voice remained steady as I said: "Hello, young man. I am delighted to make your acquaintance. My name is Mr. Poe."

In response to this salutation, the Alligator Boy merely smiled shyly and mumbled a few unintelligible words before removing his hand from my own.

"So just what did Barnum tell you, Poe?" inquired Sammy Wainwright, frowning up at me from the floor. There was a peculiar insolence in his tone, as though—existing in a state so far beyond the bounds of everyday normality—he felt unconstrained by the conventional niceties of social intercourse.

"Merely that all three of you gentlemen, having glimpsed the portrait of Isabel Somers in this morning's edition of the *Herald*, immediately recognized her as a frequent visitor to the museum."

"That's right," said Wainwright. "Picture looked just like her. To a tee. Except for the hair. She had awful pretty hair—real thick and wavy and kind of red-brown in color."

"Auburn," said the armless young man.

"Yeah," agreed Wainwright. "It was beautiful. Believe me—I got a real eye for beauty. Lots of freaks do. Right, Bruno?"

An indignant flush suffused the handsome countenance of the armless young man. "You know how I feel about that word, Sammy," he said reprovingly.

"Aw, ain't you the sensitive one?" Wainwright sardonically replied "Not me. I believe in calling a spade a spade. But all right. *Curiosities,* if it makes you feel better."

Seemingly mollified, the Armless Wonder turned to me and said, "Sammy's right. She did have very nice hair. Otherwise, her features were rather ordinary. Pleasant enough—but nothing special."

"But if there was, as you put it, 'nothing special' about her appearance," I inquired, "then what precisely brought her to your notice? Surely, there must be scores of young women who visit your exhibition each day."

"That's for sure," exclaimed Wainwright with a suggestive wink. "Some of 'em are real peaches, too!"

Gazing down at Wainwright—who was situated at my feet, the flattened base of his torso resting on the floor—I could not fail to be struck by the salacious tenor of this comment. For a man who lacked a body below the waist, he evinced a surprisingly keen interest in the fairer sex. Whether the truncated fellow retained a capacity for physical love, however, was not a question upon which I cared to dwell, and I quickly put the matter from my mind.

"You're absolutely right," said Bruno. "We do get lots of young ladies in here. But this Somers woman came around all the time."

"All the time?" I exclaimed. "Why, whatever do you mean?"

Though my query was addressed to the armless youth, it was Wainwright who answered. "We ain't saying she was here every day," he explained. "But pretty damned often. At least once a week."

"Sometimes more," added Bruno. "Isn't that so, Gunther?"

"Uh-huh," said the Alligator Boy, bobbing his head up and down.

"And precisely how did she pass the time during her visits?" I inquired.

"Just walking around and looking," said Wainwright with a shrug. "Like everybody else."

I mulled over this information for a moment before asking: "Were there any members of your troupe to whom she paid particular attention?"

"Not really," Bruno replied. "At least not that I noticed."

"She *did* spend lots of time gawking at that damned, so-called goblin kid," observed Wainwright. "But lots of women do. Must bring out the mother in 'em. Course, they don't have to listen to the godawful brat bawl all day long."

Though Wainwright's attitude seemed excessively—if not *shockingly*—harsh, I could not doubt the accuracy of his statement. Indeed, his observation about the maternal sentiments elicited by the supposed "changeling" child was entirely borne out by the behavior of my own darling Sissy, who had responded with such tender-hearted sympathy to the mere printed description of this unfortunate creature.

"Now that I think about it," young Bruno interjected in a musing tone, "I *did* notice her talking to Abel a few times."

"Yeah," concurred Wainwright. "You're right. I'd completely forgot about that."

"Abel?" I said. "And which of the performers is he?"

"He ain't one of us at all," Wainwright stated. "He's the building custodian. Abel Tomblin."

I made no attempt to conceal my surprise at this announcement. "But what business could she have possibly had with the custodian?" I exclaimed.

"It *did* seem a little peculiar, all right," observed Bruno.

Just then, a sound reached my ears—faint and far away but growing louder by the moment. It was the excited din of countless, commingled voices, emanating from below. I needed but an instant to identify its source. The museum had opened at last—the crowd had been admitted—and the eager patrons were now making their way up the main stairwell.

"Time to get to work," said Sammy Wainwright, rising on his hands. "Nice meeting you, Poe."

"Let us know if we can be of any further assistance," added the Armless Wonder.

"My thanks to you gentlemen," I replied. "Should you have any additional thoughts concerning Miss Somers, please do not hesitate to inform either Mr. Barnum or myself. In the meantime, I intend to seek out your custodian, Mr. Tomblin, and put a few questions to him. Can you tell me where I am most likely to find him?"

"Try the basement," said Sammy Wainwright. "He has a little storage room down there." He then spun about on one hand and pattered off on his palms toward the Hall of Oddities, with Bruno and the Alligator Boy following close behind.

For a moment, I stood and watched the bizarre threesome retreat into the gloom of the exhibition hall. I then turned on my heels and made for the stairwell.

CHAPTER FOURTEEN

No sooner had I begun my descent than I encountered the initial crowd of patrons, surging up the marble staircase in a great, human tide. This group was composed of a heterogeneous mix of individuals. There were complacent, middle-aged parents accompanied by their well-fed offspring—fashionably attired young couples linked arm-in-arm—dapper swells with velvet waistcoats and flashing eyes—junior clerks in threadbare brown suits—elderly tradesmen with florid cheeks and balding domes—wrinkled, bejeweled, and paint-begrimed beldames making a last effort at youth—and a smaller, though not inconsiderable, number of unescorted young females, several of whom, to judge by the brazenness of both their dress and carriage, clearly belonged to that fallen class of womanhood adept in the dreadful arts of the professional *coquette.*

Taken as a whole, this exceedingly diverse crowd exuded a palpable air of eager expectation, filling the stairwell with a continuous, excited babble. Many were already laden with bags of peanuts, peppermint candies, souvenir guidebooks, pinwheels, miniature American flags, and other trinkets, gewgaws, and mementos peddled throughout the museum. As I made my way through the press of this ascending horde, I was able to discern a number of their comments, most of which pertained to the wondrous sights they were about to behold.

"They say Barnum's giant is the biggest human in existence," remarked one young man to his pretty, female companion.

"Wait until you see the Armless Wonder," commented another to his rapt *inamorata.* "Why, he can play the fiddle, saw wood, cut paper doilies with a scissors—and all with his feet!"

One little boy of ten or twelve—his eyes aglint with mischief—was addressing his younger sister. "Now remember, Annie, keep a good distance away from the Alligator Boy," the lad was saying to the girl, whose cherubic face wore an expression of the greatest anxiety imaginable. "He's got these real big teeth, sharp as knives, and if you stand too close, he'll bite off your arm, and then you'll be a freak, too!"

Working my way through the jostling crowd—with many a muttered "excuse me" and "I beg your pardon"—I continued my descent. At length, I arrived at the main floor, which—like the stairwell—was now thronged with visitors. Thence, I proceeded to the subterranean reaches of the building.

The contrast between this portion of my descent and the preceding ones could not have been more dramatic. I was now entirely alone, the only sound the hollow echo of my boot soles against the wooden steps leading to the basement. Quickly reaching the foot of this staircase, I paused for a moment and peered into the gloom of the dimly lit corridor that stretched before me.

An aura of utter and unrelieved solitude pervaded the basement. So intense—so absolute—so sheerly oppressive was this quality that I was suddenly seized with a shudder of acute, premonitory dread. I felt, not merely alone, but completely cut off from the world of the living, as if—like the Thracian minstrel Orpheus—I had journeyed into the land of the dead. This dismal impression was heightened by the many dry, dusty, and lifeless *objets* stored in the basement and stacked against its walls: the mummified creatures, the ancient sarcophagi, the waxen effigies, the surplus taxidermical specimens.

Shaking off this unnerving sensation, I proceeded down the hallway. Once past the locked door of Barnum's office, I found myself in a wholly unfamiliar part of the basement. As I continued my search for the custodian's storeroom, the corridor became increasingly narrow and mazelike—so much so that I soon felt completely disoriented, as if I were wandering through a catacomb. My sense of confusion was exacerbated by the intensely dreary illumination provided by the flickering gas jets placed at irregular intervals high upon the walls.

I was on the brink of turning on my heels and fleeing the awful confines of the basement when my gaze suddenly fell upon a doorway several yards ahead of me. Something affixed to the center of the door shone dully in the gaslight. Stumbling forward, I quickly discovered the source of this dim, metallic glimmer: a small, brass plate engraved with the words, "Custodial Closet."

Heaving a sigh of relief at having reached my destination, I raised my fist—pounded on the door—and waited for a reply. None was forthcoming. After a brief pause, I repeated this action—but to no more effect than before. Peering down, I saw that there was no light issuing from beneath the door. Clearly, the storeroom was untenanted.

Two possible explanations immediately suggested themselves to me: either Tomblin had not yet shown up for work, or—conversely— he had arrived much earlier and was already embarked on his chores elsewhere in the building. In either case, there was no point in my remaining in the basement any longer.

Turning on my heels, I began to retrace my steps. I had only gone a short distance, however, when I was brought up short by a muted but unmistakable sound emanating from the direction of the stairwell: someone had descended to the basement and was now making his way toward me with rapid, determined strides. I knew it could not possibly be Barnum, whose errand to New Jersey would keep him occupied for most, if not all, of the day. Nor did it seem likely that it was one of the visitors to the museum. I was therefore left to conclude that the personage now approaching was none other than the very man I was seeking.

Accordingly, I cupped my hands around my mouth and called: "Hello! Mr. Tomblin?"

No one answered. Puzzled, I proceeded forward at a somewhat more cautious pace. Directly before me, the mazelike corridor took a sharp turn to the left. All at once, a figure came striding around the corner and halted several yards ahead of me. Though I could not dis-

cern his features in the dismal light of the hallway, I recognized him
at once by the distinctive mold of his physique: the immense shoulders and prodigious chest—the massive, bull-like neck—the bald and
bullet-shaped dome.

Looming before me was the exceedingly intimidating figure of
Morris Vanderhorn's fearsome aide-de-camp, the ill-natured brute
named Croley!

Astonished and alarmed in equal measure, I froze in my tracks,
while an icy chill coursed through every particle of my being. Placing
his enormous fists upon his hips, Croley regarded me in silence for a
moment before saying with a sneer: "Well, well. Must be my lucky
day."

So unexpected was the sight of this singularly menacing figure
that my organs of vocalization were momentarily paralyzed. "Wh—
what in heaven's name are *you* doing here?" I managed to stammer at
last.

"Paying a little visit to Barnum," answered Croley. "The boss
don't like strangers sticking their big snouts into his affairs. Looks
like that two-bit showman ain't here, though. Guess I'll have to settle
for *you*."

And so saying, he reached inside his coat and extracted an object
which he held at his side. Even in the intensely murky gaslight, I was
able to identify this implement with little trouble. It was a bludgeon
of the sort preferred by that inordinately debased class of ruffians
who earn their miserable livelihoods by preying on hapless and unwary pedestrians foolish enough to venture into the more sinister
neighborhoods of the city, such as the infamous Five Points district.
The handle of this weapon was wrapped in leather to afford its user
the most advantageous grip; while its shaft and head bristled with
ugly-looking protuberances carved into the wood. Its interior had undoubtedly been hollowed out and filled with lead shot to render it
even more deadly.

A malevolent chuckle issued from the lips of Vanderhorn's hulking minion as he took a step toward me and said: "This is going to be
fun."

From the days of my earliest boyhood, I had been known for my exceptional athletic prowess. As a lad, I had won the plaudits of my peers for my unsurpassed abilities as a swimmer, runner, and leaper. I was also an acknowledged master of the manly art of boxing. In any pugilistic contest conducted according to the accepted rules of civilized sportsmanship, I feared no man—not even one of much greater stature and muscular strength. I knew from long experience, however, that the world abounded in ruffians who utterly disdained such rules, and freely resorted to the most barbaric tactics imaginable when engaged in a bout of hand-to-hand combat.

That the foe now coming toward me was a stranger to the code of behavior governing *les affairs d'honneur* among civilized men could not have been more obvious. His propensity for savage modes of combat was clear not merely from the physical tokens of his previous battles (such as his partially chewed-off right ear) but—even more plainly—from the villainous implement he was now wielding. To attempt to overcome such an opponent with nothing but my bare fists and superior reflexes seemed quixotic in the extreme. Accordingly, I chose the most prudent course available: I immediately spun on my heels and fled in the opposite direction as fast as my feet could carry me.

As I ran, I could hear Croley behind me. His very manner of pursuit conveyed the utmost contempt. He did not even bother to run after me, but rather strode at a leisurely pace—as though my defeat at his hands were so predetermined that haste was unnecessary.

Continuing my mad dash along the dark and winding hallway, I quickly lost my bearings. All at once, I halted with a gasp. I had reached a dead end! Directly before me, stretching from floor to ceiling, there loomed a solid wall of crates, barrels, hampers, and innumerable surplus artifacts, all chaotically piled together.

Behind me, growing louder by the instant, I could hear the steady, inexorable tread of my pursuer. I frantically cast my gaze about the blocked and narrow passageway for some means of escape. Only one possibility presented itself. There, leaning in a far corner of the hallway—beside a carved, dragon-shaped figurehead from a Viking warship, a life-sized wax mannequin of Attila the Hun, an Esquimo kayak, and a weatherworn pillory from the era of Cotton Mather—was an ornate sarcophagus of the sort used to inhume the mummified remains of ancient Egyptian nobility. With only the briefest hesitation, I hurried to this object—swung it open—stepped inside—and pulled the heavy, elaborately wrought lid shut.

I was now completely enveloped by darkness. Silence engulfed me. By cocking an ear toward the heavy lid of the sarcophagus and straining my auditory faculty to the utmost, I could just barely make out the muffled tread of my pursuer's approaching footsteps. In another instant, they ceased. Croley had evidently come to a halt directly in front of my hiding place and was looking around in confusion for my whereabouts.

My plan—insofar as I had formed one—was to remain absolutely silent until the bloodthirsty rogue abandoned his search and retreated from the basement; whereupon I would steal from the sarcophagus and cautiously make my way back to the safety of the main floor. I had not counted, however, on Croley's extreme—his *inordinate*—persistence. For what felt like an eternity, he remained situated outside my place of concealment, while I waited in an agony of suspense for his departure.

As the moments dragged by—oh, with what torturous slowness!—the intensity of the encompassing darkness began to stifle and oppress me. The atmosphere was intolerably close. An insufferable odor of decay suffused my nostrils. I felt as if I had been encoffined while still alive! My brain reeled. A hideous dizziness overcame me. Perspiration burst from every pore.

At length, I could stand my dreadful predicament no longer. The idea of remaining immured within the black and suffocating confines of the musty sarcophagus was even more unthinkable than the prospect of facing the hulking brute, Croley. Accordingly, I placed both hands upon the wooden cover, preparatory to throwing it open.

Before I could accomplish this action, the heavy lid abruptly creaked and swung outward, seemingly of its own accord, as though my mere *wish* to escape had somehow caused it to open. Immediately, however, I perceived the true reason for this phenomenon. There—standing directly outside the sarcophagus, one meaty hand grasping the edge of the wide-flung lid—was my fearsome adversary. The expression on his visage was one of fierce and diabolical exultation.

Removing his hand from the lid, he reached inside—grabbed me roughly by the shirt just under my neck—and yanked me violently out of my narrow hiding place. Twisting the fabric of my garment tightly in his fist, he slowly drew me toward him. As he did, the knuckles of his hand dug deep into my larynx, causing me to choke.

"You slippery little son of a bitch," he hissed. "I'll teach you to run away."

With a savage outward thrust of his arm, he released his grip on my shirt and flung me backward into the wall, where I landed with a crash among a pile of boxes and assorted *objets*. Towering over me, he then raised the bludgeon high above his head and took a step in my direction.

Sprawled on the cluttered floor, I desperately cast my gaze about for a means to counter his attack. All at once, my eyes fell on the Esquimo kayak, sitting on the floor a short distance from where I lay. Resting crossways on its prow was a small spear, or harpoon, of the sort employed by these hardy aborigines to hunt seal and other aquatic creatures that form the basis of their diet. My reaction was swift as thought. Quickly rolling toward this vessel, I reached out and snatched the harpoon by its handle. Then, springing to my feet, I extended it like a lance, its serrated, razor-edged point aimed directly at Croley's brawny chest.

"Stand back," I exclaimed. "Although loathe to inflict severe bodily injury upon your person, I shall not hesitate to do so if you persist in your present course of action."

For a moment, Croley appeared utterly nonplussed by the sheer ferocity of this warning. A look of the deepest consternation spread across his intensely disagreeable visage. Slowly he lowered the fearsome weapon to his side.

"And now, Mr. Croley," I triumphantly declared. "You will kindly oblige me by raising your hands above your head and—"

I did not have a chance to complete this statement. All at once—with the speed of an attacking King cobra—Croley lashed out with his right foot, striking the shaft of the harpoon sharply with the toe of his boot. The weapon flew from my grasp and landed with a clatter on the floor. So sudden—so sheerly unexpected—was this act that, for a moment, I merely gaped down at my empty hands in stunned incomprehension.

In that instant, Croley launched himself at me with a roar, lifting the bludgeon high in the air, then bringing it down in a great, sweeping arc. Had I not raised my left arm in an instinctive, protective gesture, the ensuing blow would surely have crushed my skull. As it was, the bludgeon landed across my forearm with a sickening crack.

The pain produced by this savage assault was nothing short of blinding. I sank to my knees with a groan, my left arm hanging uselessly at my side, my right arm clutching reflexively at its grievously injured mate. An inky swirl of darkness began to spread across my vision.

"Say good-night, you damned, sorry runt," Croley growled. Looming over me, legs widespread, he made ready to deliver the coup de grace.

The lethal blow never fell. Instead, through my rapidly fading senses, I could discern a strange—a wholly unaccountable—*gurgling* sound. Gazing up stuporously, I perceived an enormous hand grasping Croley's raised wrist from behind; while a forearm as massive as a Virginia ham encircled his throat. In another moment, the bludgeon dropped from Croley's grasp—his face darkened—his eyelids fluttered—and he slid insensibly to the ground.

My rescuer now stood revealed to my sight. Even as I sank into unconsciousness, my dimming mind recognized the now-familiar features: the broad, handsome face—the full, flowing beard—the enormous physique—the red velvet dress.

"Willie!" I gasped. Then the last vestiges of strength drained from my limbs. My vision failed. An iciness of feeling pervaded my frame. Then all was darkness—and silence—and utter oblivion.

Part Three

THE GIRL WITH NO HANDS

CHAPTER FIFTEEN

"Eddie, dear. Wake up. You've been having a bad dream."

Even in my somnolent state, I had no difficulty in recognizing the surpassingly mellifluous voice of my darling Sissy, rousing me from the depths of what had indeed been a most fearful—a most *unnerving*—dream. In it, a grim, spectral creature bent on my destruction pursued me through a tunnel as narrow and circuitous as the cunning maze constructed by the fabled Athenian craftsman, Daedalus, to house the monstrous bull-man, Minotaur. As I fled down the tortuous passageways of this labyrinth, I stumbled and fell; whereupon the implacable thing at my heels threw itself upon me and sank its dripping fangs into my left forearm. I was on the verge of being devoured by this ghastly phantasm, when—like the hempen lifeline thrown to a drowning sailor—Sissy's golden voice penetrated the enveloping darkness and drew me back into the blessed world of daylight.

Now, as my eyelids fluttered open, I gazed up in an access of gratitude and relief at my angelic wife. Her incomparably lovely visage was wrought into an expression of the deepest tenderness and concern. As the mists of slumber evaporated from my mind, I grew slowly cognizant of the other sights, sounds, and sensations of my surroundings: the beneficent warmth of the sunlight—the perfumed aroma of the atmosphere—the insistent buzzing of the insects in the flower garden—the melodious chirpings of the birds in the leaf-heavy branches of the horse-chestnut trees.

All at once, I became fully aware of my actual circumstances. I was seated in a chair on the front porch of our little country cottage. Sissy was standing beside me, her cherished volume of British folk stories clutched in one hand.

"Are you all right, Eddie, darling?" Sissy inquired. "You were making such strange, frightened noises."

I smiled up at her reassuringly and replied: "How could I be otherwise when, upon awakening, I find your luminous eyes—brightly expressive as the twins of Leda—gazing down upon me with such unconcealed adoration and solicitude?"

"Oh, Eddie," Sissy said with a gentle laugh. "You have such a way with words."

Sitting upright in my chair, I began to stretch my limbs, only to be seized with a sharp, intensely searing pain in my left arm, which— I now realized—was cradled in a cotton sling suspended from my neck. Wincing, I emitted an involuntary groan of distress.

"Be careful, Eddie," said Sissy. "Doctor Beers said you should refrain from moving your poor, injured arm as much as possible."

"In my still somewhat sleep-fuddled state," I replied, "I momentarily forgot that my arm was thus incapacitated."

"Well, please try to remember," she sweetly chided. She set her book down upon the caned seat of the chair which stood beside my own and which she had evidently been occupying until disturbed by my uneasy slumber.

"I believe I've read enough for one morning," she said. "I think I'll go inside and help Muddy prepare lunch." Placing a fond kiss upon my brow, she then turned and disappeared into the house.

No sooner was she gone than I settled back in my chair and turned my gaze upon the captivating scene before me. Several yards away, our beloved feline, Cattarina, crouched in the yard, staring intently at the swarm of gaily colored butterflies fluttering about the blossoms of the flower garden. In the distance—across an extensive tract of orchards, fields, and verdant meadows—stood the spacious farmhouse occupied by our landlords, the Brennans. Behind this handsome dwelling rose a broad and swelling hill, its summit crowned by a few ancient elm trees standing alone against the cerulean sky. Even this exceedingly picturesque vista, however, could not entirely dispel the lingering agitation produced by my all-too-vivid nightmare. As I sat on the porch, waiting for Muddy and Sissy to complete their mealtime preparations, my thoughts turned inexorably to the actual events that had so clearly inspired my deeply disquieting dream. . . .

Two days had elapsed since my terrifying encounter with Morris Vanderhorn's henchman, Croley, in the basement of Barnum's museum. Of Willie Schnitzler's timely intervention—which had saved me from severe and possibly *mortal* injury—I had, of course, only the vaguest memory, having fallen into a state of utter insensibility at the very moment of her unlooked-for appearance, as the reader will recall. Only afterward did I receive a full account from her own, luxuriantly bearded lips both of the circumstances that had brought her to my rescue, and of the events that immediately followed it.

What had happened was this: Immediately after my discussion with Sammy Wainwright, Bruno Saltarino, and Gunther the Alligator Boy in the corridor outside the Hall of Oddities, the trio had returned to their respective platforms. Willie—curious as to why I had been conferring with the three performers—had put this question to the Armless Wonder, who briefly informed her of the crux of our talk and explained that I had gone down to the basement in search of Abel Tomblin. As it happened, Willie knew that Tomblin was nowhere to be found, Barnum having taken the strapping custodian along with him to New Jersey to help transport the coveted, two-headed, cyclops calf back to the museum.

Wishing to spare me the frustration of wandering around the gloomy basement in a vain search for Tomblin, Willie had therefore taken leave of her post and made her way downstairs, arriving just in time to prevent Croley from delivering a crushing blow to my cranium. Encircling his throat with her powerful forearm, she had applied sufficient pressure to his trachea to render him unconscious. Then, scooping up my own insensible form, she had borne me upstairs as effortlessly as a mother carries a swaddled infant.

After assuring herself that I had not sustained a life-threatening injury, she had dispatched several of her fellow performers—including the strongman, The Great O'Bannon—to the basement. They had returned a short while later, however, to report that they could find no trace of my attacker, who had apparently awakened in the interim and fled the premises.

By then, I, too, had regained consciousness. I found myself lying on a cot in a little room adjacent to the Hall of Oddities, where the performers relaxed between shows. My injured arm had been carefully bound in a scarf of embroidered silk which (so I subsequently learned) had been borrowed from Miss Zobeide Luti, Barnum's celebrated "Circassian Beauty."

After quaffing a cup of cold water, I had satisfied Willie's natural curiosity by providing her with a brief summary of my battle with Croley. Then—after ascertaining that I was not merely able but positively *eager* to undertake the journey homeward—she had helped me to the carriage and driven me back to my cottage.

As I disembarked from the vehicle, Muddy and Sissy had emerged from the front door and—perceiving my bandaged arm—came hurrying to my side with many exclamations of distress. Knowing that the truth would serve no other purpose than to alarm my loved ones, I had decided to prevaricate, and had enlisted Willie's co-operation in this well-meaning deceit. I therefore explained that I had sustained my injury in an accidental fall while descending the marble staircase of the museum. After receiving our profuse expressions of gratitude, Willie took her leave. Sissy and Muddy then helped me to bed and sent for the local physician, Dr. Benjamin Beers, who—after subjecting my arm to a thorough (and intensely painful) examination—pronounced it severely bruised but unbroken.

The following day, I received a visit from Barnum himself, who arrived bearing a wicker basket full of delectable foodstuffs—an entire smoked ham, a variety of cheeses, a jar of preserved quinces, a dark and exceedingly crusty rye bread, a half-dozen fresh oranges, a fragrant apple pie, a moist honey cake, and other delicacies. He was admitted to my bedchamber, where—garbed in a dressing gown, my left arm cradled in the sling contrived by Dr. Beers—I sat in my armchair, perusing Monsieur Henri Jacquemar's comprehensive (if somewhat tendentious) volume, *Histoire et théorie du symbolisme philosophique, re-ligieux, et mythologique.*

"How are you feeling, Poe, m'boy?" Barnum exclaimed as he hurried to my side. "Come—let me have a look. A little the worse for wear, I see. But not as bad as I feared. Arm's still in one piece, thank heavens. And to think—*you* took the beating intended for *me!* Brave man! I won't forget it anytime soon, I can promise you that. Why, it was a sacrifice worthy of a biblical martyr. No, no—don't deny it. Why, you're another Arnold Winkelried, Poe, m'boy—throwing yourself fearlessly in front of the enemy to shield your comrades from harm!"

Though perhaps somewhat overstated, Barnum's comparison of my behavior to that of the legendary Swiss hero—whose selfless act of bravery on the battlefield of Sempach helped spur his countrymen to their decisive victory over the Hapsburg invaders—could not fail to gratify my vanity. The stentorian volume at which this accolade was delivered, however, produced a pang of apprehension within my breast. Fearful that he might be overheard by Sissy or Muddy—who had retreated to the kitchen to unpack the basket of comestibles he had brought—I quickly motioned for Barnum to speak more softly.

He took my meaning at once, and—lowering his voice—continued with his speech. That Vanderhorn had tried to halt our investigation by such brutal means proved beyond any reasonable doubt that he was directly implicated in Isabel Somers's death, as far as Barnum was concerned. Far from serving as a deterrent, however, this crude attempt at intimidation had only served to stiffen the showman's resolve.

"I ask you, Poe," he exclaimed, "do I look like a man who can be bullied? Ha! Why, during my touring days, I had some adventures that would curl your hair. Faced down a lynch mob in Georgia, a band of river pirates on the mighty Mississip, and a whole army of savage redskins in the backwoods of Alabama! Not to mention the greatest scoundrels of 'em all—those blasted Wall Street shylocks who tried to play me for a sucker when I needed money to procure my museum. Why, if Vanderhorn thinks he can throw a scare into P. T. Barnum by sending some damned, overgrown gorilla after me, he's a bigger fool than I took him for."

As for Abel Tomblin, Barnum agreed that the intelligence I had received from Sammy Wainwright and his fellow curiosities was "worth looking into"—though he proposed that any interrogation of the custodian be deferred until I was fit enough to take part in it. I assured him that—given the nature of my injury, which was far less severe than I had initially feared—I would almost certainly be capable of resuming our investigation in a day or two.

Prior to his departure, Barnum had told me of the disappointing outcome of his trip to New Jersey. The two-headed cyclops calf had indeed turned out to be a bona fide marvel. Unfortunately—and in spite of every attention lavished upon it by its anxious owner—it had failed to survive. Barnum had arrived to find the astonishing creature preserved in a cask of pickle brine. He had gone ahead and purchased it anyway—though at a fraction of the price he was ready to pay for a living specimen. It was in the process of being mounted by Professor Pym—the museum's taxidermical specialist—for display in the Hall of Oddities, beside Barnum's other examples of grotesquely malformed animals.

"It's a wonder, all right—no doubt about it," Barnum declared, then added with a sigh: "Still, it's not what I was hoping for."

"And what precisely was that?" I inquired.

"Something awesome!—stupendous!—never before seen by mortal eyes! Something that'll make the whole blessed world gape in wonder to behold! It's out there somewhere, Poe, m'boy! And when I get my hands on it—why, I'll have to knock off the roof of my museum and add another level to the building just to hold all the people who'll come swarming to see it!"

Then, after assuring me that he would pay for any medical expenses incurred as a result of my "stupendous act of heroism," the showman had taken his leave.

Now, as I sat on my porch the day after Barnum's visit, surrounded by the tranquil beauties of the countryside, I turned my thoughts away from these recollections and focused them once again on an aspect of the case over which I had been puzzling, at intervals, for several days. I refer, of course, to the exquisite flower so incongruously left inside the mouth of the hideously butchered victim.

What meaning could possibly be attached to this bizarre detail? It will readily be recalled that the murder of the unfortunate Ellen Jennings, one year earlier, had been characterized by the same grotesque feature. It was conceivable, therefore, that the perpetrator of the Somers crime was simply acting in mindless emulation of the previous atrocity. Still, I could not help but feel that, in resolving the riddle of this singular clue, I might discover a key that would unlock the entire mystery.

Temporarily incapacitated as I was from any more physically demanding rôle in the investigation, I had employed my time during the past two days in pursuits of a strictly contemplative nature. It was for this reason that I had been consulting Henri Jacquemar's book the preceding morning at the time of Barnum's arrival. From this exceptionally learned (if frequently ponderous) work, I had discovered a great deal about the numerous, mystical meanings associated with that most lovely and symbolic of flowers, the rose.

Unfortunately, these meanings were *so* numerous—*so* diverse— indeed, so wildly at *variance* with one another—that, in the end, Jacquemar's treatise had served rather to confuse than to enlighten me. At different times and in various cultures, the rose had signified both love and death—chastity and lechery—brazenness and secrecy. To the ancient Greeks, it was associated with the carnal pleasures of the goddess Aphrodite; whereas the antique Romans employed it as an emblem of the grave. The early Christians, by contrast, drew a connection between the crimson petals of the flower and the bleeding wounds of the pierced and crucified Christ. The rose had also served to represent the paradise of Dante, the sacred *mandala* of the Hindoos, and the achievement of absolute perfection as imagined by the medieval alchemists. And these were but a few of the manifold and deeply paradoxical meanings explored by the French scholar in his massive tome.

One portion of Jacquemar's analysis, however, had inspired me to pursue a new and potentially fruitful line of inquiry. In discussing the significance of the rose as the heraldic emblem of the English throne, the Frenchman had referred to Shakespeare's dramatic treatment of the War of the Roses in *Henry VI.* This allusion had led me to ponder on the frequency with which roses appear as images and symbols in English literature.

Accordingly, I had decided to devote the morning to the examination of several anthologies of British verse in my possession. Indeed, I had been in the midst of perusing one of these volumes—Charles Eaton Ellis's *Poets and Poetry of England*—when I drifted off into the doze from which Sissy had so sweetly awakened me.

I now reopened the heavy volume on my lap and resumed my reading, searching for any poetic references to the rose that might conceivably throw light on the riddle. Earlier that morning, I had already reviewed the entirety of Geoffrey Chaucer's translation of the *Roman de la Rose* of Guillame de Lorris and Jean de Meun. Now—while waiting to be summoned to lunch—I examined several much shorter works: Robert Herrick's "To the Virgins, to Make Much of Time" (which famously counsels young maidens to "Gather ye rosebuds while ye may")—Marlowe's "Passionate Shepherd to His Love" (whose speaker beguiles his prospective mistress by promising to "make thee beds of roses/And a thousand fragrant poesies")—Edmund Waller's "Go, Lovely Rose"—Thomas Moore's "The Last Rose of Summer"—and one or two others, including Juliet Montague's immortal meditation on the cognomen of her beloved Capulet: "What's in a name? that which we call a rose/By any other name would smell as sweet." None of these, however, bore any apparent relevance to the grisly riddle whose meaning I was attempting to unlock.

I was about to abandon my examination of this volume and turn my attention to a different book I had carried out onto the porch— Charles Starrett's *Poetical Writings of the British Isles*—when I suddenly happened upon a work whose existence, until that moment, was entirely unknown to me. This was a short and exceedingly strange little piece by an obscure author named William Blake. Entitled "The Sick Rose," the poem in its entirety went as follows:

> O Rose, thou art sick.
> The invisible worm
> That flies through the night
> In the howling storm

Has found out thy bed
Of crimson joy,
And his dark secret love
Does thy life destroy.

Something about this odd little poem had a powerfully unsettling effect upon me. While its *apparent* subject was nothing more sinister than the infestation of a flower by a singularly noxious species of insect, it seemed to possess a deeper, far more disturbing *undercurrent* of meaning. This disguised, or *allegorical*, significance resounded of the darkest themes imaginable: the awful defilement and ultimate destruction of something lovely, vulnerable, and intensely feminine by a creature of sheer depravity and malevolence. To be sure, I could perceive only the most tenuous connections between the details of Mr. Blake's bizarre little piece and the particulars of the Isabel Somers murder. The unwholesome feelings evoked by the poem, however, seemed highly suggestive of the rank and unsavory atmosphere of extreme moral corruption surrounding the atrocity.

Still lost in contemplation of "The Sick Rose" I lifted my eyes from the page. All at once, my attention was arrested by a most surprising—a most *unaccountable*—sight. There, coming toward our cottage from the direction of the Brennan farmhouse, was a slender young woman. Garbed in white—her rich, auburn tresses shining in the sunlight—she appeared, at first glance, to be none other than my own darling Sissy. As I had last glimpsed my dear wife disappearing into the house behind me, my confusion upon observing this entrancing apparition may be readily imagined.

In another moment, the mystery was resolved; for—narrowing my eyes so as to intensify my visual acuity to the maximum degree—I perceived that the approaching figure was a good deal taller and skinnier than my perfectly proportioned wifey. She walked, moreover, with a pronounced limp. Clutched in one of her hands was a small, oblong package.

Shutting Ellis's anthology and setting it down upon the porch, I rose from my chair as my visitor drew closer. By now, the reason for her exceedingly uneven gait had become evident; for—glancing down at her lower extremities—I perceived that she was afflicted with *talipes equinovarus*, that unfortunate congenital deformity commonly known as "club foot."

"Hello," she proclaimed with a cheerful smile, as she came to a halt before me. She was a woman of approximately twenty-five years of age, with a somewhat *horsey*—though by no means unpleasing—countenance. Though lacking in conventional beauty, her face was suffused with a most appealing combination of qualities: intelligence, vivacity, and that intangible yet all-important essence we designate as "character."

"Are you Mr. Poe?" she eagerly inquired.

"I am indeed," I said. "And to whom do I have the honor of speaking?"

"Anna Louise Brennan—Thomas Brennan's niece," she replied with a distinct note of excitement in her voice. "And the honor's all mine. I can't tell you how *thrilled* I am to meet you, Mr. Poe."

"Is that so?" I said with some surprise.

"Oh my, yes. I'm just *wild* about your stories. 'The Pit and the Pendulum,' 'Ligeia,' 'Berenice'—they're so beautifully written. And so deliciously *creepy*. Not to mention 'The Fall of the House of Usher.' My goodness, I couldn't sleep for a week after finishing that story!"

In view of the rich, sonorous style—imaginative force—and sheer originality—of the tales to which the estimable young woman had just alluded, it may be supposed that I was fully accustomed to hearing them praised in such flattering terms. Nothing, however, could be further from the truth. To be sure, my work had received its due recognition from certain highly discerning critics, who had not failed to remark on the unique skill and artistry of my fictional compositions. From the American public at large, however, I had grown used to enduring the more-or-less utter neglect that must ever be the lot of the serious *litterateur* who refuses to cater to the Philistine taste of the masses. Indeed, while such melodramatic twaddle as Cornelius Mathews' *Wakondah: A Tale of the Great Western Prairie* had earned its author a fortune in royalties, my own, infinitely superior *Tales of the Grotesque and Arabesque* had sold barely enough copies to recoup the cost of its publication.

As a result, the young woman's unexpected words of praise fell upon my ears with all the captivating charm of one of the wildly melodious airs of Von Weber. Acknowledging her remarks with a small, gracious bow, I addressed her thusly: "It is indeed a pleasure to meet a young person of such unusual acumen and keenly sensitive taste. Tell me, have you been visiting your uncle for long?"

"Oh no. Just a few days. I arrived from Philadelphia on Monday. I come for a week every summer. It's so pretty out here. Anyway, we were sitting around the table, just finishing lunch, when someone left this package at the door. When I saw the name on the address, I couldn't believe my eyes. That's when Uncle Thomas told me that you and your family were his tenants. I nearly fell out of my chair. I immediately jumped up and came hurrying over just so I could deliver it to you."

And so saying, she reached up and held out the package, which I took in my unfettered right hand.

Glancing down curiously at this object, I took careful note of its appearance. Tightly wrapped in brown paper and secured with a length of coarse twine, it was approximately ten inches long and roughly cylindrical in shape. Its weight was not more than a pound. To judge from its size, shape, and heft, one might have deduced that it contained a small Bologna sausage. Crayoned in a bold, precise hand across the center of the package was the following address: "Mr. E. A. Poe, Brennan Farm, Bloomingdale Road, NY."

Under ordinary circumstances, I would have satisfied my curiosity as to the contents of this package by opening it at once. Having the use of only one hand, however, I was prevented from doing so. I was on the verge of passing it back to Miss Brennan and requesting that she perform this operation on my behalf when I heard the front door swing open behind me. Glancing over my shoulder, I saw Sissy emerge from the cottage.

"Sissy," I said, "this is Miss Anna Louise Brennan, the niece of our landlord, who has recently arrived from Philadelphia. She has been kind enough to bring over this package, which was delivered to her uncle's doorstep this morning.

"Miss Brennan," I continued, redirecting my gaze at our visitor, "allow me to introduce my dear wife, Virginia."

Sissy came to the edge of the porch and exchanged a pleasant greeting with the singularly perspicacious newcomer.

"I was just telling your husband how much I enjoy his stories," said Miss Brennan. "He's such a wonderful writer."

"Isn't he?" Sissy replied, placing her right hand upon my left shoulder blade and giving it an affectionate rub. "I don't think there's a better."

"I'd have to agree with you," Miss Brennan said. "Far superior to Mr. Irving, if you ask me. Even Mr. Hawthorne, good as he is, has never produced anything as gripping as 'William Wilson' or 'The Tell-Tale Heart.'" Turning back to me, the delightful young woman added: "How you dream up these stories, I'll never know."

"Oh, Eddie has quite an imagination, all right," Sissy said, with a fond little laugh.

"Ladies, please," I beseeched in a humorous tone. "I must ask you to desist at once, for such high, effusive praise—however deserved—cannot fail to fill me with an acute sense of personal embarrassment."

"Oh, Eddie," Sissy chided fondly, "you know you *love* it." Then addressing our visitor, she said: "We were just about to sit down and have lunch. Won't you join us, Miss Brennan?"

"Please call me Anna," the other replied. "And yes—I'd love to stay and chat for a while. I couldn't eat another thing, though. We just finished our own midday meal, and I'm feeling tight as a tick—to use one of Uncle Thomas's favorite expressions."

Mounting the porch steps with her brisk, if ungainly, walk—of which she seemed not the least bit self-conscious—our visitor took Sissy by the arm and accompanied her inside the house, while I brought up the rear.

We found Muddy inside the kitchen, setting a pitcher of buttermilk upon the old wooden table. Several large, earthenware platters—laden with the many delicious foodstuffs brought by Barnum on the preceding day—occupied the center of the board. I proceeded to introduce Miss Brennan to my aunt, and explained the occasion for the young woman's visit, displaying the paper-wrapped package as I did so.

"Why, whatever can it be?" inquired Muddy, gazing curiously at this object.

"I can conceive of only one certain means of finding out," I humorously replied, handing the package to my aunt. "Perhaps, Muddy dear, you will be so kind as to do the honors."

Taking the serrated knife from the bread plate, Muddy swiftly severed the twine, then carefully folded back the brown paper wrapping, exposing the contents to her view. No sooner had she done so than she emitted a shriek of such startling volume and stridency that my heart—seized with a paroxysm of terror and alarm—came to a momentary standstill.

With a wild, convulsive motion, Muddy hurled the package away from her, sending its contents flying into the air. An instant later, something landed on the table with a thud, rolled several times, and came to a rest beside a platter of sliced ham. A cry of horror burst from Sissy's lips—Miss Brennan gasped in shock—while I gaped with bulging eyes at the inexpressibly hideous thing that now lay amidst our lunch food and tableware.

It was a human hand, crudely amputated at the wrist, a segment of bone protruding from its gore-encrusted stump.

CHAPTER SIXTEEN

Less than two hours later, I was seated across from Barnum in the basement office of his museum. Lying palm upward in the center of his massive desk was the exceedingly grotesque object that had occasioned so much horror and dismay in my household shortly before.

"Must've been a hell of a shock when you tore off the paper and *that* thing tumbled out," Barnum declared, gazing intently at the crudely severed hand.

"It was my dear Aunt Maria who undid the package," I replied. "And indeed, at her first glimpse of its contents, she let loose with a scream that was nothing short of *blood-curdling*. It was my beloved wife, Sissy, however—whose sensibilities are of the most delicate organization imaginable—who had the most intense reaction. When I left for the city, the darling girl had taken to her bed."

"And how in the world did you get here?" asked Barnum.

"My landlord, Mr. Brennan, conveyed me in his farm wagon. Alerted by his niece—an unusually intelligent and cultivated young woman who was visiting our cottage at the time—he hurried over and offered to drive me to the city, so that I could inform you at once of this alarming new development."

"Good man!" Barnum said. "Deserves a show of thanks. Remind me to give you a free discount coupon for him."

Slowly shaking his head, the showman continued to stare at the grisly thing before him. "Damned if that isn't the gruesomest sight

I've ever set eyes on," he declared. "And believe me, I've seen some dillies. Why, the American Museum houses the greatest collection of
anatomical relics on the face of the earth—including the actual right
arm of Lord Horatio Nelson, amputated after the Battle of Tenerife!
And not one of 'em holds a candle to this confounded thing for sheer
ghastliness. Why, it looks as if it was removed with a dull hatchet
blade! I just hope the poor woman was already dead when the fiend
hacked it off."

"That her death took place *prior* to her dismemberment is a fact
of which we can be reasonably certain," I replied.

"And how do you figure *that?*" asked Barnum.

An engraved silver cup, standing near the center of the desk,
served as a holder for the showman's writing implements. Reaching
over to this receptacle with my free hand, I extracted a pencil, and—
employing its sharpened tip as a pointer—addressed him thusly:

"Observe both the inordinate length and tapered appearance of
the fingernails, which have been shaped in accordance with the prevailing female fashion. Now direct your gaze to the flesh of the *palm.*
The latter, you will notice, is entirely free of any scratch marks or
gouges. Had the poor victim been subjected to any form of torture
while still alive, it is likely that she would have clenched her fists in
agony, causing her long, pointed fingernails to leave marks in the
palms of her hands. That the skin is undefaced suggests that the
atrocities inflicted on Miss Somers were committed *postmortem.*"

"Fascinating, simply fascinating!" Barnum exclaimed. "Why,
when it comes to observing little details, I'd take those eyes of yours
over Mr. van Leeuwenhoek's microscope any day of the year! Do
those remarkable orbs tell you anything else, Poe, m'boy?"

"Only," I replied, "that this hand is indeed one of the extremities
taken from the body of Miss Somers, and not from any other victim."

"Well, I assumed as much, of course. But what makes you so sure?"

Again using the pencil as a pointer, I indicated the topmost portion of the middle finger, close to where the digit joined the hand.
"Permit me to draw your attention to this area of the finger, just
below the knuckle. Do you notice anything in particular?"

Leaning closer to the severed hand, Barnum briefly squinted at the place to which I was pointing before exclaiming: "Why, yes, yes—I see what you mean. She was wearing a ring. A mighty big one, too. You can see the impression, clear as day."

"Quite so," I replied. "Now, you will agree that it is quite unusual for a woman to wear a ring on her *second*, or middle, finger. Indeed, so conventional is the practice of adorning the *third* digit of the hand in this wise that it is commonly referred to as the 'ring finger.' "

"True enough. Some of your exotic races do it, of course. Take Miss Zobeide Luti, my Circassian Beauty, for instance. Sports a ring on every finger—not to mention bells on her toes, bracelets on her wrists and ankles, beads around her throat, gold hoops dangling from her ears, and Heaven knows what else! Why, the woman rattles like a junk-peddler's cart every time she takes a step. But what's this got to do with Isabel Somers?"

Reaching into the pocket of my frock coat, I extracted a piece of newsprint folded in quarters. "Here is the engraved likeness of Miss Somers that ran in yesterday's *Herald*," I said, opening the paper and passing it across the desk to Barnum. "It is based, as the caption notes, on a painting by Mr. Gilbert Opdyke, an artist noted for his competent, if exceedingly derivative, style. Here, Mr. Opdyke's utter lack of originality is evinced by Miss Somers's *pose*, which is clearly—indeed shamelessly—copied from the celebrated portrait of the Comtesse d'Hausonville by the French master, Jean-Auguste-Dominique Ingres. As in that infinitely superior work, Mr. Opdyke has depicted his subject in three-quarters profile, with her left hand raised to her face and her chin resting lightly on her fingers. You will observe that there is a handsome ring, set with a large gemstone, on Miss Somers's middle digit."

"Well, I'll be damned," exclaimed Barnum. "So there is. No doubt about it—this is the genuine, authentic, one-of-a-kind article, all right. The actual chopped-off hand of that tragically doomed specimen of poor, fallen womanhood, Isabel Somers!"

He continued to study the ghastly *objet* for a moment before wrinkling his nose in distaste. "Phew! Blasted thing gives off a mighty unpleasant bouquet. Better deodorize the atmosphere in here before it becomes intolerable. Care for a smoke?"

I responded in the negative with a decisive shake of my head.

From an elaborately carved cedarwood box that sat on a corner of his desktop, Barnum removed an enormous Havana. Then—extracting a small silver cutter from his vest pocket—he clipped off the tip, ignited the head with a phosphorous match, and settled back in his chair.

"Imagine wrapping that thing up all nice and tidy and delivering it to your home like a Christmas parcel," he declared, waving the now-glowing cigar at the dismembered hand. "Why, it's the act of a desperate man, I tell you. That devil Vanderhorn must be frightened clear out of his wits. He's grasping at straws, you see—trying everything conceivable to scare us off the case. First, he sics that plug-ugly Croley on us. Now, he stoops to *this*. I tell you, Poe, m'boy, my plan is working to perfection!"

"As far as I can determine," I said in a tone not wholly devoid of irony, "your plan is equivalent to the stratagem traditionally employed by those Bengali tribesmen, who—in attempting to lure a man-eating tiger out into the open so that they may destroy it—will tether a living kid to a stake in an open clearing. In this case, however, I have begun to feel that it is I and my loved ones who are serving as the sacrificial bait."

"Why, you wound me to the quick, dear boy," Barnum cried in an injured tone. "The safety and well-being of you and your family are my constant concern! But don't you see? The more we can goad that scoundrel into this sort of hotheaded behavior, the sooner he'll do something truly foolhardy. And then, by Jove, we'll have him!"

"I must remind you," I said, "that we have yet to establish with any certainty whatsoever that Morris Vanderhorn is the killer we are seeking."

"Not *yet*," said the showman smugly. "But we will, we will."

"In the meantime," I remarked, "perhaps I should conduct my deferred interview with your custodian, Abel Tomblin."

"You'll have to defer it a bit longer, I'm afraid. Abel's out on an errand for me. He'll be there tomorrow, though."

"Tomorrow? Why, where do you mean?"

"Isabel Somers's funeral, of course. Abel insists on going. Doesn't want to miss out on the excitement, I suppose. Oh, there's going to be quite a turnout there, I can assure you. Absolutely stupendous. Well, you can just imagine, given all the public hysteria over the case. Mourners, newspapermen, curiosity-seekers by the score. Not to mention the entire P. T. Barnum family of performers, out in full force to pay tribute to the poor woman. I was hoping you'd attend, too, m'boy. No telling what those eagle eyes of yours might pick up."

"And precisely where and at what time is this solemn occasion scheduled to take place?" I inquired.

"Green-Wood Cemetery at noon. I'd be happy to send a coach for you."

"Very well," I said after ruminating on the matter for several moments. "And now," I continued, rising from my chair, "I must return home without further delay. I am most anxious to check on the condition of my darling wife, Sissy."

"Of course, dear boy, of course," said Barnum. Leaping to his feet, he hurried around his desk and ushered me to the door. "Please send your two dear ladies my warmest regards. I will see you out in Brooklyn tomorrow."

Pausing at the threshold, I pointed my chin at the morbidly discolored hand, whose curled, slender fingers resembled the legs of a lifeless crustacean. "And what will become of *that?*" I inquired.

"That?" Barnum said off-handedly, glancing over at the desk. "Oh, don't you worry, dear boy. I'll take care of it."

CHAPTER SEVENTEEN

Barnum's declared belief that Isabel Somers's funeral would attract a large crowd of spectators struck me as nothing more than another glaring instance of the showman's penchant for wild exaggeration. Situated on Gowanus Heights in the extreme southeastern part of Brooklyn, the newly established cemetery of Green-Wood lay at some distance from the heart of the city. To reach its beautifully landscaped grounds from Manhattan, a visitor was required to ride the omnibus to the Fulton Street Ferry, cross the bay to Brooklyn, then travel by horse-car to the elaborately adorned entrance gate. That a resident of the city would undertake such an expedition merely to witness the interment of a murder victim—even one whose appalling death had excited such widespread interest—seemed to me unlikely in the extreme.

I was greatly surprised, therefore, when—upon dismounting from the carriage that conveyed me to the cemetery—I found a veritable *horde* of people gathered about the grave site. The assemblage was composed of men and women of varying ages. Nearly all were of the working- and middle-class *strata* of society. A number of them were evidently married couples who had seen fit to bring along their offspring. Some of the younger children were noisily disporting themselves on the periphery of the crowd. Others stood on tiptoe to get a better view of the proceedings, or were perched, piggyback-style, on the broad shoulders of their fathers.

It was clear at a glance that I had severely underestimated the public's intense fascination with the Somers case. Morbid curiosity, however, appeared to be only one factor in drawing so many people to the scene. Another was the sheer loveliness of the surroundings. Laid out under the supervision of a corps of landscape gardeners, Green-Wood abounded in the most exquisite scenery. The dark green of its sward—the lushness of its foliage—its stately trees—its gentle knolls—all combined to create a most serene and pastoral setting. From its highest points, the gazer could also behold an exceptionally picturesque vista: the sparkling waters of the bay—the bustling city that bordered it—and the blue ocean beyond.

Moreover—having opened for burials only a short time earlier—the cemetery was largely devoid of the countless sepulchres, tombstones, cenotaphs, and other mortuary embellishments that would overspread its grounds in later years. As a result, there was little of the morbid—the somber—the funereal—about it. Rather than a repository for the dead, it resembled an expansive and elegantly laid-out park. For the ordinary city dweller at the height of the summer, an excursion to Green-Wood offered a welcome escape from the sweltering confines of the metropolis.

I quickly discovered yet another explanation for the size—as well as the incongruously *festive* air—of the gathering. As I made my way through the crowd, I overheard several people comment excitedly on a certain item they had encountered in that morning's edition of the *New York Gazette.* Evidently, Barnum had contrived to insert a prominent front-page notice, announcing that he and his entire troupe of human curiosities would be present at the funeral to offer a special tribute to the murdered woman. This flagrant (if entirely characteristic) piece of self-promotion had produced its desired effect. The crowd that had swarmed to the cemetery in such numbers was there, not merely to gratify their ghoulish fascination, nor to luxuriate in the tranquil delights of the countryside. They were there to witness a *show.*

In this expectation, they were not disappointed. Courtesy of the incorrigible Mr. Barnum, the funeral of Isabel Somers turned out to offer as much in the way of novelty—diversion—and sheer garish spectacle as could be found outside a circus tent.

Having squeezed my way to the front of the crowd, I was greeted warmly by the showman, who was attired in a frock coat of the finest black cloth, the intensely somber appearance of which was somewhat offset by the blood-red carnation, or *boutonniere*, affixed to the lapel of this garment. As I took my place beside him, I cast my gaze about the grave site.

From the facts conveyed to me by Barnum several days earlier, I knew that Isabel Somers had been orphaned in her youth. I therefore understood that we were to be spared that most piteous of spectacles—the heart-wrenching sight of two elderly parents, grieving over the corpse of a horribly murdered child. I was not, however, prepared for the utter absence of *anyone* who could be construed as a genuine mourner. Such, however, appeared to be the case. So far as I could determine, the scene was composed entirely of observers with no ties of either friendship or consanguinity to the deceased.

There was, to begin with, the great, milling crowd of curiosity-seekers, whose holiday air was more suitable to a picnic than a burial. There was the spate of newspapermen, busily inscribing notes in their writing-pads. Finally, there were the numerous members of Barnum's company. Arrayed at the very head of the crowd, these remarkable beings constituted, without doubt, the most bizarre congregation ever assembled at a grave site.

All of the performers I had encountered during my visit to the Hall of Oddities several days earlier were present, their outlandish appearance rendered even more extreme by the striking costumes chosen for the occasion. The family of albinos, for example, was arrayed in clothing of the deepest midnight black—a shade that made their utterly livid complexions appear even ghastlier. The animal-skin costume of the "pin-head" was augmented by a ceremonial headdress consisting of three gaudy ostrich plumes that seemed to sprout from the apex of his severely tapered skull. Routh Goshen, the Arabian Giant, wore a long, flowing robe of the finest white silk, embroidered with golden filigree; while the diminutive "King of Lilliput" was garbed in a purple velvet cape trimmed with ermine.

Sammy Wainwright's coat (tailored, as always, to expose his grotesquely truncated physique to the fullest extent) was of lustrous, dark blue satin. Upon his head, he wore a broad-brimmed, black felt hat trimmed with a silver cord and tassel. By contrast, Gunther the Alligator Boy was hatless. His shoulders, however, were draped in a heavy traveler's cloak of shimmering jade-green material. The Lobster Boy, who stood next to Gunther, was dressed in a tight-fitting coat, whose bright red hue very aptly resembled that of a freshly boiled member of the genus *Homarus.*

My friend and savior, Willie Schnitzler, was there, her prodigious form enveloped in a dress of billowing, black satin. Upon her head, she wore a surpassingly charming bonnet of pink silk, tastefully garnished with black ribbon and lace. Her luxuriant beard had apparently been groomed with a dollop of pomade and glistened softly in the noonday light. As my gaze met hers, she lifted one hand to shoulder level and wiggled her plump fingers in a fond salutation. Raising my left arm—still bandaged but now free of its restraining sling—I returned the greeting with a little wave of the hand. Seeing this improvement in my condition, Willie clasped her hands over her bosom and beamed with satisfaction.

Barnum's other curiosities were also present: Bruno the Armless Wonder—the Amazing Murray Midgets—the wild Australian children, Hoomie and Iola—Crowley the Man-Horse—Slim Jim McCormack, the Living Skeleton—John Hanson Craig, The Carolina Fat Boy—Charley Dockery, The Man with Two Bodies—and the rest.

In addition, the showman was accompanied by a large number of his other performers, whom I recognized from my initial visit to the museum with Sissy: his jugglers and acrobats, magicians and mind-readers, Bohemian glass-blowers, and Swiss bell-ringers. Indeed, apart from the beasts in his menagerie, every living member of Barnum's organization appeared to be present—and I could not help but feel that, had the Fulton Ferry been capable of accommodating pachyderms, the impossibly brazen impresario would have shown up with his pack of trained elephants, too!

In looking about, I observed one individual among Barnum's company whom I had never before laid eyes upon. Compared to the human anomalies surrounding him, his appearance was unexceptional. Considered by himself, however, he cut a most imposing figure. His height was no less than six feet four inches—his chest and shoulders massive—his arms unusually long. His head was square and blocklike, with a heavy, underslung jaw and a huge shock of blond hair that sprouted from the crown. The enormously broad and calloused hands that protruded from the cuffs of his threadbare gray frock coat were covered with a mat of thick, yellow hair resembling the fur of a South American squirrel-monkey of the species *Saimiri sciureus.* He kept his eyes downcast, occasionally shifting his weight from foot to foot. From both his size and obvious muscular strength—as well as from the exceedingly rough condition of his hands—I inferred that he worked in a manual capacity, and I wondered if I might not be gazing upon the very person of Barnum's custodian, Abel Tomblin.

At length, the service got under way. It began with a moving, if somewhat protracted, eulogy delivered by the officiating minister, the Reverend Titus Higgins—a small, portly fellow with the most wildly irregular teeth I had ever seen in a human mouth. Following his speech, Reverend Higgins led the crowd in a rendition of the venerable hymn, "There Is a Land of Pure Delight"—a performance much enlivened by the enthusiastic vocalization of Miss Flora Mayfield, Barnum's famed "Carolina Songbird," whose warbling contralto was clearly audible above the general chorus.

No sooner had the final strains of this hymn faded into silence than a quartet of rough-hewn and raggedly attired workmen stepped forward and approached the polished, walnut casket, which awaited its final disposition. Bending low, they took hold of the ropes and made ready to consign the coffin to its final resting place. The dank and sour aroma of freshly dug earth came wafting from the open grave, assaulting my nostrils.

As the workmen commenced to lower the casket into the yawning pit, I was seized with a sudden paroxysm of dread. Every fiber of my being recoiled from this all-too-vivid demonstration of the hideous end that awaits every mortal. To lie, for all eternity, within the confines of a narrow box, deep inside the earth, surrounded by the unseen but all-pervading presence of the Conqueror Worm! The mere thought of this awful eventuality caused my heart to quail—to cringe—to *sicken*. I gasped for breath—perspiration burst from every pore—my soul was possessed with a vague yet intolerable anguish!

Averting my eyes from this intensely unnerving sight, I turned and looked behind me. A short distance away, a grassy hill sloped gently upward, its summit affording an ideal vantage point from which to view the funeral service. Silhouetted on the hilltop was a vehicle I had not previously observed—an elegant brougham, drawn by a handsome coal-black steed. Curious, I squinted my eyes to obtain a better view of this conveyance—only to be thrown into a state of even greater consternation than before! For seated on the driver's box was a thickset figure who appeared to be none other than my erstwhile adversary—Morris Vanderhorn's implacable minion, Croley.

The noonday glare, however, was so exceedingly bright that I could not be absolutely sure. Raising my right hand as though in a military salute, I placed it across my brow to shield my eyes from the sunlight. At that moment, the occupant of the coach leaned forward and peered out the window. From the distance at which I stood, I could discern his features only imperfectly. I saw enough, however, to convince me that the countenance at the carriage window was indeed the grotesquely bifurcated visage of Vanderhorn himself!

Trembling in every fiber, I spun forward again and gazed abstractedly at the ground, my mind racing furiously. What reason could there possibly be for Vanderhorn's wholly unanticipated appearance at the interment? Was it yet another sign of his culpability in the young woman's appalling death? The inner compulsion that causes certain cold-blooded killers to revisit the scenes of their crimes was a well-known and widely documented phenomenon. Could a similar motive—born of either deep-seated guilt or the overweening arrogance of a hopelessly depraved criminal—be responsible for Vanderhorn's decision to attend his victim's funeral? Or might there be some other, entirely different explanation? Whatever the case, Vanderhorn's presence at the scene offered further proof that a deep—if as yet unexplained—relationship existed between the monstrously malformed businessman and the horribly slaughtered woman.

I was distracted from these ruminations by a sudden, excited stir among the crowd. Lifting my gaze, I saw that a number of Barnum's human curiosities had walked to the edge of the grave (or, in the case of Sammy Wainwright, toddled forward on his hands) and arranged themselves around its periphery. All at once, a black-cloaked gentleman whom I recognized as Mr. Joseph Pentland, Barnum's master of legerdemain, stepped forward. Raising his arms, he made a great flourish of his hands and, as if from nowhere, produced an enormous bouquet of beautiful yellow roses—a feat that brought a spontaneous outburst of awed ejaculations from the spectators.

Striding from one of the anomalous beings to the next, Pentland distributed a blossom to each—stooping low to place one in the doll-sized fist of the Lilliputian King, rising on tiptoe to hand one to the Arabian Giant (in whose colossal fingers the full-blown yellow flower seemed no larger than the diminutive blossom of a buttercup plant). Bruno the Armless Wonder took the stem between his teeth; while Charley Dockery, The Man with Two Bodies, accepted a pair of the flowers, one for each of his conjoined torsos.

Following a moment of silent meditation, the assembled curiosities then drew back their hands (except, of course, for the Armless Wonder, who cocked his head sharply to one side), and—at a signal from the magician—simultaneously tossed their roses into the open grave, where they rained down upon the lid of the casket.

"Farewell, fair flower, that for a space was lent,/then taken away unto eternity," declaimed Mr. Pentland with a slight but audible catch in his voice, quoting from Mistress Bradstreet's intensely moving elegy on the untimely death of her infant granddaughter, Elizabeth.

"Farewell! Farewell!" the freaks chimed in. Then—heads still solemnly lowered—the performers returned to their places at the head of the crowd, while the audience rewarded them with a prolonged round of applause.

It was now Barnum's turn to speak. Striding to the foot of the grave, he swiveled about to face the crowd and assumed the pose of an actor about to deliver a Shakespearean soliloquy: chest outthrust, right hand clutching the lapel of his coat, left extended upward. Then—speaking in a voice sufficiently loud to be heard by the entire assemblage—he addressed his listeners thusly:

"Friends—fellow New Yorkers—gentlemen and ladies. We are gathered here together on this solemn occasion to show our pro-found—our *heartfelt*—respect for the dear departed, a young woman tragically snatched from this vale of tears in the very prime—the very *flower*—of her existence. Lord bless me, but it was a horrible crime—the worst I ever heard of! Well, all right, maybe not the *worst*. But certainly a very terrible crime, absolutely appalling. I needn't go into the gruesome details. I'm sure you've read all about them in the dailies, many of whose fine representatives I see among the crowd.

"Now unless I miss my guess, I bet you're thinking: why has P. T. Barnum—a man with so many obligations, so many pressing demands on every waking minute of his day—why has P. T. Barnum taken the time to travel all the way out here to the wilds of Brooklyn this morning? What's he to Isabel Somers, or Isabel Somers to *him*? And it's a good question, too, a very good question. And do you know what the answer is? The answer is—because Isabel Somers was *family*. Not in any literal sense, of course. Never met the woman in my life. Wouldn't recognize her if I bumped into her on Broadway in the full light of a summer day. Still, as I say, I feel as if the poor girl were my own dear, precious daughter. Assuming I had one.

"Now, I can tell what many of you are saying to yourselves right now. You're saying to yourselves—'Well, that's mighty strange. That's mighty peculiar. Why in heaven's name would P. T. Barnum feel that way about a person he never even set eyes on?' Well, all right, fair enough, that's a sensible question. Deserves an honest answer, too. So here it is. Because Isabel Somers, like thousands of other satisfied people from every quarter of the globe, was a regular visitor to the American Museum. And at the American Museum, we treat *everyone* like family. That's right. For the mere cost of twenty-five cents—children and servants half-price at all times—visitors are not only treated to the most amazing collection of marvels ever assembled under one roof. They're treated with the same respect, courtesy, and caring attention they'd expect from their own kin. 'Treat the customer like family!' That's P. T. Barnum's motto.

"Now, some of you good folks have no doubt read the scandalous lies and accusations spread by one or two unscrupulous individuals who are a disgrace to the otherwise noble profession of news-paper publishing, as exemplified by the many good and honorable re-porters present here today. Well, I have just one word to say to those libelous calumniators—those craven, cowardly mudslingers. *Hogwash!* Why, the truth is just the opposite! Think about it! Would the poor, martyred woman—whose tragic and untimely death we have come here to memorialize—would a woman such as *that* have visited the American Museum not once, not *twice*, but on numerous separate oc-casions if she was in danger of being exposed to anything that wasn't absolutely pure and uplifting? Of course not!

"Why, it's a well-known fact that the American Museum offers the most wholesome and instructive entertainment to be found in Christendom—suitable for the young and old, male and female, chil-dren of all ages! Don't believe me? Come see for yourselves next Monday afternoon, when we'll be holding our second annual Baby Show—the most angelic display of juvenile humanity ever staged for the delight and delectation of the public! Liberal cash prizes of up to five dollars apiece for the first-place winner in each of five separate categories: the Fattest Baby—the Cutest Baby—the Handsomest Baby—the Sweetest Baby—and the Finest All-Around Baby. Contest open to all and sundry!

"No, my dear friends, no. You'll find nothing harmful or in the least bit immoral in the American Museum. The poor girl whose tragic demise we have come here to mourn was destroyed by some-thing evil existing elsewhere in our great but hazardous city. Exactly who and what that evil thing is, I can't tell you just at present. But it's only a matter of time before I bring the vicious perpetrator of this heinous deed to light. Mark my words. Once I set my mind on a mat-ter, I won't rest for an instant until it's settled. The word 'quitting' just isn't part of P. T. Barnum's lexicon. So you can rest assured that this case is as good as solved. In the meantime, I hope to see each and every one of you at the American Museum, Broadway and Ann Street, open daily from ten A.M. to midnight. Thank you all for com-ing here today. And now, my friends—farewell!"

At several points during this remarkable speech, I cast my gaze about to observe the reaction of the crowd, most of whom appeared to be utterly transfixed by the showman's oratory. One person in particular attracted my notice. This was a small but exceedingly *wiry* fellow who had been a member of the work crew responsible for lowering Isabel Somers's casket into the ground. Apart from a purple birthmark on his right cheek in the shape of a crescent moon, there was nothing especially noteworthy about him. His expression, however, was striking in the extreme. Throughout Barnum's address, he stared at the showman with a look of the greatest intensity imaginable, while chewing continuously on his lower lip in a manner that betokened the highest degree of impatience.

No sooner had Barnum concluded his talk than this roughly dressed individual rushed over to the showman and began speaking to him in urgent tones. At first, Barnum seemed somewhat nonplussed to be so accosted—but as the little graveyard worker continued to speak, Barnum's brow contracted—he raised a hand thoughtfully to his chin—and began to attend to the speaker with a look of the deepest interest.

Standing at some distance from the pair, I could not discern the content of the little man's remarks. The service having concluded, the crowd began to disperse all around me. Perhaps, I thought, I could now make my way closer to the hill and confirm that the occupant of the mysterious brougham was indeed Vanderhorn.

When I turned and looked behind me, however, the carriage was gone.

CHAPTER EIGHTEEN

The following morning—an unusually chill, dreary Wednesday, when the clouds hung oppressively low in the heavens—I returned to the American Museum. On this occasion, however, I was not alone, being accompanied by Muddy, Sissy, and our landlord's niece, Miss Brennan, with whom my darling wife had formed an immediate bond of friendship. The motive for my visit was my determination—following the unavoidable delays of the past several days—to question the custodian, Abel Tomblin, about his reported familiarity with Isabel Somers.

Contrary to my original intention, I had not, in the end, spoken to this personage at the cemetery. The solemnity of the occasion—as well as the demeanor of Tomblin himself (who, of all Barnum's employees, seemed the most visibly agitated)—had discouraged me from accosting him at the conclusion of the funeral service. I therefore resolved to travel downtown early Wednesday morning and interrogate him at the museum. Owing to the purely businesslike nature of the trip, I had no intention of inviting my loved ones along. When I announced my plan over breakfast, however, my dear wife immediately clasped her hands in a prayerful attitude and began bouncing up and down in her seat.

"Oh, please say you'll take us with you, Eddie dearest," she sweetly implored. *"Pleeeease."*

"But is it wise to subject yourself to the intense stimulation such an outing would undoubtedly entail?" I asked in a tone of the deepest concern. "After all, Sissy darling, you are only now beginning to recover from the shock inflicted upon your supremely delicate nervous system by the deplorable incident of several days ago."

"But that's all the more reason to bring me!" Sissy exclaimed. "I can't think of anything that would make me feel better. And I know that Muddy's just *dying* to visit Mr. Barnum's museum. Isn't that so, Muddy?"

"Well," answered Muddy, with an indulgent smile. "*Dying* may be putting the matter too strongly. Still, it *would* be fun to see Mr. Barnum's marvels, after all that I've heard about them. And I don't suppose a little outing would do either of us any harm, Eddie dear."

These heartfelt appeals could hardly be resisted. "By all means, then," I declared. "We shall make it a family excursion."

Leaping from her seat, Sissy threw her arms about me and hugged me warmly to her bosom. "Oh, thank you, Eddie dearest," she cried, then added excitedly: "Can I ask Anna Louise, too? I'm sure she'd *love* to come with us."

"Whatever you desire, Sissy dear," I fondly rejoined. "Heaven forfend that I should deny your slightest wish."

After rewarding me with an incomparably sweet kiss upon my brow, Sissy immediately turned and hurried out in the direction of our landlord's abode, returning a short time later with the news that Miss Brennan had been delighted both to receive and to accept the invitation.

Though I had originally meant to depart immediately after breakfast, the unanticipated alterations in my plan necessitated a protracted delay while my three distaff companions made ready for the trip. As a result, we did not arrive at the museum until shortly after noon.

Owing to the exceedingly raw and blustery weather, I had assumed that a smaller crowd than usual would be gathered on the street, awaiting admission. This supposition proved wholly mistaken. The scene outside the museum was as lively as ever. Even as they shivered in the unseasonable cold, the long line of customers chatted gaily amongst themselves, their excited voices adding to the encompassing clamor of Broadway.

Shouting to make himself heard above the din was the tow-headed newsboy who regularly patrolled the sidewalk in front of the museum. "Extree! Extree!" he cried, as I ushered my three charming companions toward the entranceway. "Boy dies in horrible fall! Read all about it in the *Daily Herald!*" Though these words penetrated my consciousness, they did not make a particularly forceful impression upon it, my mind being preoccupied with thoughts of my impending interview with Abel Tomblin.

Once inside the museum, my companions and I determined upon a course of action. While I attended to my business, Sissy (who had brought along the souvenir guidebook I had purchased for her on our earlier visit) would take Muddy and Miss Brennan on a tour of the museum. As I had no accurate conception of how much time my mission would require, it was agreed that the four of us would rendezvous at three o'clock at the Hall of Aquarial Science, Muddy having a particular desire to see Barnum's performing seal, "Ned," who—in addition to his prodigious skills at balancing—could play a very creditable version of "Yankee Doodle" on the xylophone. Bidding good-bye to my loved ones and Miss Brennan, I made for the stairwell, while the three delightful women immediately hurried across the lobby to view Barnum's famous "Cosmorama" exhibit, each of whose porthole-shaped windows opened onto a breathtaking scene of some natural or man-made wonder, from the roaring cataracts of Niagara to the Great Pyramids of Egypt.

I descended to the basement and rapidly made my way to Barnum's office. Finding the door ajar, I rapped it with a knuckle to announce my presence, then stepped inside.

I found the showman seated in his usual place. Head bent, he was perusing a newspaper that lay open on the desk. I perceived at once that something had worked him into a state of extreme agitation. The very skin of his balding dome was suffused with an angry flush, while his hands were clenched so tightly that the knuckles showed white. As I crossed the floor, he raised one of his fists to shoulder level and brought it down upon the desktop with such force that his writing implements rattled in their pewter cup.

"Damn the fellow!" he thundered. "Damn his black heart to hell!"

"Why, what is the matter?" I exclaimed, considerably taken aback by the sheer *violence* of the showman's outburst.

"Ah, so it's you, Poe," said Barnum, gazing up at me with a look in which outrage and sorrow seemed equally commingled. "Didn't hear you come in. I was too busy showering curses upon the head of that damned infernal reprobate, Vanderhorn."

"So I overheard. But what in Heaven's name has happened?"

"I underestimated the man," Barnum said in a tone of surpassing bitterness. "Took him for a mere cold-blooded scoundrel. But that's doing him too much credit. He's the devil himself, I tell you. You know what they say, Poe—you oughtn't to judge a book by its cover. Well, that doubtless applies in certain cases. But not in this one. Why, the man's a downright monster—inside *and* out. You can talk all you want about your Heliogabalus, your Torquemada, your Attila the Hun. Ha! Amateurs, m'boy, rank amateurs. Why, next to Vanderhorn, Caligula himself looks no worse than a mischievous schoolboy, putting tacks on his teacher's seat or dipping some poor little girl's pigtails into an ink pot!"

"But what precisely has provoked your indignation to such an inordinate degree?" I cried.

"Here," Barnum said grimly, thrusting the newspaper toward me. "Read this. Better take a seat first, though. You're in for a shock, m'boy."

My curiosity, by this point, having been raised to an acute pitch, I snatched the newspaper from his hands. It was a copy of that morning's *Daily Herald*. Obeying the showman's directive, I lowered myself onto the chair beside his desk and began to peruse the front page. My attention was immediately seized by the following story:

DREADFUL ACCIDENT!
Youth Plunges to Death!
Brokenhearted Mother Collapses
Upon Hearing News of Tragedy.

A terrible accident came to light yesterday evening when the shattered corpse of Master Franklin Plunkitt, thirteen years of age, was found in an alleyway on Thomas Street. Young Plunkitt, who resided with his family at Number 14, was last seen by his mother several hours prior to the calamity, when he announced that he was going outside to play a game of "ring-a-levio" with his cronies. When the lad failed to return home for dinner, his anxious mother dispatched her eldest daughter, twelve-year-old Dessie, to fetch him.

An Awful Discovery

It was Dessie who made the awful discovery. After coming upon the lifeless corpse of her older sibling in the narrow alleyway separating Number 14 from the neighboring building, the horrified girl ran screaming back home. The scene that ensued was wrenching to the last degree. Neighbors, alerted by the hysterical screams of Mrs. Plunkitt, hurried over and found the poor woman lying unconscious on her kitchen floor, where she had collapsed after learning from her daughter that young "Frankie" would return home no more.

Police Question Chums

Two officers of the law, Constables Berry and Mc-Cormick, were summoned at once to the scene. In attempting to ascertain the cause of the ghastly mishap, they sought out and spoke to several of the victim's playmates. One of these, Master Tommy Watkins of 48 Broome Street, tearfully told the officers that young Plunkitt was well known for his reckless audacity. "Frankie wasn't scared of nothing," Watkins declared. "He was always doing something to prove how brave he was—like going into graveyards at midnight all by himself, or hitching rides on the back of moving horse carts. He kept bragging about how he was going to jump between the two rooftops one day, just to show he could do it. But no one believed him."

Youthful Recklessness to Blame?

From this statement and other indications, the constables concluded that the victim had plummeted to his doom while attempting to accomplish this daredevil feat. As Constable McCormick stated, accidents such as these are, regrettably, an all-too-common occurrence, the natural physical exuberance of the typical, red-blooded, American youth often leading him to undertake deeds of the most daring and hazardous nature, without regard for his personal safety.

So *this* was the awful fatality to which the tow-headed newsboy had been referring when I arrived at the museum, and to which I had barely attended at the time! Lowering the paper, I stared absently at the floor, while my brain teemed with a multitude of thoughts. In my mind's eye, I saw the precociously shrewd, if unprepossessing, visage of young Frankie Plunkitt during our sole encounter in the very alleyway where his poor, broken body would be found only a few days later. Though his manner—no less than his appearance—had produced a decidedly unfavorable impression upon me at the time of our interview, I could feel nothing but sadness at his tragic and untimely death.

Still, the question remained: was Barnum justified in assuming that—contrary to the conclusions of the police—young Plunkitt had been murdered either by or at the behest of Morris Vanderhorn? That the singularly *brash* lad might well have fallen to his death while attempting to leap between two rooftops seemed not at all implausible to me. After all—as he himself had recounted—it was while sneaking home late at night from precisely one such youthful escapade that he had caught his fateful glimpse of the hideously deformed Vanderhorn. Perhaps, as in that former case, one of his chums had "double dared" him to make good on his boast, and young Plunkitt had accidentally perished while accepting this foolhardy challenge.

I conveyed these thoughts to Barnum, who considered them in silence for several moments before responding thusly:

"Yes, yes. I see what you mean, of course. I had the same idea myself. After all, the lad was a regular scamp. Plucky as the dickens. Reminded me of myself in my younger years. Always ready for some daring exploit, the riskier the better. Still and all, Poe, m'boy, there's something awfully *funny* about the timing, wouldn't you agree? We tell Vanderhorn that a neighbor of Isabel Somers observed him leaving her apartment—and just a few days later, that very witness goes tumbling to his death from the rooftop! Mighty big coincidence to swallow, I'd say. Yessir, as coincidences go, I'd call that one a whopper. Why, the Great Zambini, my Neapolitan sword swallower, would have trouble getting it down his throat."

"You may, of course, be entirely correct in your supposition," I replied. "In any event, the death of young Plunkitt—whether by tragic accident or malevolent design—does not materially alter the course of our investigation. We must continue to pursue every possible lead in the hope that it will eventuate in the quick resolution of this mystery. And with that end in view, I have traveled here today to question your custodian, Mr. Tomblin, in order to ascertain the precise nature of his purported relationship with the murder victim."

"You'll find him upstairs, fixing the tank that holds my giant South American iguana," said Barnum. "Damned thing managed to pry open the lid and work its way free just before closing time last evening. Bless my soul, but you should have seen the pandemonium! Why, you'd have thought there was a man-eating tiger loose on the premises. It's a fearsome-looking critter, I'll admit, but no more harmful than a kitten. Anyways, we rounded him up in short order and stuck him in a packing crate overnight. Abel's up there now, in the Hall of Reptiles, working on the tank. I'd come along with you, but I'm expecting a fellow on a matter of urgent business any minute now. Could turn out to be something mighty big, Poe, m'boy. Absolutely immense."

"Then I will proceed on my own to the reptilian exhibit without further delay," said I. Rising from my chair, I dropped the newspaper back onto the desk and made for the doorway.

As I stepped into the corridor, I encountered a small, somewhat shabbily dressed fellow waiting just outside the office, a bulky, paper-wrapped bundle clutched in his hands. There was something strangely familiar about him, though—in the dim illumination of the hallway—I could discern his features only imperfectly. As I nodded to him in passing, however, I perceived something that immediately made his identity clear to me: a crescent-shaped birthmark on his right cheek. It was the wiry, little gravedigger who had spoken so intently to Barnum immediately following the funeral service.

Was this the person from whom Barnum was so eagerly expecting a visit? If so, what "urgent business" could the little gravedigger possibly have with the showman?

As I made my way upstairs, my thoughts turned from this mystery and reverted to the subject of young Frankie Plunkitt's death. That a lad of so tender an age had come to such a grim and tragic end was, of course, dismaying in the extreme. The mere thought of his mother—who, even now, must be suffering the most excruciating throes of anguish—caused my own heart to thrill with a pang of the purest sympathy; for after all, as the immortal Euripides states in his flawed, if intensely moving, drama, *The Suppliant Women:* "What greater pain can mortals have than this:/To see their children dead before their eyes?"

That any sane man—even one as hopelessly lost to all sense of personal decency as Morris Vanderhorn—might deliberately, and with malice aforethought, contrive the cold-blooded murder of a thirteen-year-old child seemed so utterly heinous to me as to be nearly inconceivable. If the showman were correct in his assumption, then Vanderhorn must indeed be counted among the vilest wretches ever to have sullied the world with his mere existence—a being of such utter turpitude and depravity as to have forfeited any hope of salvation, even by the all-merciful God of forgiveness!

I had now arrived at the third-floor landing. Thrusting the subject of young Plunkitt's death from my mind, I forced myself to focus on my imminent interview with Abel Tomblin.

The Hall of Reptiles was one of the most popular attractions at the American Museum. Crossing the threshold, I paused for a moment and searched for the custodian. As it was at every hour of the day, the great room was packed with visitors, who stood in clusters around each of the exhibits, raptly gazing at Barnum's vast collection of living, exotic specimens: his giant boa constrictor and colossal anaconda; his African crocodile and Florida alligator; his monitor lizard, Gila monster, and great spotted salamander; his diamondback terrapin, Galapagos tortoise, and rare, Pacific sea turtle. And much, much more.

All at once, my gaze fell upon a powerfully built individual of such exceptional height that he loomed, head and shoulders, above the rest of the crowd. From his imposing size—as well as from the great shock of coarse, yellow hair that covered the top of his massive skull—I immediately recognized him as the troubled-looking personage I had observed at Isabel Somers's grave site on the previous day.

Making my way through the exhibition hall, I came to a halt before him. He was standing beside a large, glass-sided tank containing a plump, green lizard, approximately three feet in length, that resembled a diminutive version of one of the fearsome, fire-breathing dragons so prevalent in the mythologies of the ancient world. Dressed in work clothes, the enormous fellow was in the process of returning several carpenter's tools to a wooden chest that sat at his feet, having evidently just completed his repair work on the tank lid.

"Mr. Tomblin?" I inquired.

"Yeah?" he said, standing erect and regarding me with a look of the keenest suspicion. "Who wants to know?"

"My name is Edgar Poe," I said, gazing upward into his narrowed eyes. "I am working in association with your employer, Mr. Barnum, on a matter of extreme importance."

"Oh, yeah. Mr. B said you'd be coming to see me. Didn't say what for, though."

"I will be happy to explain. Perhaps, however, we can find a more secluded place to talk. The subject I wish to broach is sufficiently sensitive as to require a certain degree of privacy."

"All right," Tomblin said in a somewhat grudging tone. Grabbing the handle of his tool chest, he led me to a remote corner of the hall, devoid of all displays, where he set the heavy box down on the floor, then turned to me and brusquely demanded: "So what's this all about?"

"It concerns Miss Isabel Somers," I replied, "the poor woman whose savage—and thus far unresolved—murder has provoked so much excitement among the populace of the city. It has been established beyond question that Miss Somers was a frequent visitor to the American Museum. According to several eyewitnesses—whose identities I am not at liberty to divulge, but whose veracity I have no reason to doubt—Miss Somers was seen on several occasions in your own company, deeply engrossed in conversation."

As I made these observations, Tomblin's visage underwent a very striking transformation. His intensely *wary* expression was replaced with a look of the most extreme agitation. His face flushed—his mouth twitched—his eyes darted about nervously. "Wh-what? Who?" he stammered. "Why, the lyin'—. I don't know what the hell you're talkin' about, mister. Why, I never set eyes on the woman in my life. The only reason I come to the graveyard yesterday was 'cause Mr. B told us to. Wanted to put on a show for the newspapers, I guess."

Reaching into the side pocket of my coat, I extracted the newspaper portrait of Miss Somers and, unfolding it, held it out for Tomblin to see.

"Here is a likeness of Miss Somers. Are you quite sure that you have never seen or spoken to this person before?"

Without even so much as glancing at the picture, Tomblin raised his massive right hand across his chest and swatted my own hand aside.

"I already told you," he said with a menacing growl. "I never seen the woman in my life. Wouldn't know her from Adam. Whoever told you otherwise is a damned filthy liar. They just better pray I don't never find out who it is, that's all I gotta say."

Without another word, he swiftly bent down, snatched up his heavy toolbox, and strode off across the hallway, elbowing his way through the crowd so rudely that several of the male patrons hurled indignant comments at his receding back.

For several minutes following the custodian's departure, I remained rooted in place, brooding on the scene that had just transpired. That Tomblin had not been candid with me could scarcely be doubted. Everything about his reaction—from his intensely agitated *mien* to the inordinate vehemence of his parting threat—suggested that he was lying. Indeed—as was invariably true in cases where the subject of an interrogation "doth protest too much"—the very intensity of his denials only served to persuade me of the opposite.

In seeking out the custodian, I had been motivated, less by any belief in his possible guilt, than by a professional obligation to leave no stone unturned in my investigation. Now, however, I found myself possessed with the deepest sense of suspicion—an absolute conviction that, while Tomblin might not be directly involved in the crime, he certainly knew a great deal more than he was revealing.

I resolved to share these conclusions with Barnum. First, however, I decided to discharge an obligation that had been weighing on my mind for several days. The reader will recall that—following my violent encounter with Vanderhorn's brutish underling, Croley—Willie Schnitzler had tended to my wounded arm by wrapping it in a costly silk scarf borrowed from Miss Zobeide Luti, Barnum's renowned Circassian Beauty. Having no further need of this item, I was eager to deliver it back to its owner, along with my sincere expressions of gratitude. I had therefore made certain to place it in my pocket before departing from our abode that morning. As I was already on the third floor of the museum—very close to the Hall of Oddities, where Miss Luti was on display—I thought it convenient to perform this brief errand before returning to the basement.

Accordingly, I proceeded without delay to the cavernous chamber housing Barnum's unparalleled assemblage of human anomalies, zoological curiosities, and other specimens of grotesque and bizarre malformation, both living and preserved. Passing inside, I immediately spied Willie Schnitzler, occupying her draperied little stage with an air of queenly repose. On a platform nearby, Bruno the Armless Wonder, was seated upon a three-legged stool with a violin tucked under his chin. He was scratching out a very passable rendition of the "Radetzky Waltz," his right foot moving up and down the neck of the instrument, while his left worked the bow.

All at once, as I continued to glance about the chamber, I observed a sight so unexpected that I started with surprise. For there, not far from Bruno's platform, stood a trio of women I recognized at once as Muddy, Sissy, and Miss Brennan. They were closely inspecting something that I could not—from my present vantage point at the threshold of the exhibition hall—perceive, their closely huddled figures obstructing it from view.

Immediately, I made my way toward them and halted directly behind Sissy, standing in such close proximity to my darling wife that I was nearly pressing against her back. Her gaze was so firmly riveted upon the display before her, however, that she—along with her companions—remained completely oblivious of my presence. Peering over Sissy's shoulder, I now saw what had so transfixed their attention. It was Barnum's purported "goblin child." It lay on its back in the elaborately carved wooden crib, rhythmically clutching at the air with its large, clawlike hands. Its black—bulging—seemingly *pupil-less*—eyes stared unblinkingly upward. From its mouth (which, in spite of the evident youth of the infant, positively *bristled* with enormous, yellow teeth) there issued a succession of weird, unearthly groans.

At length, resolving to make my presence known to my loved ones, I reached up a hand and gently tapped Sissy on the shoulder. She gave a little jump, as though startled from a reverie, and swiftly turned to face me. I saw at once that the surpassingly luminous eyes of the dear, tenderhearted creature were moist with tears.

"Sissy," I declared, "I confess that I am very much surprised— and not a little concerned—to find you here. Much of what can be found in this hall is disturbing to the highest degree, and entirely unsuited for a sensibility as delicately organized as your own."

At the first sound of my voice, Muddy and Miss Brennan had immediately swiveled to face me. Like Sissy, the two women appeared visibly upset, their countenances wrought into expressions of extreme pity and dismay. Although my comment had been addressed to my beloved wife, it was Miss Brennan who answered.

"Oh, please don't be cross with Virginia, Mr. Poe," she said in a tremulous voice. "*I'm* the one who insisted we come up here to see the changeling baby."

"Now, now, Anna Louise," Sissy gently protested. "That's not true, and you know it."

"It was the *both* of them, Eddie," Muddy interjected. "And I'm as much to blame as anyone. You know how much Virginia and I have always fancied stories about pixies and goblins and whatnot."

"As have I," exclaimed Miss Brennan. "I absolutely *adore* Mr. Tyler's collection of faerie legends. Why, it's probably my second-favorite book in the whole world—after your own *Tales of the Grotesque and Arabesque*, of course," she endearingly added.

"Well," said Muddy, "I suppose each one of us was just as curious as the other when Virginia told us there was a genuine changeling baby on show up here."

Turning back toward the little platform upon which stood the weirdly ornamented crib with its grotesque occupant, the good woman muttered: "Strange. I almost can't bear to look at it. And yet, I can't seem to take my eyes off it, either."

"Why, that's just exactly how *I* feel, Mrs. Clemm," said Miss Brennan. "It breaks my heart and makes my blood run cold at the same time."

"The poor, horrible, pitiful thing," Sissy said, patting her eyes with a handkerchief. "Do you think it can possibly be *real*, Eddie?"

"The answer to that question," I replied, "is entirely contingent upon the way in which one defines the meaning of the exceedingly equivocal term, 'real.' That the creature before us is an actual, flesh-and-blood infant can scarcely be doubted. Certainly, it is no mere mechanical contrivance, like the uncannily lifelike *automata* to be found elsewhere in the museum. If your query, however, refers to the child's purportedly supernatural origin and nature, then I must emphatically reply in the negative."

At that moment—as though speaking up in support of this observation—a disembodied voice coming from somewhere very near at hand declared: "Things aren't always what they seem at the Barnum museum."

Looking about to discover the source of this surprising pronouncement, I saw that it had come from none other than Bruno the Armless Wonder, who—having completed his musical performance—was now standing on the very edge of his platform, signing autographs with a pen held between the first and second toes of his naked right foot.

"Hello there, Mr. Poe," he called cheerfully, as he finished affixing his signature to the last of the engraved likenesses being held out to him by his admirers. "I couldn't help overhearing what you were just saying."

"Good afternoon, Bruno," I replied. Turning toward my two loved ones and Miss Brennan, I addressed them thusly: "Come, ladies. There is a remarkable young gentleman over here whom I would very much like you to meet." I then extended an arm—escorted them over to the little platform a short distance away—and introduced them to Bruno.

He was dressed somewhat in the manner of a Regency dandy, with close-fitting black pantaloons and ruffled white shirt whose empty sleeves were pinned up to his shoulders. As I gazed upward at him, I was struck anew by the exceptional, almost *feminine*, beauty of his features: the fine-boned face—the graceful mouth—the surpassingly warm and lustrous brown eyes, which were fixed, at that moment, upon the angelic creature standing beside me, my darling Virginia.

Perceiving the stricken expression that still lingered on her lovely countenance, Bruno pointed his finely molded chin in the direction of the nearby platform upon which the supposed "goblin baby" was on display. "Don't be upset, dear lady," he said gently. "That little fellow over there is not as badly off as he seems. If there's one thing you can say about Mr. Barnum, he makes sure his attractions are well taken care of. Believe me, there are children in this world that aren't treated a fraction as well."

Glancing over at Sissy, I saw her face brighten perceptibly at these reassuring words.

"Say," Bruno suddenly declared. "I have a favor to ask of you three, lovely ladies. Would you mind posing for me?"

So unexpected was this request that, for a moment, my companions merely looked at him in mute surprise. It was Miss Brennan who finally replied. "Why, of course," she said cheerfully. "It would be an honor."

"Excellent," said Bruno. "It's not often I have the opportunity to create silhouettes of three such fetching subjects."

Returning to his stool, he perched himself on the seat and, using both feet, removed a sheet of stiff, black paper and a pair of scissors from the little table beside him. He then requested that Miss Brennan turn sideways, and—after taking a single glance at her left profile—began snipping away at the paper, which was clamped between the first and second toes of his right foot. The dexterity with which he wielded the scissors—whose handles he gripped with the digits of his opposite foot—was nothing short of astounding.

After repeating this process with both Muddy and Sissy, he replaced the scissors on the table, hopped off the stool, and stepped to the edge of the platform, the three silhouettes held loosely in this mouth. He then leaned forward and distributed them to the eagerly awaiting women, who plucked their respective portraits from his lips and—after scrutinizing them for a moment—broke into a chorus of astounded exclamations.

"Why, it's incredible," cried Miss Brennan. "You've caught me *exactly.*"

"And me as well," said Muddy, shaking her head in amazement as she stared down at the picture in her hand. "I really can't believe it."

"Oh, Mr. Bruno," Sissy said delightedly. "You really *are* a wonder!"

Glancing over at the silhouette clutched in Sissy's hand, I saw that—while no mere artistic representation could possibly capture the unequaled loveliness of my dear wife's countenance—Bruno had indeed managed to reproduce the contours of her profile with a remarkable fidelity, particularly in view of the extraordinary handicap under which he labored.

"Permit me to add my congratulations to those of your three models," I said to the handsome youth, who gazed down upon us with a look of intense satisfaction. "Rarely have I encountered a more skillfully rendered specimen of the silhouette-maker's art. Your talents as a portraitist are as formidable as your many other capabilities."

While talking to Bruno, I had my right hand thrust into the side pocket of my frock coat and was idly fingering the folded sheet of newsprint containing the engraved illustration of Isabel Somers. This circumstance—coinciding with my use of the word "portraitist"—must have triggered a particular train of associations deep within my mind; for, all at once, I was struck with a sudden inspiration.

By this point, a small crowd had gathered around Sissy, Muddy, and Miss Brennan to exclaim over their portraits. Drawing my aunty aside, I explained that there was an unforeseen matter which demanded my immediate attention. I then asked if she and her two companions were content to remain at the museum for as long as my business required.

"Oh my, yes," she replied. "We're having such a wonderful time. Why, we'd be happy to stay here all day!"

"Then I will see you sometime later this afternoon," I said with an indulgent smile. From the sheer, childlike excitement in her voice, I could tell that the good woman had completely succumbed to the vulgar enchantments of Barnum's gaudy wonder-world.

Then—bidding her to say farewell to Sissy and Miss Brennan (who were still happily displaying their silhouettes to the people around them)—I turned to take my leave.

CHAPTER NINETEEN

Before departing, I decided to discharge the errand that had brought me to the Hall of Oddities in the first place. I therefore made my way across the room to the little cubicle within whose tapestried walls sat Barnum's celebrated "Star of the East," Miss Zobeide Luti.

She was garbed in a voluminous gown of shimmering blue satin, and reclined on a settee upholstered in the same richly patterned, crimson material that hung on the walls and served as a carpet on the floor. She was a creature of wildly exotic beauty, with great, dark eyes even fuller than the gazelle eyes of the tribe of the Valley of the Nourjahad—skin resembling the purest ivory—and raven-black, glossy, luxuriant tresses setting forth the full force of the Homeric epithet, "hyacinthine." Keeping watch over her was an exceedingly tall, turbanned eunuch, who stood directly behind her settee, his massive arms crossed over his bare, powerfully muscled chest, his features arranged into a look of glowering menace.

Pressing my way to the front of the crowd that surrounded her platform, I drew Miss Luti's attention by loudly pronouncing her name. I then extracted the scarf from my pocket and held it aloft. With a languorous motion of one hand, she signaled to her bronze-skinned attendant, who immediately strode to the edge of the little stage—plucked the silken kerchief from my fingers—and returned it to his mistress.

As the bare-chested eunuch resumed his post behind the settee, I drew myself up to my fullest height and addressed Miss Luti thusly: "Allow me to convey both my sincerest gratitude and deepest respects. To permit your finery to be used as a mere *bandage* by a total stranger bespeaks a rare generosity of spirit. I trust that you will henceforth regard me as one who is forever in your debt."

Though the precise *meaning* of my words may have eluded the beauteous Circassian female—whose knowledge of the English language was evidently of the most rudimentary sort—she could hardly fail to grasp the appreciative *tenor* of my remarks. Draping the scarf about her long—slender—surpassingly elegant—neck, she favored me with a placid half-smile that, for sheer, exquisite loveliness, nearly rivaled that of Da Vinci's immortal *La Gioconda*.

With a farewell bow to the ravishing maiden, I then spun on my heels—hastened from the hall—descended to the basement—and proceeded rapidly down the corridor to Barnum's office. The door standing wide open, I strode directly inside without bothering to knock.

Instantly, I froze in shock!

The showman—whom I had expected to find seated in his usual place—was nowhere to be seen. Crouched upon his desk, however, was a creature that might have sprung from one of the bizarre, phantasmagoric conceptions of the wildly eccentric, medieval genius, Hieronymus Bosch: a hideous, vermilion-winged beetle of such gigantic proportions that its body covered a significant portion of the desktop!

A numbness, an iciness of feeling pervaded my frame. My breast heaved—my knees tottered—I grew deadly sick. A shriek of the purest horror rose in my throat and burst from my lips. As I staggered backward in a paroxysm of terror, I suddenly became cognizant of the sound of rapidly approaching footsteps in the corridor outside. In another instant, someone burst through the doorway behind me—a steadying hand clutched me by the arm—and the showman's familiar voice spoke urgently into my ear:

"Good Lord! What in Heaven's name has come over you, Poe?"

"Th-that *thing!*" I stammered, pointing a trembling finger at the monstrous insect.

"Why, yes, I can see where it might have startled you a bit," said the showman, glancing toward the desk. "She's a queer-looking critter, all right. Not a bit of harm in her, though. Dead as a doorpost. Come on over here, m'boy, and have a seat. I'll tell you all about it."

Still grasping me by the arm, he attempted to urge me toward the chair that stood beside his desk—but to no avail. I continued to stand rooted in place, refusing to move a single step closer to the monstrously oversized beetle.

"I would be grateful," I said in an unsteady voice, "if you would bring the chair over *here*."

"Why, certainly, m'boy, certainly," said Barnum obeying my request. "I must admit, however, that I'm just a tad surprised at you, Poe. Can this be the same stout-hearted fellow who stood up so valiantly to that club-wielding ruffian, Croley? The same bold and dauntless spirit who fought with the ferocity of an enraged Serengeti lion defending his pride?"

"As disconcerting as my reaction may be to you, it is far more so to *me*," I declared, carefully lowering myself into the chair. "And yet, there is nothing I can do to control my feelings. From childhood on, I have been prey to an anomalous species of terror in regard to certain members of the order *Coleoptera*, of which I believe this insect to be an extraordinarily overgrown specimen."

This statement was nothing less than the all-too-painful truth, my mental condition having been morbidly affected by a singularly unsettling episode during my boyhood, when—as a punishment for some minor infraction—my brutish guardian, the Richmond merchant John Allan, had locked me in the cellar of our house, where I had spent several torturous hours, listening in an agony of superstitious dread to the rapid, scurrying movements of the large yellow cockroaches that inhabited those dank and lightless precincts.

I briefly recounted this incident to the showman, who—after seating himself behind his desk—frowned darkly and shook his head in evident disbelief.

"Bless my soul, but that's a horrible tale," he exclaimed, clucking his tongue sympathetically. "Why, the man should have been horse-whipped. Imagine mistreating a youngster so!"

"Indeed," I replied in a voice that quavered with emotion, "without wishing to indulge in self-pity, I may say without exaggeration that the indignities I was made to suffer as a poor orphaned child were of the most deplorable nature."

"Well, Poe," said Barnum, "I can certainly understand why this king-size *Coleoptera* bug, or whatever you call it, would give you the willies. From where *I'm* sitting, though, the view is different. Considerably different. Know what *I* see when I look at it?"

This query being of a clearly rhetorical nature, I made no effort to answer.

"Money!" Barnum exclaimed after a momentary pause. "Heaps of it! A fortune that'll make the fabled treasure of King Midas look like pocket change, mere pocket change!" And here, he gave the monstrous beetle a look of such tender regard that I would not have been surprised to see him reach out and fondly pat the grotesque creature on its head.

Accustomed though I was by now to Barnum's love of overstatement, I was nevertheless surprised by the extravagance of this claim. To be sure, the gigantic insect was remarkable to behold—but no more so than a dozen other anomalous creatures in the showman's collection: his hornless, dwarf rhinoceros, for example, or six-legged armadillo.

Moreover, as the recent, ill-fated episode involving the two-headed, cyclops calf made clear, the value of even the most extraordinary freak of nature diminished dramatically once it was deceased. Had the enormous beetle been alive, Barnum's faith in its money-making potential may have been justified. Unfortunately for him (though much to my *own* relief), the ghastly creature was—as he himself had put it—"dead as a doorpost."

I expressed my confusion to Barnum, who responded in a most unexpected way. Breaking into a broad, delighted smile, he clapped his hands together and exclaimed: "Why, bless your heart, Poe, but that's exactly the point! Picture a bug identical to this one—only twice as big and alive as you or me! Why, it would be the wonder of the ages! The greatest marvel in the universe! Make the Colossus of Rhodes look like a child's pull-toy!"

The mere thought of such an insect caused a shudder of revulsion to pass through my frame. "I have no doubt that a living beetle of that magnitude would produce quite a sensation. But surely no such creature exists."

"Ah, but it does, m'boy, it *does*—at least, if Mr. Charlie McDougall is to be believed. And I see no reason to doubt him, no reason in the world. If there's one thing P. T. Barnum prides himself on, it's being a keen judge of human nature. And I judge Mr. Charlie McDougall to be as straight and honest a fellow as ever drew breath."

"Charlie McDougall?" I said with a frown. "I fear I am unfamiliar with that appellation."

"Chap from Green-Wood Cemetery," said Barnum. "Gravedigger by trade. Buttonholed me after the service yesterday. He was the visitor I was expecting this morning."

"Of course," said I. "I encountered him outside your office when I left." All at once, I was struck with a realization. "So this exceedingly curious specimen was the object contained in the bundle he was carrying."

"Why, yes," said Barnum. "That's what he was so all-fired eager to tell me about at the funeral yesterday. Seems there's a whole family of these critters living at the cemetery. And this one here is just the *runt* of the litter. McDougall swears he's seen one at least twice as big."

Arranging my features into an intensely skeptical look, I inquired as to the precise details of the gravedigger's story.

"Well, there's not much to tell," said Barnum. "Seems he was crossing the cemetery one evening about a week ago. Just finished filling in the last grave of the day—some poor soul who'd been planted right before sunset. So there he is, trudging back to the toolshed—when all of a sudden, he spies a whole pack of these critters scampering over the grass. Well, you can imagine how he reacted. Nearly jumped out of his skin—same as you, Poe, m'boy.

"He soon got hold of himself, though. Calculated there might be a world of money to be made from such an astonishing bug. Right then and there, he decides to try bagging one. So off he goes, chasing after the monster of the bunch—a regular behemoth, six feet from end to end if it's an inch. McDougall swears it's true—and I have no reason to doubt the man's veracity, none at all. But the blasted thing burrowed underground and got away.

"This feller here wasn't quite so nimble," Barnum continued, pointing his dimpled chin at the lifeless insect on his desk. "McDougall whacked it on the head with his shovel blade—dispatched it with a single blow. Here, take a look. You can see where the head's dented in. And the right feeler's missing—broken clean off.

"McDougall and I haggled over it for a while. He was here until just a few minutes ago—I was seeing him out when you showed up. Claimed he wouldn't take a penny less than a hundred for it. Think of it, Poe! Playing *me* for a sucker! Why, do I look like the kind of man who'd pay one hundred dollars for a damaged giant beetle? Twenty-five dollars, take it or leave it—that was my final offer. As you can see," he concluded, gazing contentedly at the monstrous insect, "he took it."

Subduing the instinctive sense of revulsion aroused in me by the mere sight of the creature, I turned my eyes upon it and scrutinized it narrowly. Even apart from its phenomenal size, it was of a most distinctive appearance, with a flattened, elongated body—a bright red tuft on the tip of its surviving antenna—and a pair of vermilion bands, zigzag in shape, running width-wise across its wing-case. After studying its anatomical features closely for several moments, I turned to Barnum and declared:

"Though I am unable to account for its grotesquely enlarged dimensions, there seems little doubt that this creature belongs to that common, if singularly *odious*, order of insect, the *Necrophorus*, more familiarly known as the *burying* or *sexton* beetle. Its name derives from its characteristic habit of digging a hole beneath the dead body of any small creature it happens upon—bird, snake, mouse, mole, etc. The corpse having sunk into the ground, the beetle then covers it entirely with a mound of dirt. The buried carrion is then employed as fodder for the insect's developing larvae. So skilled are the *Necrophori* at their mortuary task that, in his classic *Introduction à l'enotomologie*, the great French scientist, Jean Théodore Lacordaire, refers to them as the 'undertakers of the insect world.' "

"Well, I'll be," said Barnum in a musing tone, scratching the side of his bulbous nose with the fingernail of his left pinky. "I suppose that explains why they'd turn up in a graveyard."

"Though seemingly logical, there is, I am afraid, not the slightest scientific basis for your assumption," I replied. "As the burying beetle requires an *exposed* cadaver upon which its larvae may batten, a human graveyard—with its casketed remains—offers no apparent benefit to the insect. Even more puzzling is the staggering size of this specimen, which is literally thousands of times larger than the average *Necrophorus.*"

"Well, the world is full of mysteries, Poe," Barnum declared. "Chock full of them. Who can say where these colossi of the insect world originated? The equatorial jungles of darkest Africa? The vast, infernal reaches of the Gobi Desert? The sunken continent of Atlantis?"

All at once, the showman's eyes grew wide, and a delighted look spread over his ruddy countenance. "That's it! Of course! Why didn't it occur to me sooner? Just think of the come-on: 'Ladies and gentlemen! Prepare to behold the most remarkable living curiosity of all time! The last surviving member of a species long thought to be extinct! Worshipped as a deity by the pagan people of antiquity! The Giant Sacred Beetle of Lost Atlantis! Brought to these shores at incalculable expense! Now on display exclusively at Barnum's American Museum!' Why, the public will be *battling* to get in! The place will be *besieged*. It'll make the storming of the Bastille look like a model of civic restraint!

"Of course," he continued, "McDougall has to supply me with a living insect first. But I have perfect faith in the man. Especially with a five-hundred-dollar offer dangling in front of him."

"Five hundred dollars!" I exclaimed.

Barnum made a dismissive gesture with one hand. "Pshaw. Mere pocket change. I'll earn every penny of it back within a week. Assuming he brings me a decent-sized specimen, that is. Not another pipsqueak like this fellow here. Of course, capturing a monster like that won't be easy. That's why I plan to send Abel Tomblin out to Green-Wood to assist him."

By this point, it was clear that the showman had completely forgotten about my interview with Tomblin, his enthusiasm over the giant insect having driven all else from his mind. I therefore seized this opportunity to remind him of it.

"Speaking of the custodian," I said. "Permit me to recall your attention to the main purpose of my visit here this morning—to wit, my questioning of the latter as to the nature of his relationship with the Somers woman."

For a moment, Barnum merely looked at me blankly. All at once, he nodded his head vigorously and declared: "Why, of course, of course. Tell me all about it, m'boy. I'm just bursting with curiosity to hear."

As the showman listened attentively—his fingers formed into a steeple and placed against his tight-pressed lips—I proceeded to deliver a *précis* of my brief, intensely unsatisfactory interview with Tomblin. I reported that—while I had approached the talk with no preconceptions about the custodian—I had come away with my suspicions deeply aroused. I described his inordinately violent reactions to my queries, and explained that it was the very vehemence of his denials that had, in the end, persuaded me that he was lying.

For several moments, the showman remained silent, his brow deeply furrowed, his mouth arranged into a ruminative frown. At length, he looked at me and said: "Well, it sounds mighty peculiar, all right. Still, I don't believe that Abel Tomblin had anything to do with that horrid murder. Don't believe it for an instant. Why, the man's as tender-hearted as they come. Oh, yes, he *looks* strong. And he *is* strong, too—strong as an ox. Why, I'd wager he could hold his own against The Great O'Bannon himself in a wrestling match, if it came down to that. But there's not a drop of meanness in him."

"I do not say that he was directly implicated in the murder itself," I replied. "I am convinced, however, that, in absolutely disavowing any familiarity with the victim, he is distorting the truth—in short, that he is concealing *something*. Answer me this—precisely how long have you known him?"

"Just a little over three years," said Barnum. "Ever since the museum opened its doors in the spring of '41. Put an ad in the *Herald* for a handyman, and Abel was the first candidate to show up. Hired him on the spot. Never had cause to regret it, either. Why, the man's as reliable as the sunrise. Ask him to do anything, anything in the world, and he manages it without a peep of complaint. Wish all my employees were that dependable. Why, you wouldn't believe the aggravation I get from some of these people. Take Lean Bear, my genuine, full-blooded Cheyenne chief. Damned Indian refuses to perform his war dance unless he gets a home-cooked meal of ham steak, boiled potatoes, and corn every morning. Blasted *prima donna.* Why, you'd think—"

"Apart from Tomblin's commendable qualities as a handyman," I said, interrupting the showman before he became utterly swept away on the tide of his indignation over the recalcitrant savage, "do you know very much about him?"

"Well, no, now that you mention it. One thing about Abel—he keeps pretty much to himself. Lives alone in a little flat on the Bowery. Shows up for work first thing in the morning, and leaves when the place closes up for the night. Other than that," Barnum added with a shrug, "I can't say that I know the first thing about the man."

A few moments of silence passed while I contemplated this information. "That Tomblin has revealed so little of himself to you in the course of three years may indicate nothing more than a marked, temperamental inclination to privacy," I said at length. "Nonetheless, it strikes me as somewhat peculiar that the details of his personal life, both now and in the past, are shrouded in such utter obscurity. While it would be premature to draw any sinister inferences from this fact alone, I feel strongly that further investigation into the custodian's background is warranted."

"Well, yes, I see your point," said Barnum, albeit in a somewhat grudging tone. "I'm sure it'll turn out to be a complete waste of our time, but I don't suppose it can do any harm to look into the matter."

"In the meantime, I have been struck with another idea," I said, drawing from my pocket the newspaper illustration of Isabel Somers and displaying it to Barnum. "As you know, this engraving was based on an oil painting by the well-known society portraitist, Mr. Gilbert Opdyke."

"Yes, I've met him a time or two. Dreadful fellow, the worst kind of snob. Pretty handy at daubing, though, I'll give him that."

"It occurs to me," I said, "that Mr. Opdyke must have spent a considerable amount of time in Miss Somers's company while she posed for him. Thus—while far from certain—it is at least *conceivable* that he may possess some piece of information about the victim which may prove useful to us."

"Well, it's a long shot, all right," said the showman. "But nothing ventured, nothing gained, as the saying goes. Might as well call on the fellow and ask him a few questions. His studio's just a few blocks away from here, on Warren Street."

"Well, then," I declared, slapping my thighs and getting to my feet. "Shall we be off, then?"

"What?" exclaimed Barnum. "Right this minute?"

"There's no time like the present—that's P. T. Barnum's motto, is it not?"

"So it is, so it is," said the showman with a chuckle. Grabbing his walking stick, he rose from his seat—strode around his desk—and took me by the elbow. Then—after casting one last, affectionate gaze at the monstrous bug on his desktop—he ushered me from the office and locked the door behind us.

CHAPTER TWENTY

Opdyke's residence, which stood at Number 37 Warren Street, was an elegant brick edifice, two stories high, with green window shutters and a pair of sculpted, Oriental dragons flanking the doorway, like the chimerical sentries that once stood guard at the entrance of the great Ziggurat of Kish during the reign of Nebuchadnezzar II. A polished brass knocker wrought into the shape of a bull's head was affixed to the center of the green-painted door. Ignoring this object (as was his wont), Barnum raised his walking stick and made ready to deliver an annunciatory rap.

Before he could accomplish this act, however, the door was opened from the inside by an elderly servant, garbed in knee-breeches and a gray, swallowtail coat. With a deferential bow, he stepped to one side; whereupon, an exceedingly corpulent female of approximately fifty years of age swept from the house. Her face was heavily powdered—her hair elaborately coiffed—her gown of such opulent material and voluptuous design that it would not have seemed out of place at one of the dissolute revels held nightly at the palace of Versailles during the reign of the Sun King. Perhaps her most noticeable feature, however, was a large, fleshy growth—somewhat resembling the cap of a newly sprouted mushroom of the genus *Lactarius piperatus*—that protruded from the tip of her nose.

Striding haughtily past us—as if she were, indeed, a member of that high, aristocratic class that regards the ordinary man as barely worthy of notice—this flamboyantly costumed woman proceeded directly to a magnificent four-in-hand carriage that waited at the curbside. At her approach, her liveried coachman leapt from his seat, hurried around to the side of the vehicle, threw open the escutcheoned door, and assisted the imperious woman in clambering aboard. He then remounted the box, and—with a cluck of the tongue and a jerk of the reins—directed the chequered steeds into the traffic.

After watching the gaudy vehicle drive off, Barnum and I turned our attention back to the doorway. Extracting one of his calling cards from his vest pocket, the showman presented it to the grizzled servant, who scrutinized it minutely. Then—after inviting us to step inside the house—the old fellow went off to notify his master. He reappeared a few minutes later and announced that—though busily engaged in his painting—Mr. Opdyke was willing to take a respite and grant us a brief interview. The old man then turned on his heels and—shuffling ahead of us—led us upstairs to the second floor.

After passing through a brightly lit hallway—whose walls were hung with several massively framed still lifes in the manner of the sixteenth-century Flemish master, Jan de Beer—we were shown into a spacious, high-ceilinged apartment that served as the antechamber to Opdyke's studio. The servant taking his leave, Barnum and I turned our attention to the decor of this remarkable room.

In both its architecture and embellishments, the evident intention had been to dazzle and astound. The eye wandered from object to object, and rested upon none—neither the grotesque statuary of the ancient Etruscans, nor the sculptures of the best Italian days, nor the huge carvings of untutored Egypt. Upon the floor there lay a carpet of rich and liquid-looking cloth of Chili gold. Each window was fashioned of a single pane of crimson-tinted glass, and hung with heavy draperies, which rolled from their cornices like cataracts of molten silver. The walls were covered with dozens of paintings, from the Greeks to Cimabue, and from Cimabue to the present hour. Many of these artworks had been chosen with little deference to the opinions of conventional propriety, though all served as fitting tapestry for a chamber of such wildly unorthodox—if not *fantastic*—design.

Approaching a table of richly enameled silver upon which stood a curiously fashioned clay vase—vaguely suggestive in its contours of a voluptuous female torso—Barnum turned to me as though to render an opinion on our surroundings. Before he could utter a word, however, a shrill burst of laughter erupted from behind us.

"Ha! ha! ha! I see that you are astounded at my apartment—at my statues—my pictures—my originality of conception in architecture and upholstery! Am I right, gentlemen?"

Swiveling about to discover the source of this surprising utterance, I found myself facing a person of most unusual appearance. Framed in the doorway that opened into the adjacent room, he was thin to the point of emaciation. His profuse, silken hair—so blond as to seem nearly white—was parted in the middle, and of such inordinate length that it fell to the level of his shoulders. His countenance was long—narrow—and utterly devoid of color. The extreme pallor of his complexion was rendered even more striking by its contrast to the peculiarly roseate hue of his mouth. His bow-shaped upper lip was adorned with a slender mustache whose ends had been heavily waxed and combed upward into a symmetrical pair of curlicues. He wore a loose-fitting painter's smock that reached almost to his knees—pants of the most stylish cut and fabric—and ankle boots that had been buffed to a high polish. In his right eye, he sported a monocle, and his face was suffused with an expression of perfect *ennui.*

Assuming this singular personage to be Mr. Opdyke himself, I replied to his comment thusly: "Your collection is exceptional indeed. I am especially impressed by this Madonna della Pietà. Is it not Guido's own?"

Arching one, pale eyebrow, Opdyke regarded me with a look of somewhat amused curiosity. "Why, what have we here? A connoisseur? How delightful! And what is your name, my good sir?"

Ignoring the supercilious note in his voice, I politely answered: "Poe. Mr. Edgar A. Poe."

"Ah, of course. The critic. I read your essay on 'The Canons of

Good Breeding' in *Burton's*. I must say, I found it a trifle long-winded, although not entirely without interest.

"And you, sir," continued the insufferable fop, gazing languidly at the showman. "I take it that you are the celebrated Mr. Barnum, who has contributed so *very* much to the cultural life of our fair city."

Whatever umbrage Barnum may have taken at the smirking tone of this latter remark, he evinced no outward sign of it. "At your service, sir, at your service," he said pleasantly. "I believe our paths have crossed once or twice before—though I'd hardly expect a great genius like yourself to remember a mere showman like me. Can't tell you how honored I feel just to be here. Why, I've heard the most remarkable things about your abilities. Painter extraordinaire! America's most accomplished living artist! Makes Leonardo and that whole Renaissance crew look like a bunch of butterfingered amateurs!"

So unbounded was the extent of Opdyke's self-conceit that he took this rank hyperbole for the sincerest flattery. Bowing his head slightly—as if to acknowledge Barnum's wildly extravagant praise as nothing less than his due—he remarked: "May I assume, then, that you are here to commission an original Opdyke?"

For the merest instant, a somewhat flustered look passed over Barnum's countenance. Swiftly recovering himself, he exclaimed: "Why, yes, yes, to be sure. Two portraits, to be exact. One of me, one of Mrs. Barnum. A matched set, to be hung over the mantelpiece in our country estate. Have to move our Tintorettos to make room for them, of course. But that's no sacrifice, no sacrifice at all. After all, who wants some old Italian claptrap cluttering up the walls when he can have a spanking new pair of original Opdykes?"

"Well, I suppose it can be done," Opdyke replied with a weary sigh. "Of course, there is a rather lengthy waiting list, the demand for an original Opdyke being what it is. Fortunately, I am very close to completing my current work—a portrait of Mrs. Henry Beekman, commissioned by her as a twenty-fifth wedding anniversary gift for her husband." The very nonchalance with which Opdyke referred to this personage—a member of one of the city's oldest and most illustrious knickerbocker clans—was clearly meant to impress us with his own importance.

Playing up to the painter's unblushing self-conceit, Barnum emitted a soft whistle and exclaimed: "Beekman, eh? Mighty hoity-toity, all right. Blood doesn't run any bluer than that, not in this town, anyway."

Opdyke waved his hand dismissively, as if to suggest that, among his many wealthy patrons, there were far grander names than that of Beekman. "She was just here for her daily sitting. Perhaps you gentlemen saw her as she was leaving. Tiresome woman. Frightfully unattractive. It's taken me *forever* to find a way to make her appear less gruesome. Come. Would you care to see my latest work in progress?"

"Heavens, yes," said the showman. "It would be a privilege."

As Opdyke turned and disappeared into the studio, Barnum cast me a look as if to say: "Try to keep a straight face, Poe, for we must go along with this charade if we are to learn anything from this popinjay." He then took me by the arm and led me through the doorway.

Opdyke's studio was characterized by the clutter typical of a professional *atelier*. Canvasses of various dimensions were stacked against the walls. A long, oaken worktable held a multitude of brushes, palette knives, charcoal sticks, paint jars, and other accoutrements of the artist's craft. In one corner stood a fluted pedestal, topped with a marble bust of Marcus Aurelius. The other furnishings of the room included a dressing screen, chiffonier, settee, and washstand, along with a tall display cabinet whose shelves contained an array of highly detailed anatomical models, molded of plaster and wax. Affixed to the walls was a promiscuous assortment of rough drawings and more highly polished preliminary studies, rendered in pencil, watercolor, and charcoal.

In the center of the studio stood a small wooden platform upon which Opdyke's subjects posed. It was covered with a thick rug of intricate Oriental design and held a comfortable-looking armchair, whose seat-cushion still retained the impression of its most recent occupant. Facing the platform was an easel, upon which rested the nearly completed portrait of Mrs. Beekman. Situating himself beside the picture, Opdyke beckoned to us with a languid wave of one long, slender hand.

"Come have a look, gentlemen," he said as we came up and stood beside him. "Tell me, does she not seem to live and breathe?"

Had honesty, rather than expedience, been my guide, I should have unhesitatingly answered with an emphatic "no." The picture before us was a mere head and shoulders, done in what is technically termed a *vignette* manner, much in the style of the favorite heads of Sully. The arms, the bosom, and even the ends of the hair melted imperceptibly into the vague yet deep shadow which formed the background of the whole. Though willing to concede (however grudgingly) that the painting evinced a fair degree of technical skill, I perceived at once that Opdyke utterly lacked that gift which distinguishes the truly great portraitist from the mere journeyman: to wit, the all-important ability to infuse his subjects with a convincing illusion of life. There was a stiffness—a brittleness—a hopelessly academic quality—to the image.

Even so, I could understand why Opdyke was so fervently admired by his aristocratic clientele. Besides the superficial polish of his style, he was clearly able to render his subjects in a manner most flattering to their vanity. His portrait of Mrs. Beekman, for example, managed to capture the lineaments of her visage, while transforming her into an infinitely more elegant creature than the lumbering female I had seen emerging from his house. In addition, her appearance had been materially improved by the removal of the fungus-shaped wart from the end of her nose.

"So, gentlemen," he urged. "What do you think?"

"Bless my soul, but it's sublime," cried Barnum. "Most astonishing thing I've ever seen. Why, she looks as alive as you do!"

"Yes," said the painter complacently. "It is a classic example of the famed Opdykean style."

"A style that must be viewed in all its original glory to be fully appreciated," I said in a tone of intense, if utterly feigned, admiration. "Newspaper reproductions of your work, such as the one published earlier this week, simply cannot do justice to the vigor—the grace—the sheer, overwhelming brilliance—of the Opdyke technique."

"I take it," said the painter with a look of distaste, "that you're referring to that hideous engraving of the Somers woman that ran in Monday's *Herald*."

"That is, indeed, the picture I had in mind."

Opdyke made an exaggerated shuddering motion. "What an abomination. Done completely without my permission, of course. Why, it bears as much resemblance to my painting as a child's chalk-drawing does to the ceiling of the Sistine Chapel. Here," he continued, motioning for us to follow him. "I can't show you the original, of course, but I have one or two rough sketches that will give you some hint of the finished version."

Leading us over to a lacquered highboy that stood against the far wall of the studio, Opdyke slid open the center drawer and, after rummaging through the contents, extracted a large sheet of drawing paper, which he then carried over to one of the several undraperied windows that provided the studio with an abundance of natural light. Arranging ourselves on either side of him, Barnum and I peered closely at the picture, which he held up for our perusal.

Though reluctant to give the vaunting Opdyke any more credit than he deserved, I was forced to concede that his skill as a draughts-man was considerable. The penciled study possessed a freshness and vigor entirely missing from the lifeless oil portrait of Mrs. Beekman. As I scrutinized the face of the young woman in the picture, something about her features—and in particular, about the distinctive shape of her finely molded chin—struck me as strangely familiar. I was at a loss to say, however, precisely where I might have encountered a physiognomy of such formation before.

"It is indeed a very excellent drawing," I remarked to Opdyke. "Most expressive. Am I correct in discerning a certain melancholy cast to her eyes?"

"Good for you, Mr. Poe," Opdyke said, in a tone so intensely patronizing that it required the greatest exertion on my part to keep from administering a savage rebuke to the fellow. "That was indeed the effect I intended. To all outward appearances, the woman was extremely vivacious. But the truly great portraitist must be more than a mere virtuoso of the brush. He must be an adept in the hidden workings of the heart—the innermost secrets of the soul. Beneath her superficial gaiety, I perceived a deep well of sorrow in Miss Somers."

Though this surpassingly pompous remark had been addressed to me, it was Barnum who responded. "Well, I don't doubt your word, sir, don't doubt it for a minute. Still and all, I can't see for the life of me what she had to be so almighty sorrowful *about.* From all I've heard about the woman, she was living like royalty. All the comforts that money can buy—splendid digs, high-class furnishings, fashionable clothing. Good heavens—how many mortals are fortunate enough to have their pictures painted by the shining ornament of the American art world, the incomparable Opdyke himself?"

"As to the cause of her unhappiness, I really couldn't say," responded Opdyke in his characteristically *blasé* manner. "My connection with Miss Somers was of a purely professional nature."

"Nevertheless," I remarked, "it must have come as a terrible shock when you read of her death."

"Not particularly," Opdyke replied with the greatest nonchalance. "From what little I saw of the woman, she kept company with certain highly questionable associates."

"Really?" Barnum exclaimed. "What sort of associates?"

My companion's overeager tone elicited, for the first time, a wary reaction on the part of the painter. Regarding the showman with narrowed eyes, Opdyke said: "I must say, you seem strangely interested in the woman, Mr. Barnum. Why *is* that?"

Arranging his features into an ingenuous look, the showman replied: "Why, there's nothing the least bit strange about it. *Everyone's* interested in the Somers case. Why, it's the talk of the town! Grisliest crime since the Jennings murder! Bless my soul, it would be strange if I *weren't* curious."

For a moment, the painter weighed this answer in silence. At length—having evidently accepted it as a sufficiently plausible explanation—he declared: "I visited her apartment only once, to deliver the finished painting and ensure that it was properly hung. While I was there, she had a male caller. Quite an unsavory-looking fellow."

"Unsavory?" Barnum said. "In what way?"

"Why, as a matter of fact," said Opdyke, "he looked like something that might be found in your very own museum, as you call it. A great, hulking creature, well over six feet tall. Big, square head with a simian jaw and a thatch of blond fur sticking up from his skull. Altogether repulsive. Looked like he might have been sired by an ourang-outang."

At this description, Barnum and I exchanged a sharp look. In every respect, it corresponded to the distinctive physical appearance of the museum custodian, Abel Tomblin.

"Sounds like a rough customer, all right," said the showman. "Wonder what he was doing there."

Opdyke shrugged. "I don't have the slightest idea, though it was obviously something of a fairly personal nature; for after greeting him, she led him into the privacy of her bedroom, where they remained for five or ten minutes behind the closed door until he left."

"Didn't happen to catch his name by any chance?" Barnum asked.

The painter thought for a moment before replying: "It was a biblical name, as I recall. Aaron—Adam—something of the sort."

"Abel?" Barnum ventured.

"Perhaps," said the painter, looking at the showman with renewed suspicion. When he spoke again, a distinct note of impatience had entered his voice. "And now, Mr. Barnum, if we can finally get down to the business at hand—"

"Great Scot!" Barnum suddenly burst out.

"What in the world is the matter?" cried the startled painter.

"Business!" Barnum exclaimed, pulling out his pocket watch and checking the time. "There's a fellow coming to see me in—good heavens!—in a mere fifteen minutes from now! Completely slipped my mind, I've been so dazzled by your work. My deepest apologies, Mr. Opdyke, but Poe and I must be off this very minute. Can't afford to miss this appointment. Enormous proposition, absolutely huge! Whole oceans of money in it! But I'll be back, my dear sir, I'll be back. You can depend upon it."

And so saying, Barnum grabbed me by the arm and hurried me out of the studio, as the painter looked on in astonishment.

Leading me briskly downstairs and out of the house, Barnum spoke not a word until we were back on Broadway, where we paused beneath the awning of a tobacconist's shop. Beside us, atop a small pedestal, stood the carved wooden figure of a tawny Indian brave, a panther's skin about his loins, a quiver full of arrows on his back, an eagle's feather in his raven hair. In one hand, he clutched a bow; while, with the other, he proffered a sheaf of cigars to all passersby.

Extracting his own cigar from the inside pocket of his coat, Barnum bit off one end—ignited the other—and took a deep draw before speaking. "Lord bless me, what an ordeal. Rather spend all of eternity in Dante's purgatory than another minute in the company of that damned milksop.

"Poe," he continued, taking another great puff of his cigar, "forgive me for doubting you. Don't know what came over me. You were right about Abel, no question about it."

"Indeed," I replied, "Opdyke's testimony leaves little doubt that the personage he observed at Miss Somers's residence was none other than your custodian."

"It certainly looks that way," Barnum said with a sigh. "Why in the world Abel would lie to you in such a flagrant manner, I just don't understand. Wish I did, but I don't. Of course, there's one thing we mustn't lose sight of—just because he was acquainted with the woman doesn't mean he had anything to do with her murder."

"True enough," I replied. "Nevertheless, from both Opdyke's observation and that of Bruno the Armless Wonder—who first apprised me of the relationship—it would appear that Mr. Tomblin and Miss Somers were more than mere acquaintances. Moreover, as I have already suggested, there was something distinctly suspicious about the peculiar intensity of Tomblin's reaction to my questioning."

"Well, we'll have to put our heads together, you and I, and figure out how best to proceed," said Barnum. "I still don't believe that Abel Tomblin is the party we're after. Don't believe it for a minute. But *something* funny's going on, no doubt about it. 'There's no smoke without fire,' that's what I always say. We—"

All at once, the showman broke off in midstatement, and a look of utter astonishment crossed his visage.

"Poe!" he cried, pointing to a spot across the street. "Look there!"

Under ordinary circumstances, the great thoroughfare of Broadway was so clogged with a dense and continuous tide of conveyances—sulkies and stanhopes, broughams and barouches, charcoal-wagons, farmers' carts, and carriages of every imaginable variety—that a person standing on one side of the street could catch only the most partial and fleeting glimpse of the opposite curb. At the moment, however, the situation was markedly different. Directly before us, an ancient and skeletal dray-horse, hitched to a rickety hay-cart, had collapsed in the middle of the street, bringing the tumultuous flow of vehicles to an abrupt halt.

It was not this mishap, however, to which Barnum was directing my attention. Rather, he was pointing to a remarkable sight on the sidewalk directly across from us, now accessible to our view as a consequence of the sudden break in the traffic.

Two people, male and female, had just emerged from a druggist's shop. For a moment—before striding off in opposite directions along the street—they stood together in the entranceway of the shop and exchanged a few hurried words, the woman leaning down toward her companion and whispering in his ear in a singularly intimate manner.

Her gentleman companion was as handsomely garbed as any Broadway gallant. Even from the distance at which I viewed him, I recognized him instantly—not, however, from his somewhat ostentatious clothing, but rather from his unmistakable *physique*. It was Morris Vanderhorn's hunchbacked secretary, whose painful humiliation at the hands of his employer Barnum and I had been made to witness several days earlier.

The other figure—an inordinately thin and pallid female, clad in the deepest, funereal black and clutching an enormous volume to her narrow bosom—was Mrs. Vanderhorn herself!

CHAPTER TWENTY-ONE

The reader may easily imagine my startled reaction to the sight of this exceedingly incongruous pair. What, I wondered, was the unearthly Mrs. Vanderhorn doing at a druggist's shop in the company of her husband's grotesquely malformed assistant? And what was one to make of the strange bond of familiarity that appeared to exist between them?

It quickly occurred to me, however, that—in spite of the vaguely conspiratorial air that seemed to surround them—there might, in fact, be no cause at all for suspicion. Perhaps they were there on a perfectly legitimate errand. In any case, my knowledge of the Vanderhorn household—its inner workings and various occupants—was far too meager to allow me to draw any sinister inferences.

After watching the cadaverous woman and her hunchbacked companion go their separate ways, Barnum and I hurriedly repaired to his office, where—after engaging in a brief and inconclusive discussion of the surprising sight we had just witnessed—we turned our attention back to the more pressing subject of the custodian. Before long, we had settled on a plan.

I then took my leave of the showman and went off in search of Muddy, Sissy, and Miss Brennan, locating them on the second floor, in the Grand Skeleton Chamber, where they were marveling at a display of mounted mastodon bones. By this point, the three women—and my darling wifey in particular, whose constitution, even in the best of circumstances, was delicate in the extreme—were in a state of near-exhaustion from their protracted stay at the museum. Their fatigue, however, did not prevent them from chattering excitedly during the entire ride home; while I reclined in a corner of the jouncing cab, silently ruminating on my plans for the morrow.

Twenty-four hours later, in accordance with my prearranged scheme with Barnum, I was back in the heart of the city. On this occasion, however, my destination was not the museum, but rather that crude—teeming—distinctly disreputable quarter into which the more refined members of the populace rarely, if ever, ventured. I refer, of course, to the Bowery.

I was on my way to the residence of Abel Tomblin.

In the aftermath of our interview with Opdyke, one fact had become abundantly clear to Barnum and me: we must do everything within our power—and as swiftly as possible—to ascertain the nature of the custodian's relationship to Isabel Somers. How to achieve this goal was less apparent. Nothing was to be gained from another direct interrogation of Tomblin. The latter's angry response to my earlier questioning proved the futility of such an approach. Only one expedient suggested itself. We must somehow gain entrance to the custodian's living quarters while he was absent, and search for any evidence that might offer a clue to the mystery.

Needless to say, such an investigation had to be conducted under conditions of the greatest secrecy. It was for this reason that the showman had disqualified himself from any direct participation in the undertaking.

"I'd come along in a flash, Poe, m'boy, but I'm afraid of being recognized. When you enjoy the immense—the *extraordinary*—fame that I do, it's hard to walk the streets without attracting attention. Why, you've seen it for yourself—the sort of public adulation that's showered on me wherever I go. It's the curse of celebrity. Now, I'm not saying I don't enjoy it, because I *do*—can't get enough of it, it's mother's milk to me. Still, there are drawbacks, definite drawbacks. Be grateful for your obscurity, m'boy. It's a blessing in disguise!"

Having thus determined that I would carry out this venture on my own, we were next faced with the question of *when* it should be attempted—and here, too, the matter was readily decided. For on the very afternoon following our visit to Opdyke's studio, Tomblin was to be dispatched to Green-Wood Cemetery, where he would assist in the pursuit of the giant insect so coveted by the showman. This undertaking (which included several hours of travel-time to and from Brooklyn) was bound to keep him occupied for much, if not all, of the evening, thus affording me ample opportunity to enter and explore his apartment without fear of discovery.

These, then, were the circumstances which had led to my present situation—striding briskly along the Bowery toward Canal Street, where the custodian made his home.

Since residing in New York City, I had largely avoided this noisome and degraded district, and now, as I made my way along the street in the gathering twilight, I was filled with an inexpressible sense of revulsion at the vile sights—sounds—and smells that assaulted me from every side. A dark and dismal mist, compounded of dust, smoke, and the reek of squalid gutters seemed to envelop the neighborhood. In place of the bright and handsome shops found elsewhere in the city, the sidewalks here were lined with the most tawdry establishments imaginable: dilapidated lodging-houses, cheap clothing stores, oyster cellars, beer gardens, concert saloons, pawn shops, dance halls, billiard rooms, gambling dens, bowling alleys, hack-stables, and assorted houses of the most evil repute.

The vast sea of humanity that surged along the street was, if anything, even more noisy and tumultuous than that which swept along Broadway. Sporting men and street beggars—sailors and tramps—barflies and bootblacks—gamblers and coal-heavers—porters and peddlers—and dissolute, frowzy females in all imaginable, flaunting, immodest dresses swarmed about me. The vast globe seemed to have emptied itself onto this single thoroughfare. The air was filled with a clatter and confusion of accents and tongues that rivaled the cacophony of Babel: English, French, Spanish, Irish, Portuguese, Italian, Chinese, and Hebrew. On all sides could be heard drunken male and female voices spewing forth words and phrases unrepeatable in God's sunlight. Pedestrians making their way along the street were compelled to run a gauntlet of brazen enticements: sidewalk "sharpers" peddling brass watches as solid gold and paste trinkets as diamond jewelry—shrill-voiced "touts" proclaiming the delights to be found within the many tawdry palaces of sin—and flagrant, heavily rouged women beckoning from shadowy doorways.

As I hurried toward Canal Street, I kept my right hand thrust deep within my pants pocket and my fingers tightly clenched around the singular object it contained. This was a shiny, brass "skeleton key" which the showman had inveigled from his famed escape artist, the Amazing Grimaldi, and which would—so the showman swore—ensure my entrance into the custodian's apartment, no matter how securely it was locked.

Having arrived at length at my destination, I paused for a moment to take stock of the building before me. It was a four-story, wooden tenement, indistinguishable in its overall air of dilapidation from the other ramshackle structures that lined the block. Ignoring the openly hostile glares of several formidable women with uncombed hair and tattered dresses who stood gossiping on the curb outside the building, I climbed the rickety stoop and stepped into the cramped, dismal entranceway.

Immediately, my olfactory senses were assaulted by the most disagreeable odors imaginable—a rancid mix of boiled cabbage, stale tobacco, and privy-smells. Grimacing at this *foetor,* I made my way up the murky staircase, each sagging, wooden step of which creaked loudly under my tread. At length, I arrived at the third floor. The hallway being shrouded in absolute gloom, I removed from my coat pocket one of the dozen phosphorous matches I had brought along for just such a contingency, and, after striking it, quickly located the apartment I was seeking—number 8. For a moment, I stood motionlessly outside the door, listening intently to the noises emanating from the other flats: the dismal wailing of babies—the thumping of footsteps in unseen rooms—the muffled curses of an inebriated woman, followed by the splintering of crockery.

Extracting the "skeleton key" provided by Barnum, I inserted it into the hole of the door-lock and turned it this way and that. Nothing happened. I cursed inwardly. In spite of the showman's assurances, I had remained unconvinced that this implement—secretly

employed by the Amazing Grimaldi in his seemingly miraculous escapes from padlocked containers, iron manacles, and other re-
straints—would prove to be an "open sesame" to Tomblin's residence.
Now, my misgivings appeared to have been borne out. I was on the
brink of abandoning my efforts, when I gave the key one last, decisive
twist—and the lock abruptly yielded with a loud click. Swiftly dousing my match (which had burned so low by this point that the tips of
my right thumb and forefinger had begun to smart from the flame), I
slipped inside and softly closed the door behind me.

A single inhalation was all that I needed to determine one fact
about Tomblin: however efficiently he might perform his janitorial
duties at work, his personal habits were of the most negligent sort.
The atmosphere within the apartment was, if anything, even more offensive than that of the hallway—strongly indicative of a tenant who
paid little heed to the benefits of regular house-cleaning, routine
bathing, or adequate ventilation. Intermingled with the miasmic smell
of mildew, dust, and human exudation were other, even more noxious
aromas, a full description of which I shall spare the reader.

Subduing the paroxysm of nausea that immediately seized me, I
extracted another of my matches, struck it, and held it aloft. The
sight thus revealed to me confirmed what I had already deduced from
my sense of olfaction. Even for a bachelor's quarters, devoid of the
holy influence of womanhood, the sheer squalor of the place was excessive.

Close to where I stood was a low-slung, single cot, its stained and
sagging mattress visible beneath a rumpled blanket and execrable
sheet. Filthy, evil-smelling clothing was strewn everywhere around the
uncarpeted floor. The peeling, ancient wallpaper was badly discolored
with mold; while the windowpanes were so thickly coated with grime
as to obviate the need for curtains.

In addition to the cot, the only other furnishings were a battered
oaken bureau that listed sharply to one side—a rickety chair—and a
small, square dining table, cluttered with dirty, unwashed crockery,
greasy utensils, and a chipped, earthenware platter holding the sod-
den fragments of a half-eaten meal. An oil lamp occupied one corner
of the table. Intending to ignite it, I took a step toward the table—

whereupon, a small army of cockroaches suddenly swarmed from the platter and scurried for cover, causing my heart to quail and my right hand to tremble so violently that my match was extinguished.

Quickly striking another one, I hurried over to the lamp—raised the glass chimney—and placed the wavering match-flame to the wick. The apartment being fully illuminated, I now perceived something that had previously been obscured. Suspended from a ceiling hook in a far corner of the room was a handsome gilt cage containing an unusually well-fed canary. The bird, which had evidently been asleep, now stirred and began to chitter excitedly. That Tomblin regarded this creature as his single most precious possession—and treated it with corresponding tenderness and care—was evident not only from its robust physical appearance, but from the condition of its cage, whose gilded bars shone with an immaculate purity that contrasted sharply with the surrounding squalor.

Having been assured by Barnum that the custodian would be absent for several hours (at least), I knew that I could proceed in my search without haste. Even so, I had no wish to linger within the oppressive confines of the apartment. Its intensely malodorous atmosphere had already begun to induce in me a vague but palpable sense of queasiness. Moreover—though prompted by the highest motives (i.e., the desire to bring a heinous killer to justice)—I could not help but feel exceedingly uneasy at committing what was, after all, an act of criminal trespass.

Impelled by these considerations, I therefore resolved to complete my errand without further delay. Fortunately, the apartment was so meagerly appointed that there were only a few places in which any incriminating evidence might be concealed. The bureau being the most obvious, I stepped directly to this tottering piece of furniture—pulled open each of the three drawers in succession—and made a thorough search of the contents.

For the most part, these consisted of a pitiful collection of work shirts, stockings, and underclothes, indistinguishable from the deplorable garments scattered everywhere on the bare wooden floor. At the bottom of the center drawer, however, I *did* make an unexpected discovery: a bone-handled hunting knife in a frayed leather sheath.

Removing this implement from its case, I noted that its long, serrated blade was discolored with a reddish-brown substance—though whether this was paint, rust, or blood it was impossible to say.

In the last drawer, I found something even more surprising—a large, burlap pouch, bulging with coins. Pulling open the draw-string and peering inside, I was startled to see that it was crammed with silver dollars—perhaps as many as a hundred! How the custodian had come by this fortune I could not begin to guess. Even in view of his obvious frugality, it seemed exceedingly unlikely that he could have managed to save so considerable a sum out of the modest wages he was undoubtedly paid by the pennywise showman. For many moments, I simply stared down at the glistening coins, mulling over this latest mystery.

At length, I restored the knife and money-sack to their respective places, then closed all three drawers and cast a look around me. From my present vantage point, the far side of Tomblin's bed was now clearly visible. Lying on the floor by the head of the cot was a small stack of newspapers. They were carelessly piled atop one another, and seemed to bulge in a peculiar way at the center.

Stepping toward the bed, I squatted on my haunches, removed the topmost paper from the stack, and perused its front page. What was my surprise to discover that it was the very issue of the *New York Herald* containing the engraved portrait of Isabel Somers which Tomblin had denied ever seeing! I quickly inspected the next newspaper, and the next. Each was a copy of a city gazette—the *Mirror*, the *Transcript*, the *Courier*, the *Sun*—devoted to the lurid details of the Somers crime.

Here, then, was definitive proof—as though any more were needed—that the custodian had been utterly lying to me. Even so, the mere presence of these newspapers indicated nothing about the custodian's possible involvement in the crime. From our interview with Opdyke, Barnum and I had already established that Tomblin was concealing some still-unexplained relationship with the slain woman. Under the circumstances, it was only to be expected that he would take a particularly keen interest in her brutal demise. In short, I had discovered nothing that I did not already know or suspect. Certainly

I was no closer than before to linking Tomblin directly with the murder.

I have previously mentioned that, instead of lying flat, the small stack of newspapers had a strange bulge at the center. Now, as I removed the last issue, I discovered the reason for this peculiarity. Concealed beneath the papers was a book. This in itself was somewhat surprising, since the enjoyment of literature did not appear to be a pastime of Tomblin's, whose apartment was otherwise devoid of reading matter.

Picking up this volume, I examined its exterior. Garishly bound in yellow cloth, it was of the most shoddy manufacture conceivable. I was puzzled to see that neither the title of the work nor the name of the author was stamped upon the cover. Frowning, I opened to the title page. *The Confessions of Mary Anne Temple*, it read. *Being the Private History of an Amorous and Lively Girl of Exquisite Beauty and Strong Natural Love of Pleasure! By the Author of "Fanny Greeley; or Memoirs of a Free-Love Sister" and "The Ladies' Garter."*

Instantly, my countenance was suffused with a hot flush of shame. That the volume I now held in my hands was of that sordid and licentious class of literature whose very existence is an affront to human decency there could be little doubt. Still, I could not be *absolutely* certain of this fact without investigating the matter more closely. Accordingly, I rose to my feet and carried the book over to the little table, where I might peruse it by the glow of the lamplight. I then seated myself upon the rickety chair and flipped the book open.

All at once, my eyes lit upon a passage so shameless—so salacious—so sheerly *obscene*—that I was shaken to the very core of my being. The narrator—evidently a young woman of the most hopelessly degraded character—was describing a visit from a male paramour named Pierre Duval. The passage in question, which I quote here *verbatim* solely in the interest of conveying its almost unimaginable lewdness, read as follows:

> As I reclined upon my velvet settee, my ripened form enshrouded in the light folds of a diaphanous night-robe, the bold Monsieur Duval kept his hungry gaze riveted upon the

soft, velvety orbs of my bosom. All at once, with a growl like
that of a wild jungle-beast, he sprang upon me, tore open my
garment, and—putting his lips to my rose-tipped hillocks—
caused me the most thrilling pleasures. I sank prostrate beneath him overpowered with delight, and, sighing deeply,
returned his passionate kisses. Let it not be supposed for an
instant that I was a mere passive instrument in his nimble
hands. No! I hugged and kissed him with a voluptuous eagerness that, when I once began, was carried to the extreme by my
uncontrollable passions!

As I sat there, reading and re-reading this passage and others of
an equally dissolute stamp, my feelings were of the most tumultuous
kind. My heart raced—my hands trembled—sweat burst from every
pore. At length, I slammed the vile book closed and—with an exclamation of disgust—hurled it across the room, where it hit the wall,
then landed on the floor beneath the dangling birdcage. For several
moments, I was incapable of coherent thought, so profoundly disconcerting was the effect of this outrageously prurient matter upon
my sensibilities. At length, my agitation having somewhat subsided, I
was able to refocus my mind upon the question of the custodian's
possible culpability.

It was, of course, an article of faith with me that a person's literary preferences bore no direct correlation to his actual behavior. A
saint might enjoy a respite from his life of stainless virtue by indulging in the titillating pleasures of a Gothic romance; while villains
of the deepest dye have been known to be assiduous readers of Scripture. My own tales of the grotesque and arabesque, after all, were
filled with every imaginable horror and atrocity, from bodily dismemberment to premature burial. And yet—except when provoked by the
libelous insults of one of the many talentless literary *poseurs* who
could find no other way of venting their envy than by attacking the
man of true genius—I was a person of the most amiable, easy-going,
and forbearing temperament.

That Tomblin enjoyed wallowing in the rankest imaginable
pornography could not, I therefore believed, be taken as evidence of

criminal behavior on his part. Even so, it was hard to avoid perceiving his taste for such odious fare as yet another dubious reflection on his character.

So absorbed was I in these reflections that I had become entirely oblivious of my surroundings. Now, as I removed my handkerchief from my pants pocket and dabbed the perspiration from my brow, my attention was suddenly riveted by a dim but distinct noise emanating from the hallway.

Someone was standing just outside the apartment door!

Instantly, I froze in place, my mind in a ferment. Had the custodian returned unexpectedly from his mission to Brooklyn? Moving with the greatest imaginable caution—so as not to cause the rickety chair to creak—I slowly bent forward in my seat, leaned over the lamp-chimney and, with a single, sharp exhalation, blew out the flame, plunging the room into darkness. Barely daring to breathe, I sat there in a state of rigid immobility, straining my auditory faculties to the utmost in an effort to hear what was taking place in the hallway.

One fact immediately became apparent: whoever was out there was, in fact, a man. I could hear him mumbling to himself in exasperation, like someone searching fruitlessly through his pockets for his door-key. Judging from its timbre, I also deduced that the voice belonged to a *big* man. More than that I could not say. Certainly, I could not identify the voice as belonging to Abel Tomblin—with whom, after all, I had only engaged in a single conversation.

As the moments passed by—oh, with what torturous slowness!—I clutched reflexively at the table. All at once, I felt something tickle the back of my right hand. Immediately, my blood ran cold, my nape-hairs stood erect, and my bosom heaved with the sudden onset of insufferable anxiety—for I knew at once what was causing this peculiar sensation.

Emboldened by the dousing of the lamplight, the odious vermin that had scattered at my first appearance had now reemerged from their hiding places. A cockroach was crawling over my hand!

As the reader will recall from my violent, initial reaction to the overgrown beetle in Barnum's office, I was afflicted with a morbid dread of certain members of the order *insecta*. So deep and instinctive was the revulsion aroused in me by the mere touch of the cockroach that all my efforts to maintain a stealthy silence were in vain. As the odious creature crept over my flesh, I leapt from my chair (which fell backward with a crash)—emitted a shriek of the purest terror—and shook my hand wildly, sending the loathsome insect flying into the air.

Trembling violently in every limb, I clamped both hands over my mouth to stifle the ragged, high-pitched whimpers issuing from my throat. But my presence had already been betrayed. Instantly, there came a loud, insistent knocking on the door, followed by the sound of a gruff male voice:

"Hey! What the hell's goin' on in there? Everything all right?"

My alarm at having been thus discovered was accompanied by a certain sense of relief. For, even with the blood pounding loudly in my ears, I could recognize that the voice was not Abel Tomblin's, but that of an entirely different man—presumably another tenant. Removing my hands from my mouth, I drew several deep breaths and exhaled them slowly until I felt calm enough to respond.

"I am perfectly fine," I called back, simulating, as best I could, the timbre of Tomblin's voice. "Thank you for your concern. It is, however, unnecessary for you to continue to linger outside my doorway."

My statement produced the desired effect, for—after muttering something unintelligible—the unseen individual shuffled across the landing, then made his way up the stairwell to the topmost floor. In another moment, I heard a door creak open, then slam shut overhead.

No sooner was I alone again than I reignited the lamp and made a hasty examination of the few remaining places in the apartment that remained to be searched. I peered under the sagging bed— groped beneath the odious mattress—poked through the piles of clothing that lay strewn upon the floor—and even rummaged in the pockets of the threadbare greatcoat that hung from a peg on the wall beside the doorway. My efforts, however, turned up nothing of relevance.

By now, my desire to flee the fulsome, vermin-infested apartment had reached a pitch of the highest intensity. Extinguishing the lamp, I dashed from the room—locked the door behind me—rushed down the three flights of stairs—and hurried into the street. For several moments, I merely stood on the sidewalk, drawing deep, grateful breaths of the acrid city air, which—however unwholesome in itself—seemed positively refreshing in comparison to the unbearable miasma of the custodian's living quarters.

At length, I turned away from the building and strode back in the direction from which I had come, ruminating on the significance of my discoveries. Though I had not established any *definitive* link between Tomblin and Miss Somers, my mission could not, I felt, be deemed a total failure. The mysterious sack of dollars that I had found inside his bureau hinted strongly at his involvement in some secret, if not illicit, enterprise. Moreover, my discovery of the obscene volume proved beyond a doubt that—in spite of Barnum's glowing testimonial to his employee's character—the custodian could in no respect be regarded as a paragon of morality.

As I bent my steps along the Bowery, I suddenly became sensible of how deeply I had been affected by the events of the evening. The inherent strain of my undertaking—combined with the turbulent feelings aroused in me by Tomblin's scandalous book and my intense, instinctive reaction to the loathsome touch of the cockroach—had left me in a state of extreme agitation. Under the circumstances, it seemed exceedingly unlikely that I would be able to enjoy the sweet nepenthe of slumber without some means of quieting my overwrought spirit.

In short, I was in desperate need of a drink.

As I had recently explained to the showman, my constitution was so finely organized that—to a far greater degree than the ordinary man—I was highly susceptible to the demoralizing effects of alcohol. As a result, I strove to maintain a consistent and rigorous temperance. On rare occasions, however—when suffering from a particularly incapacitating bout of nervous anxiety—I permitted myself to imbibe a moderate quantity of alcohol, strictly for its medicinal properties.

Having decided that the present was just such an occasion, I was now faced with the question of *where* to satisfy this need. My pecuniary circumstances being (as always) pitifully straitened, I could not afford to drink at one of the elegant "watering holes" of Broadway. The Bowery, of course, offered no paucity of cheap saloons. If anything, the problem here was avoiding one of the many squalid "dives" for which the neighborhood was infamous.

All at once, as I approached Chatham Square, I came upon a taproom that, from the outside, appeared altogether suitable. Its windows glowed with a warm, inviting light, and a convivial din issued forth from inside. As I drew nearer, the door swung open and a pair of perfectly respectable-looking, middle-aged gentlemen—their arms linked together and their faces flushed with merriment—stepped onto the street. Seeing me standing before the tavern, one of them held the door open for me. I thanked him for his courtesy and crossed inside.

No sooner had I entered, however, than I realized with a start that I had entirely misjudged the character of the place. Far from being the decent, if humble, drinking establishment that I had taken it for, it was a gin mill of the most infamous type. The chief item of furniture in the cramped and low-ceilinged room was a rough wooden counter, furnished with bottles of variously colored raw whiskey. A crowd of men, most of them clearly of the laboring classes, stood hunched at the counter, tossing down tumblers of the evil-looking drink, and occasionally leaning over to expectorate gobs of tobacco juice directly onto the floor-planks. A few fetid camphene lanterns, hanging at dreary intervals along the walls, exhaled a shower of lamp-black into the air. In addition to this noxious soot, the atmosphere seemed largely composed of the reek of unwashed bodies, commingled with the smoke of cheap cigars. Above the raucous din of voices could be heard a shrill, discordant sound, produced by a pair of purported musicians who sat in a corner of the room, one scraping on a villainous fiddle, the other punishing a rheumatic piano.

For several moments, I stood in the doorway, taking in this deplorable scene. I could only infer that the two respectable-looking fellows I had seen emerging from this den of infamy belonged to that peculiar class of men who enjoy a perverse titillation from "rubbing elbows" on occasion with the most dissolute and abandoned elements of society. As I had no desire to emulate their example, I made ready to leave.

All at once, however, I was possessed with the singular conviction that someone was staring at me. Glancing around, I saw a trio of exceedingly rough-looking individuals occupying a small table in a far corner of the room. One of them was fixing me with a look of such pure, undisguised animosity that the blood in my veins instantly turned to ice.

A gasp of sheer, horrified bewilderment escaped my lips. Turning on my heels, I dashed from the barroom and did not slacken my pace until I had reached the relative safety of Broadway.

The fellow who had been glaring at me with such intense—such *venomous*—hatred was none other than Abel Tomblin.

CHAPTER TWENTY-TWO

During our planning of my mission, Barnum had suggested that—once my search of Tomblin's apartment was completed—I remain overnight in the city. "Heaven knows how late it will be by then," the showman had observed. "Midnight, for all we know. Maybe later. Mighty dreary hour to be driving all the way back up to the country."

Though reluctant to be separated from my loved ones, even for the span of a single night, I had recognized the wisdom of this proposal. Accordingly, I had allowed him to secure a suite for me at the Astor House, located only a short distance from the museum on Broadway. It was to this celebrated hostelry that I now bent my steps, casting frequent, nervous glances behind me to make sure that I was not being pursued by the custodian. Arriving safely at the imposing, granite-walled establishment, I hurried inside its magnificent lobby and quickly made my way upstairs to my third-story rooms.

In regard to the sheer luxury of its accommodations, the Astor House easily rivaled—and, indeed, in many ways surpassed—the finest hotels of London and Paris, offering every imaginable amenity for the comfort of its guests. I was in no condition, however, to appreciate the elegant appointments of my suite—the trying experiences of the evening having reduced me to a state of excessive bodily and mental fatigue.

Hurrying into the bedroom, I threw off my garments—pulled

back the sumptuous bedclothes—and flung myself onto the wonderfully soft, commodious mattress. For many minutes, I lay in the dark, reflecting on the startling coincidence that had just occurred. How was it that—out of all the saloons I might have conceivably chosen—I had picked the very one where the custodian sat drinking? Given the inordinate variety of drinking establishments to be found along the Bowery, I could not help but feel that something more than mere chance was involved in my seemingly random decision—something akin to the workings of *Fate*. Moreover, Tomblin's very presence in the neighborhood at that hour was deeply perplexing. Had his errand to Brooklyn been abandoned for some reason? Or had it, on the contrary, been so expeditiously concluded that he had been able to return to his home territory at a much earlier time than anticipated? I was at a loss to answer these questions at present. This inability, however, did not prevent me from revolving them, over and over again, in my mind.

At length, I fell into a profound, if exceedingly troubled, slumber. My dreams were of the most unsettling—the most *harrowing*—sort, populated by a host of wildly deformed and freakish beings. Some of these fell into that teratological category technically known as *monstres par défault:* writhing, limbless humans with serpentine torsos and the anguished faces of the damned. Others, by contrast, were *monstres par excès:* women with a dozen, tentacular arms—men with multiple heads sprouting from their shoulders—and mere babes sporting supernumerary eyes in the center of their foreheads.

Still others were grotesque beings whose anomalous physiques combined both human and bestial features. Foremost among the latter was a gigantic, apelike creature whose thickly muscled body was entirely covered in coarse, yellow fur. He was crouching by the prostrate body of a white-clad, young woman. All at once, this half-human monstrosity raised its head—looked directly at me—and grinned with a fiendish delight. Aghast, I saw that its mouth was slathered in blood, and that it had been battening upon the throat of the lifeless young woman, whose face—I now perceived to my inexpressible horror—was that of my own dearest Sissy!

Awakening with a groan, I sat bolt upright in bed and glanced wildly around me, uncertain as to my whereabouts. By slow degrees my confusion ebbed, and I grew sensible of my surroundings. A feeling of the deepest relief suffused my bosom as I realized that the ghastly vision of my poor, slaughtered wife was naught but a hideous nightmare.

With a sob of gratitude, I rose from my bed—staggered to the ornate washstand—and performed my morning ablutions. After donning my garments, I strode to the window and drew back the curtains of rich crimson silk. From the sheer brilliance of the sunlight that instantly flooded the room, I deduced that the morning was already well advanced—an inference reinforced by the acute hunger-pangs in the pit of my stomach of which I had suddenly become all-too-painfully aware.

Departing from my suite, I made my way downstairs and inquired the time of the somewhat officious young desk clerk. What was my surprise to discover that it was already nearly half-past noon! Ignoring the audible growls emanating from my abdominal region, I hurried out onto the bustling sidewalk, carefully made my way across the traffic-clogged street, and approached the main entrance of the museum.

As usual, the ticket booth was manned by Barnum's cheerful living skeleton, Slim Jim McCormack, who was outfitted in his customary pair of tight-fitting red "long johns."

"Morning, Mr. Poe," he croaked. "Or 'good afternoon,' I suppose I should say. Mr. B told me to keep an eye out for you. Wants you to meet him upstairs in the menagerie storeroom. You'll find it way back of the hall. Door marked 'No Entrance.' Just knock twice and sing out your name."

With an acknowledging nod, I turned toward the doorway. All at once, I was struck by a thought. Pausing at the threshold, I looked back at the cadaverous fellow and addressed him thusly: "Tell me, Slim Jim, have you seen Mr. Tomblin today?"

Arranging his mouth into an exaggerated frown, McCormack raised his right hand to his exceedingly narrow countenance and thoughtfully stroked his long, pointy chin. So entirely devoid of flesh were his fingers that each separate phalangeal bone was clearly visible beneath the tight-drawn, nearly translucent skin.

"No sir," he answered. "Don't believe I have. Been sitting here all morning, too. Reckon ol' Abel has took the day off."

This intelligence could hardly fail to please me. I was eager to avoid a confrontation with the custodian, and his apparent absence meant that I could move freely about the museum without anxiety. Thanking the skeletal ticket-seller, I entered the museum and proceeded to make my way up the crowded main staircase to the third floor, where the menagerie was located.

Barnum's impressive zoological collection never failed to attract a large crowd of visitors, who—in their eagerness to view such exotic specimens as his Royal Bengal Tiger, White Himalayan Mountain Bear, Silver-striped Hyena, and Double-Humpbacked Bactrian Camel—did not seem to mind the intense barnyard aroma that pervaded the cavernous hall. Following the directions of Slim Jim, I pressed my way through the crowd toward the rear of the gallery, where the single most popular display in the entire menagerie was located. This was Barnum's so-called "Happy Family": a wildly heterodox assortment of creatures, both predators and prey, living together in a manner suggestive of Edward Hicks's much-beloved painting, *The Peaceable Kingdom.* Here—though the viewer might not behold the proverbial "lion dwelling with the lamb"—he would nevertheless be treated to the remarkable sight of cats and rats, owls and mice, eagles and rabbits, hawks and small birds, and other natural enemies all peacefully coexisting within the confines of a single cage.

I worked my way around the throng of people clustered about this singular attraction until I found the door that Slim Jim had indicated, and announced my presence with several sharp raps. A moment later, a voice—which I recognized at once as Barnum's—called out from the other side: "Who's there?"

"It is I," I replied. "Edgar Poe."

Instantly the door sprang open, a thick hand emerged, and I was yanked unceremoniously inside.

As the door slammed shut behind me, I cast my gaze about. The room in which I now found myself was lined with cages of varying sizes in which Barnum housed his surplus creatures—llamas and leopards, monkeys and mountain goats, porcupines and pumas, and dozens more. Large, barred windows placed at regular intervals along the walls provided the necessary sunlight—and the even more essential ventilation.

Turning to look at Barnum, I saw that his countenance was permeated with an expression of the most intense excitement. His eyes gleamed, his roseate cheeks were even more deeply flushed than usual, and his mouth was wrought into a look of barely suppressed elation, as though he were strenuously resisting the impulse to burst out with a loud, celebratory cheer.

"Where have you been, m'boy? I've been waiting all morning for you to show up!"

I began to explain the reason for my lateness, commencing with the anxious events of the preceding evening, which had left me so physically and emotionally depleted. Before I could complete my first sentence, however, Barnum cut me off with an impatient wave of his hand.

"Yes, yes, of course, I'm eager to hear all about it—down to the very last detail," he said. "But not right at this moment. There's something I want to show you first. Here, come this way."

Taking me by the arm, he led me across the storeroom. A large object—which, from both its size and shape, I deduced to be yet another animal cage—stood at the far end. I could not identify it with absolute certainty, however, as it was completely hidden beneath a heavy, canvas tarpaulin.

Positioning me directly before this mysterious object, Barnum stepped to its side—stooped—and grasped one corner of the tarpaulin in his right hand. He then straightened up and addressed me thusly:

"Brace yourself, m'boy. Get a good grip on your breath. You're about to witness the most staggering sight ever viewed by mortal man. The greatest marvel in all creation! The eighth wonder of the world! Behold"—and here, with a mighty tug, he pulled the tarpaulin from its place, revealing the object underneath—"the Giant Sacred Beetle of Lost Atlantis!"

A gasp of the utmost astonishment escaped my lips as I stared at the extraordinary—the nearly *incredible*—sight that now stood exposed before me. The tarpaulin had indeed covered an iron cage, one of such capacious size that it could easily have accommodated a member of the species *Hippopotamus amphibius*. The creature it contained, however, was not anything as prosaic as a mere pachyderm. It was an insect identical in nearly all respects to the grotesquely oversized *Necrophorus* beetle I had recently viewed in Barnum's office. I stress the word "nearly" because there were two highly significant ways in which it differed from its predecessor. First, it was at least twice as large, measuring approximately six feet long by three feet wide.

Second, and even more startling—it was alive! Its feathery, red-tipped antennae—so large that they resembled the plumes of an ostrich's tail—twitched spasmodically; its ferocious-looking mandibles opened and closed like a giant pair of blacksmith's tongs; its fat, segmented abdomen wriggled and pulsed.

Of such stupendous—such *colossal*—size was the creature that, even in a cage big enough to hold a hippo, there was little room for it to move. It hunkered on its belly, its six legs scraping angrily on the hay-strewn floor, its vibrating, vermillion-tipped wings giving off a low, angry buzz, or hum. I could see at a glance there was no possibility of its breaking free of its prison. The bars of the cage were of the stoutest iron, and so closely spaced together that the massive beetle could not conceivably squeeze through the gaps. Even so, the mere proximity of such a monster caused my heart to quail and the blood to congeal in my veins. Instinctively, I retreated several paces from the cage, while a shudder of the deepest revulsion coursed through my frame.

The showman, who had been watching me narrowly while I scrutinized his amazing acquisition, now stepped to my side, threw one arm about my shoulders, and declared: "I ask you, Poe—was I exaggerating? Why, it's the most astonishing thing that ever crawled, swam, or soared through the heavens! The public will go absolutely *wild* over it. The gold will be *cascading* in, I tell you—riches that'll make the mines of Golconda look like a dried-up coal shaft! Why, if John Jacob Astor himself showed up and offered me his entire fortune in exchange for this beauty, I'd turn him down in a flash!"

"Permit me to congratulate you," I said, mustering whatever enthusiasm I could. "It is indeed a most remarkable creature."

"*Remarkable?*" scoffed the showman. "Ha! The word doesn't do it justice! The press will have to come up with a whole barrel of new superlatives once P. T. Barnum's latest sensation is revealed to the world!"

"I take it, then," I said, "that last night's expedition went precisely as planned."

"Lord, yes," said Barnum. "It was a glorious success! Even Charlie McDougall and Abel were surprised at how smoothly things went. They lured the critter out of hiding with a big slab of horse meat they'd brought along as bait. Then—bam!—tossed a big net over it, wrestled it into a specially built wooden crate, and hauled it straight back home. Showed up before the museum even closed! You can imagine how I felt when I saw it. Why, I haven't been that excited since I first set eyes on the Feejee Mermaid!

"Even so," he continued, "I was mighty anxious on your account, Poe, m'boy. Did my damnedest to stall Abel for as long as I could. But after a while, he just picked himself up and headed for home."

One mystery, at least, had thus been resolved—to wit, how Tomblin had come to be back on the Bowery at such an unexpectedly early hour the preceding night.

"In regard to the custodian," I said, "I have much to communicate to you concerning my search of his abode. May I suggest that we retire to your office without further delay?"

In truth, my eagerness to depart from the storeroom was motivated, less by an urgent need to apprise Barnum of the results of my investigation, than by a desperate desire to get away from the gigantic insect. The sheer, appalling size of the monstrous beetle was beginning to overwhelm me—to take a heavy toll upon my already overstrung nerves. I felt slightly faint—a condition exacerbated by my extreme state of hunger (for it had now been nearly twenty-four hours since any form of sustenance had last passed my lips).

Something in either my tone of voice or facial expression must have alerted Barnum to this fact, for—regarding me with a look of the deepest solicitude—he declared: "Yes, yes, of course, m'boy. My apologies. In my excitement over the beast, I'd clean forgotten about your own sensitivities. Come along now, come along. We'll head down to the basement and have ourselves a powwow. I'm bursting at the seams to hear every detail of your adventures."

After calling a fond farewell to the colossal, caged insect—as though the six-legged monster were a much-beloved pet—Barnum led me from the storeroom and out into the menagerie. As we began to make our way across the densely packed hall, the showman was immediately recognized by various members of the crowd, who greeted him with cheers and exclamations, insisted on shaking his hand, and even held up their children in their arms, so that the little ones might get a better view of the great man himself. Beaming with satisfaction, Barnum lingered to bask in the adulation of the crowd, dispensing handshakes, autographs, and discount coupons by the dozen, and repeatedly declaring that—as the humble servant of the great American public—his only desire was to provide them with the grandest, most spectacular entertainment on the face of the earth.

By the time we arrived at the basement, a full twenty minutes had elapsed since we had departed from the storeroom. Unlocking the door to his office, Barnum stepped inside. I was just about to follow him across the threshold when I paused at a sudden, unexpected sound. Someone had just descended the stairwell and was now approaching rapidly along the corridor. Turning, I saw a tall, broad-shouldered figure stride purposefully in our direction.

"It appears that we have a visitor," I said to Barnum, who came immediately to the doorway and peered outside.

A moment later, the stranger came to a halt before us. He was a ruddy-faced fellow with eyes of the palest blue and thick, mutton-chop whiskers. When he spoke, I could not help notice that his teeth were in the most deplorable condition imaginable, appearing to be covered with a thick, greenish substance, like tree moss.

"You're Barnum, right?" he asked the showman in a harsh, gravelly voice.

"Indeed I am," said the latter. "And you are—?"

"Constable Marcus Hayes," the fellow said brusquely. Then, turning to me, he added: "You must be Poe."

"Why yes," I exclaimed in surprise. "How on earth did you deduce *that?*"

"They told me I'd you find you here. You're the one I'm looking for."

"Me?" I exclaimed, suddenly seized with a sense of the deepest apprehension.

"Yeah," said the gruff-voiced fellow. "You'd better head on home. There's been a murder."

This dread—this *appalling*—announcement struck me with the shock of a galvanic battery. "Murder!" I gasped. "But who—how—?"

"Don't know much more about it," said the constable with a shrug. "Someone's been killed, that's all I been told. A young woman."

"A young woman!" I cried. "You cannot mean—it cannot be—"

My wife, I intended to say. The words, however, refused to emerge from my throat. My brain swam—I grew deadly sick—I felt the strength drain from my limbs.

I did not, however, succumb to insensibility. Exerting my will to the utmost, I fought back the black tide of oblivion that threatened to engulf me—turned to the showman—clutched him by the arm—and cried: "For the love of God, my friend! Let us be off at once!"

CHAPTER TWENTY-THREE

Few things in life are more difficult—more productive of the extremes of mental and emotional distress—than to be reduced to a state of helpless passivity during a crisis. When that crisis involves an endangered loved one the situation becomes even harder to bear, progressing from the merely painful to the actively intolerable.

This was the exceptionally trying—if not *torturous*—circumstance in which I now found myself.

No sooner had Constable Hayes delivered his alarming intelligence than the three of us hurried out onto Broadway, where the showman had quickly flagged down a cab, offering the driver a bonus of five dollars above his ordinary fare to convey us uptown with the greatest possible dispatch. To avoid slowing down the vehicle with extraneous weight, the burly police officer—who had been officially detailed to the investigation and wished to accompany us to the crime scene—agreed to ride separately on horseback.

In spite of the great velocity at which our vehicle traveled, the trip up to Eighty-fourth Street seemed interminable. Never, surely, was there a more excruciating state of anxiety and suspense. For the duration of the journey, I sat huddled on the seat of the violently bouncing carriage, silently gnawing on the nail of my left thumb, while exerting every shred of willpower to prevent myself from imagining the worst. Even the normally voluble showman spoke not a word. Seated beside me, his countenance furrowed with concern, he occasionally reached out a hand and patted me comfortingly on the knee, as if to say: "There, there, m'boy. Don't succumb to despair. Things may yet turn out to be less calamitous than you fear."

At length, we reached the rutted dirt path leading from Bloomingdale Road to the Brennan farmstead. As our carriage drew closer to our cottage, I leaned my head out the window and saw a sight that filled me with inexpressible dread.

Gathered in our front yard was a small crowd of men, perhaps a dozen in all. Some of these I recognized at once as neighbors of the Brennans. Others, unfamiliar to me, appeared to be members of the local constabulary. Several of the latter were moving slowly about the yard, their eyes riveted on the ground, as though searching for clues. The countenance of every man present was taut with a mixture of sorrow, indignation, and grim determination.

Lying in the grass at the center of this somber congregation was the motionless form of a young woman. From my elevated vantage point in the seat of the approaching cab, I could see that the bosom of her white dress was drenched in red, as though someone had hurled an entire bucketful of crimson paint directly at her breast. Her head was bent at such a grotesque and ghastly angle that I could not perceive her features. In the glare of the noonday sunlight, however, I saw that her hair was a delicate shade of auburn—the same color as the incomparably lovely tresses of my darling Sissy!

The intensity of the anguish which possessed me at that instant is folly to attempt describing. Before the cab had even drawn to a halt, I had thrown open the door—leapt to the ground—and dashed wildly toward the lifeless figure sprawled on the grass. At my approach, several of the men turned in surprise. Strong hands gripped me, as though to prevent me from getting too close to the body.

"Let me through!" I exclaimed with a sob. "I am Mr. Poe—the husband of this poor, horribly butchered young woman."

Even as I struggled with my captors, I gazed in horror at the figure in the grass. The gore that imbrued the front of her garment, I now perceived, had come from a fearful wound to her throat, which had been so dreadfully mutilated that the corpse's head seemed attached to the body by a few mere filaments of flesh. Both hands were missing, her wide-flung arms terminating in ghastly, blood-caked stumps. Though her features, as I have said, were turned away from me, I could see—protruding upward from what was clearly the lower portion of her face—the clipped end of a flower stem.

A shriek of the purest anguish arose in my throat. Before it could burst forth from my lips, however, my gaze lighted upon something which I had not noticed until that moment. Visible beneath the hem of her dress were the lower extremities of the poor victim. I now perceived that her right foot was shod in a grotesquely oversized shoe of the sort required by those suffering from the anomalous condition, *talipes equinovarus.*

The dreadfully slaughtered young woman was club-footed!

Tearing myself free of those who sought to constrain me, I stumbled forward and dropped to my knees in front of the corpse. I was now in a position to view the features of the victim, whose identity, of course, I had already surmised. With tears welling up in my eyes, I looked upon the sweetly familiar countenance of Miss Anna Louise Brennan, now contorted into an expression of extreme—of unendurable—torment. Her glazed eyes bulged from their sockets—her mouth was twisted into an agonized grimace—and her square, perfectly white teeth were clamped around the killer's bizarre and inexplicable trademark: a long-stemmed, crimson rose.

A wave of heartsickness overcame me as I gazed upon the doleful sight. It would be disingenuous of me, however, to pretend that this was my only response; for—commingled with my sorrow, horror, and pity—was an entirely different emotion: a palpable sense of relief at the discovery that the victim was not my own precious wife.

As I stood erect, a strong hand was laid upon my shoulder. Turning, I saw that it belonged to the showman, who had come up behind me, and was now staring in horror at the hideously mutilated corpse at our feet.

"Bless my soul," he gasped. "What a gruesome sight. But look!—it's not your little woman after all!"

"No," I replied. "It is our landlord's niece, Miss Brennan—a thoroughly admirable young woman with whom my darling Sissy had formed an immediate and inseparable friendship."

"Dreadful, perfectly dreadful," said Barnum, shaking his head. "I tell you, Poe, it makes me think the Spanish Inquisition wasn't such a bad idea after all. Why, mere hanging's too good for the fiend who did this! He should be flayed, quartered, and boiled in oil!"

"He must be apprehended first," I remarked. "And the sooner the better, for it appears that he has now turned his malignant attention on those nearest to me."

"Don't worry, m'boy. We'll nab him," said Barnum. "But tell me—where *are* your dear wife and auntie?"

"Yonder in the house," someone croaked in reply. Swiveling, I saw that the comment had come from an elderly farmer named Hawkins, a neighbor of the Brennans, who—standing a few feet away among a small group of onlookers—had overheard Barnum's query. "Your womenfolk is all right, Mr. Poe. Leastways, they ain't hurt none."

"And where are Mr. and Mrs. Brennan?" I inquired.

"Holed up back home," he said, pointing his white-stubbled chin at the handsome farmhouse visible across the broad expanse of meadow. "They're mighty broke up over the poor gal. Doc Phillips is up there right now, tendin' to the missus."

I turned back to the showman and said: "I must go see my dear ones at once."

"Go ahead, m'boy, go right ahead," he replied, patting me on the back. "I'll remain out here and see what I can find out."

I cast a last, mournful glance at the horribly mangled corpse that had so recently been the mortal habitation of a mind and a spirit of singular vivacity. Then—after uttering a silent prayer on behalf of her Heaven-bound soul—I turned, hurried up the steps of our front porch, and burst into the cottage.

I found my two loved ones in the parlor, seated side by side on the sofa. My dear aunt's fleshy right arm encircled the frail shoulders of my wife, whose face was buried in her mother's bosom. A few, weak, muffled sobs shook Sissy's delicate frame, as though she had wept herself into a state of near-exhaustion. All at once, as I stepped toward the sofa, she glanced up at me with a stricken expression— sprang to her feet—and threw herself into my arms.

"Oh, Eddie," she cried. "Did you see poor Anna Louise? It's simply too horrible to bear!" And so saying, she lay her head against my chest and burst into clamorous tears.

"There, there, my sweetest," I said, my heart replete with pity to see my darling so overcome with sorrow. "Grieve not for your friend. She has gone to that empyrean where supernal beauty dwells."

"But why—*why*—would anyone want to harm her?" Sissy wailed. "She was the kindest, sweetest creature who ever lived!"

"It is a mystery all insoluble," I said gravely. "Evil abounds in this harsh—this *care-laden*—world of ours. And the pure, the good, the innocent are its most cherished prey. For His own unfathomable reasons, God wishes it to be so.

"But come, dear Sissy," I continued with a sigh. "You must try to rest. I fear that you will make yourself ill."

Leading my darling wifey into her room, I helped her settle into bed. "Close your eyes, sweet one," I said. "Muddy and I will be right outside, in the parlor." Then—after placing a tender kiss upon her alabaster brow—I turned and left the room, softly closing the door behind me.

I found Muddy where I had left her—seated on the sofa, her normally ruddy complexion now ashen with distress. From the crimson hue of her eyes, I could see that she, like Sissy, had given way to ungovernable grief.

As I lowered myself onto the cushion beside her, she reached out and clutched me by the hand.

"Thank God you're here, Eddie," she said hoarsely. "It's been the very worst morning of my life."

Giving her chapped hand a reassuring pat, I said: "Tell me, Muddy, precisely what transpired here."

"Very well," she said in a tremulous voice. "Poor Anna Louise was here for supper last night. Before leaving, she promised to return bright and early, so that she and Sissy could go berry-picking. I intended to make my special blackberry cobbler, the one you are so partial to."

"Indeed," I said with a gentle smile, "it is a particular favorite of mine."

"Well, this morning," continued Muddy, "I slept much later than usual. You know me, Eddie—I'm a regular early bird. But I had such a terrible time falling asleep last night. I just couldn't stop fretting about *you*, dearest boy—all this worrisome business you've been up to with Mr. Barnum, investigating murders and whatnot. Finally, I fixed myself a nice glass of hot milk and managed to doze off.

"I was awakened by a fearful scream. I sat bolt upright in bed, terribly confused. It felt like only minutes since I had fallen asleep, but I saw at once that the morning had come, for the room was bathed in sunlight. I listened with all my might, but I could hear nothing. For a moment, I thought I must have been dreaming. But then I *did* hear something—a man's voice crying, 'Hi! Giddup!' and the sound of pounding hoofbeats, disappearing into the distance.

"I leapt from bed and dashed out onto the front porch. That's when I saw the poor child, awash in her own blood like a butchered lamb."

Here, Muddy's voice faltered, and she was obliged to pause for several moments until she had regained her composure. At length, she drew a deep, ragged breath and continued thusly:

"It was all I could do to keep from fainting. I must have let out a terrible scream, because young Thomas Hawkins—Mr. Hawkins's grandson, who was walking down Bloomingdale Road—came dashing over. He was the one I sent to inform poor Mr. and Mrs. Brennan. I understand that he was later dispatched to the city on horseback to notify the police."

"And what of Sissy?"

"My scream must have awakened her, too," Muddy answered. "Before I knew she was even there, she had come running out onto the porch. I tried to prevent her from looking at the horrid sight, but it was too late."

For several moments, I merely stared at the floor, pondering Muddy's story in silence.

"Was there anything else you heard or saw?" I asked at length. "Anything that might assist us in identifying the perpetrator of this heinous—this *unspeakable*—atrocity?"

Muddy shook her head sadly. Then gazing at me intently with her red-rimmed eyes, she said: "Tell me truthfully, Eddie—it was *he* who did this, wasn't it? The monster you and Mr. Barnum have been seeking."

"So it would appear," I grimly acknowledged.

"But why, oh why, would he want to harm poor Anna Louise? The sweet, dear child didn't have a dislikable bone in her body."

A candid answer to this question would have caused my darling Muddy the greatest possible dismay. I therefore made no reply. My effort to protect her from the truth, however, was futile. So closely bound was my own soul to that of the dear, maternal creature that she often appeared capable of reading my very thoughts.

So it proved on this occasion. All at once, her eyes grew wide, her mouth fell open, and—placing a hand to her mouth—she gasped: "Oh no! It wasn't poor Anna Louise that he was after, was it? It was . . . Sissy!"

Reaching out both hands, I clutched her by the shoulders and exclaimed: "Do not fear, Muddy. I promise you that no harm will come to her. Prudence dictates, however, that certain precautions be taken. It will no longer do for you and Sissy to remain here in the country. The very attribute that has made our little cottage so delightfully appealing—its isolation from the hurly-burly of the city—has now become its greatest disadvantage. Barnum has secured a suite of rooms for me at the Astor House that can serve as a temporary lodging for the three of us."

Rising from the sofa, I continued thusly: "I will go inform the showman of my plans. In the meantime, you must pack a bag of belongings for yourself and Sissy." Then, after bending down to bestow a reassuring kiss upon the good woman's broad, deeply wrinkled brow, I hurried from the parlor and outside onto the porch.

I immediately observed Barnum standing several yards away among a small group of men whose number included the newly arrived Constable Hayes. One of the bunch—a short, squat fellow wearing the distinctive garb of a city marshal—was holding out something in his right hand, which the others were inspecting closely.

Approaching this assemblage, I came to a halt beside Barnum and stared down at the object in the marshal's extended palm. It was a grass-stained pouch of Red Horse chewing tobacco, decorated with the distinctive trademark of a prancing, crimson-hued steed.

As I scrutinized this article, Barnum suddenly became aware of my presence. "Ah, there you are, Poe," he said, turning to face me. His countenance, I observed, was clouded with worry.

"Tell me, m'boy," he continued. "This tobacco isn't yours, is it?"

"Certainly not," I replied. "Indeed, I am somewhat surprised at your question. To a person of fastidious habits—such as you know me to be—the practice of 'chewing and spitting' is the most vulgar, if not *repulsive*, of all addictive vices."

"Yes, of course, just double-checking," Barnum said with a sigh. "Marshal Comstock found this pouch lying in the grass, not far from the poor victim's body."

"Perhaps, then," I proposed, "it fell from the killer's pocket during the perpetration of the atrocity."

"That's our notion, too," Barnum said, sounding strangely troubled. For a moment, he remained silent, seemingly lost in thought, his gaze directed downward. At length, he looked up at me again and inquired after Sissy and Muddy.

"They are doing as well as can be expected under these exceptionally difficult, if not appalling, circumstances," I replied. Then, drawing him aside, I explained my plan to convey my loved ones to the city.

"Sensible, very sensible," Barnum said when I was finished. "You go on ahead and take the cab, m'boy. Don't worry about me—I'll make my way back all right. I'll get word to you just as soon as I arrive."

Acceding to this suggestion, I took leave of the showman and hurried back into the cottage. I found Muddy in Sissy's bedroom, packing a carpetbag with various articles of my wife's clothing. Sissy herself lay on her side in bed. Though a blanket concealed her body from the shoulders down, I could see that she had arranged herself into the same position that an unborn child assumes within its mother's womb: back hunched, knees drawn up to her chest, clasped hands pressed to her chin.

Retreating to the kitchen, I took a moment to fortify myself with some desperately needed sustenance: an apple, a large slice of cheese, a piece of brown bread, and a glass of milk. Feeling much refreshed, I then returned to Sissy's room, helped her to her feet, and led her out to the waiting cab. Muddy followed close behind with the carpetbag in one hand and, in the other, a small, ventilated box holding our family's beloved feline, Cattarina.

As we approached the vehicle, I glanced over and saw that several more people had now appeared on the scene and were gathered around the cadaver. Several of these men were obviously newspaper reporters, who were scribbling furiously in their notepads. Another of the new arrivals—an elderly gentleman dressed in a somewhat thread-bare brown coat—was kneeling beside the body, scrutinizing it with an expression of professional detachment. I took him to be the coroner's physician, there to conduct the postmortem examination.

During our ride back into the city, the atmosphere within our carriage was somber in the extreme. Sissy sat mutely between Muddy and me, her head upon my shoulder. From time to time, she would shiver uncontrollably, and a rivulet of tears would trickle down her drawn, exceedingly pallid face.

When Muddy was not tending solicitously to her daughter—softly stroking her hair, or gently drying her cheeks with a handkerchief, or carefully arranging the plaid, woolen traveler's blanket over her lap—she stared sadly out the window, emitting an occasional heartbroken sigh that seemed to emanate from the very core of her soul.

For the most part, I said nothing, my own thoughts being entirely preoccupied with the urgent matters raised by that morning's dire developments. There was little or no doubt in my mind that the motive behind the atrocity was a desire to inflict the gravest possible wound upon *me*. What better way to do so than by harming the person dearer to me than my own life? That Sissy had been the intended target of the fiendish assassin I was firmly convinced. Only the chance appearance of poor Anna Louise Brennan—whom the madman evidently mistook for my own darling wife—had spared her from the appalling fate that befell her innocent friend.

Was Barnum's custodian, then, the likely perpetrator of this heinous deed? That the murder had followed so closely on the heels of my encounter with Tomblin seemed suspicious, to say the least. On the other hand, Morris Vanderhorn's remorseless aide-de-camp, Croley, could not be entirely ruled out as a suspect. If Barnum's theory about young Frankie Plunkitt were correct—i.e., that the lad had been viciously murdered at Vanderhorn's behest—it was not inconceivable that this latest atrocity had been committed out of similarly vindictive motives.

There was, of course, a third possibility as well: that the culprit was neither Tomblin nor Croley but some still-unknown party. Whoever the killer might be, one fact was appallingly clear: the package he had previously sent me—containing the amputated left hand of Isabel Somers—had been meant, not merely as a vicious taunt, but as a *threat*. And that threat had now been all-too-horribly fulfilled.

CHAPTER TWENTY-FOUR

Having arrived at length at our destination, I climbed from the carriage, then helped Sissy and Muddy onto the sidewalk. Even in their stricken state they could not help but gape in wonder at the magnificent granite façade of the Astor House. Carrying the carpetbag, I ushered them inside the lobby and upstairs to my suite.

Having settled my little wifey in bed, I consulted with Muddy in the sitting room. Deeply concerned over Sissy's ever-fragile health, we decided that I should obtain some soothing medication that would help the dear, overwrought child sleep more peacefully. I therefore headed back outside and proceeded to the same small but well-stocked pharmacy on Greenwich Street that I had patronized several months earlier, shortly after our arrival in the city. I was briefly tempted to purchase another bottle of Mayhew's Miracle Cold Remedy, which had produced such immediate, soporific effects upon both Sissy and myself. Recalling Barnum's derisive opinion of this popular tonic as a mere concoction of hard liquor and pseudo-medicinal flavorings, however, I settled on a bottle of laudanum.

I took some time on the way back to purchase a pint of ripe strawberries from one of the many sidewalk "patterers" peddling their wares on Broadway. This small treat was intended to help lift the spirits of my loved ones, both of whom were exceedingly fond of this particular fruit.

Returning to our suite with my purchases, I threw open the door and entered the sitting room. What was my surprise to see—occupying the entire expanse of the elegant, Chippendale settee—the colossal figure of Willie Schnitzler!

"Mr. Poe," she exclaimed, rising to her feet and coming toward me with outstretched arms. "I'm so sorry to hear about your friend."

Before I could respond, she enveloped me in her arms and hugged me to her body. Though touched by the simple, spontaneous warmth of this gesture, I was somewhat disconcerted to find myself thus embraced, with my face tightly pressed against her coarse, bosom-length beard.

"Your condolences are deeply appreciated, Willie," I said, freeing myself from her hold and taking a step backward. "But what, pray tell, has brought you here?"

"Mr. B sent me to fetch you," she replied. "He's just back from your farm." She clucked her tongue and shook her massive head slowly. "He told me what happened up there. Dreadful, just dreadful. Why, I was chatting with that poor girl just the other day, when they visited the museum—her and your pretty little wife, and your auntie. Couldn't ask for a nicer person. Tell me, Mr. Poe," she continued with a catch in her voice. "Who in the world would do such a horrible thing to a sweet, harmless creature like that?"

"That is the question Mr. Barnum and I are so urgently endeavoring to answer," I solemnly replied. "And now, Willie, you must excuse me. I must tend to my wife before going to meet with your employer."

"Please tell her that I'd love to say hello," said Willie. "Maybe help cheer her up a bit. But only if she's feeling up to it."

Acknowledging this gracious offer with a nod, I turned and entered the bedroom. I found Muddy perched on the mattress beside Sissy, who lay with her head cushioned on the voluminous down pillow, her pallid face framed by her rich, auburn tresses, her luminous eyes staring upward. Curled at the foot of the bed in an attitude of utter repose was Cattarina.

"I have brought you something to make you feel better, Sissy dear," I said, displaying both the amber-hued medicine bottle and the container of strawberries. "How are you feeling?"

Turning her gaze in my direction, she tremulously replied: "Heartsick."

I reached down and stroked the peak of her brow consolingly. "I am afraid I must leave you for a brief period, to go confer with Mr. Barnum," I said gently. "In the meantime, you have a visitor—Miss Schnitzler."

"Yes, I know," Sissy said. "Muddy told me."

"She is most eager to see you. I am sure that, if you so desire, she will be happy to regale you with some diverting anecdotes about her life as an entertainer."

"I do not know that I have the strength for it right now," said Sissy. "But please tell her to come in, so that I can at least thank her for her visit."

Raising my dear wife's right hand to my lips, I pressed a fervent kiss upon her fingers. Next, I bid farewell to Muddy and hurried into the sitting room, where I informed Willie that Sissy—though too debilitated for a prolonged visit—wished to say hello. I then left the suite and made my way out of the hotel.

Moments later, I was back in front of the museum. Though the hour was already late, customers were still filing past the ticket booth, where Slim Jim McCormack remained at his post. As I approached the entranceway, the skeletal fellow looked up at me and called out: "Evenin', Mr. Poe. Heard about the troubles up to your place. Mighty nasty business. Glad none of your kinfolk was hurt."

"Thank you, Slim Jim."

"By the by," he said, as though suddenly struck with an afterthought. "Abel Tomblin has showed up after all. Thought you'd want to know, seein' as how you was askin' after him earlier on today."

This surprising news caused a pang of the sharpest apprehension to course through my bosom. "Is that so?" I exclaimed. "When did he arrive?"

"Not more'n half-an-hour ago. I asked him why he'd bothered comin' to work at all when it's nearly closing time."

"And what was his reply?" I inquired.

Slim Jim gave a shrug of his inordinately narrow shoulders. "Said there was something he needed to attend to upstairs amongst the oddities."

Thanking him for this information, I crossed into the museum and immediately repaired to Barnum's basement office.

I found the showman striding back and forth across the center of the room, arms behind his back, one hand clasping the wrist of the other. His extreme agitation was evident not only from his ceaseless movement (which put me in mind of the constant pacing of the caged Bengalese tiger that constituted one of the prized attractions of his menagerie), but also from the intensely troubled expression on his face.

Noticing my presence, he halted abruptly and said: "Ah, there you are, Poe. I've been waiting for you. Got back not long ago with Officer Hayes. He'll be here in a moment. He's—ah—taking care of some urgent business."

From the insinuating tone of this latter remark, I deduced that the constable was availing himself of the privy.

"Tell me, m'boy," Barnum continued, "how are those two dear ladies of yours?"

"Safely ensconced in my suite," I replied. "As you can readily imagine, the unspeakable murder of her friend has left my dear wife, Virginia, prostrated with grief. Indeed, I have only now returned from a visit to the druggist's shop, where I purchased some medication for her."

"Medication, eh?" said Barnum. "Wouldn't mind a little swig of something soothing myself right now. To tell you the truth, Poe, it's times like these that I wish I weren't a teetotaler. Of course, that's just between you, me and the walls. Wouldn't want Mrs. Barnum to hear me say it. She's the one who got me to take the pledge in the first place, bless her heart. Best thing I ever did, too. Still . . . a little nip of brandy—just a *smidgen*, mind you—would do my nerves a world of good at the present moment."

Here, he inhaled deeply and let out a long, weary sigh before continuing thusly: "Lord, but I can't get the picture of that poor, butchered girl out of my head. What a horror—what an absolute, unmitigated horror! Believe me, Poe, I've seen one or two ghastly things in my day. Had a fellow in here once who could pop his eyeballs clean out of their sockets so they'd be hanging down his cheeks by a thread—then shove 'em back in place the way you'd stick a cork back in a wine bottle. Wanted me to hire him for my Hall of Oddities. 'Young man,' I says to him, 'I'm here to attract customers, not scare them away!' I tell you, Poe, it was a bloodcurdling thing to behold. But nothing compared to *that* poor girl."

That Barnum had been so deeply affected by the sight of the dreadfully mutilated corpse came as no surprise to me. Though he prided himself on the unparalleled realism of the waxworks manikins in his Hall of Crime and Punishment, no mere sculptural representation could possibly capture the sheer, ghastly awfulness of an actual flesh-and-blood atrocity such as the one to which Miss Brennan had been subjected.

One thing, however, continued to puzzle me: the response he had evinced to the pouch of Red Horse chewing tobacco found on my premises. The discovery of what might prove to be an important clue to the identity of the perpetrator should have been a cause for rejoicing. Barnum, however, had appeared singularly distressed. When I now queried about this reaction, he answered thusly:

"So you noticed, eh? Well, I'm not surprised. Nothing escapes those hawk-eyes of yours. Yes, it's true. The minute I laid eyes on that pouch of Red Horse, I felt sick—sick to my stomach. And I'll tell you why. It's the same kind Abel Tomblin chews."

"Aha!" I exclaimed. "I should have guessed as much."

"Now, mind you," Barnum hastily declared, "that doesn't *prove* anything. After all, Red Horse is a mighty popular brand, one of the biggest around. Sells by the wagon-load. That pouch could have fallen from the pocket of any one of a thousand different men."

"It is entirely true," I said, "that Tomblin cannot be conclusively linked to the crimes by this or any other, single piece of evidence uncovered thus far. Still, the sheer accumulation of these clues cannot be ignored—particularly in light of certain discoveries I myself made while searching through his apartment."

"You never did get around to telling me what you turned up in there," said Barnum.

"Permit me to do so without further delay," I said. I then proceeded to describe the results of my investigation, laying particular stress on the wildly pornographic volume I had found beneath the newspaper pile. So vile—so rank—profoundly shocking—were the contents of this work that entire passages had seared themselves upon my memory, allowing me to repeat them nearly verbatim. As I did so, the showman's complexion grew absolutely scarlet.

"Yes, all right, no need for more—I get the idea," he interjected at length, just as I reached the point in my recitation where the brazen Miss Temple wantonly submits to the impassioned embraces of the hopelessly debauched Monsieur Duval, returning his kisses with a "voluptuous eagerness" that matches his own.

"I tell you, Poe, it makes my blood boil," he declared with a scowl, as he removed a handkerchief from his pocket and mopped his florid brow. "All this outcry in the newspapers about the corrupting effects of my museum—*my* museum, the most wholesome and edifying showplace on the face of the planet! And meanwhile, real filth like that can be found all over the city. Why, it's as common as road apples on Broadway!"

Returning his handkerchief to his pocket, he slowly shook his head and continued thusly: "Well, I don't hesitate to say that I'm pained, deeply pained, to find out that Abel reads that sort of trash. Of course, he's still a bachelor. The beastly instincts haven't been tamed in him yet. Takes a few years of marriage to cure a man of his carnal longings. Still and all, that's no excuse for indulging in such foulness. No sir, it's another black mark against the man's character, there's no two ways about it."

"Are you aware," I said, "that he is even now in the building?"

"No! Really? How do you know?"

"I was apprised of the fact by Slim Jim, who indicated that Tomblin arrived only within the last half-hour or so. Evidently, there was some business that required his attention in the Hall of Oddities."

"That's strange," said Barnum. "That's mighty peculiar. I told him to take the day off. He'd earned it after that safari out to Brooklyn last night."

All at once, I was struck with an idea. "Tell me," I said. "When was the last time you had occasion to examine his custodial closet?"

"Never been in there at all, not that I can remember," Barnum replied. "It's just a storage room for his tools and cleaning supplies and whatnot. Why do you ask?"

"As Tomblin must now be considered a major suspect in these butcheries," I replied, "it behooves us to be as thoroughgoing as possible in our search for incriminating evidence. Have you a key to the room?"

"Of course," said Barnum. "It's my building, ain't it?" Striding around to the front of his desk, he pulled open a drawer and, after rummaging around for a moment, extracted a large ring of keys.

"Let's go," he said, marching to the doorway and gesturing for me to follow.

We made our way along the cramped, dismal corridor until we arrived at the door bearing the small brass plate marked CUSTODIAL CLOSET. Bending close to the lock, Barnum tried one key after another, muttering in annoyance with each successive failure. At length, just as he appeared ready to abandon the effort in an access of frustration, I heard a sharp, metallic click.

"At last!" he exclaimed, and threw open the door.

We could see the interior of the room only imperfectly, as the sole illumination came from a wall-mounted gas jet in the hallway. It appeared to be at least as large as Barnum's office, though I could not gauge its dimensions with any accuracy, its farthermost reaches being entirely steeped in shadow.

"Must be a lamp in here somewhere," my companion remarked, stepping over the threshold. An instant later, I heard him strike a match, which flared in the darkness of the chamber.

"Ah, here we are," said Barnum, who had located a lantern resting upon a small wooden shelf. Raising the glass chimney, he applied the match-flame to the wick. As the light suffused the room, I crossed inside and gazed around.

Apart from the narrow area that the showman and I now occupied, the room was crammed with all the equipment necessary for the maintenance of the building. There were janitorial supplies of every variety: mops and brooms, buckets and pails, barrels of granulated soap and vats of lye. There were paint cans by the score and jars of varnish by the dozen—barrels of tar—bushels of nails—huge coils of rope—ladders and lathes and even a sawhorse. Every species of tool lay stacked on the shelves, or hung from wooden pegs on the walls: axes and augers, chain blocks and chisels, hammers and hand-saws, crowbars, planes, mallets, trowels, and countless more.

As I turned to survey the rear of the room, I was struck by the exceptional orderliness of Tomblin's work space, so markedly in contrast to the inordinate squalor of his living quarters. Barnum, too, must have been similarly impressed, for at that very moment he observed: "Well, I'll say one thing for Abel. He runs a mighty tight ship."

"Indeed, I was only now remarking on the same fact," I replied. "Evidently, your custodian is far more scrupulous about his professional duties than his personal housekeeping, for—"

All at once, I ceased to speak, for I had suddenly become cognizant of a most unnerving circumstance.

Someone had entered the room and was now standing directly behind us!

Quelling the spasm of terror that had seized my heart, I quickly spun around, expecting to find myself in a direct—and no doubt highly unpleasant—confrontation with the custodian himself. The reader will easily imagine my sense of relief when I saw that the person who had come upon us in so stealthy a manner was Officer Hayes.

"Sorry to startle you gents," said the gruff-voiced constable. "No one was in your office, Barnum. Didn't know where the hell you went 'til I spotted the light coming from over here. What's going on?"

"Doing a bit of investigating while you were otherwise engaged," Barnum replied. "Poe here is of the opinion that my custodian—fellow named Tomblin, Abel Tomblin—might have something to do with all this unpleasantness. Thought we'd look around a bit, have a little peek at his storage room."

"Oh yeah?" demanded Hayes. "And just what makes you think this Tomblin fellow is involved?"

Since my suspicion of the custodian was partly founded on a wholly unauthorized search of his living quarters, Barnum was obliged to be circumspect. As he replied to Hayes's query with a carefully edited version of the truth, I continued to survey the room.

Several feet away stood a battered and paint-stained worktable, upon which sat a lidless pine box, approximately two feet long and eight inches wide, and outfitted with a wooden handle. I recognized this item at once as the tool chest belonging to the custodian. I had seen him with it several days earlier in the Hall of Reptiles, where he was engaged in repairing the cage of Barnum's tropical iguana.

All at once, my attention was riveted by a peculiar object that rested atop the other contents of the chest. At first glance, this appeared to be nothing more than a bunch of old, badly discolored rags, rolled up into a roughly cylindrical shape. There was something about the appearance of this bundle, however, that caused a vague but palpable feeling of premonitory dread to stir within my bosom. It took me a moment to recognize the source of this exceedingly anxious sensation.

Not very long ago, I had encountered another object very much like this one—wrapped, however, not in rags but in brown paper. It had arrived at our home on the day I had first met Anna Louise Brennan. Indeed, she had been the unwitting bearer of the grisly thing.

This realization struck me with the force of an electrical charge from a galvanic battery. Stepping to the table, I removed the suspect object from the tool chest. The moment I took it in my hands, my deepest fears were confirmed; for—entirely swathed though it was in old rags—I knew without doubt, from both its contours and heft, precisely what it was.

I must have emitted an audible gasp, for both Barnum and Constable Hayes immediately materialized at my side.

"Good gracious, m'boy," exclaimed the showman. "What in heaven's name is the matter?"

"Find something, Poe?" demanded Hayes.

Without speaking—for the sheer horror of the situation had temporarily robbed me of all power of vocalization—I lay the bundle upon the table and, with trembling hands, undid the rags that enclosed it. As the inconceivably hideous object came into view, the two men beside emitted simultaneous exclamations of stunned amazement.

It was a woman's right hand, so freshly amputated that the blood had not entirely congealed upon the ragged stump, out of which protruded a splintered fragment of wrist-bone.

For what seemed like an eternity, the three of us merely gaped at the extremity, which—even in its current, dreadfully butchered state—I recognized as the small and exceedingly elegant hand of poor Anna Louise Brennan. It was Constable Hayes who finally broke the horror-struck silence.

"Quick man," he said to Barnum in a voice hoarse with urgency. "Where can we find this custodian of yours?"

CHAPTER TWENTY-FIVE

Even in the murky illumination of the storage room, I could see that Barnum's face had gone ashen. "Up on the third floor," he said in reply to Hayes's query. "Among my human curiosities. Isn't that right, Poe?"

"So I was informed by Slim Jim," I said softly, having somewhat recovered the use of my voice.

Without a word, the burly constable turned toward the doorway. Before he could take a step, however, Barnum reached out and grabbed him by the arm.

"What's your plan, Hayes?" asked the showman.

"Plan?" growled the officer. "Why, to arrest the son-of-a-bitch."

"That might be harder than you suppose. Abel's no milksop. Why, the man's a veritable Goliath. Got the strength of three ordinary mortals. Once he sees we're on to him, he's likely to put up quite a battle."

Arranging his mouth into a sneer of the purest disdain, Hayes reached down and patted the large, ugly "billy" club sheathed in his belt. "We'll see about that," he said. He then did an about-face and made swiftly for the doorway, Barnum and I following close on his heels.

As we ascended the main stairwell, Barnum was greeted by the usual cries of excited recognition. So grimly bent was he on our mission, however, that—for once—he appeared entirely oblivious of his adoring public.

Moments later, we were standing at the threshold of the Hall of Oddities. Hayes slipped his "billy" from his belt and held it inconspicuously at his side; then the three of us crossed into the cavernous salon.

As always, a hushed, almost churchlike atmosphere pervaded the gallery. The hour being so late, the crowd consisted mostly of adults, many of them fashionable young couples out for a romantic evening on the town. Though a visit to a "freak show" would not seem conducive to love-making, the opposite—as countless swains had discovered—was the case; for, at the mere sight of Barnum's human monstrosities, the typical young women would invariably draw closer to her escort and clutch his arm in the most charming way imaginable.

Failing to see the custodian, I swept my gaze about the room, taking note of the performers on their raised, partitioned platforms. A distinct air of lassitude seemed to surround them—unsurprisingly, since (apart from the occasional respites they were permitted) they had been on display since early that morning. Hands on hips, the albino family stood side-by-side at the front of their little stage, their snow-white faces arranged into matching expressions of absolute *ennui*. Willie Schnitzler had returned from her visit to Sissy. She was seated upon her oversized stool, folded hands resting on her prodigious belly, eyes half-lidded, as though she were subsiding into sleep. The grotesquely truncated half-man, Sammy Wainwright, was perched on his little swing, languidly puffing on an enormous cigar and paying no attention whatsoever to the gaping spectators below.

Only Bruno the Armless Wonder was occupied in an activity. He was in the process of eating his supper, which consisted of a porterhouse steak—a baked potato—and a mound of black-eyed peas. The manner in which he ate this meal was singular in the extreme. Seated upon a small bench, he leaned as far backward as possible and raised both bare feet to the level of the tabletop. With his right toes, he clasped a fork; with his left, a sharp, glittering knife. Wielding these implements with his usual, astonishing dexterity, he was able to slice, scoop, and spear his food—then bring each forkful to his mouth—as effortlessly as any ordinary diner.

All at once, as I continued to survey the room, my gaze fell upon the object of our search. To my great surprise, he was standing upon the platform of the purported "goblin child," peering intently into the elaborately carved crib.

"There he is!" I said, pointing across the room.

"You two stay here," commanded Hayes. Tightening his grip on his weapon, he pushed his way through the crowd until he had reached the foot of the platform. He then placed his free hand on the edge of the little stage and vaulted onto its surface with surprising agility for so burly a man.

Rising to his full height, he came up beside the custodian. "Abel Tomblin?" he gruffly inquired. In the muted atmosphere of the hall, I had no difficulty discerning his words, in spite of the distance that separated us.

"Who's asking?" Tomblin demanded.

"Constable Marcus Hayes," replied the other. "No trouble now, Tomblin. Just come along quietly." And so saying, he reached out a meaty hand and laid it upon the custodian's right arm.

"I ain't goin' nowheres with you," growled Tomblin, yanking himself free of the constable's grasp.

Uttering a profane imprecation, Hayes swiftly raised his "billy" above his head, clearly intending to subdue the custodian by force. Before the club could descend, however, Tomblin drew back one massive fist and unleashed a fearsome blow that struck the constable squarely on the chin. With a loud grunt, Hayes collapsed backward into the crib, knocking it over on its side and sending its bizarre little occupant sprawling onto the platform.

As may be imagined, this altercation produced an immediate commotion among the crowd. All at once, the room was filled with a cacophony of startled cries—frightened shrieks—and bewildered exclamations. Intermingled with these sounds could be heard the unnerving wail of the weirdly misshapen baby, which lay on its back, waving its clawlike extremities in the air.

And then, something exceedingly peculiar transpired. With his adversary lying stunned at his feet, Tomblin could easily have made his escape. Instead, he swiftly bent over—scooped up the moaning baby—and raised the fallen crib back into an upright position. Only after gently depositing the supposedly supernatural creature back inside its crib, did he make for the edge of the stage.

By then, however, the constable had somewhat recovered from the blow, and was on his hands and knees, slowly shaking his head. As Tomblin hurried past, Hayes suddenly lunged at him, throwing both arms about the custodian's legs and bringing him down with a crash. Rolling wildly upon the platform, the two combatants began to exchange a flurry of blows, while a stream of savage oaths issued from their throats.

Standing helplessly in the doorway, Barnum looked desperately around for assistance. All at once, his gaze lit on the massive figure of Ajeeb Salaama, the enormous, turbanned eunuch who stood perpetual guard over the Circassian Beauty.

"Ajeeb!" called Barnum, pointing frantically at the two combatants who were now struggling furiously at the very edge of the platform. "Come, man! You must help stop Abel."

Moving with the grace of an Amazonian jaguar, the half-naked eunuch immediately sprang from his post and hurried across the hall toward the scene of the battle.

By this point, Tomblin had achieved the dominant position. He was on his knees, straddling the chest of his opponent and delivering a succession of blows to the latter's face. Though Hayes still retained possession of his "billy" club, he was unable to employ it in his supine position. All at once, Tomblin ceased his pummeling—reached down with both hands—and, with a savage cry, wrested the weapon out of the constable's hand. Before the latter could lift his arms in self-defense, the custodian raised the club and brought it down with a sickening crack upon the skull of his adversary, rendering him totally unconscious.

Struggling to his feet, Tomblin leapt from the platform, scattering the crowd of spectators who had gathered about the little stage to watch the ferocious struggle. Before he could take another step, however, he found himself face-to-face with the hugely muscled form of the bare-chested eunuch.

"Out of my way, Ajeeb!" Tomblin cried. At that moment, the custodian was the very picture of wild desperation. His clothes were in a state of excessive disorder, his hair badly disheveled. There was a half-crazed look in his eyes—perspiration dripped from his brow—and he was panting as loudly as an overtaxed horse.

His menacing appearance, however, in no way seemed to intimidate the eunuch, who merely shook his head slowly from side to side, and reached for the handle of the great, crescent-bladed scimitar which was sheathed in his wide leather belt.

Ajeeb's fingers had barely curled around the grip of his weapon, when Tomblin—moving with astonishing celerity—lunged forward like a fencer and thrust the extended "billy" club into the eunuch's solar plexus. As Ajeeb doubled over with a groan, the custodian stepped forward, reached down with his free hand, and withdrew the sword from his adversary's belt. He then used the "billy" to deliver a swift coup de grace to the skull of the eunuch, who dropped to the floor as heavily as a sack of feed.

In a cleared space amid the cowering crowd, Abel now stood by himself, brandishing a weapon in each hand.

"Anyone who wants to die, just try and stop me!" he shouted. All at once, as he continued to look wildly about the hall, his maddened gaze came to rest upon *me*.

"You!" he cried. Then, with the scimitar raised high above his head, he emitted a bloodcurdling scream and sprang in my direction.

"Abel, no!" shouted a voice that—even in that moment of imminent and deadly peril—I recognized as Willie Schnitzler's.

I squeezed my eyes shut, steeling myself for the fatal sword-stroke that was sure to decapitate me. In that instant, I heard a high, *whooshing* noise directly over my shoulder. This was followed by a kind of liquid *thud* and a cry in which agony and amazement seemed equally commingled.

Opening my eyes, I saw an astonishing—an unaccountable—sight. Tomblin stood only a few feet in front of me, staring down with a look of utter incredulity at the center of his chest, from which protruded the wooden handle of a knife, whose blade was entirely embedded in his body. An instant later, his knees buckled—his eyes rolled back in their sockets—and, with a fluttering moan, he dropped lifelessly to the ground!

Amid the cries—gasps—and screams of the spectators, I looked about in confusion, searching for the person responsible for this extraordinary turn of events. When I finally saw him, my eyes widened in amazement.

Leaning so far back on his little bench that he was nearly horizontal, Bruno the Armless Wonder sat with his right foot resting on the edge of his dining table, his toes still clutching a fork. His left leg, by contrast, was extended directly outward. His bare foot was pointed in the direction of the fallen custodian. His sharp, glittering steak knife was missing from his toes.

Part Four

ROSE

CHAPTER TWENTY-SIX

The slaying of Abel Tomblin—or "The Killer Custodian," as the penny papers were quick to denominate him—provoked an unparalleled excitement among the populace of the great city. Indeed, I can call to mind no other similar incident producing so general and intense an effect. For more than a week, even the most momentous political events of the day were forgotten in the discussion of this one, all-absorbing theme. In every gathering place throughout the metropolis—in business offices and barbershops, alehouses and oyster cellars, public parks and private parlors—the exceedingly dramatic circumstances surrounding the custodian's fiendish crimes and violent death formed the dominant topic of conversation.

The newspapers, of course—and particularly James Gordon Bennett's *New York Herald*—contributed greatly to the widespread fascination with the case, covering their front pages with seemingly endless stories about Tomblin's diabolical career of cruelty and bloodshed. The irony of this situation was not lost upon Barnum, who never tired of railing against the flagrant hypocrisy of Bennett.

"Can you believe it, Poe? Why, the man has no shame! Imagine! Attacking *me* as a crass exploiter of crime—then filling that blasted rag of his with every last, grisly detail about Tomblin and those poor women he butchered. Why, the nerve—the brass—the complete, unmitigated gall of the fellow! I tell you, Poe, it's a scandal! Greatest outrage since Herod slew the innocents!"

That Barnum—a man in whom audacity knew no reasonable bounds—could work himself up into such a paroxysm of righteous indignation was, to be sure, no small irony in itself. Still, it could scarcely be denied that the press indulged in a veritable orgy of sensational reporting on the case. Day after day, the *Herald* and its competitors featured headlined stories that portrayed the late custodian as a monster of nearly mythic dimensions—a creature who had conducted a reign of terror unparalleled since the Sphinx laid waste to Thebes.

In their avid pursuit of information relating to the "Killer Custodian," reporters had managed to uncover a number of surprising details about his past. Foremost among these was the fact that, as a young man, Tomblin had spent time in prison for having committed an indecent assault upon a female of his acquaintance. Though he had steadfastly maintained his innocence at his trial—insisting that his accuser had willingly consented to his advances and only turned on him in spite when he had subsequently spurned her for another woman—he had been judged guilty and incarcerated for a period of nearly two years. To Barnum (who had not inquired into Tomblin's background before hiring him and so was utterly ignorant of this unsavory episode), this revelation served as the final confirmation that he had sadly misjudged the custodian's character all along. The showman was now firmly of the belief that, as he put it, Tomblin was "guilty as all get-out."

Not everyone, however, shared this opinion. Willie Schnitzler, for one, continued to express her conviction that—in spite of all evidence to the contrary—Tomblin could not possibly have perpetrated the atrocities of which he stood accused. It was Willie who had ministered to the mortally wounded custodian in his final moments. Hurrying down from her platform with an agility that belied her enormous girth, she had lowered herself onto the floor and cradled her dying friend in her massive lap, while copious tears flowed down her face and dampened her beard. Afterward, when additional police officers had arrived and the custodian's blood-soaked corpse had been carried off to the municipal dead-house, she had taken me aside and poured out her heart to me:

"I just don't believe it, Mr. Poe, and I never will. It don't make a lick of sense. Why, he was the nicest, kindest fellow you'd ever hope to meet. A real gentle giant, you might say. Why, just look at the way he took care of that poor, miserable creature," she cried, indicating the "goblin child" in its extravagant crib. "That's why he dropped by here today—to see how the little feller was faring. It's been feeling mighty poorly of late—sneezing and coughing something fearful. Abel had a real soft spot for the poor little thing. He was always looking in on it. You can't tell me a man like that is the kind to go 'round chopping up young women."

Even those who never questioned Tomblin's culpability for an instant were somewhat uncertain about the full *extent* of his crimes. That he was responsible for the savage murder of Anna Louise Brennan seemed incontestable. Moreover—as his connection to Isabel Somers had been firmly established by the unflagging efforts of Barnum and myself (efforts which the showman lost no time in publicizing by sharing the details of our investigation with sympathetic members of the press)—it seemed equally definite that he had been the agent of that atrocity as well.

The uncertainty concerned his involvement in the earlier slaying of the beauteous Ellen Jennings. Not even the most assiduous reporter was able to discover a link between Tomblin and the horribly butchered harlot. In the end (partly, I suspected, because the judicial authorities were loath to admit that they had hanged the wrong man), a consensus emerged that, in all likelihood, Tomblin had been innocent of the Jennings crime. The murders of Isabel Somers and Anna Louise Brennan, it was felt, had constituted depraved imitations of the earlier, much-publicized atrocity.

As for my own opinion, I remained vaguely troubled by a number of unresolved questions relating to the case. Foremost among these was the rôle of Morris Vanderhorn. In our pursuit of the mystery, Barnum and I had been so persuaded of the latter's complicity in the crimes that I now found it difficult to cease viewing him as a suspect. I also remained exceedingly puzzled by what was, perhaps, the single most bizarre component of the murders: the inexplicable need of the killer to leave long-stemmed roses clamped between the teeth of his victims. Certainly, nothing had been discovered about Tomblin's life that would suggest an affinity with that or any other variety of flower.

Moreover, I could not help but wonder why Tomblin had been so incautious as to leave poor Miss Brennan's severed right hand displayed so prominently in his custodial closet. And where was its mate?

The former question, at least, I was able to answer to my own satisfaction. In depositing the incriminating object directly on top of his toolbox, Tomblin may well have been counting on a singular phenomenon of our nature: to wit, our tendency to overlook precisely those objects which are *too* palpably and obtrusively self-evident—which are *inordinately* conspicuous—in short, which escape detection by being deposited immediately beneath our noses! Or perhaps he simply believed that there was no reason to take any unusual precautions in concealing his ghastly trophy. After all—as Barnum himself had testified—no one besides the custodian ever ventured into the storage room.

In the end, the mere presence of poor Miss Brennan's horribly mutilated hand in Tomblin's sanctum—coupled with the sordid and shocking discoveries I had made during my search of his abode—convinced me that, in spite of my few, lingering doubts, the custodian had indeed been the guilty party. I could thus take pride in knowing, that—largely through the bold initiative of the showman and myself—the monster's reign of terror had at last been brought to an end.

As far as the press and the public were concerned, however, the real hero was neither Barnum nor myself, but rather Bruno the Armless Wonder, whose prowess was hailed as nothing short of miraculous. To the precise degree that Tomblin was transformed by the newspapers into a creature of almost supernatural evil, Bruno was portrayed as a latter-day Perseus or Jason—a figure on a par with the fabled monster-slayers of antiquity. Even Heracles himself (according to one infatuated writer for the *Morning Transcript*) could scarcely compare to Bruno; for in performing his prodigious feats—the killing of the many-headed Hydra, the capture of the great Erymanthian boar—the former enjoyed an advantage denied to the Armless Wonder: i.e., the full use of all *four* of his limbs!

As a result of such *lionizing,* Bruno quickly became one of the museum's star attractions, drawing spectators in unprecedented numbers to the Hall of Oddities. This circumstance did nothing to endear him to certain of his colleagues. Sammy Wainwright in particular seemed exceedingly resentful of Bruno's new-found celebrity. Barnum, however, could not have been more pleased.

Indeed—for all his grumbling about the supposed hypocrisy of the papers—the showman clearly reveled in their ceaseless coverage of the Tomblin affair. It served to provide him with a benefit he valued above all others: an abundance of free publicity. The crowds who now flocked to his establishment were larger than ever. What brought them to the museum was not merely the opportunity to view the city's newest sensation, the celebrated Armless Wonder. They were equally eager to see at first hand the actual sites where the infamous "Killer Custodian" had hoarded his grisly treasure and met his ghastly end. It is hardly necessary to add that—with his unsurpassed genius for exploiting the public's most morbid and prurient impulses—Barnum was only too ready to oblige.

Within days of the bloody culmination of the tragedy, he had converted the custodian's gloomy basement storeroom into a brightly lit exhibition gallery, where (as Barnum himself would exclaim to the crowd) visitors could "see the hidden, subterranean lair of the notorious Killer Custodian, whose horrid deeds of bloodshed and torture outstripped those of the legendary Bluebeard himself!" Needless to say, customers were subject to an additional charge for the privilege of viewing the custodian's workplace, the tariff amounting—in Barnum's words—to a "mere thin dime" above their initial twenty-five-cent admission fee.

The ostensible highlight of this tour was a glimpse of Tomblin's actual tool chest, containing—as the showman put it—"an object so gruesome, so shocking, so absolutely bloodcurdling that those of you with a faint heart, weak stomach, or a delicate nervous system are advised to reconsider the advisability of subjecting yourselves to the awful spectacle! That's right, my friends! You will see with your own two eyes the genuine, chopped-off hand of the madman's poor female victim, precisely as it was discovered in this very room!"

As was so often the case at the American Museum, customers gullible enough to believe the showman's every word did not get precisely what was promised. This is not to say that they were victims of an outright *hoax*. Those willing to invest the additional ten-cent fee to enter the storeroom were indeed confronted with the grotesque sight of a real human hand resting atop Tomblin's toolbox.

This anatomical relic, however, did not belong to Anna Louise Brennan (whose corpse had been interred in as complete a state as possible, the recovered body part having been reattached to its limb by the local mortician). Rather, it was the preserved hand of Isabel Somers—the very one which had been sent to my home, and which I had then turned over to Barnum under the (inordinately naïve) expectation that he would decently dispose of it.

At all events, his customers seemed unconcerned about the exact provenance of the lurid relic. No one who entered the custodian's private lair came away feeling cheated. They had received what they had paid for—a titillating peep at the unspeakable.

As Barnum never tired of proclaiming, even when he duped the public, he always gave them their money's worth.

One week had elapsed since the maddened custodian—brandishing a deadly weapon in each enormous hand—had been felled by the perfectly aimed throw of Bruno's projectile. It was now Sunday, the ninth of July. Two days earlier, Muddy, Sissy, and I had packed up our belongings and journeyed back to our cottage. Our return was attended with a singular mixture of emotions. Despite (or rather *because* of) its inordinate elegance and luxury, the Astor House offered few of the comforts of home. To escape from the city and move back to our rural abode, therefore, was a palpable relief for all three members of our little family (*four* counting Cattarina, who seemed equally excited to be in the country again, where she had grown used to having the free run of the outdoors).

At the same time, a distinct atmosphere of melancholy now pervaded the farmstead, which had been the scene of so frightful—so *appalling*—a tragedy. Even on the most brilliantly sunlit afternoon, the memory of the charming and vivacious young woman—and of the ghastly fate that had befallen her—cast a dreary pall over the surroundings.

While the spirit of Anna Louise Brennan continued to haunt the premises, her corpse had been transported home for inhumation in her family burial plot. Her uncle and aunt, having accompanied the casketed remains, had not yet returned from their journey, having evidently decided to remain in Philadelphia to condole with their grieving relations. Muddy, Sissy, and I were therefore alone on the farm—a not entirely unwelcome circumstance, since the presence of our heartbroken landlords would only have exacerbated the still-sorrowful mood of my darling Sissy.

At approximately two P.M. of the day in question—Sunday, July 9—I had just set off on my usual, daily ramble. Though preferring to hike at a much earlier hour, I had been compelled to defer my normal exercise until the afternoon, a violent morning thunderstorm having rendered any outdoor activity impractical. I might add that—while bringing some much-needed rain to the area—the storm had produced no discernible effect on the temperature, which remained exceedingly sultry.

My intended destination was a small, enchanting brook that lay deep in a wooded area of the Brennan's property. Owing to the intense heat—which was rendered even more oppressive by the density of the undergrowth through which I was compelled to pass in order to reach the little stream—I was perspiring heavily by the time I arrived at my destination. As I was utterly alone in the woods, however—with no witnesses about, apart from a pair of scampering chipmunks—I felt free to comport myself in whatever manner I chose, even to the point of gross immodesty. With a wild cry of abandon, I therefore undid my shirt collar and pulled it open to its widest extent. I then knelt by the brook and—extracting my pocket handkerchief—soaked it in the water and applied the invigorating compress to the back of my neck.

Next, I found a bed of moss beneath a towering tree and stretched myself upon it, hands laced behind my head. For many minutes, I merely lay there, staring upward, taking idle notice of the many details of my surroundings. In the perfect solitude of the woods, each sight—sound—and smell—was suddenly endued with a singular intensity of interest. In the quivering of the leaves—the humming of the bees—the breathing of the wind—the faint odor emanating from the wild honeysuckle that grew at the base of the great tree—there came a whole universe of suggestion, a motley train of rhapsodical and immethodical thought!

How long I remained immersed in my reveries, I cannot say with certainty. By slow degrees, however, my mind began to turn away from these random impressions and focus on a far more pressing matter—one which had, during the preceding days, begun to weigh heavily on my mind.

For the past several weeks—ever since I first became involved with the showman—I had not set pen to paper, the urgent demands of our investigation taking precedence over all other areas of my life. Given the sheer degree of struggle and frustration that invariably attends the act of composition, it might be supposed that this enforced hiatus from my labors represented a welcome respite. The opposite, however, was true. Those who are blessed (or cursed) with the need— or more properly, the *compulsion*—to create art know perfectly well that any prolonged suspension of their efforts can be a source of the deepest anxiety and unease.

Now that the murder case had been resolved, I was exceedingly eager to resume my work. I was faced, however, with the question of *what* I should write: an essay, a short story, or a poem. As the urge to express myself in a *lyrical* manner seemed most exigent at the moment, I had decided upon the latter. Moreover, I was resolved to compose a poem that should suit at once both the popular and the critical taste.

The difficulty now lay in choosing an appropriate topic. As I lay upon my back—gazing upward at the limpid patch of blue visible through the branches overhead and meditating on this problem—I began to reason thusly. *That* pleasure which is at once the most pure, the most elevating, and the most intense is clearly derived from the contemplation of the Beautiful. It must further be acknowledged that Beauty of whatever kind, in its *supreme* development, invariably excites the sensitive soul to tears. We must thus conclude that *melancholy* is the most legitimate of all poetical tones.

Next, I posed to myself the following question: "Of all melancholy topics, what, according to the universal understanding of mankind, is the *most* melancholy?" The obvious reply was—*Death.*

"And when," I then asked myself, "is this most melancholy of topics most *poetical?*" Here, too, the answer was obvious—"When it most closely allies itself to *Beauty.*" By such assured, unimpeachable logic, I quickly arrived at the conclusion that the single most poetical topic in the world was, without question, the death of a beautiful young woman.

I had thus decided on the general theme of my work. My next task was to determine the most effective means of *embodying* this supremely poetical topic. Keeping originality always in view, I said to myself, "Of all the imaginable situations involving the death of a beautiful young woman, which shall I select?" Here, however, the very profusion of choices served as an obstacle; for, faced with a nearly limitless range of possibilities, I was at a loss to settle on any particular one.

I had been reclining on the ground, engaged in these reflections for goodness knows how long, when—all at once—I was startled from my thoughts by the harsh, cawing sound of a large bird of the species *Corvus corax* that had alighted on a branch directly overhead. The raucous cry of this ebony fowl—shattering the serenity of the secluded little grove—caused me to sit up abruptly in a state of some annoyance.

As it happened, the appearance of this grim, ungainly raven proved to be a blessing in disguise. Roused from my contemplations, I decided to consult my pocket watch. When I saw that it was nearly four o'clock, I leapt to my feet with a small cry of dismay, and—after restoring my loosened shirt-collar to its properly buttoned state—immediately bent my steps toward home. I did not want to be late. I was expecting a visit from Barnum.

I had received a letter from him two days earlier, informing me of his intentions to travel up to the cottage on Sunday afternoon. "Look for me around dinnertime," he had written. "And tell those dear ladies of yours they needn't bother to cook—I'll supply the grub. We'll have ourselves a regular *blow-out*—a feast that'll make a Roman bacchanalia seem like fast day at a monastery! Keep your appetite handy, m'boy—you'll need it! See you anon!

"Oh—one thing more. I've invited a guest. There's a little idea he and I want to discuss with you."

Needless to say, this missive had greatly piqued my curiosity. As any attempt to construe its significance, however, would be nothing but mere *guess-work*, I had promptly put it from my mind. Now, as I hurried in the direction of my abode, I found myself puzzling once again over the matters to which it made such mysterious and tantalizing reference: i.e., the possible nature of Barnum's unspecified "idea," and the identity of his unnamed guest.

CHAPTER TWENTY-SEVEN

As I approached the cottage, I observed Sissy seated on the front porch. She was perusing a book, which she clutched with her left hand. With her right, she was idly stroking the back of our beloved tabby, who lay curled upon her lap. So perfectly—so *profoundly*—contented was the slumbering feline that, as I crossed the yard, I could clearly discern her continuous, low-throated *purring* from at least a dozen feet away.

Sadly, my darling wife's spirits were not nearly as untroubled as those of Cattarina. Though sufficiently improved since the day of the tragedy to have resumed the least demanding of her daily activities, she remained deeply bereaved by the loss of her friend, and subject to sporadic bouts of unbridled grieving—fits of such violent intensity that I feared for her always-fragile health.

Even now, her face wore an expression heavily tinged with melancholy. She was reading her cherished anthology of faerie stories—a work that never seemed to loosen its bewitching hold on her imagination. Indeed, so engrossed was she in its pages that she had failed to take note of my arrival. From the somber look on her face, however, I could see that the innocent, childlike pleasure she had formerly derived from the book had now (and perhaps *forever*) been severely eroded. For all its captivating charm, Mr. Tyler's volume could hardly fail to remind her of her horribly murdered friend, who had shared with Sissy an abiding love of all things related to the myths and legends of faerieland.

It was not until I mounted the porch—stepped beside her chair—and gently kissed the peak of her alabaster brow—that Sissy became aware of my presence. Looking up from her book, she smiled sweetly and said: "Oh, hello, Eddie dearest. How was your walk?"

"Exceedingly pleasurable," I replied. "My ramble took me to the banks of the most exquisite little brook imaginable. You must accompany me there some day soon, Sissy. We will recline upon the grassy sward, and there—like Marlowe's impassioned shepherd—'I will make thee a cap of flowers, and a kirtle embroidered all with leaves of myrtle.' "

"Just what I've always wanted," Sissy said with a mischievous sparkle in her luminous eyes. "A kirtle embroidered with myrtle. Delightful as it sounds, though, I'm afraid we'll have to wait until I feel a little stronger, Eddie. I'm not up to hiking through the woods quite yet."

"Of course," I replied. "I remain hopeful, however, that the salubrious effects of the country air—combined with the loving care and attention supplied by myself and our ever-devoted Muddy—will greatly expedite your recovery. And where *is* Muddy at present?"

"In the kitchen," Sissy answered. "Making a blueberry pie."

"Ah," I replied. "So my sense of olfaction has not been deceiving me after all." From the moment I had stepped onto the porch, I thought I had detected the faint but unmistakable aroma of freshly baked pastry wafting through the open window of the house. "But why is she bothering? In his letter to me, Mr. Barnum insisted that she not go to any trouble in regard to culinary preparation. Indeed, he was quite emphatic on the subject."

"You know Muddy," Sissy said fondly. "She doesn't believe that guests ought to supply their own food—even when they *do* invite themselves to dinner."

"Perhaps I shall go inside and see how she is progressing."

"Very well," said Sissy, turning back to her book. "I'll stay out here a bit longer. I'm just finishing up this wonderful story, 'Sir Gilbert and the Faerie Banquet.' It's about a knight who goes on a quest and comes upon a tribe of faeries, who are about to feast on all kinds of strange and magical foods."

"To judge by the delectable aroma issuing from our abode," I said, "our own feast promises to be every bit as marvelous as any that might be concocted for the King of Faerieland himself."

Taking leave of my wifey, I entered the cottage and made directly for the kitchen, where I found Muddy in the act of removing a bubbling, lattice-topped pie from the stove.

"Hello, Muddy dear. I see that you have been exceedingly busy in my absence."

"You mean *this?*" she said, placing the pie on the windowsill to cool. "Why, it took me no time at all. Just a little something I whipped together for dessert."

Closing my eyes, I took a deep breath before declaring: "To characterize it as a 'little something' is not unlike describing the celestial strains of Handel's *Messiah* as a pleasant little ditty. Rarely, if ever, has my olfactory organ been treated to a finer—a more *sublime*—fragrance than the wingéd odor emanating from your ambrosial creation."

"Well, there's nothing like a fresh-baked blueberry pie," she said with a smile. "How was your walk?"

I proceeded to regale her with a concise description of my visit to the secluded little stream. Then, glancing down at my hands, I declared: "Excuse me, Muddy, while I retire to my chamber. I am in need of some washing-up as a result of my exertions."

"Of course, Eddie, dear. I'll go outside and sit for a while with Virginia."

Repairing to my bedroom, I filled my washbasin with water and proceeded to perform my ablutions. I had just finished drying my hands and face with a towel, when, through my wide-flung window, I heard the sound of a rapidly approaching vehicle.

Immediately, I hurried out onto the porch, where I found my loved ones gazing expectantly at the rutted dirt path that led from Bloomingdale Road to our doorstep. An instant later, a buggy drove into view. At our first glimpse of this conveyance, each of us emitted a simultaneous gasp of astonishment—for seated upon the driver's box, holding the reins between his teeth, was none other than Bruno the Armless Wonder!

As the buggy drew up to our cottage, the extraordinary youth leaned sharply backward on his seat, drawing the harness taut and bringing the steed to an easy halt. Then, leaping from his perch—his mouth still retaining hold of the reins—he lashed them to the hitching post with a few deft movements of his head.

In the meantime, Barnum had emerged from the buggy with a large, wicker picnic-hamper clutched in his hands.

"Poe! Ladies!" he exclaimed in his great, booming voice. "Delighted to be here! Perfectly delighted!"

Striding up to the cottage, he paused at the foot of the porch and—smiling up at Sissy—declared: "Bless my life, but you're looking well, my dear. A little thin, perhaps, just a little—but that's only to be expected. I know how hard hit you were by your dear friend's tragic demise. Still, there's nothing to be gained from making yourself sick over it. Won't bring the poor child back. No amount of grieving will. Might as well get on with the business of living. Banish care—on with the show! That's P. T. Barnum's motto. You'll be the healthier for it every time—that's been my experience, and I've seen a good deal of this world.

"And you, Mrs. Clemm," he continued, turning his attention to Muddy. "Always a pleasure to see you, my dear woman—an absolute pleasure! And don't you look *radiant!* Why, when I stepped from my carriage just now and saw you standing up there, I thought—What on earth is my Circassian Beauty doing here at Poe's house? You look *that* splendid! Well, I'm just glad Mrs. Barnum isn't here to listen to me rattle on this way. Flies off the handle if I so much as smile at another woman. Lord, what a jealous streak that woman has! Why, Othello was a paragon of unwavering conjugal trust by comparison."

By this point, the Armless Wonder had stepped to Barnum's side. He was dressed in an elegant frock coat of the finest black cloth, whose empty sleeves hung straight down at his sides. His fine—surpassingly handsome—countenance was arranged into a look of the utmost affability.

"Welcome, Bruno," I declared. "I confess that I am surprised—if exceedingly pleased—to see you. I had no idea that you would be accompanying Mr. Barnum on his visit."

Acknowledging my greeting with a little bow of the head, the armless youth graciously replied: "The pleasure's all mine, Mr. Poe. Good afternoon, ladies. Charming place you have here."

"Told you I'd be bringing a guest," Barnum exclaimed, glancing over at Bruno with a fond, proprietary smile. "Didn't say that it would be New York's man-of-the-hour, though. Bless my soul, you wouldn't believe what a celebrity the lad's become. Why, the whole city's gone wild—positively wild—over him. Greatest hero since David toppled Goliath with his slingshot."

"*Please,* Mr. Barnum," Bruno protested, a flush spreading over his smooth, almost girlish cheeks.

"Well, it's true, m'boy," said Barnum. "No sense in pretending otherwise! Opportunity like this doesn't come knocking every day! You've got to fling open the door and welcome her with open arms! That's why we're here, ain't it? Well, we'll talk about all that later. In the meantime—let's eat! I've brought along quite a little banquet here—a regular Epicurean feast!"

And so saying, he mounted the porch and offered his free arm to Muddy, who—with a titter of girlish pleasure—looped a hand over it and accompanied him into the cottage.

As Bruno followed the showman up the steps, he glanced over at Sissy, who was in the act of rising from her chair. Taking note of the volume in her hands, he let out a little cry of recognition and remarked: "I see that you're reading Mr. Tyler's faerie stories."

"For about the hundredth time," Sissy laughingly replied.

"I know what you mean. I was *mad* about that book when I was younger. Couldn't get enough of it. A few of the stories used to give me the chills, though."

"Oh my, yes," said Sissy. "There's some awfully gruesome stuff in here."

"Tell me—which is your absolute favorite?"

"My favorite?" Sissy said with a charming frown. "Goodness, that's a difficult question. Let's see—"

And thus chatting merrily away, Sissy and the Armless Wonder disappeared into the cottage, while I brought up the rear.

Though gross exaggeration came as naturally to Barnum as

breathing, he proved to be as good as his word on this particular occasion; for the food he had brought with him was indeed ample enough to have satisfied the most gluttonous disciple of Epicurus. Setting the wicker basket down on our kitchen table, he opened its lid and—like a prestidigitator extracting an entire colony of rabbits from his magical hat—proceeded to remove a veritable *cornucopia* from its interior. There was cold veal and ham steak, smoked beef and roasted chicken, hard-boiled eggs and several varieties of cheese, dark rye bread and great puffy rolls, a jar of preserved plum and another of quinces, fresh strawberries, two honey cakes, and a batch of doughnuts.

At length, the hamper was emptied of its contents. Rubbing his hands together with the avidity of a miser gloating over his hoard, Barnum contemplated the table—now transformed into a veritable *groaning-board*—and declared: "Lord bless me, but that's a handsome spread, if I do say so myself! I don't know about you folks, but I'm just about ready to *perish* of hunger. Why, my mouth is watering like a cannibal contemplating a missionary. Come, friends—let's dig in without delay!"

For the most part, our dinner proved to be an exceedingly pleasant affair. Though somewhat overwhelmed by the profusion of foodstuffs—the sheer number of which typified the showman's love of all that was lavish and excessive—I fully entered into the intensely congenial spirit of the evening. Barnum was at his most entertaining, regaling us with a host of amusing anecdotes about his singularly colorful and venturesome life.

One story in particular made a vivid impression upon me. It concerned his maternal grandfather, Mr. Phineas Taylor, after whom the showman had been named. This gentleman, it appeared, was an inveterate prankster, who—as Barnum put it—would "go further, wait longer, work harder, and contrive deeper to play a practical joke than any man alive!" All those with whom he came into contact—neighbors, friends, relations—were liable to fall victim to his elaborate deceptions. Indeed, he did not scruple to make his very own grandson and namesake the butt of an especially extravagant hoax, which Barnum—interspersing his story with many a wry and self-deprecating chuckle—now proceeded to relate:

"Might've been yesterday—that's how clearly I recall it. I was a mere lad, just four years of age. Oh, I was full of spunk, I tell you! Bright-eyed and bushy-tailed. Well, Grandpa Taylor comes up to me one day and takes me by the shoulder—bless my soul, but the man had a grip like a blacksmith! Never seen him look so serious before. Says he's decided to bestow a very special gift upon me. Something wonderful—absolutely stupendous! You can imagine how excited I was! What in the world could it be? A gold pocket watch? My own pony?

"Well, he reaches into his pocket and pulls out . . . a piece of paper! My heart sinks clear down to my feet—heavy as a stone dropped into a millpond. Then, very slowly and deliberately, he proceeds to unfold it and hand it to me. Of course I can't read a word of it. Heavens, I've just turned four! So he takes the paper back, clears his throat, and reads it to me. It's a gift-deed to a place called Ivy Island. And the deed has been made out to—*me!*

" 'Do you know what this means, Phineas?' says Grandpa, looking down at me oh-so-solemnly. 'It means that you are now a property owner. Ten acres of prime farmland, which will become yours on the day you turn twenty-one.' Then, with great ceremony, he shakes me by the hand and says, 'Congratulations, m'boy. You are now the richest lad in Fairfield County!'

"Well, from that moment on, hardly a day went by that I didn't hear talk of my precious patrimony. Grandpa Taylor never tired of telling anyone who'd listen, stranger or friend, about my remarkable good fortune—how I'd inherited the whole of Ivy Island, the richest farm in all of Connecticut! My own parents continually spoke of it. 'Well, at least we don't have to worry about our old age,' they'd say. 'Not with such a wealthy child to support us.' Neighbors would come up to me all the time and express the fear that I'd refuse to play with their children anymore, because I owned an island, and *they* didn't!

"I don't have to tell you what effect all this puffery had on a boy of my tender years. I couldn't have gotten any more stuck-up if I'd been the young dauphin himself!

"Well, after four or five years of this, I reached the point where I just couldn't stand it any longer. In all that time, I'd never so much as glimpsed this fabulous realm of mine. So one fine summer morn, just after my ninth birthday, I begged my grandfather to take me to the island.

" 'All right,' says he, after stroking his chin for a while. 'You must promise me one thing, however. When you finally set eyes on your property, you mustn't make yourself sick with excitement over it. Remember, m'boy—rich as you are, it'll be a dozen more years before you come into possession of your estate.'

"I swore that I'd stay calm and reasonable—and off we went!

"The old man must've been pushing seventy by then. Still spry as a schoolboy, though. Even *I* had trouble keeping up with him—and I was no slouch when it came to hiking. Oh, he was a remarkable old fellow, by jings—absolutely extraordinary!

"Well, we walked and we walked, until finally we arrived at an area known as East Swamp. Gazing around in some perplexity, I asked my grandpa where Ivy Island was.

" 'Yonder, just north of this meadow,' he said pointing to a spot some distance away. 'We're almost there, m'boy! Excited?'

" 'Oh my, yes, Grandfather!' I exclaimed. Winded as I already was, I began to pick up my pace. The promised land was within sight! Why, Moses of old couldn't have felt more eager to reach his destination!

"As I approached the north end of the meadow, however, I noticed something peculiar. The ground just kept getting wetter and wetter. After a while, it was nothing but bogs. It wasn't long before I found myself waist deep in brown, mucky water.

" 'Keep on going, lad,' called my grandfather, who was striding along just as easily as if he were taking a noonday stroll along the main street of Danbury. 'You're off the regular track, but never mind—just keep wading through, and you'll hit it.'

" 'Wade?' I cried 'Why, the water's almost over my head! I shall be drowned!'

" 'Don't be silly,' said he. 'Why, the water isn't more than four feet deep at the deepest.'

"So on I plunged, until I reached a little clump of semidry land. No sooner did I set foot on it, though, than a whole army of hornets came swarming up out of the grass and laid siege to my face. Screaming and flailing my arms like a Bedlamite, I swatted them away—but not before one vicious rascal stung me right on the tip of my nose. With a great shriek of pain, I fell backward into the water with a mighty splash!

"'C'mon boy,' called Grandpa. 'Quit fooling around. We've almost reached your domain. Just another quarter-mile of wading and you'll be there!'

"Groaning with pain and exhaustion, I continued slogging on as best I could. After another fifteen or twenty minutes of floundering through the morass—now stepping on a piece of submerged wood, now slipping into a hole—I finally rolled out upon dry land, covered with mud, out of breath, looking considerably more like a drowned rat than a human being.

"'Here we are at last!' exclaimed Grandfather.

"'Oh, my poor nose,' I moaned.

"'Never mind that, m'boy. We have only to cross this little creek, and you'll be upon your own valuable property at last!'

"Looking around, I saw that we were at the margin of a stream at least twelve feet wide.

"'Good heavens!' I cried. 'Is my property surrounded by water?'

"'Why the devil would it be called Ivy *Island* if it weren't?' said Grandpa.

"Striding up the bank a ways, he located a series of stepping-stones that formed a natural bridge across the stream. Nimble as a mountain goat, he skipped his way across to the other side. When I tried following, however, my foot slipped and I went plunging into the water.

"'Help!' I shouted. 'I'm drowning!'

"Roaring with laughter, Grandpa called: 'Swim, m'boy, swim! You're almost there!'

"With every last ounce of strength in my body, I managed to make it to shore, where I lay spread-eagled on my back, panting like a played-out plowhorse.

"'Up—up on your feet, m'boy!' shouted Grandpa. 'We're here—Ivy Island! Your personal kingdom! What do you think of it?'

"Dragging myself onto my hands and knees, I gazed all about me.

For a moment, I couldn't make sense of what I was seeing. Instead of a rich and fertile domain—a land of milk and honey, of rich forests and lush, green fields—all I could see was a barren stretch of ground with a few stunted ivies and some straggling trees. At that moment, the truth flashed upon me—my precious Ivy Island was nothing but an inaccessible wasteland, not worth a farthing! And I realized something else, too. Everyone I knew—my parents, my friends, the whole town—had been in on the joke from the beginning! I had been the laughingstock of my family and neighbors for years!

"As I knelt there on the sandy soil—my visions of future wealth and greatness all gone up in smoke—I spotted a monstrous black snake come slithering toward me, with upraised head and piercing green eyes. With a shriek of terror, I leapt to my feet and took to my heels, flying over the stepping-stone bridge, while the roar of Grandfather's laughter boomed out behind me.

"And that," the showman concluded with a chuckle, "was my first and last visit to Ivy Island!"

For several moments after this singular tale was completed, the rest of us looked speechlessly at the showman. I, for one, was at a complete loss as to how to respond. Barnum himself seemed to regard this childhood episode as nothing more than an amusing illustration of his grandfather's irrepressibly mischievous character. It was difficult to avoid the suspicion, however, that an experience involving such profound and public humiliation *must* have left a lasting mark upon him—accounting, perhaps, for his lifelong terror of being 'played for a sucker.' It was also apparent that, while he may not have inherited a ten-acre farm from his Grandfather Taylor, the old man had evidently bequeathed him something even more valuable—a flair for brazen and outrageous chicanery that the showman had exploited with unparalleled success.

It was Sissy who finally broke the uncomfortable silence that had descended upon our little party, politely asking our other guest about *his* family background.

"Yes, Bruno, m'boy," said Barnum. "Go ahead and tell us all about it. After all," he added cryptically, "that's why we're here."

Prior to seating ourselves at the table, the young prodigy had removed his footwear, so that he could enjoy the unencumbered use of his pedal extremities while dining. Now, he raised his right foot to his face and—with his linen napkin clutched between his big and second toes—fastidiously dabbed at his mouth before replying.

"There isn't much to tell—that's just the problem," the young man replied. "Certainly nothing as diverting as Mr. Barnum's stories."

"Oh, but we'd *love* to hear it just the same," Sissy sweetly implored.

"Very well," said the young man, smiling charmingly at Sissy. "I was born in Boston twenty-one years ago, the youngest of four children—three girls and myself. The midwife, so I've been told, swooned when I emerged from the womb. My father, a cabinet-maker by trade, didn't faint when he first laid eyes on me; he did something far less forgivable. Within days of my birth, he abandoned his family, and was never seen nor heard from again.

"With four little ones to care for—including a newborn that some people couldn't even bear to look at—my poor, sainted mother labored night and day to support us. Even so, she found time to shower us with tenderness and love. Especially me. Far from repelling her, my deformity only seemed to make me more precious in her eyes. Oh, I shall always be grateful for what that dear woman gave me! It was the greatest gift in the world—she made me feel *ordinary*. Not a freak, not a joke of nature, not something to be shuddered at, or pitied. Just a normal, beloved child.

"And then she was gone. Dead of heart failure at the age of thirty-four. Killed before her time—by care and overwork and a husband's terrible cruelty."

At this point in his narrative, I happened to glance over at Sissy and observed that her eyes were glistening with moisture. I, too, found myself deeply moved by the young man's recitation—unsurprisingly, since I could empathize so easily with his childhood sufferings. Though spared his grotesque physical handicap, I had also been sired by an unfeeling brute, who had cruelly abandoned his poor wife and little children shortly after my birth. And like Bruno's maternal ancestor, my own dear mother had succumbed to a tragic and untimely death, leaving her children as orphans.

Lowering his head to the glass that sat before him on the table,

Bruno clenched the rim between his teeth—tilted the drinking vessel upward—and moistened his throat with a sip of the surpassingly refreshing lemonade that Muddy had fixed for our meal. He then set the glass back down on the tabletop and continued thusly: "I was five years old when Momma died. My sisters and I were sent off to different institutions. I ended up in the Boston Asylum for the Care of Homeless Boys. I was treated much like any other orphan. Coldly—callously—with nothing resembling real tenderness or concern. Certainly, I was afforded no special dispensation on account of my condition. I was expected to perform all the usual chores and responsibilities—peel potatoes, wash dishes, scrub floors, mend clothing, darn my socks. But strangely enough, that sort of treatment turned out to be the best thing in the world for me. Out of necessity, I became remarkably adept at using my feet in place of my absent hands—so much so that, by the time I was ten, I was regarded as a genuine prodigy.

"Word about my talents spread far and wide. One day, the owner of a traveling circus showed up at the asylum. Somehow, he'd gotten wind of my accomplishments while passing through Boston. The following morning, I learned that I had been 'placed out' to him. Not adopted—*indentured.* Next thing I knew, I was the star of his show. Eventually we ended up here in New York City—and that's where I've been ever since.

"So there you have it, ladies. As I said, it's not a very entertaining tale. Not nearly as amusing as inheriting a barren, snake-infested bog that I had been led to believe was Eldorado!"

His protestations notwithstanding, his story was, in fact, replete with interest and drama. Aside from the inherent pathos of his situation, there was the matter of his own extraordinary efforts to achieve the unparalleled skills he now possessed. The very reticence with which he had related this part of his story—entirely omitting the almost-inconceivable struggles that he *must* have endured—only added to the power and poignancy of his tale. In spite of the almost *effeminate* cast of his surpassingly fine-featured countenance, it was clear that the young man was endowed with the most iron-willed and stoical character imaginable. Truly, his was a life story guaranteed to inspire the keenest feelings of both sympathy and admiration in any-one who heard it. Indeed, not only Sissy, but Muddy as well now sat staring at him with moistened eyes.

Perceiving how deeply affected my loved ones were by Bruno's recitation, Barnum responded in a most unexpected way. He emitted a loud, triumphant, "Ha!"

As the rest of us swiveled our heads in surprise to look at the show-man, he clapped his hands together and exultingly exclaimed: "Just look at those faces, Bruno, m'boy! Go on, go on—take a good, long gander! Have you ever seen such compassionate—such *pitying*—expressions? Why, they can barely hold back their tears! What did I tell you? Bless my soul, but there's whole *worlds* of money to be made from a life story like yours. Assuming it's all written out in the proper manner, of course, with the tragedy and the triumph—the tears and the laughter—the heartache and the heroism played up for all they're worth! Lord bless me, it would sell by the wagonload! 'They cry, they buy'—that's P. T. Bar-num's motto. Why, that's what always made my goblin child such a huge—such an *irresistible*—draw. The public couldn't get enough of it. Especially the weaker sex. Loved to gather around its cradle and shed crocodile tears over the pathetic little creature."

Patting her eyes dry with a corner of her napkin, Muddy asked: "And just how is that poor, miserable child, Mr. Barnum?"

"Dead," responded the showman with a sigh.

At this wholly unanticipated pronouncement, Muddy and Sissy gasped simultaneously in shock.

"Took sick a couple of weeks ago," Barnum continued with a frown. "He seemed to be improving nicely at first. All of a sudden, he just went into a decline. Next thing I knew—bang!—he was gone. Happened just like"—here, he raised a hand and, pressing his thumb and middle finger tightly together, produced a sharp, snapping noise—"*that!*"

Hearing this surprising news, I immediately called to mind the remarks made to me by Willie Schnitzler immediately following Abel Tomblin's death. In defending the character of her slain friend, she had expressly pointed to his inordinately tender and caring treatment of the supposed "goblin child." Was it possible, I now found myself wondering, that the connection between Tomblin and the grotesquely malformed infant was even deeper than Willie had suspected—that the strange little being had been *so* dependent on the custodian's attentions that it could not survive his demise?

Sissy in the meanwhile shook her head sadly and, clucking her tongue in sympathy, said: "I'm so sorry, Mr. Barnum. It's all so terribly, terribly sad."

"Yes, it's a blow, all right," answered Barnum. "The little critter was a tremendous moneymaker for me. Why, you wouldn't believe the number of people who came to the museum just to ogle the thing. Still," he continued, breaking into a cheerful smile and reaching out to pat the Armless Wonder on the knee, "I've got young Bruno here to take up the slack! The public can't get enough of him! That's why I want Poe here to write up his life story!"

This surprising pronouncement roused me from my ruminations. "I beg your pardon?" I exclaimed.

"Why, yes," said Barnum. "That's what we've come to see you about. The little idea I mentioned in my letter. After all, m'boy, you *did* agree to come work for me. Not that you haven't been pulling your weight! Heavens, no! Why, the assistance you rendered in helping me solve the Jennings case was everything I'd hoped for—and *then* some! *Still,* our agreement did include your services as a writer."

I could scarcely take issue with the showman on this point. Indeed, I had initially accepted his offer of employment precisely so that I might apply my own literary skills to his otherwise deplorable publications, thereby bringing some small measure of taste and cultivation to his hopelessly vulgar enterprise. To be sure, I would be forced to defer the project I was most truly interested in pursuing— i.e., the composition of a poem dealing with the death of a beautiful young woman. Such a delay, however, would only be temporary, as a biographical pamphlet of the sort that Barnum wished me to write could easily be produced in a week—two at the most.

"Very well," I replied after reflecting on the matter for several moments. "I shall be pleased to discharge my obligation to you by undertaking this task."

"Excellent, m'boy, excellent," said Barnum, raising his glass of lemonade as if offering a celebratory toast. "Exactly what I was hoping you'd say."

He drained the tumbler dry, then set it back on the table. "Just remember, Poe," he continued. "No need to be a stickler for every dry, dusty, tedious detail. A dash of added color—a little poetic license, if you will—never hurts. Something to tug at the heartstrings—make the blood pound a little faster in the veins. For instance—is it so far-fetched that Bruno might have learned his remarkable skills from an Indian yogi after running away from his brutal life at the orphan asylum and making his way to Bombay by whaleboat? Perhaps surviving a shipwreck somewhere in Polynesia and being taken captive by man-eating headhunters for a spell? Why, it's all perfectly plausible! Might've happened that way—might *easily* have happened. And it gives a nice little touch of *spice* to the story, if you see what I mean. Not that I'm telling you how to go about your business, mind you. Heaven forfend! Wouldn't dream of such a thing! No more than I'd want your advice on running the world's greatest museum. You're the artist, after all. And a mighty splendid one, at that!"

As Barnum drew to the end of this speech, I exchanged a pointed look with the Armless Wonder, who rolled his eyes upward, shook his head slowly from side to side, and grimaced wryly.

"I am curious about one aspect of your tale in particular, Bruno," I said. "You mentioned that you were indentured to the owner of a traveling circus. Who precisely was this gentleman?"

"Why, Alexander Parmalee," replied the other.

"Parmalee!" I cried. "You mean Mr. Barnum's despised rival?"

"Why, yes, I thought you knew that," said Barnum. "Parmalee was an itinerant showman like me, until he settled here in Manhattan and opened the Gotham Museum. Poor Bruno was forced to slave away in that dump for five long years. Might be working there still, if *I* hadn't come along and sprung him. Parmalee never forgave me. Accused me of stealing away his prized attraction! *Stealing!* Ha! Saving the lad from bondage is more like it! The damned scoundrel is *still* contriving ways of getting even! Surely you've heard of his latest outrage," Barnum added, his voice heavy with scorn. "His 'Amazing Harmonizing Insect Choir,' as he calls it."

305

"I fear I am completely ignorant of the matter to which you allude," I replied.

"Of course, of course, I keep forgetting how isolated you are up here," said Barnum. "Seems Parmalee found out about my latest phenomenon—you know the one I'm talking about, m'boy. My Giant Sacred Beetle of Lost Atlantis."

"It would have been awfully hard for Parmalee *not* to find out about it," Bruno said in a tone of amusement. "There are posters for it everywhere you go!"

"True enough," chuckled the showman. "Wait'll you see 'em, Poe. Splendid full-color announcements of the most stupendous exhibition ever viewed by human eyes! Why, the entire populace is in an absolute uproar over the big event! Well, the next thing you know, Parmalee is running a full-page notice in every paper in town, announcing *his* latest attraction—a whole blessed chorus of giant cockroaches that can *sing!* Couldn't believe my eyes when I came across that advertisement. Most ridiculous thing I ever saw. Shows a bunch of big happy insects, standing upright on their hind legs, arms around each other's shoulders, harmonizing like a barbershop quartet!"

"Singing roaches?" I exclaimed. "Can such things exist?"

"Tell you what, Poe," said Barnum. "Let's go see for ourselves. I'll bet dollars to doughnuts that the whole thing is a complete and utter fraud! Singing bugs! Ha! *Humbugs* is more like it! And while we're there, you can get a firsthand look at the Gotham. See for yourself the kind of wretched conditions poor Bruno here was forced to endure until I came along and saved him!"

At that moment, Muddy—who had risen from the table several moments earlier and disappeared into the kitchen—returned to the dining room bearing her blueberry pie, which she set down on the table.

"Aha!" cried Barnum rapturously. "So *that's* what I've been sniffing since I entered your home. Heavens and earth, but it smells divine—absolutely celestial! Reminds me of the time Baron Poniatowski invited me to dinner at his ancestral castle overlooking the Rhine. Lord, but that man knew how to live! Ever tell you folks that story? No? Well, then. . . ."

CHAPTER TWENTY-EIGHT

It was already fully dark when our guests took their leave. Before departing, Barnum informed me that—as there was no point in delaying our visit to Parmalee's establishment—he would send a carriage to fetch me on the morrow. The following day, shortly before noon, a buggy arrived at our cottage, and—after bidding farewell to my loved ones—I climbed aboard and was swiftly conveyed to the tumultuous heart of the city.

At length, the vehicle came to a halt directly before the American Museum. As I dismounted at the curb, my attention was riveted by the building's ostentatious façade. To its other flamboyant adornments—the array of colorful world flags that waved from its rooftop; the wrought-iron balcony from which blared the deafening cacophony of Barnum's egregious brass band; the scores of oval animal paintings mounted in the spaces between its windows—had now been added an enormous advertising banner, portraying a beetle the approximate size of Mount Aetna, looming over the rooftops of New York City.

"Extraordinary Attraction!" read the garishly painted sign, which stretched across the entire west side of the building's second floor. "The Giant Sacred Beetle of Lost Atlantis! The 8th Wonder of the World! Live! For the First Time Ever! World Premiere Exhibition, Wednesday, July 12!"

As I stood on the sidewalk, studying this remarkable sign, Barnum suddenly emerged from the museum, walking stick in hand. Striding directly to my side, he clapped me heartily on the shoulder.

"What do you think of her, Poe, m'boy?" he declared, pointing toward the banner with his walking stick. "Ain't she a beaut?"

"Indeed, it is a most striking—a most impressive—advertisement. I do not recall, however," I added dryly, "that the creature in question, however prodigious in size, was of *quite* such colossal dimensions."

"Yes, yes, I see your point," mused Barnum, as though this consideration had never before occurred to him. "I suppose the artist *did* get a tad carried away. Still, there's nothing wrong with embellishing things just a bit to attract the public's notice—not as long as you end up giving 'em their money's worth. And believe me, m'boy, the customers won't come away disappointed—I absolutely guarantee it. No one's ever been cheated at the American Museum! That's the difference between P. T. Barnum and other so-called showmen like our friend Alexander Parmalee. Heavens and earth, I'm just *bursting* to see these so-called harmonizing bugs of his. Why, I'll wager a full week's profits that they're a complete and utter hoax! Come! Let's be off!"

And so saying, he took me by the elbow and ushered me briskly up Broadway in the direction of Lafayette Street.

Within minutes we had arrived at the Gotham Museum. It was housed in a distinctly decrepit-looking building, three stories high, whose dark and dingy façade was adorned with a few crudely rendered banners depicting the supposed marvels within: a living sea serpent—Ziggo and Montano, the "Aztec Children"—Baron Ernest Malgri, the "Astonishing Double-Horned Man"—George the Turtle Boy—and several other equally bizarre curiosities. A large, brightly painted wooden sign was propped against the wall by the entranceway. It portrayed the museum's latest attraction—"The Amazing Harmonizing Cockroach Choir! The Wonder of the Insect World! You Won't Believe Your Eyes or Ears! The Greatest Natural Marvel in New York!" Stationed beside this garish advertisement was a gaunt—red-whiskered—rather shabbily dressed fellow, whose job was to lure passersby into the museum, and whose "patter" consisted of a string of doggerel couplets, recited over and over again in a lilting, singsong cadence:

> "Ladies and gents,
> for only ten cents
> you can see all the sights.
> And there on your right
> is the great fat lady;
> my, but she's a healthy baby,
> weighing three hundred pounds—
> she's six foot around!
> Her husband is the living
> skeleton—see him shivering!
> The dog-faced boy
> will bring you all joy!
> The human horse
> is a wonder, of course!
> And I'll show to you
> the boxing kangaroo!
> The tattooed lady
> will drive you crazy!
> Lydia's her name—
> She's got pictures across her frame!
> And our singing bugs are a wonder to hear—
> They'll be music to your ear!"

Passing into the entranceway, we purchased our tickets at the counter and proceeded within.

Unlike Barnum's spacious and brightly illuminated galleries, the halls of the Gotham were cramped, dim, and smoky. They were also far less crowded. Indeed, in several of the halls, Barnum and I found ourselves entirely alone. What few customers we *did* encounter appeared to belong to a much less prosperous class than those who patronized Barnum's establishment. As we passed through the museum, we came across more than one raggedly attired fellow reeking of cheap cigars and gin; as well as several females whose painted faces—

tawdry dress—and brazen manner—clearly marked them as members of the most debauched and fallen species of womanhood.

The attractions at the Gotham were, if possible, even more *outré* than those routinely featured at the American Museum. Apart from the living performers, both human and animal—the freaks and jugglers, boxing kangaroos and waltzing dogs—the exhibits consisted largely of grotesque anatomical curiosities. Display case after display case was filled with preserved medical anomalies of the most sensational kind: the charred stomach of a French noblewoman who had died of spontaneous combustion after imbibing a bottle of brandy—three spotted newts, a horned toad, and a large black snake that had been extracted from the intestines of a German peasant—a two-pound kidney stone resembling an Irish potato—a twelve-headed tapeworm measuring 238 feet in length—an ovarian cyst weighing more than 150 pounds—the embryo of a hydrocephalic child—an immense swarm of bot-fly larvae that had burst from a boil on the neck of a twelve-year-old Scandinavian boy—and much more.

As we made our way through the galleries, peering intently at the various bizarre and unwholesome displays, a continuous stream of disparaging sounds issued from my companion's lips. These ranged from mild *tuts* of disapproval, to nasal *snorts* of incredulity, to loud exclamations of unreserved scorn. Perhaps his most intense reaction was reserved for a glass case containing three taxidermically preserved bunnies, indistinguishable in every respect from the common brown rabbits of the genus *Sylvilagus* that I encountered on my daily rambles through the countryside. A hand-lettered sign on the wall beside the case identified these perfectly unremarkable specimens as "The Astonishing Toft Triplets!"

"What in heaven's name do you make of *this*, Poe?" Barnum asked, squinting through the glass at the trio of stuffed rodents.

"Unless I am mistaken," I replied, "these three, rather moth-eaten creatures are some of the purported offspring of Mrs. Mary Toft, the notorious eighteenth-century 'rabbit breeder.' "

"Offspring? Great Scot! You don't mean to say that this Toft woman is supposed to have given birth to bunnies?"

"So it was averred at the time," I said. "Mrs. Toft was a poor peasant woman, residing in Surrey, England, in the early 1700s. According to her testimony, she was startled by a hare while working in the fields during the fifth week of her pregnancy. Shortly thereafter, she developed an overwhelming craving for rabbit meat. When she finally gave birth, the creature that emerged from her womb was the first of several dozen rabbits she begat during the next few years. Word of these miraculous births soon spread from her village, eventually reaching the ears of no less a personage than King George himself, who dispatched his court physician, Nathaniel St. André, to check on the phenomenon. After examining Mrs. Toft's claims, Doctor St. André came away utterly convinced, and proceeded to publish a book on the subject, *A Short Narrative of an Extraordinary Delivery of Rabbits*, which became an immediate sensation. Before long, the 'rabbit-breeder' was the talk of all London. In the end, of course, she was exposed as a flagrant fraud. She died in disgrace, while St. André incurred the merciless ridicule of his contemporaries."

"Fascinating," Barnum exclaimed. "Amazed I never heard the story before. There's an important moral to be learned from it, too!"

"And what might that be?" I inquired.

"Never underestimate human gullibility," said Barnum. "Why, it's astounding what folks'll believe in—positively staggering! Mermaids—unicorns—females who can spawn whole colonies of cottontails! And it's not just folks today—not just here and now—but always and everywhere. Been that way since the beginning of time. Started in the Garden of Eden. From the minute the serpent smooth-talked Eve into believing that one bite of that sweet, juicy apple would do wonders for her, there's never been a shortage of suckers in the world!"

"Nor of those," I said pointedly, "who devise ingenious means of exploiting the almost limitless credulity of their fellow man."

Far from offending Barnum—who might have been expected to interpret this as a sly *dig* at himself (which, in fact, it partially *was*)—my remark merely elicited a hearty chuckle from the showman.

"Who knows?" he said. "Maybe there's more to Parmalee than I thought. Imagine—sticking a few dead bunnies inside a display case and claiming they're the hundred-year-old relics of a world-famous hoax. Brilliant! Why, it's almost enough to make me admire the man!

"But look there," he suddenly cried, pointing to the opposite side of the gallery, where a hand-lettered placard was affixed to the wall beside the exit. "This Way to the Amazing Harmonizing Bug Choir!" it read.

Following this sign, we soon found ourselves inside a small, circular room, containing the largest congregation of customers we had thus far encountered—perhaps twenty-five people in all. They were gathered around a small stage upon which stood a table draped in red velvet. Posed behind the table was an elderly, hollow-cheeked fellow with lank, white hair that hung nearly to the level of his shoulders. He was very formally dressed in a black frock coat, gold vest, and white cravat. In his right hand he clutched an ebony baton with a shiny brass tip.

Arranged before him on the table was a row of clear glass jars, eight in number, each containing a specimen of a most remarkable-looking insect. These creatures were wingless—oblong in shape—and armored in thickly plated carapaces the approximate color and texture of polished mahogany-wood. I recognized them at once as members of the species *Gromphadorhina portentosa*, more commonly known as the Giant Hissing Cockroach of Madagascar—so-called because of the distinctive noise they produced from their spiracles when angered or alarmed.

It was this latter characteristic that accounted for their ostensible musical abilities. Since the size of the roaches varied considerably— the smallest measuring barely one inch, the largest more than four times that length—each produced a sound with a distinctly different *pitch*. By sharply striking the jars with his brass-tipped baton, the old man could thus elicit a series of loud, sibilant "notes" from the insects. By this means, he was able to produce crude, if recognizable, renditions of a variety of tunes, from "Three Blind Mice" to "Rule, Britannia."

The conclusion of each number was greeted with a few tepid hand-claps from the audience. The elderly gentleman would acknowledge this half-hearted applause with a little bow—gesture at the row of insects like a symphony conductor paying tribute to his soloists—then launch into his next selection.

After listening to this singular concert for five minutes or so, Barnum—who spent the entire time shaking his head in disbelief and chortling to himself—leaned close to me and said: "Come, Poe—let's be on our way. No need to subject ourselves to another instant of this travesty. I'll say one thing for Parmalee—just when you think he can't sink any lower, he comes up with *this!* You've got to hand it to the man—not everyone could dream up something as stupendously dreadful! Why, it's almost a form of genius!"

Having no wish to remain any longer than was absolutely necessary in the presence of the fearsome-looking (if, as I knew, entirely harmless) insects, I readily acceded to this suggestion.

Taking me by the arm, Barnum steered me briskly from the little room. No sooner had we stepped over the threshold, however, than we came face-to-face with a stout, middle-aged gentleman with a florid, somewhat porcine countenance. I recognized this individual at once as none other than Alexander Parmalee himself, whom—as the reader may recall—I had glimpsed several months earlier during my initial visit to the American Museum.

"Barnum!" he cried in astonishment, coming to an abrupt halt before us.

"Afternoon, Parmalee," said the showman. "Why, I was just talking about you. Telling Poe here what a genius you are!"

"Oh, yes, I'm *sure* those were your very words," said the other sardonically. "I must say, Barnum, you certainly have your nerve, showing your face around here."

"Nerve?" exclaimed the showman. "Heavens and earth, but there's the pot calling the kettle black! Poe and I just got done listening to those hissing humbugs of yours. The 'Amazing Harmonizing Insect Choir.' Ha! Why, that's like describing a common garter snake as the Legendary Sea Serpent of Loch Ness!"

"Or a stuffed monkey with a dried-up fishtail sewn on it as a beautiful, bare-breasted mermaid, eh, Barnum?" sneered Parmalee.

"That's a low blow, Parmalee, a mighty low blow! You know as well as I do that I was utterly persuaded of the complete and absolute authenticity of my Feejee Mermaid! Why, I spent a small fortune to have her examined by the greatest scientific experts of the age! And every single one of 'em—well, *nearly* every one—assured me that she was the genuine article! How was I to know different? Why, if anyone was victimized by that unfortunate episode it was *me!*"

"Yes, yes, I've heard it all before," said Parmalee. "But that still doesn't explain what you're doing here. Come to see if there's anything new you can steal from me?"

"Steal? Why, that's rich. That's amusing. Who's the thief, I ask you? Here you are, trying to steal *my* thunder with those ridiculous performing cockroaches of yours, just when *I'm* about to debut the greatest insect attraction the world has ever seen!"

"I resent that, Barnum!" cried Parmalee. "Resent it clear down to my bones! Why, I've been planning to display those magnificent musical creatures for months—long before you started covering the whole city with those absurd posters of yours! Acquired 'em way back in May from a ship's captain just returned from a voyage to darkest Africa. Paid a king's ransom, for 'em, too!"

"Oh yes, I believe you," Barnum said with heavy sarcasm. "Thousands wouldn't."

"Barnum," said Parmalee, drawing himself up to his full height. "I shall be glad to refund your admission fees, but I must ask you and your companion to leave at once. You are not welcome here."

"Keep the money, Parmalee," said the showman with a sneer. "Judging from the size of your crowd, you need it more than I do." He then gripped me by the elbow—turned on his heels—and led me away.

To reach the exit, we were compelled to pass through a long, narrow corridor lined with glass-fronted cabinets. As we made our way along this hallway, I suddenly drew to an abrupt halt, my attention having been caught by one especially curious object resting on one of the cabinet shelves. It was a large glass jar of the sort that might be found in a chemist's laboratory. It was filled with a pale, yellow fluid. Floating within was a gray, furrowed object I instantly recognized as the complete cerebral organ of a human being! A hand-lettered card beside the receptacle read: "Actual Brain of the Heinous Murderer

Lemuel Thompson, Showing Characteristic Anatomical Structure of the Born Criminal."

As I stared at this grisly specimen—which had evidently been removed from the young man's corpse following his execution for the savage murder of the beautiful prostitute, Ellen Jennings—Barnum came up beside me and said: "Ah, I see you've spotted Thompson's brain. Fascinating article, ain't it? Wouldn't mind owning it myself— make a marvelous addition to the Jennings display in my Hall of Crime and Punishment. Tried my damnedest to get my hands on it. Offered to buy it from Parmalee for—well, I won't even tell you how much I offered him; you'd think I was out of my mind, the amount was so generous. But I can't help it, Poe, that's just the way I'm built—when I want something badly enough, I'm willing to go whole hog, pay whatever it costs. 'Spare no expense!'—that's P. T. Barnum's motto. Didn't work out, though. The scoundrel refused to part with it. Claimed it had too much sentimental value. Couldn't bear to part with something that belonged to his own kin."

"Kin?" I cried in astonishment. "What in heaven's name do you mean?"

"Why, Thompson was Parmalee's nephew," said Barnum. "Thought you knew that. Worked around his museum, doing odd jobs and such. Of course, if you ask me, it shows mighty poor taste to keep your own nephew's brain on display in a jar! But that's Parmalee for you—man hasn't got a decent bone in his body. Well, come on, Poe, let's be off. Don't like to linger in a place where I'm not wanted."

Moments later, we found ourselves back out on the street, each of us absorbed in his own ruminations as we made our way along Broadway. My own thoughts were preoccupied with the intelligence just related to me concerning Parmalee's relationship to Lemuel Thompson. It was undeniably true that there was something intensely unseemly— if not actively *ghoulish*—about Parmalee's willingness to put his own nephew's brain on public display. Even so, Barnum's high-minded reproof of his rival struck me as intensely amusing, since I was sure that he himself would not have hesitated for a moment to exhibit the stuffed cadaver of his own grandmother if it would have drawn customers to his museum.

All at once, as Barnum and I reached the intersection of Broadway and Barclay Street, I was roused from my thoughts by the shrill call of a newsboy standing on the corner. "Extree! Extree! Read all about it! Murder most foul! Morris Vanderhorn killed!"

A startled gasp escaped my lips. Barnum turned to look at me, his countenance wrought into an expression of the utmost astonishment. Hurrying to the newsboy, he handed him a coin and snatched a paper from his grasp. He then carried it to my side, and—standing in the center of the sidewalk, oblivious to the tide of pedestrians streaming around us—we read the following:

MURDER BY POISON!

MORRIS VANDERHORN DEAD

ARSENIC FOUND IN BODY

Wife Suspected

A terrible crime came to light today, when arsenic was discovered in the stomach of Morris Vanderhorn, who died yesterday morning at his elegant home on Union Square Park, one of the city's most fashionable neighborhoods. Mr. Vanderhorn, who had been severely indisposed for the better part of a week, was at first believed to have perished of natural causes. However, a postmortem examination conducted by the coroner, Dr. Wakeman, revealed the unmistakable presence of poison in the digestive organs of the unfortunate Mr. Vanderhorn, proving beyond a doubt that he was the victim of foul play.

According to those familiar with the case, it has been nearly a week since Mr. Vanderhorn began exhibiting the symptoms that eventually culminated in his demise. These included severe nausea, dizziness, and vomiting. During his apparent illness, Mr. Vanderhorn was treated by his business partner, the celebrated Dr. Archibald

Mayhew, purveyor of the highly popular medicinal tonic that bears his name. For nearly a week, Mr. Vanderhorn was fed frequent doses of Dr. Mayhew's newest product, Mayhew's Revitalizing Vegetable Cordial. As it was necessary to administer these doses at regular intervals—three spoonfuls every four hours—the task fell to Mr. Vanderhorn's seemingly devoted wife, Emmeline, the daughter of Mr. and Mrs. Cornelius Steenwyck. According to Mr. Chester Croley—described as the "right-hand man" of the deceased—Mrs. Vanderhorn was very diligent in the performance of her duties, never failing, day or night, to administer the required dosage with her own hands.

Far from improving, however, Mr. Vanderhorn's condition grew steadily worse, until—after six days of terrible suffering—he lapsed into unconsciousness and died. Questions were immediately raised about the efficacy of Dr. Mayhew's potion. Though refusing to divulge its exact ingredients, Dr. Mayhew insisted that his elixir contained nothing more harmful than a modicum of alcohol, and demanded that an autopsy be performed at once on the corpse. The latter operation revealed a lethal amount of arsenic in the digestive system of Mr. Vanderhorn, making it clear that the victim had been slowly poisoned over the course of the preceding week. In spite of her reputation for piety, Mrs. Vanderhorn was very naturally deemed a likely suspect. When police sought her out for questioning last evening, they discovered, to their great consternation, that she was no longer in the country, having absconded several hours earlier on board the ship, the *John Donaldson*, bound for Liverpool, England! Also on board the passenger vessel, it was learned today, was Mr. Vanderhorn's personal secretary, Mr. Hiram Flagg.

Friends of Mrs. Vanderhorn—renowned for her docile temperament and charitable work—vehemently deny that she could possibly be guilty of such a heinous deed; although even they are at a loss to explain her sudden flight in the company of Mr. Flagg.

Mr. Vanderhorn was a well-known figure about town. Though afflicted with a dreadful facial deformity, he made it his business not to shun the public eye. On the contrary, he was exceptionally fond of attending society dinners and other engagements, in spite of the chilling effect his frightfully disfigured visage had on the more tender-hearted guests.

Having reached the end of this article, Barnum and I turned to each other and exchanged a wordless look. It was unnecessary to speak—each knew what the other was thinking.

We were recalling the day, several weeks earlier, when we had observed Mrs. Vanderhorn and her husband's hunchbacked assistant—whose name, we had just now learned, was Mr. Hiram Flagg—emerge together from a shop on Broadway and hold a brief, furtive conversation before departing on their separate ways. The shop they had been visiting was Ludlow's Pharmacy, which—like every other druggist in the city—sold commercial arsenic to the public as both a rat-killer and a nervous stimulant, no questions asked.

CHAPTER TWENTY-NINE

For the next several days, New Yorkers seemed to talk of little else besides the murder of Morris Vanderhorn. The public's all-absorbing interest in the case was not to be wondered at, in view of the many sensational elements of which it was composed. Not only was the victim himself a person of great notoriety, but the circumstances surrounding his death were such as to excite the most intense—if prurient—fascination.

There was, to begin with, the alleged involvement of the socially illustrious—reputedly unimpeachable—Mrs. Vanderhorn. This ostensible paragon of wifely devotion and Christian virtue now stood exposed not merely as a remorseless killer but as a brazen adulteress as well! The man in whose company she had fled, moreover—her apparent lover and co-conspirator—was none other than her husband's grotesquely deformed personal secretary. These circumstances, combined with the vicious manner in which Vanderhorn had been dispatched (slow poisoning by arsenic being a particularly unpleasant form of death) were guaranteed to provoke the greatest imaginable excitement in the mind of the masses, whose appetite for the titillating—the sensational—and the sordid—was well nigh inexhaustible.

My own reaction to the news of the murder was exceedingly mixed. On the one hand, I could hardly fail to be shocked by a crime of such callousness and cruelty as the deliberate, cold-blooded poisoning of a man by his supposedly devoted helpmate. On the other hand—having witnessed at first hand the malice and contempt with which Vanderhorn routinely treated both his wife and employee—it was hard for me not to feel a certain measure of sympathy for his alleged killers. I also found it peculiarly fitting that Vanderhorn should meet his death by unwittingly imbibing a lethal potation, since he himself had made his fortune by peddling adulterated spirits to countless abject wretches in thrall to the Fiend Intemperance!

My strongest emotion, however, was one of regret. Though more than a week had elapsed since the resolution of the Isabel Somers murder case, I continued to be tantalized by the question of Morris Vanderhorn's connection to that savagely slaughtered young woman, and I greatly lamented the fact that—with his death—the answer to that riddle had forever been swallowed by the grave.

As for Barnum, his reaction was as divided as my own—though for different reasons. So extreme was his antipathy toward Vanderhorn that he could scarcely contain his glee over the murder, which—to the showman—constituted nothing less than sheer, poetic justice. As a *connoisseur* of human hypocrisy—who relished nothing more than watching the self-righteous brought low by disgrace—he also took particular delight in the scandalous revelations concerning Vanderhorn's wife, whose façade of saintlike self-abasement and purity had now been so completely stripped away.

At the same time, he was deeply galled by the degree to which the Vanderhorn case had overshadowed every other topic in the city, including the impending debut of his monstrous insect. To regain the attention of the public, Barnum redoubled his publicity campaign—increasing the size and frequency of his newspaper advertisements—posting even more and larger placards around the city—and sending a virtual army of men in sandwich-board signs to patrol the streets. Before long, it was difficult, if not impossible, to cast one's gaze anywhere in Manhattan without encountering a gaudy announcement for the upcoming, world premiere exhibition of *The Giant Sacred Beetle of Lost Atlantis, the Greatest Living Wonder Ever Beheld by Human Eyes!*

At length, the big day arrived. At approximately six o'clock that evening, a handsome brougham pulled up at our cottage to transport

Muddy, Sissy, and myself to the American Museum, Barnum having invited us to attend the premiere as his special guests. Both of my loved ones had attired themselves in their finest apparel for the occasion, and as I escorted them out to the waiting vehicle, my bosom swelled with a sense of nearly overpowering adoration for the two radiant and angelic creatures at my side.

Our trip to the city was intensely pleasant. The evening was one of indescribable loveliness. With its windows fully lowered, our carriage was suffused with a warm and perfumed fragrance that seemed to be the aromatic distillation of summertime itself. Muddy and Sissy chattered and laughed continuously, while I inwardly rejoiced to see them both so animated and cheerful—particularly my darling wife, whom I had not observed in such high, such seemingly carefree, spirits since the tragic slaying of her friend.

My own mood was singularly buoyant, tempered only by a slight twinge of apprehension at the prospect of spending the evening in such close proximity to a six-foot specimen of the genus *Necrophorus.* Barnum had assured us that—as his personal guests—we would be seated in the very front row of the theater, mere feet away from the stage. In view of my instinctive aversion to beetles of even normal size, the reader will easily understand why I experienced a distinct sense of misgiving as I contemplated the evening ahead.

Arrived at length at our destination, I saw at once that Barnum's intensified efforts to work the public into a state of frenzied anticipation over his gigantic insect had been an unqualified success. Gathered outside the museum was an enormous crowd, composed of people of every age and social class, from young ragamuffins—who had evidently broken open their piggy banks to obtain the price of admission—to fashionably attired members of the *beau monde.* One and all, old and young, their excitement was palpable.

Above their heads, on the wrought-iron balcony (which had been draped with red-white-and-blue bunting), Barnum's brass band was rending the air with an unusually vigorous (if typically inept) performance of "Yankee Doodle"; while his rooftop-mounted Drummond light swept the streets with its broad and dazzling beam. Several members of Barnum's acrobatic troupe had been outfitted so as to suggest bizarre, anthropomorphic insects. Wearing grotesque *papier mâché* masks and bulky costumes onto which had been sewn a few floppy appendages resembling spider legs, they frolicked and capered about the sidewalk, much to the merriment of the youngest members of the crowd. Altogether, an intensely festive, even *carnivalesque*, atmosphere prevailed.

Dismounting from the carriage, Sissy, Muddy, and I strolled directly toward the entranceway and into the museum, under the envious gaze of the horde of people waiting to purchase tickets. We found Barnum just inside the lobby. He was formally clad in a handsome coat of expensive black material, a gray-striped vest, and a white cravat. His portly face beamed with pleasure, and there was a sparkle of wild, almost feverish, excitement in his full—dark—liquid eyes.

After greeting us warmly and exclaiming over the unsurpassed loveliness of my companions, he turned to me and—gesturing toward the crowd outside his doors—addressed me thusly:

"Ever seen anything like it, Poe? What a turnout! Bless my soul, it's even more stupendous than I imagined! Why, it beats the multitude that showed up for my Grand Buffalo Hunt in Hoboken last spring—beats it all hollow! There must be a thousand people out there at the very least! Auditorium only has nine hundred seats, too. Have to squeeze the rest of them in somehow—stick 'em in the aisles, stand 'em in the balconies! Lord, there'd be a riot if I turned even a single one of them away! Been standing out there for hours. Well, they won't be sorry they waited. Mark my words, Poe, they'll be telling their grandchildren about this in the years to come—'Yessiree, I was present when Barnum's magnificent gigantic beetle was first revealed to an astonished and awestruck world!' Oh, there'll be pandemonium when they see it—sheer pandemonium! Make the crowds at the old Circus Maximus seem as sedate as a Unitarian prayer-meeting!

"Here," he continued, reaching into the side pocket of his coat. When he withdrew his hand an instant later, it was clutching three large, pasteboard tickets of a bright vermillion hue, which he then distributed to Muddy, Sissy, and myself. "Best head upstairs right away and avoid the stampede. Just hand these to the usher. He'll show you to your seats."

Thanking the showman—who promised to see us backstage following the show—we climbed the grand marble staircase to the third floor, and proceeded to the auditorium. Posted outside the entrance were several handsomely attired individuals who had evidently been enlisted to serve as ushers. One of these was Slim Jim McCormack, whose skeletal frame was clothed in a specially tailored costume consisting of a dark blue, satin dress coat—a waistcoat of cream-colored cashmere—a white cascade necktie—and linen pantaloons. He was conversing with a tall, broad-shouldered fellow, garbed in an even more resplendent coat of richly embroidered red velvet—white breeches with gold knee buckles—white silk hose—and gold-buckled patent leather slippers.

The physiognomy of this latter individual was singular in the extreme. In the mold of his fine, classically regular features—the brilliancy of his piercing, brown eyes—the luster of his naturally curling, chestnut-colored hair—he possessed a dark, brooding, masculine beauty of nearly Byronic dimensions. His dashing appearance, however, was severely mitigated by his extraordinary complexion, which was entirely covered with a baroque filigree of bizarre and exotic markings—stylized figures in indigo and cinnabar of reptiles, birds, fish, and jungle animals, interspersed with indecipherable hieroglyphics. From this remarkable facial ornamentation, I deduced at once that this gentleman was none other than Captain Conrad Coughlin, the so-called "Miracle of Mortal Marvels," every inch of whose body was tattooed with nearly four hundred different designs. According to the account of his life included in Barnum's official guidebook, these tattoos—requiring more than seven million individual punctures—had been inflicted as a form of torture lasting almost six months, following his capture by the fiendish Khan of Kashgar in Chinese Barbary.

As we stepped up to the entrance, Slim Jim bid us welcome; while—with an urbane smile that caused the intertwined serpents on his upper lip to appear to writhe in a most disconcerting manner—his companion asked to see our tickets.

"Please come this way," said the tattooed gentleman after briefly perusing the tickets. He then preceded us into the auditorium and ushered us to our front-row seats.

323

"Enjoy the show," he said, presenting each of us with a pro-gramme card. As I took mine from his hand, I observed that his en-tire extremity, including the palm, was inscribed with a wild webwork of zoological designs. Only the fingernails were untouched.

"Oh, Eddie, isn't it splendid?" exclaimed Sissy, as the tattooed marvel swiveled on his heels and returned to his post.

Indeed, Barnum's auditorium was as impressive as any theater to be found in the city. It featured an enormous stage—approximately fifty feet deep by ninety feet wide—upon which, in any given month, a staggering variety of entertainments were held, from fat baby con-tests and beauty pageants to temperance lectures, Shakespearean tragedies, minstrel acts, magic shows, and appearances by touring classical vocalists. The hall itself was exceedingly lavish, with plush, red velvet seats, Corinthian columns, elaborate white-and-gold deco-rations on the proscenium and stage boxes, and a half-dozen crystal chandeliers depending from the arched ceiling, which was painted with a neoclassical landscape scene in the manner of Poussin.

As I surveyed the richly appointed surroundings, I suddenly be-came cognizant of a growing *din* emanating from just outside the the-ater. An instant later, Captain Coughlin and his fellow ushers began to lead a stream of visibly excited patrons to their places—Barnum having evidently opened the doors for general admission immediately following our arrival. As the seats around us began to fill, I turned my attention to the programme card. Elegantly printed on heavy, royal blue pasteboard, it read as follows:

BARNUM'S AMERICAN MUSEUM PROUDLY PRESENTS

"THE LOST CITY,
Or, THE FALL OF ATLANTIS!"

A Great Dramatic Pantomime Full of Magical Scenes, Marvelous
Incidents, and Wondrous Sights!

CULMINATING IN THE MOST THRILLING SPECTACLE
EVER WITNESSED BY MORTAL EYES!

The Giant Sacred Beetle of Lost Atlantis!

The Colossus of the Ancient World!

A LIVING MIRACLE!

THE MARVEL OF THE AGES!

MORE AWESOME THAN THE LEVIATHAN OF SCRIPTURE!

═══════════

Programme begins promptly at 9:00 o'clock in the evening.

═══════════

CHARACTERS

Salamo, King of Atlantis . . . Mr. W. I. Jamison

Prince Hassanbad, his Son . . . Mr. Clarence Hardaway

Aurora, A Beautiful Slave Maiden . . . Miss Flora Graham

Critias the Athenian . . . Mr. Milnes Prior

Ugliana, Wife of Critias . . . Mrs. Prior

Tartarro the Troubadour . . . Mr. Elbridge Brothwell

Papillo, A Merry Sprite . . . Mr. Lyman Hutchins

Fatalio the Sorcerer . . . Mr. Abner Bridgeman

Giants, Witches, Dwarfs, Sorcerers, Seers, etc. . . . . Colonel
Routh Goshen, Mr. Raddo Schauf, Signor Bruno Saltarino,
Miss Wilhelmina Schnitzler, Madame Cleo Ben Dib, Mr. Waldo
Toft, Messrs. Hoomie and Iola, Mr. Sammy Wainwright
Madame Maria Macart, Miss Zobeide Luti.

Synopsis

ACT I

The Palace of Salamo. The Greek Emissary. The Sacrilege.

ACT II

Picturesque Landscape by Moonlight. Aurora's Lament. Tartarro's Reply.
Merry Dance and Chorus.

ACT III

The Invasion. Terrific Broadsword Combat. The Defeat of Hassanbad.

ACT IV

The Sorcerer's Cave. Incantation of the Witches.
Dreadful Catastrophe Foretold.

ACT V

The Fall of Atlantis! The Dance of the Pagan Priestesses! Blood Sacrifice to
the Monster! The Vengeance of Zeus!

━━━━━━

By the time I finished perusing the card, the auditorium was already nearly packed to overflowing. Such was the magnitude of the crowd that—as Barnum had perceived—there were not nearly enough seats to accommodate them all. For whatever reason, however—whether greed or a sincere desire not to disappoint, it was impossible to say—the showman seemed determined to admit each and every individual who had shown up for the grand event. Long after the final seat was taken, people continued to arrive, until there were spectators occupying every conceivable space—standing in the very rear of the auditorium, leaning against the walls along the periphery, and even (in the case of a dozen or so limber young men) sitting cross-legged in the aisles.

Though nine o'clock was the announced starting-time for the show, another twenty-five minutes elapsed before the very last customer had been squeezed into the hall. It was already half-past the hour when the gas jets illuminating the auditorium were finally lowered, leaving the proscenium bathed in the bright glow of the footlights. An instant later, the orchestra struck up a rousing version of "Hail Columbia"; whereupon Barnum strode onto the stage to thunderous applause. For several moments, he basked in the adulation of the crowd, smiling, bowing, and waving to the audience. At length, the music ceased—the clapping subsided—and, after loudly clearing his throat, Barnum addressed the house thusly:

"What a magnificent ovation—absolutely grand. From the bottom of my heart, dear friends, I offer you my thanks. I also offer my congratulations. That's right—*congratulations*. For tonight, you will be privileged to witness a sight that has been vouchsafed to no one else now living on the planet!

"Now, you'll sometimes hear it said that P. T. Barnum is given to gross exaggeration—even outright fabrication. Well, that's pure hogwash, of course—a dastardly lie perpetrated by my enemies. Still, I'd be less than candid if I didn't admit that, on one or two occasions, I *may* have made a claim that deviated just a tad from strict, one-hundred-percent accuracy. Never knowingly, of course—never out of a calculated effort to mislead or deceive, Heaven forbid! It's just that—well, every now and again, I get carried away over some extraordinary new attraction I've acquired, and I let my enthusiasm get the better of me.

"Tonight, however, there's no need for exaggeration. Tonight, I can say to you, without fear of overstatement, that you will be witnessing a phenomenon whose significance is nothing less than earthshaking! You will be present at an event that can fairly be described as a landmark in human history! A spectacle whose sheer momentous importance rivals the greatest scientific milestones of all time—the discovery of fire!—the invention of the wheel!—Newton's law of universal gravitation! Yes, my friends—you and you alone will see with your own astonished and disbelieving eyes a living marvel straight out of myth and legend! And you will be the first to learn the answer to a riddle that has baffled the greatest minds of the ages—namely, what caused the destruction of the fabled kingdom of Atlantis?

"Now, ladies and gentlemen, for those of you who may not be entirely familiar with the subject, permit me to offer a few words by way of introduction to the astounding and unforgettable spectacle you are about to witness. According to the highest classical authorities—Plato, Solon, that whole Greek crew—Atlantis was the most splendid place the world's ever known. Oh, it was just glorious, I tell you—palaces gleaming with emeralds and rubies, houses made of the finest marble, streets paved with gold. Why, it made Nebuchadnezzar's Babylon look like the wretchedest kind of gypsy encampment! And then one day—*poof!*—it was gone! Vanished under the waters, leaving no more trace than a bubble bursting on the waves.

"From that day to the present, the mystery of what became of Atlantis has been the greatest enigma ever to torment the mind of mortal man. Philosophers and historians, scientists and theologians have devoted their entire lives to studying the question. One theory kept coming up again and again. According to the deepest thinkers on the subject, Atlantis was destroyed by a vengeful God, who smote the citizens of that proud, pagan kingdom for committing sacrilege, just the same as the ancient Israelites were punished for worshiping the Golden Calf. Only the deity that the ancient Atlanteans were worshiping wasn't anything as ordinary as a graven idol. It was something far, far worse. They were worshiping *bugs!* That's right—hideous, monster beetles that came crawling out of the very center of the earth! And when the Lord saw that, he just pulled the plug on the whole godless city and sent it to its everlasting doom, the same as He did with Sodom and Gomorrah!

"Well that was just a theory, of course—an educated guess. In all the centuries that followed, no one's ever been able to *prove* anything. Until tonight!

"Yes, ladies and gentlemen—tonight, you will view with your own wonderstruck eyes the living evidence of that theory. Believe it or not, one of those creatures managed to survive! Made it to shore—crawled underground—and hibernated for a few thousand years.

"Now, as everyone knows, Barnum's museum employs a whole army of agents who scour the globe day and night, three hundred sixty-five days a year, searching for the greatest curiosities and attractions in existence! Well, one of these fellows heard rumors while traveling through darkest Africa. According to these stories, an actual living specimen of the Giant Sacred Beetle of Lost Atlantis—long thought to be extinct—had been spotted in the impenetrable jungles of the Congo! At great personal risk to life and limb, this bold and intrepid fellow managed to track down and capture the monster. It was then shipped back here to New York City at unimaginable trouble and incalculable expense. Amazing story, simply amazing! Wish I had time to share it with you. Those of you who are interested can read all about it in the lavishly illustrated souvenir pamphlet, costing a mere twenty-five cents, on sale in the lobby following tonight's performance.

"One last thing, ladies and gentlemen, before the show begins.

Please be assured that no expense has been spared to protect you, the public, from any danger posed by this ferocious, carnivorous monster. It is housed in a specially designed cage, constructed of the most powerful, indestructible iron bars in existence. Why, a herd of rampaging elephants couldn't put a dent in it! So please try to hold back your screams of terror when you set eyes on the creature.

"And now, without further ado, I have the pleasure and honor of presenting to you the grandest, most astounding, most spectacular entertainment ever staged! Ladies and gentlemen," he concluded with a flourish, " 'The Lost City, or, The Fall of Atlantis!' " He then bowed again to the audience and exited the stage.

Though accustomed by now to hearing the most outlandish claims imaginable issue from the showman's lips, even I was not prepared for the sheer *nonsensicality* of the presentation he had just made. In my incredulous reaction to its absurdity, however, I appeared to be alone. Far from responding in the way I would have expected—with outraged catcalls and hoots of derision—the crowd rewarded Barnum with an ovation even louder than the one that had greeted his entrance.

As the orchestra struck up the fanfare from Beethoven's *Fidelio*, the velvet curtains parted to reveal a sight that brought a chorus of awed and delighted gasps from the audience. Even my darling Sissy—at whom I cast a quick, sideways glance—was seated forward in her seat, her eyes wide, her interlaced hands clasped excitedly to her bosom, her inexpressibly lovely mouth parted in wonder. To give the showman his due, it was evident at a glance that he had gone to considerable expense in putting together his show—the props, scenery, costumes, and appointments being of the most costly and even extravagant order. The problem lay not in the *elaborateness* of his production, but rather in its overall *conception*, which seemed—in its gaudy, fantastical vulgarity—to have sprung from the mind of a ten-year-old child with an excessively active, not to say overheated, imagination.

The scene was the palace grounds of the King of Atlantis, the architecture and embellishments of which were composed of the most wildly incongruous elements—Corinthian columns, Arabian minarets, Chinese pagodas, Egyptian statuary, Gothic spires. The players themselves were accoutred in what appeared to be garishly dyed togas of variegated hues, which—for modesty's sake—were supplemented with tight-fitting undersuits of white linen. Apart from the king himself— who wore an enormous, towering crown adorned with brightly colored paste jewels—each of the men sported a golden, winged helmet, similar to the one worn by the god Hermes in the famous statue by Giovanni Bologna. Swords, scepters, staffs, and tridents completed the colorful, if utterly preposterous, costumes.

The pantomimed drama that proceeded to unfold over the course of the next hour was, if anything, even more of a *farrago*. Try as I might, I could scarcely make sense of the proceedings. The story appeared to have something to do with a terrible doom visited upon the people of Atlantis, whose ruler has rashly insulted the religion of the Athenian ambassador, thereby bringing down the wrath of Zeus upon both himself and his kingdom. To counter the curse, the Atlantean ruler invokes the aid of his own pagan deities by sacrificing a number of living fowls to the giant, carnivorous beetle-demon that resides in a cave beneath the palace. In a subordinate plotline, a beauteous slave maiden of Atlantis is smitten with a handsome wandering troubadour from the Peloponnesian city-state of Sparta—an ill-starred infatuation that terminates in a predictably tragic dénouement.

At various points in the drama, several of Barnum's most popular curiosities appeared on stage in a variety of subsidiary rôles—as gigantic warriors, dwarfish jesters, bearded witches, hermaphroditic soothsayers, and the like. They were attired in the same pseudo-Etruscan garb as the other cast members, albeit modified to accommodate their grotesque physical anomalies. The garment worn by Bruno, for example, was completely covered at the shoulders, so that it bore a closer resemblance to a multihued potato sack than a toga. Only Sammy Wainwright, the Amazing Half-Man, appeared to have been improperly fitted for his costume, the hem of which dragged behind him like the train of a wedding gown as he scuttled about the stage on his inordinately powerful hands.

Though falling short of the truly *spectacular*, the cataclysm featured in the final act of the drama was, it must be said, rather impressively staged. By means of an ingenious, rocking platform upon which it had been erected, the palace of the Atlantean king was made to sway violently, as though shaken by a violent earthquake. The mighty walls trembled and collapsed—the pillars toppled—the Doric entablature fell with a crash. While the orchestral instruments simulated the tempestuous sounds of a raging thunderstorm—kettle drums pounding, cymbals clashing, violins shrieking—an enormous bolt of undulating, dark blue, satin fabric was used to suggest the gigantic billows of an approaching tidal wave.

It was at this point that the drama reached its much-anticipated climax. Seeking to avert the impending catastrophe, the king of Atlantis decides to perform a desperate, blood-sacrifice to the monstrous, cave-dwelling beetle-demon, and orders several of his most able-bodied servants to bring him the creature. The four largest of the performers immediately hurried offstage: Colonel Routh Goshen, the "Arabian Giant"—the Great O'Bannon, the "World's Strongest Mortal"—Ajeeb the Eunuch—and Willie Schnitzler (differentiated from the others by the exceptionally modest cut of her toga, which, in contrast to the knee-length garments worn by the males, extended all the way down to her ankles).

Several acutely suspenseful moments elapsed, while the audience kept its eyes riveted upon the stage. The orchestra had fallen silent, save for a single—low—ominous note played insistently on the cello. By slow degrees, the other instruments joined in. As the orchestra reached a dramatic crescendo, the four performers suddenly appeared—backs bent with strain—each with a length of thick, nautical rope drawn tautly over his or her right shoulder. An instant later, the object they were hauling—an enormous cage mounted upon a wheeled, wooden platform—rolled into view. Through its bars could be seen, squatting at the bottom of the enclosure, the colossal vermillion-winged insect.

At their first glimpse of the prodigious beetle, there arose from the audience a loud buzz or murmur of astonishment. Women shrieked—children squealed—and a number of people half-started from their seats, as though ready to bolt from the theater in terror.

Intermingled with these reactions, however, were others of a far less awestruck nature. Indeed, as the seconds ticked by, there could be heard a growing chorus of discontented—even derisive—noises. To some degree, the showman himself was to blame for this *grumbling.* For weeks, the public had been bombarded with posters and newspaper advertisements depicting the creature as a monster of Brobdingnagian dimensions, looming over the very rooftops of Manhattan. To those credulous enough to take Barnum at his word, the six-foot-long beetle—however extraordinary in its own right—could hardly fail to come as a disappointment.

Moreover, unlike the rampaging monster of the advertisements, the enormous bug now on display appeared to be singularly inert. It was housed (despite Barnum's assurances to the contrary) in what was very clearly an ordinary menagerie cage of the sort used to exhibit the largest of his mammalians. This was a circular enclosure approximately ten feet in diameter, with iron bars rising to a height of eight feet. There was no roof or covering of any sort on the cage, the top being completely open to the air. Though this latter feature might have seemed exceedingly ill-advised—offering an unobstructed avenue of escape for the giant bug—there appeared to be little or no cause for alarm. So circumscribed were the dimensions of the cage that the creature could not possibly have maneuvered itself into an upright position, even if it had been inclined to bestir itself from its torpor.

The rationale for placing the beetle in an open-topped enclosure soon became apparent. No sooner had the cage been rolled into place than a trio of females—apparently meant to represent the pagan votaries of the beetle-demon—swept onto the stage and began to execute a wild, gyrating dance around the monster. These characters were played by three of Barnum's most beauteous performers: Madame Cleo Ben Dib, his Egyptian snake-lady—Madame Maria Macart, his internationally acclaimed exotic danseuse—and his Circassian Beauty, Miss Zobeide Luti.

As they cavorted about the stage—in a manner so *flagrant* as to cause my entire countenance to flush with embarrassment—a slender male figure suddenly appeared on the catwalk directly above the cage. In his arms he bore a large, covered, wicker basket. From my vantage point in the front row, I easily recognized him as Barnum's "frog swallower," "English Jack" McMurphy, whose highly popular—if singularly unsavory—act consisted of ingesting fully grown members of the species *Rana catesbeiana.*

All at once, "English Jack" threw open the lid of the basket—reached inside—and pulled out a living hen of the Rhode Island Red variety by its legs. He then extended his arm, dangling the squawking fowl upside-down over the cage. As the audience gasped in horror, "English Jack" opened his fingers and let the unfortunate chicken drop directly in front of the giant beetle. The sluggish insect instantly stirred to life, its legs twitching—its mandibles clicking—a loud, angry hum emanating from its thoracic region. It immediately set upon the hen, which was quickly rent to pieces in a spray of blood, feathers, and bone fragments.

Three more chickens were sacrificed in the same, grisly fashion. The last of these poor creatures having been devoured, the orchestra broke into a deafening cacophony, suggestive of the utter, catastrophic breakdown of all harmony and order. As the instrumental din reached a nearly intolerable pitch, a painted curtain—depicting the final collapse of the island kingdom of Atlantis—descended upon the stage. The chaotic noises died, the houselights came on. The performance was over.

A sustained ovation—mixed with a few, highly audible boos—issued from the crowd. As the spectators filed from their seats, the theater was filled with the sound of their chatter. To judge from the comments that I managed to overhear, the general reaction to the show was exceedingly favorable, the vast majority of the audience clearly believing that they had gotten more than their money's worth from the garish and overblown spectacle. Only a few of the spectators voiced their disapproval, though they did so in the most emphatic manner, denouncing the entire production—and particularly the much-trumpeted giant insect—as little more than a shameless swindle.

Muddy and Sissy were most certainly *not* among the disgruntled portion of the crowd. As we rose from our seats and made our way to the steps leading up to the proscenium, they exclaimed enthusiastically about every aspect of the production, which had evidently made the deepest impression upon them. Having no wish to diminish their enjoyment by asserting my own, far harsher and more critical judgment, I resolved to keep my true opinion to myself. Accordingly, when Sissy turned to me and asked how I had enjoyed the show, I merely replied: "Rarely, if ever, have I witnessed so unique—so *unprecedented*—a spectacle."

Arrived at the backstage area, we found Barnum busily congratulating his performers.

"Bravo, one and all!" he exclaimed. "Splendid job, absolutely splendid! Never saw anything like it! Brought tears—actual tears—to my eyes. What poignancy!—what majesty!—what grandeur! And all of it achieved without a single spoken word of dialogue! Amazing! Incredible! Why, even Shakespeare himself had to fall back on poetry and whatnot to get his ideas across! Just think of it, ladies and gentlemen—what you have accomplished here tonight may well be the single most remarkable feat in the entire history of the dramatic arts!

"Aha!" he suddenly cried out, having become cognizant of our presence. "Here's Poe and his fair ladies, come to join the celebration!" Striding in our direction, he threw his arms open wide, as though intending to gather the three of us within his embrace. "Well, m'boy, what did I tell you? Didn't I say it would be a triumph? Good lord, have you ever heard such applause? Why, it was loud enough to drown out the thunderous roar of Niagara!"

"There can be no doubt," I replied, "that, based upon the reaction of the crowd—which was indeed vociferous (if by no means unanimous) in its appoval—your production must be accounted a great success."

"And here's a young man who contributed mightily to that success," said Barnum, smiling over my shoulder at someone who had just come up behind me. Looking around, I saw that it was none other than the Armless Wonder. He had already shed his sacklike costume and was dressed in his usual, stylish attire.

"Stunning performance, Bruno, m'boy—simply breathtaking," declared Barnum. "Nearly stole the show!"

"Hardly," replied the other, with self-deprecating amusement. "But I appreciate the compliment, Mr. B."

In point of fact, the showman's flattering remark was only slightly hyperbolic; for Bruno's rôle in the production—though minor—had been greeted with a particularly tumultuous outburst from the audience. He had played the part of a heroic, if dreadfully disabled, young warrior of Atlantis, who—having lost both arms in an earlier battle—nevertheless managed to help defend his country against the Grecian invaders by wielding a bow and arrow with his feet.

"Oh, no!" Sissy protested. "He's right—you were wonderful. And that costume of yours. Why, I've never seen anything so—so—"

"Ridiculous?" said Bruno.

Sissy let out a small laugh of surprise. "Not at all! It was quite becoming."

"Oh yes," added Muddy. "And very authentic-looking, too. Just exactly how I imagined they dressed back in those days."

"Well, you're both very kind," said Bruno. "Say—would you care to have a closer look at Mr. Barnum's monster? It's really quite a remarkable specimen."

"Oh my, yes!" exclaimed Sissy, clapping her hands in excitement.

"Marvelous idea, Bruno," exclaimed Barnum. "You take charge of the ladies for a spell, while Poe and I repair to my office. I feel like celebrating with a fine Havana."

As Bruno led my loved ones off in the direction of the large, circular cage—where the gigantic beetle had subsided into its usual lethargy—I followed Barnum out of the theater and down the stairs to the basement. As we approached his office, I observed that the door was standing ajar, sending a wedge of light into the dimly illuminated corridor.

"That's mighty odd," Barnum said with a frown. "I *always* douse the light and shut the door behind me when I leave."

The mystery was resolved an instant later—for as we stepped across the threshold, we were astonished to observe a man seated behind Barnum's desk. Leaning back in the chair, with his feet propped on the desktop, he was puffing contentedly away at a cigar which he had evidently removed from the showman's silver receptacle.

For a moment—having been rendered mute with astonishment—Barnum merely gaped at this figure. I, too, stood there mutely, in a state of extreme—of *utter*—consternation. It was not merely the unexpected presence of this figure that I found so unnerving—nor even the exceedingly insolent manner with which he had made himself at home in Barnum's sanctum. No. It was his *identity* that sent a spasm of dread through every fiber of my being!

The man now regarding us narrowly through a dense cloud of cigar smoke was none other than the late Morris Vanderhorn's brutish aide-de-camp—Chester Croley!

CHAPTER THIRTY

The intensely dismaying effect produced by the sight of Croley is not to be wondered at when the various circumstances are taken into account. During our previous encounter, after all, he had done his best to dispatch me with a wooden club. Only the timely intervention of Willie Schnitzler had saved me from certain death. I had every reason to believe, therefore, that he had now returned to complete the job.

Instinctively, I cast my gaze about the office, searching for a weapon with which to fend off the anticipated attack. No more than a foot away from where I stood, Barnum's elephant-headed walking stick leaned against the wall. Very slowly and (I hoped) inconspicuously, I began to move my hand in its direction.

Croley, however, apparently perceived my intent. Clamping the cigar between his teeth, he swung his feet off the desk and rose slowly from the chair. Immediately, I snatched up the walking stick and extended it outward in a threatening posture.

"Advance no further," I warned, arranging my features into an expression of fierce, of *unflinching*, resolve. "This time, it is *I* who am wielding a bludgeoning implement, and *you* who are—to all outward appearances, at least—unarmed. You may rest assured that—should you lift a hand against either my companion or myself—I shall not hesitate to inflict the greatest possible damage upon your person!"

The ferocity of my words—no less than of my aspect—produced the desired effect. Croley raised both hands in a mollifying gesture, and—with the cigar still protruding from a corner of his mouth—said: "Take it easy, Poe. I ain't looking for trouble. Hell, you're right—I ain't even armed." Unbuttoning his coat, he pulled it open to reveal that there were no weapons hidden about his person.

"Maybe I *did* mean to rough you up a bit that time," he continued. "But only 'cause the boss ordered me to. But now that he's dead . . ." Here, he shrugged his massive shoulders, as if to say that he no longer had a reason in the world to wish me harm.

The showman, however, was clearly unimpressed by Croley's conciliatory attitude. "Don't listen to him, Poe," he angrily declared. "Why, he's the devil himself—nothing but a cold-blooded child-killer!"

Croley plucked the cigar from his mouth. "What the hell are you talkin' about, Barnum?" he exclaimed, his face flushed with indignation. "I ain't never hurt a kid in my life!"

"Oh really?" Barnum scoffed. "I suppose that little Frankie Plunkitt threw *himself* off the roof."

"Plunkitt?" Croley said, his singularly unprepossessing countenance wrinkled with perplexity. "You mean that punk from Isabel Somers's building—the one that took a header onto the sidewalk? Hell, *I* didn't have nothing to do with it. Saw it in the papers. Far as *I* know, he was just showing off for his chums—proving what a big man he was, just like the papers said. Hell, crap like that happens every day in this town."

Though offended by the extreme vulgarity of Croley's language, his protestations of innocence struck me as plausible. After all, I myself had entertained the selfsame theory in regard to the manner of young Plunkitt's death.

I therefore lowered my weapon and addressed him thusly: "Though having little or no reason to trust your word, I shall extend you the benefit of the doubt. Be advised, however, that I remain ready to employ this imposing, brass-headed implement in the most devastating manner conceivable, should your behavior necessitate such action on my part."

"Anything you say, Poe," Croley replied, curling his thick, rather simian lips into the crude approximation of a friendly smile.

"All right, Croley," growled Barnum. "State your business."

"Got something here I thought you gents might be interested in," replied the other, reaching down for an item that lay upon the table in front of him. So thoroughly had my attention been fixated on Croley that I had previously failed to notice it. It was, I now perceived, a slender volume, bound in red morocco.

"What's that supposed to be?" inquired Barnum.

"Isabel Somers's private notebook," Croley answered nonchalantly, holding up the volume for our inspection. "Found it in her apartment. Mr. Vanderhorn sent me up there right after the killing. He was mighty pleased when I came back with it, too."

Barnum and I exchanged a rapid look. During our inspection of the Somers abode, I had concluded—from several small but telling pieces of evidence—that just such a volume *must* have been among the items removed from the premises at Morris Vanderhorn's behest following the murder. That my deduction had now been confirmed in so dramatic a fashion could not fail to infuse me with a keen sense of vindication.

"And whatever gave you the idea," said Barnum with studied indifference, "that my associate and I are at all interested in such an article?"

"You kidding?" Croley snorted. "The way you two was snooping around?"

"Well," Barnum said in the same off-handed tone, "I suppose we might be *mildly* curious—just a *tad*, mind you. Enough to offer, say, twenty dollars for it."

Croley barked out at a nasty laugh. "You're a nervy bastard, Barnum, I'll say that for you. I had me a slightly higher price in mind—two hundred, to be exact."

"Two—two hundred!" Barnum sputtered. "Surely you can't be serious! Why, it's the most preposterous—the most *outrageous*—thing I've ever heard! And believe me, sir, I've heard some dillies! Why, I didn't pay that much for my unique, ten-foot-high sculptural facsimile of the Liberty Bell, composed of over three million individual seashells!"

"Take it or leave it," said Croley.

"And how can we be sure that it is the genuine article and not some rank forgery?" Barnum said.

"Just have to take my word for it," said Croley. "Ain't this a face you can trust?" he added with a smirk.

"Whatever else might be said of your physiognomy, Mr. Croley," I said with withering sarcasm, "it is hardly designed to inspire confidence in your veracity. Nevertheless," I continued, turning to address the showman, "I believe that, in this instance, we can take our visitor at his word. The volume in question is, I am convinced, genuine."

At this unexpected assertion, Barnum looked at me in surprise. He then pursed his lips thoughtfully and, turning to Croley, declared. "One hundred dollars, and not a penny more."

Croley took a long draw on his cigar, then expelled the smoke in a slow, steady stream. "Lucky for you, I'm hard up for cash," he said at length. "Ain't got a job no more, thanks to that bible-totin' bitch and that filthy little humpback she run off with. Shit, what I wouldn't give to get my hands on them two! All right, Barnum—a hundred it is. Fork it over."

Crossing the floor, Barnum squatted before the iron safe that stood in a far corner of his office. Making sure that his body was positioned in such a way that it blocked Croley's view, he proceeded to undo the lock—swing open the door—and extract the requisite sum. He then secured the safe, rose to his feet, and—approaching the desk—handed the money to Croley.

After carefully counting the bills, the latter thrust them into the pocket of his trousers. He then passed the notebook over to Barnum and made for the door.

Throughout this transaction, I had remained standing near the threshold. As Croley approached, he came to a sudden halt and leaned his face in such close proximity to mine that I could clearly distinguish every individual pore on his small, badly misshapen nose.

"You was right about one thing, Mister Poe" he hissed. "If that fat freak hadn't come along and snuck up behind me, I would've cracked open that friggin' skull of yours like a damned eggshell. Would've enjoyed every second of it, too."

Then, with a grin of sheer—of *overpowering* malevolence—he tipped his hat and strode from the room.

No sooner had he gone than I slammed the door behind him and threw the lock. Exhaling a sigh of relief, I turned to Barnum, who was now situated behind the desk in the place that Croley had been occupying.

"Good riddance to bad rubbish," commented the showman. "Nasty customer, that Croley. One of the worst I've ever run across. Say—you don't think *he* killed Vanderhorn, do you? Slipped him some poison and put the blame on the wife?"

"I very much doubt it," I replied. "When seeking to establish the guilt of a suspected killer, the investigator must prove the existence of *three* crucial elements. He must show that the suspect had an *opportunity* to accomplish the crime—access to the *weapon* with which it was committed—and a plausible *motive*. In Croley's case, the last of these was utterly lacking. On the contrary, as his livelihood was entirely dependent upon Vanderhorn, it behooved him to do everything in his power to protect the latter from harm."

"Yes, I reckon you're right," Barnum said. "But tell me, m'boy, what in heaven's name made you so certain that this notebook is the genuine article?"

Stepping to Barnum's side, I addressed him thusly: "You will recall that, during our examination of Miss Somers's apartment, I noted the presence of a faint but unmistakable discoloration upon the surface of her desk, evidently created when the contents of an overturned ink pot pooled around the corner of a book in which she had been writing. Indeed, it was the discovery of this stain that led me to deduce the existence of the missing notebook.

"Examine, now, the front cover of the volume you hold in your hands. You will observe that the upper left-hand corner is badly stained with ink—in precisely the way that I surmised the missing notebook would be. I noticed the tell-tale stain at once when Croley held out the proffered volume for our inspection."

"Great Scot, you're right!" Barnum exclaimed, closely scrutinizing the cover of the notebook. "Splendid work, m'boy—absolutely tip-top! Well, now, let's have a peek inside. See what I spent my hard-earned money on."

As Barnum opened the book and stared down at its contents, a look of utter bewilderment spread over his countenance. Rapidly, he began to turn the pages, his expression growing more dismayed by the moment.

Perceiving his confusion, I peered over his shoulder and saw the following:

```
;48 9$*8: 5((6+8 I($9 + ;$&5:--5*& *$; 5 9$98*; ;$$
)$$*! 6; 6) )$ I(634;I?00: 8!.8*)6+8 ;$ 06+8 ;48 ~5:
$*8 ~6)48) 6* ;46) -6;:. ;48 ;4(88 4?*&(8& ~600 25(80:
)88 98 ;4($?34 ;48 8*& $I ;48 9$*;4. ;48 8*+80$.8 ~5)
&806+8(8& 2: 46) 05-=8:, -($08:. 3(?8)$98 I800$~! 5
08;;8( ~5) 8*-0$)8&, 8!.(8))6*3 ;48 4$.8 ;45; + 5*& 6
95: $*8 &5: 28 (8-$*-608&. ~800, ~8 )4500 )88 52$?;
;45;!
```

"We've been *had*, Poe!" the showman bitterly exclaimed. "Played for the greenest kind of suckers! Why, it's nothing but gibberish— pure gobbledygook!"

"No," I replied, studying the seemingly meaningless scribblings. "It is *code*."

CHAPTER THIRTY-ONE

That Isabel Somers had composed her journal entirely in secret code was a source of great frustration to Barnum.

"Heavens, what a jumble!" he exclaimed. "Makes my head spin just looking at it. Why, the fellows who worked on the Tower of Babel had a better chance of understanding each other than you or I have of making sense of these blasted hieroglyphics!"

It will come as no surprise to the reader that—in this matter as in so many others—I did not share Barnum's feelings. Indeed, my reaction differed so markedly from his as to constitute its nearly complete antithesis. Far from being daunted by the complexity of the cipher, I looked forward to unraveling it with positive *relish*. That I could do so with comparatively little difficulty I felt reasonably certain. I was equally confident that the results would more than justify my efforts; for it appeared self-evident to me that Miss Somers would not have resorted to so inconvenient a system of writing unless she had something significant to conceal.

Accordingly, I replied to Barnum in the following manner: "I concur that, to *some* persons, the unriddling of a cryptographical puzzle of such seeming complexity would prove inordinately difficult, if not impossible. To those of us, however, who have been blessed with analytical powers of more than ordinary force, there is no such thing as an unbreakable code. Indeed, it may be roundly asserted that human ingenuity cannot construct an enigma of the kind which human ingenuity may not, by proper application, resolve."

Though remaining somewhat skeptical of my ability to do so, Barnum agreed that I should make every effort to decipher the journal. He was, after all, as curious about its contents as I—perhaps even more so, having invested such a substantial sum in its acquisition. Nevertheless, he urged me to defer the attempt until I had accomplished a task that, in his estimation, took precedence over all others—to wit, the completion of the Armless Wonder's biography.

" 'Strike while the iron's hot'—that's P. T. Barnum's motto! Bruno's a big star right now, one of the biggest I've ever featured. Heaven only knows how long that'll last, though. The public's a fickle mistress, m'boy—and fame as fleeting as the morning dew! You've got to snatch at every opportunity when it comes along—snatch it with both hands! 'Gather ye rosebuds while ye may,' as the poet says. 'And ye profits, too,' as *I* say!"

In point of fact (though I did not confess this to Barnum), I had yet to commence work on the pamphlet. Making a silent resolution to do so without further delay, I assured him that he would have the promised work in his possession no later than the following week.

As I prepared to depart, Barnum proposed that I borrow one of his buggies for our trip back to the country. "No need to return it right away, m'boy," he said. "Just bring it back next week, when you drop off your finished manuscript!"

It was already past midnight by the time Muddy, Sissy, and I arrived back at our cottage. While my dear wife readied herself for bed, I repaired to my study with Isabel Somers's journal, which Barnum had turned over to my care. After taking one final glance at its contents in order to satisfy myself that its seemingly inscrutable writing was, in fact, completely susceptible of solution, I retired for the night.

The following morning, I awoke with a start from a hideous dream in which Sissy was pursued through a dark and labyrinthine tunnel by a colossal, carnivorous beetle intent on rending her limb from limb with its razor-sharp mandibles. Sitting upright with a groan, I gazed about wildly, my terror subsiding as I saw—to my inexpressible relief—that my dear one was slumbering peacefully in the neighboring bed.

Rising somewhat shakily from my mattress, I quickly performed my morning ablutions—donned my clothing—and made for my study, where I immediately settled down at my desk and commenced to work on the Armless Wonder's life story. For the remainder of the day, I wrote furiously, taking only a brief respite at Muddy's insistence to consume a light supper late in the afternoon. Heeding Barnum's wishes, I allowed my imagination free rein, concocting incidents and anecdotes of the most wild—the most *thrilling*—nature.

The sun had already set when I finally laid down my pen and—after stretching the fingers of my writing hand several times to uncramp their overworked muscles—picked up the manuscript and began to read what I had thus far composed.

"My baptismal name is Bruno," the narrative began.

I am the descendant of a race whose vigor of fancy and ardor of passion have at all times rendered them remarkable. My forebears have been called a line of visionaries; and in many striking particulars—in the character of the family mansion—in the frescos of the chief saloon—in the tapestries of the bedchamber—but most especially in the gallery of antique paintings and contents of the ancestral library—there is more than sufficient evidence to warrant the belief.

From my earliest infancy, however, I gave evidence of possessing a temperament radically—if not diametrically—opposite to that of my progenitors. Indeed, I have often been reproached for the aridity of my fancy. A deficiency of imagination has been imputed to me as a crime. And it can scarcely be denied that, upon the whole, no person could be less liable than myself to be led from the severe precincts of truth by the *ignes fatui* of superstition. I have thought it proper to premise this much, lest the incredible tale I have to tell should be considered rather the raving of a crude imagination than the positive experience of a mind to which the reveries of fancy have been a dead letter and a nullity.

Having thus introduced Bruno to the reader by means of this crisp and vividly evocative introduction, my narrative proceeded to relate the leading (if wholly fictitious) particulars of his exceedingly adventurous early life: His experiences as a young stowaway upon a whaling vessel bound for the coast of Australia. His discovery by savage mutineers who cast him overboard. His death-defying swim through shark-infested waters. His arrival at an uncharted tropical isle and capture by bloodthirsty cannibals. His days of inhuman torture, culminating in the slow amputation of his arms with sharpened clam shells. His agonizing recovery under the care of a sympathetic witch-doctor. His initiation into the arcane tribal wisdom of Melanesia, and his gradual acquisition of unheard-of pedal abilities under the tutelage of his native mentor.

Pleased with what I had thus far accomplished—though exceedingly weary from my exertions—I retired for the evening. The following morning, immediately after breakfast, I resumed my labors. So assiduously did I apply myself to my work that, by the end of the second day, I had arrived at the point in Bruno's story where he was rescued from his inhuman bondage to his former employer by the merciful intervention of Barnum (whom I made sure to portray as a deeply benevolent and compassionate individual, motivated solely by his humanitarian concern for Bruno's well-being).

As I laid down my quill and leaned back in my chair—stretching my arms over my head and exhaling a deep, self-satisfied sigh—I realized how little I actually knew of my subject's present circumstances. Though Barnum had encouraged me to invent an extravagantly colorful past for the Armless Wonder, I felt that—in describing Bruno's current existence—I should keep my embellishments to a minimum and adhere as closely as possible to the facts. But what *were* the facts? What sort of life did Bruno lead outside the museum? What were his interests? What pastimes did he enjoy? Who were his friends? Did he live by himself, or was he—like a number of Barnum's human anomalies—married? So entirely ignorant was I of the most rudimentary details of Bruno's life that I did not even know *where* he lived. Though some of Barnum's performers lodged in the museum itself (which featured a sort of dormitory on the upper floor), others chose to reside elsewhere, either in nearby boardinghouses or their own, private homes.

It suddenly occurred to me that—in view of the friendship she had established with Bruno—Sissy might know the answers to at least some of these questions. I therefore rose from my chair and quit my study.

No sooner had I stepped into the hallway than I heard Muddy's voice emanating from the parlor. Her words were indistinct. From the tone of her voice, however, I could tell that she was admonishing Sissy in an unusually emphatic manner.

Hurrying into the parlor, I saw my auntie standing in the center of the room. In her left hand, she clutched a volume that I recognized at once as Sissy's beloved collection of faerie stories. My darling wife was seated on the sofa, her ineffably lovely visage wrought into a look of extreme distress. Muddy herself appeared to be equally distraught as she addressed her daughter in a voice that quavered with emotion.

"No, I will *not* give it back, Virginia," my aunt was exclaiming. "You are making yourself sick with it!"

"What in the world has happened, Muddy dearest?" I cried, stepping to the good woman's side.

"Oh, Eddie," she said in a beseeching tone. "Perhaps you can talk some sense into the child. I came into the parlor a few minutes ago and found her bawling over one of these foolish tales. Here," she continued, opening the book to a place she had marked off and thrusting it into my hands. "Read this. Why, it's even worse than those ghastly horror stories of *yours*."

Lowering myself onto the sofa beside Sissy—whose stricken expression elicited a sharp pang of sympathy in the depths of my bosom—I quickly perused the offending tale.

Its title alone was sufficiently unsettling to make me understand Muddy's reaction. It was called "The Girl Without Hands." Like so many of the stories in Tyler's collection, it was replete with all the elements that appeal to the peasant mentality—shocking cruelty, primitive superstition, and an unquestioning faith in the miraculous workings of Providence.

The plot concerned a poor miller who is tricked by the devil into bargaining away his own daughter. When the Evil One comes to collect his prize, the beautiful, pious girl keeps him at bay by standing

347

within a magical, protective circle and washing her hands clean with water. To counter this stratagem, the devil commands the father to chop off the girl's hands. The selfish man—fearful for his own soul—performs the dreadful deed. Even so, the maimed girl defeats the devil by weeping so copiously upon her bloody stumps as to render them perfectly immaculate.

Leaving the home of her despicable parent, she becomes an outcast and a wanderer. At length, she is discovered by a tender-hearted king, who falls immediately in love with her—takes her to wife—and has silver hands made for her. Many more ordeals and reversals are visited upon the poor woman, though the story, like all such tales, ends triumphantly, with the heroine restored to happiness, material comfort, and even bodily wholeness, her hands being miraculously regrown through the grace of God.

Closing the volume, I turned to my dear wife and addressed her thusly: "There can be no doubt that this tale has many commendable qualities. Indeed, the very artlessness and *naïveté* with which it is told endows it with a singular enchantment. Nonetheless, I must concur with Muddy. In view of the ghastly mutilation to which its heroine is subjected, it can serve no other purpose than to cause you great and unnecessary dismay."

"I suppose so," Sissy said in a tremulous voice. "When I saw the title, my curiosity got the better of me."

"Perhaps it is time for you to devote your attention to an altogether different work of literature," I gently suggested. "I fear that, for now at least, Mr. Tyler's book is fraught with too many painful associations."

"All right," Sissy agreed after a momentary pause. "I will put it aside for a while."

"Oh, Virginia," Muddy exclaimed with a catch in her voice, "I am so glad to hear it. Forgive me for scolding you. I was just so upset when I walked in and found you crying over this silly book. You know how much I worry about you, dear."

"I know," Sissy replied, reaching out and giving her mother's hand a gentle squeeze.

"Well, then, that's all settled," Muddy said, greatly relieved.

"Now, why don't I make us all a nice pot of tea? It'll be just the thing before bedtime!"

"A soothing cup of your excellent pekoe would be most welcome," said I.

Bending down, Muddy bestowed a kiss upon her daughter's brow, just below the point of Sissy's widow's peak. Then, straightening back up, she turned and went bustling off into the kitchen.

"Thank you, Sissy," I said after the good woman was gone. "You have lifted a great burden of care from our dear Muddy's heart."

"I suppose Bruno was right," Sissy observed with a sigh. "Some of those old peasant tales are enough to give you nightmares. That's just what he was saying the other night, when he was here for dinner with Mr. Barnum."

"Yes," I said. "I recall overhearing some conversation to that effect. As it happens, my motive for seeking you out just now relates directly to our friend Bruno."

"Oh, really?" said Sissy. "How so?"

"As you know, I am in the process of composing the biographical pamphlet that Mr. Barnum desires me to write. My narrative—which, of course, relates the story of Bruno's life in strict, chronological fashion—has very nearly reached the present moment. Unfortunately, I am in possession of few, if any, real facts about his current circumstances, and am loath to include information that the public may easily discover to be utterly fallacious."

"I'm sorry that I can't be of much help, Eddie," Sissy replied. "I know very little about him myself. He *did* mention at one point that he lives by himself in a boardinghouse on Leonard Street, just off Broadway."

"I see. I take it, then, that he is not married?"

"Why, no," Sissy exclaimed in a somewhat surprised tone. "As far as I know he has no family whatsoever. Certainly not a wife!"

"Perhaps," I mused aloud, "I shall pay a visit to this boardinghouse on Leonard Street. By speaking to Bruno's landlady and others familiar with his daily, household habits, I may well garner details that will greatly enhance the verisimilitude of my narrative."

"When are you planning to go?" Sissy inquired.

"Why, the sooner the better," I replied. "Perhaps as early as to-morrow morning."

All at once, Sissy—whose mood had been rather subdued since the start of our conversation—grew intensely animated. "Oooh, Eddie," she exclaimed. "Can I come along with you to the city? You can leave me off at the museum. Bruno has offered to show me a room where Mr. Barnum keeps his special treasures—things that are hardly ever put on display, they're so valuable."

For a moment, I merely regarded my dear wife in silence. That she evinced such palpable excitement at the mere prospect of seeing Bruno again was, I confess, a source of some vexation to me. Though not inordinately susceptible to the "green-eyed monster," I could hardly fail to feel somewhat jealous of Sissy's growing fondness for the deformed—albeit exceedingly handsome, charming, and alto-gether remarkable—young man.

At the same time, however, I could scarcely begrudge her a friendship that brought her so much pleasure, and that served to dis-tract her from her continuing grief over the murder of poor Anna Louise Brennan.

"Very well," I said, just as Muddy reappeared, bearing a tray that held three steaming mugs of her fragrant decoction. "We shall make our visit on the morrow."

CHAPTER THIRTY-TWO

The sky was exceedingly overcast when Sissy and I departed early the next morning. I therefore took the precaution of equipping myself with the blue-cotton umbrella I had purchased several months earlier, on the day we had first arrived in Manhattan from Philadelphia.

No sooner had we turned from Bloomingdale Road onto Broadway than a drizzle began to descend from the overhanging clouds. By the time we arrived at our destination, the rainfall had developed into a full-fledged downpour.

I know not how it was but, at my first glimpse of the museum, a sense of insufferable gloom pervaded my spirit. Partly this was due to the strangely forlorn—even *desolate*—air that seemed to surround the building. Owing no doubt to the inordinately inclement weather, the sidewalk was entirely devoid of its usual crowd of excited customers. The gaudily painted banners normally draped across the façade had been removed, so as to protect them from the ravages of the storm. Even the blaring brass band that added so clamorously to the carnivalesque feel of the place had been driven from its perch on the balcony. In lieu of its characteristic atmosphere of gay, not to say *garish*, festivity, the great, looming edifice had the grim—the foreboding—aspect of a medieval *keep*.

Shaking off the dreariness of spirit that had so suddenly possessed me, I quickly climbed down from the vehicle—hurried around to the opposite side—and helped my dear wife to dismount. Sheltering her under the canopy of the umbrella, I then led her to the entranceway.

Barnum's skeletal ticket-seller, Slim Jim McCormack, was missing from his post—as had also been the case when Sissy and I first visited the museum. On that occasion, the showman himself had taken over for his absent employee. This time, McCormack's place was occupied by one of his fellow performers—Gunther the Alligator Boy, who sat behind the counter with a look of perfect *ennuyé* upon his grotesquely scaly visage.

Approaching the dermatological curiosity, I greeted him thusly: "Good morning, Gunther. I see that you are filling in for Slim Jim this morning. Is he again—ah—indisposed?"

"Don't know nothin' about *that*," Gunther replied. "I expect he's sleepin' off another drunk, though. He's mighty fond of the bottle, Slim Jim is."

"Given the intensity of Mr. Barnum's aversion toward alcoholic overindulgence," I observed, "I marvel that he has tolerated Slim Jim's behavior for so long."

"Mr. B don't cotton to drinkin', that's for sure," said Gunther. "He sure does like his money, though. And us oddities is mighty popular with the customers. Lots of folks come here just to see Slim Jim and me and the rest of us."

"You are no doubt correct in your analysis," I replied. "There do not appear to be many customers here today, however."

"No sir, there ain't. Rain's keepin' 'em at home. Kind of surprised to see you and the missus here on a day like this."

"I have a matter to attend to that will brook no delay," I explained. "My wife, in the meantime, intends to visit Bruno."

"Go right on in, missy," said Gunther to Sissy. "You'll find him upstairs in the usual place."

Telling Sissy that I would return for her as soon as I had completed my undertaking, I bade her good-bye and watched as she disappeared inside the museum.

"Tell me, Gunther," I said to the anomalous young man after Sissy was gone, "do you happen to know the exact address of Bruno's residence?"

"No sir, I don't," replied the Alligator Boy. "All's I know is, he don't live here at the museum, like lots of us do."

For a moment, I considered following Sissy upstairs to the Hall of Oddities and putting the question directly to Bruno. In the end, however, I decided against this approach. Though the young man had acceded to Barnum's desire that I compose his official biography, he had provided me with only scant details about his personal life. In view of this reticence, I feared that he would take an exceedingly dim view of my investigation into his domestic arrangements, regarding it as an unwarranted invasion of his privacy. I believed, moreover, that—knowing the approximate whereabouts of his residence—I would have little or no trouble locating it once I reached the designated block.

Bidding good-bye to Gunther, I therefore reopened my umbrella—stepped onto the sidewalk—and hurried along the rain-drenched pavement in the direction of Leonard Street.

As the meager attendance at Barnum's museum clearly demonstrated, the inclement weather had discouraged all but the most determined amusement-seekers from venturing out-of-doors. No mere downpour, however, could impede the frenetic *commercial* activity of the city. Fewer women may have been out and about; but the great thoroughfare of Broadway teemed with the usual mass of male pedestrians—merchants and tradesmen, attorneys and clerks, stock-jobbers and common laborers. Grimly bent upon their business, they hurried along the pavement with their shoulders hunched, their eyes cast low, while rainwater streamed from the brims of their hats, or spilled from the domes of their umbrellas.

When I rounded the corner onto Leonard Street, however, the crowd instantly diminished. Indeed, compared to the sheer *press* of humanity on Broadway, the narrow block was virtually deserted. Peering around from beneath my umbrella, I scanned the street for the house that might serve as Bruno's lodging place. To my surprise, I saw only two dwelling places on the entire block—a modest, three-story brick edifice, evidently divided into individual apartments; and, standing directly across from it on the opposite side of the street, an exceedingly small, framed house, scarcely larger than the tiny cottage occupied by Muddy, Sissy, and myself. The remainder of the street was occupied by warehouses, stables, shops, and a small church.

At first blush, neither of the two dwellings appeared to be a boardinghouse. For a moment, I stood rooted in place, unsure as to how to proceed. All at once, an elderly, round-shouldered woman emerged from the front door of the three-story brick building, and, after opening her umbrella, slowly descended the stoop. As she shuffled along the sidewalk, I briskly approached her, and—planting myself directly in her path—addressed her thusly:

"Pardon me, my good woman. I am searching for a boardinghouse that, according to my informant, is situated on this very street. I am having some difficulty in locating it, however. I would be very much obliged if you could assist in this matter."

Tilting back her umbrella, the ancient woman peered up at me with rheumy eyes and, cupping her free hand behind one ear, loudly replied:

"Eh? What's that? Speak up, young man. I can't hear a blessed thing in this deluge!"

Bending closer, I repeated my question at a greatly elevated volume.

"Boardinghouse?" she replied with a frown. "Not on *this* block. Looking for a room, are ye?"

"No, no," said I. "I am seeking the residence of a young man named Bruno Saltarino."

"Bruno? The armless fellow? Why, he don't live in a boardinghouse," she said, pointing an inordinately gnarled index finger in the direction of the low, framed house across the street. "He lives over there. With his mother."

So unexpected was this statement that a full half-minute elapsed while I merely gaped at the old woman in astonishment. "His mother?" I exclaimed at length. "Surely you must be mistaken. Bruno is an orphan!"

"Mistaken?" she cried. "Why, you whippersnapper! I've lived on this street for forty years! Reckon I know my own neighbors. Now, get out of my way and let me go about my business." And so saying, she nudged me aside and shambled off down the street, muttering bitterly under her breath.

For several moments, I remained where I was, my mind in a ferment as I sought to account for the old woman's startling assertion. Was it possible, I wondered, that she was in the throes of advanced *senile dementia*, an affliction that wreaks such terrible havoc on the minds of the elderly? To judge from her inordinately withered appearance, her age could not have been less than seventy years. Perhaps, in her pitiable condition, she genuinely believed that Bruno's long-deceased mother was still among the living. I was forced to admit, however, that—despite the old woman's physical frailty—her mental faculties appeared fully intact.

There was, of course, a direct and definitive means of resolving the matter. Crossing the gutter, I approached Bruno's ostensible residence, unlatched the gate of the picket fence that surrounded the premises, and strode up the walkway to the front porch.

From my initial vantage point on the opposite side of the street, the little dwelling had appeared reasonably well-kept. Now, upon closer inspection, I saw that it was far more dilapidated than I had thought. Many years had elapsed since the house had last been painted, and its exterior had a cracked and peeling look that put me in mind of the scabrous complexion of Gunther the Alligator Boy. Mold of a sickening greenish hue grew in great, irregular patches upon the walls. The little yard was rank with weeds and untended grass. Altogether, a general air of neglect and decay hung about the premises, relieved only slightly by the presence of a handsome, flourishing rosebush that stood by the ramshackle fence.

Climbing the three, sagging steps onto the weatherbeaten porch, I closed my umbrella, rested it against the wall, and announced my presence with several sharp raps upon the door.

When my knocking brought no response, I repeated my action—but to no more effect than before. Convinced that no one was at home, I was on the brink of abandoning my effort and returning to the museum, when I thought I detected, from the interior of the house, the muffled sound of approaching footsteps. An instant later, the door swung in upon its hinges. Framed in the doorway was a woman of advanced middle years.

Any doubts I had harbored about the mental capacities of the crone with whom I just conversed were instantly banished—for I saw at a glance that the female now standing before me could be none other than Bruno's parent. She was far from youthful, having already reached—according to my estimate—the fifth decade of her allotted span. Even coarsened by age, however, her features bore an unmistakable resemblance to those of the armless prodigy.

In other important respects, however, she appeared wholly unlike her son. From what I had seen of Bruno—whose manners and mode of dress were never less than impeccable—he was a young man of fastidious habits. By contrast the personage now standing in the doorway was unkempt to the point of shamelessness. She was garbed in a loose-fitting dressing gown, or *peignoir,* that exposed her bosom in the most scandalous fashion. Her graying auburn hair hung in wild disarray about her face, as though she had just emerged from bed. Even more disconcerting to me than her slovenly style of dress, however, was the reek of alcohol that she exuded. I could only surmise that—despite the earliness of the hour (which had yet to reach noon)—she had already been drinking!

"Good morning, madam," I declared, politely doffing my hat. "I am looking for the abode of Mr. Bruno Saltarino, Mr. P. T. Barnum's celebrated 'Armless Wonder.' I have been led to believe that he resides at this address."

"Maybe he does, maybe he don't," the bleary-eyed slattern responded, her breath redolent of whiskey. "Who wants to know?"

"My name is Poe," I replied. "Mr. Edgar Poe."

"Poe," said the woman in a musing tone. "Seems like I heard that name before. Ain't you the one with the pretty young sister I been hearing about?"

Though my initial response to her query was one of the greatest surprise, I quickly deduced the source of her misunderstanding.

"The personage you mean," I explained, "is not my sister, but rather my darling wife, Virginia, who has formed a close bond of friendship with young Mr. Saltarino. Your confusion derives, no doubt, from the fond appellation by which I call her—i.e., 'Sissy.' "

"My, my, ain't you a talker," said the bibulous woman. "Handsome, too."

The sheer unblushing frankness of this latter observation left me somewhat flustered. Quickly recovering myself, I declared: "Allow me to explain the reason for my visit. I have been retained by Mr. Barnum to compose Bruno's life story, and have come here to seek out additional facts about his personal background." As I spoke, I stared fixedly at her slack, fleshy, countenance, keeping my gaze deliberately averted from the flagrant *déshabillé* of her dressing gown.

For several moments, she stood mutely in the doorway, regarding me with a bold, appraising look peculiarly unsettling in a woman. At length, she placed one hand upon her outthrust hip—extended the other in a welcoming gesture—and, in a tone of exaggerated cordiality, said: "Sure. Come on in. Glad to do a favor for a nice gentleman like you."

Thanking her for her cooperation, I stepped over the threshold and followed her voluptuous, carelessly draped form down a small corridor and into her parlor.

In view of her inordinately unkempt appearance, it came as no surprise to find that she was an equally negligent housekeeper. A stale—musty—distinctly unwholesome atmosphere pervaded the little parlor into which she conducted me. It had evidently been many months since the room had been subjected to the ministrations of a dust mop or a broom. The windowpanes were thick with grime, and cobwebs hung in dirty strands from the corners of the ceiling. Though of decent quality, the furnishings—a sofa, a high-backed Windsor chair, a claw-footed tea table, and an old grandfather clock (whose hands were stopped at a quarter-past-five)—were much the worse for wear. Several long-dead roses protruded from a chipped porcelain vase that stood on the mantel. Brown, withered petals lay scattered on the floor at the foot of the fireplace.

That this dreary little abode was, in fact, Bruno's residence I could tell at a glance—for the walls of the parlor were decorated with a half-dozen or so gaudy (if somewhat tattered and dog-eared) advertising posters from the various circuses and dime museums at which the Armless Wonder had performed in the course of his career. I inferred from their presence that—however lacking in traditional womanly virtues she may have been—my hostess was not entirely without redeeming feminine qualities; for she clearly took a mother's deep and natural pride in her son's accomplishments.

"Make yourself comfortable," said she, gesturing toward the sofa. "Want something to drink? Tea? Or maybe," she continued with a suggestive wink, "something a tad stronger?"

To be thus offered an alcoholic beverage (for there could be no mistaking her meaning) only confirmed my impression of the woman's hopelessly dissipated nature. With a curt refusal, I lowered myself onto the sofa, which was upholstered in a threadbare fabric of sickly green hue.

"Suit yourself," she said. "Now don't you go anywheres. I'll be back in a flash." And so saying, she swiveled on her heels and bustled from the room.

Gazing about the little parlor in her absence, I noticed a small shelf affixed to the wall beside the grandfather clock. Among the dozen or so works it contained were a copy of Bunyon's *Pilgrim's Progress*, several of Scott's Waverly novels, and a well-worn volume I instantly recognized as Tyler's *Traditional Faerie Legends of the English and Scottish Peasantry*, which—as Sissy had informed me on more than one occasion—had been a favorite of Bruno's as a child.

A moment later my hostess reappeared, clasping a tumbler that held an ample measure of amber-colored liquid. The Windsor chair being situated only a few feet away from the sofa, I fully expected her to seat herself upon this article for our interview. What was my surprise—and dismay—when she proceeded to lower herself onto the cushion directly beside me!

"So," she said. "What would you like to know?" As she spoke, she crossed one leg over the other, exposing the uppermost limb in a manner that was not merely immodest but positively indecent!

Displaying none of the shock and indignation that I felt at this unseemly display, I calmly declared: "I am interested in learning any details that might assist me in creating a full and vivid picture of your celebrated son's life."

"Why not ask *him?*" she inquired, taking a sip of her brandy (for so, from its distinctive aroma, I perceived her drink to be).

"I have done so," I replied. "The information that he volunteered, however, was exceedingly meager." I did not add that it was also exceedingly *misleading*, inasmuch as he had insisted that he was orphaned at an early age. Of course—having now met the young man's mother—I could easily understand the reason for his deception. Undoubtedly, he wished to conceal from the world the shameful truth of his parentage—i.e., that he was the offspring of a female who was nothing less than an abject slave to the Fiend Intemperance!

"Well, I guess there's a reason he didn't tell you much," she remarked, taking another swig of her drink. "And the reason is—there ain't that much to say!" As she raised the glass to her lips, I perceived that the third finger of her right hand was adorned with a resplendent gold ring, set with a large, semitransluscent emerald surrounded by small diamonds. In its sheer costliness and elegance, it contrasted sharply with the overall shabbiness of her appearance. Something about the ring seemed oddly familiar to me, as though I had encountered one of identical design in the recent past. For the life of me, however, I could not remember where.

"He never had no father to speak of," she continued, growing suddenly lachrymose. "The Good Lord took my husband off just after Bruno was born. Cut himself with an old handsaw blade and perished of the lockjaw. Left me without a man. It ain't easy for a lone woman in this world, especially not with a damned brat to feed. Worked day and night, and *still* never had a pot to piss in. Never even had a bed to call my own. Had to share one with Bruno 'til he was big enough to start bringin' in money with his act. I gave up my life for that boy—did everything for him."

All at once, her countenance underwent a most striking—and disconcerting—transformation. From maudlin self-pity, her expression shifted in an instant to one of brazen coquettishness, if not outright *lubricity*. Reaching down with her beringed right hand, she laid it upon my knee and, in a low, insinuating voice, said: "Tell me, handsome. Anything I can do for *you?*"

So startled was I by both her gesture and remark that I immediately leapt to my feet and strode to the opposite side of the room, where I halted before the fireplace. Though my mind was in a tumult, I attempted to strike a pose of perfect nonchalance, not wishing my hostess to see how thoroughly she had unsettled me. I therefore leaned my elbow against the mantelpiece and cast a *blasé* look back at the woman, who regarded me with an amused expression, while she imbibed another mouthful of her brandy.

As I waited for my inner agitation to subside, I pondered on the ever-deepening mystery of Bruno's life and character. That a young man's attitude toward the fairer sex was shaped by his earliest maternal experiences there could be little doubt. My own case might serve as an example. Though cruelly deprived in childhood of my dear mother, the celebrated actress Eliza Poe, my loving memories of that sainted creature had endowed me with a lifelong veneration of womanhood.

In utter contrast to the angelic female who bore me, the personage now seated across the room was a grotesque travesty of all that was holy and pure about the sacred estate of motherhood. To be raised by such a vile being could hardly fail to infuse a growing boy with a deep and general detestation of the entire sex. And yet, such did not seem to be the case with Bruno. On the contrary, to all outward appearances, he was a young man of singularly tender-hearted, not to say *chivalrous* nature. How, I wondered, had he escaped the dire consequences of his upbringing? It was a mystery all insoluble. I could only conclude that his evident fondness for, and gallantry toward, the opposite sex was further evidence of his exceptional nature—as marvelous in its way as the pedal skills he had developed to compensate for the absence of his upper limbs.

At that moment, my ruminations were interrupted by a remark from my hostess. "Careful you don't knock over that vase," she said, her words increasingly slurred from the effects of the alcohol.

Glancing to my left, I saw that my elbow was resting only inches away from the receptacle in question.

"Guess I ought to change those flowers one of these days," she continued. "Poor little roses." Raising the tumbler to her lips, she imbibed the remainder of the brandy, then ran her tongue over her lips.

"That's my name, you know," she abruptly declared.

"Your name?" I said, frowning in puzzlement at this seeming *non sequitur.*

"Rose," she said.

"I-I beg your pardon?" I stammered, feeling the blood abruptly drain from my countenance.

"Rose," she repeated. "That's me."

All at once, a realization struck me with the force of a physical blow. I now recollected precisely why the piece of jewelry on her right hand had looked so familiar to me.

"Th-that ring," I gasped. "Where did you get it?"

"This?" she said, glancing down at the ring as though seeing it for the first time. "Why, my boy gave it to me. Thinks the world of me, he does."

By this point, my throat was so constricted with dread that it was only by exerting myself to the utmost that I managed to utter: "When? When did he give it to you?"

"I don't know. Last month, I guess," she replied with a shrug.

It would be folly to attempt to describe the emotions that now possessed me. A thousand harrowing thoughts came thronging to my brain and drove the blood in torrents upon my heart. Could it be true? But how was it possible?

All at once, the answer flashed upon me, filling my bosom with a species of horror and dread for which the language of mortality has no sufficiently energetic expression.

"You're lookin' awful strange, mister," said the woman, staring at me intently. "Something wrong?"

"Miscreant!" I shrieked. "Vile, unnatural woman! You have created a *fiend!*" Then—as the wretched creature shrank back on the sofa—I bolted from the room and dashed headlong through the rain-drenched streets toward the American Museum.

CHAPTER THIRTY-THREE

Within minutes, I had arrived back at the museum. Gunther, who was in the act of selling a pair of admission tickets to an elderly couple, glanced at me in surprise as I sprinted past his counter and—without addressing so much as a word of greeting to him—rushed inside the building.

Up the main staircase I bounded, taking the marble steps two at a time. Attendance at the museum being much sparser than usual, I encountered relatively few patrons during my rapid ascent. One of these—a stout, ruddy-faced fellow with luxuriant side-whiskers—cursed at me bitterly as I shouldered him aside in my haste.

Moments later, I reached the third floor and burst into the Hall of Oddities. The sight that greeted me caused the very marrow to freeze in my bones.

Bruno's platform was empty—and Sissy was nowhere to be seen!

As I stood there panting wildly—my clothing so saturated with rainwater that a puddle instantly formed at my feet—I heard a voice nearby me say: "Mr. Poe! For Heaven's sake, what's wrong?" Even in my distracted state, I recognized the speaker at once as Willie Schnitzler, beside whose little stage I had come to a halt.

"Willie!" I cried, turning toward the enormous, bearded female who was gazing down at me with a look of intense concern. "Where is Bruno?"

"Taking a little break," she replied. "He left just a few minutes ago."

"And have you seen my wife, Virginia?"

"Why, yes. She was here for the better part of an hour, I'd say. Watching Bruno's act. They left together."

A sensation of uttermost terror instantly pervaded my frame. "Tell me, Willie," I urgently demanded in a voice trembling with agitation. "Where is Mr. Barnum's special room—the one in which he stores those artifacts too rare and precious to be placed on public display?"

"Special room?" Willie said, a look of the deepest perplexity suffusing her broad, bewhiskered countenance. "Why, I've never heard of such a thing. As far as I know, Mr. B keeps all his extra stuff stored in the basement."

"But according to Sissy—" I began to say. I did not, however, manage to complete my sentence; for I was suddenly struck with a realization so dire—so sheerly *appalling*—that my powers of speech totally failed. *The basement!* Of course. There was indeed a storage room down there—a room which, as I now had reason to believe, Bruno was only too dreadfully familiar.

With a strangled cry of horror, I spun on my heels—bolted from the hall—and went hurtling down the stairs to the bottommost level of the building.

Through the cramped and mazelike basement I flew. As I drew near Barnum's office, the showman himself emerged into the corridor, apparently bent on some errand.

"Poe!" he cried in astonishment. "What in Heaven's name—?" In his intensely alarmed facial expression, I saw reflected the wild, if not *desperate*, appearance I must have presented.

"The custodial closet!" I shouted, without slackening my pace. "Quickly!"

With the showman at my heels, I continued to race through the murky precincts of the basement. Within seconds I had reached the storeroom formerly used by Barnum's late employee, Abel Tomblin. I instantly grabbed the knob and turned—but to no avail. The door was securely locked!

"Here!" Barnum said, as he came up beside me and extracted his key ring from the pocket of his trousers.

At that instant, from the opposite side of the door, there issued a sound that caused every separate hair on the nape of my neck to stand erect in terror. A female voice—*Sissy's* voice—cried out: "Help! Oh, God! Please help!"

"Stand aside!" I shouted to Barnum, who was frantically searching for the correct key. Imitating a maneuver that my erstwhile companion, Colonel David Crockett, had once performed in my presence, I raised my booted right foot to the level of the doorknob and—with a savage kick—broke open the lock. The door flew in upon its hinges—revealing a sight that caused my brain to reel with horror!

In the middle of the room stood Bruno. He was naked from the waist up, having divested himself of his jacket and shirt, which lay in a heap at his feet. Having already deduced the truth about the nefarious young man, I was unsurprised by the sight of his exposed upper torso. Barnum, however, emitted a loud cry of amazement as he gaped at Bruno's physique.

The Armless Wonder was not armless at all. On the contrary, his two upper limbs were fully intact and perfectly formed, as were the hands in which they terminated.

In his right hand he clutched a large knife, which was pointed directly at my darling Sissy, who cowered before him, her own two hands clasped tightly before her bosom, as though she were imploring him for mercy.

"Oh, Eddie!" she sobbed, turning her tear-streaked countenance in my direction. "Thank Heavens you're here!"

"Incredible!" Barnum muttered, as though speaking to himself. "I see it with my own two eyes, but I just don't believe it!"

Making no move to lower his weapon, Bruno regarded the showman with a look of sheer, gloating malice.

"The Great Barnum!" he scoffed. "King of humbugs! *Ha!* Guess I humbugged *you* pretty well!"

He then turned toward me. "I suppose you think you're pretty damned smart, eh, Mr. Poe?" he said in the same, sneering tone. "How the hell *did* you figure it out?"

My feelings at that moment can scarcely be conveyed in words. To stand helplessly by while my darling wife quailed in terror before the knife-wielding madman was almost more than I could bear. With every fiber of my being, I longed to leap at the villain—wrest the weapon from his hand—and vent my fury upon his depraved and hateful person. I knew, however, that any precipitate action on my part would place my loved one in the gravest jeopardy. Exerting my willpower to the utmost, therefore, I subdued my raging emotions, and—speaking in as level a voice as I could manage—replied thusly:

"I shall be pleased to describe the chain of ideas and observations that led me to my conclusion. Before I do so, however, I must demand that you lay down your weapon and release my wife, who has ever treated you as a trusted friend. It is time, Bruno, to give yourself up."

"What for?" replied the half-naked rogue, his handsome visage contorted into an expression of pure malevolence. "To hang?"

"But you cannot possibly escape," I said.

"We'll see about that," he answered.

With shocking suddenness, he thrust out his free hand and grabbed my wife by the hair. She shrieked in pain as he yanked her roughly toward him—spun her around so that she was facing away from him—and placed the point of his knife directly against the base of her surpassingly delicate throat.

The sight of my poor, helpless wife being so brutally manhandled aroused my fury to a nearly intolerable pitch. And yet, I was utterly powerless to take effective action. Although the walls were hung with tools—hammers and axes, crowbars and handsaws, mallets and chisels, all within easy reach—I dared not seize one and use it as a weapon; for with the fiend's knife pressed against my darling's throat, any sudden movement on my part might result in her death.

"Don't try anything stupid, Mr. Poe," snarled Bruno, as though discerning my thoughts. "Now, both of you—out of my way!" Then, using Virginia as a shield, he worked his way past us and backed out of the room.

No sooner had he disappeared into the hallway than Barnum and I quickly followed.

Anticipating our pursuit, Bruno continued to move backward down the corridor, so that he could keep an eye on Barnum and myself. "Stay back!" he cried from over Sissy's shoulder. Though my darling wife said nothing, the imploring expression on her visage tore at my very soul.

"Fear not, dear Sissy," I cried in a tremulous voice. "No harm shall come to you!"

These words had scarcely issued from my lips when I perceived something that made my heart leap with sudden hope. From out of the shadows behind Bruno, there emerged a massive figure I recognized at once as Willie Schnitzler! As she had done on a previous occasion—when her timely appearance had saved me from certain death at the brutish hands of Croley—the good-hearted woman had evidently come looking for me out of concern. She was now stealthily approaching Bruno from behind; while he—oblivious of her presence—continued to move backward in her direction. In another instant, they would be in close enough proximity for Willie to seize the young man and disarm him.

At that very moment, however, something dreadful occurred. Apparently sensing the looming presence of the enormous figure behind him, Bruno abruptly released his hold on my wife—whipped around—and, with a savage cry, plunged the knife into Willie's bosom! As she collapsed with a groan, he scrambled over her fallen body and bolted toward the stairway.

Emitting simultaneous shouts of dismay, Barnum and I rushed toward the fallen woman. Sissy, meanwhile, dropped to her knees and raised poor Willie's head into her lap.

Taking only a moment to assure myself that my dear wife was unscathed, I cried out to her and Barnum: "Stay here and attend to Willie. I shall go after Bruno!" Then, leaping over the enormous form of the bearded woman (who lay moaning in pain, one hand clutched to the carved knife-handle that protruded from her bosom), I raced down the corridor to the stairwell.

I was halfway up the steps when, from the landing above, I heard a sudden eruption of shrieks and exclamations. Arriving at the main floor, I found a small group of patrons standing about, their faces registering varying degrees of shock and confusion. One young woman appeared to have swooned at the sight of the fleeing, half-naked madman. Eyes closed, head hanging limply to one side, she was being supported in the arms of her male companion.

"Which way did he go?" I cried as I reached the little group.

"Up there! The stairs!" they exclaimed, accompanying their words with frantic, pointing gestures.

Instantly, I made for the staircase. Up the marble steps I rushed. All at once, I heard a new outburst from above: more startled cries and ejaculations, mingled this time with another sound—the shattering of glass. The source of this latter noise became immediately clear when I reached the second floor and saw that one of the display cases, situated in the hallway not far from the head of the stairs, had been vandalized. Its glass panels had been utterly smashed and lay in jagged shards on the floor.

Hurrying over to the case, I saw that its contents were missing, except for the hand-printed explanatory card that still stood on a little wooden easel. "Actual Pistol Used by Aaron Burr to Slay Alexander Hamilton in Their Famous Duel, July 11, 1804," it read. From the indentations on the red-velvet cushion upon which the missing items had rested, I deduced that the case had contained, not merely the handgun itself, but its various accoutrements—powder flask, ammunition pouch, etc.

Far from causing me the slightest hesitation, the awareness that my quarry was now armed with a deadly weapon only filled me with a greater sense of urgency. Within moments, I had bounded upstairs to the third floor. Several customers were standing in a little cluster on the landing, gazing in consternation at the entrance to the auditorium, where Barnum's gaudy theatrical extravaganza was staged every evening.

"Some crazy-looking feller just ran in there!" cried one of the patrons, a gaunt young man whose somewhat threadbare habiliments identified him unmistakably as a member of the city's laboring class. "Naked as a jaybird above the waist. Looked like he had some kind of pistol in his hand, too."

"The police must be notified!" I exclaimed. "One of Barnum's performers has been desperately wounded. Even as we speak, she lies bleeding in the basement. In the meantime, I shall pursue the perpetrator of the foul deed and attempt to subdue him until help arrives." Then, as the gaunt-looking young man turned and hurried down the staircase, I made my way to the auditorium and cautiously slipped inside.

The great hall lay steeped in shadows, a pair of glowing, wall-mounted gas-jets on either side of the entrance providing the sole illumination. The vacant seats stretched before me, row upon row of them, receding into the darkness that enveloped the front of the theater. For several moments, I remained standing at the very rear, just inside the entrance, allowing my vision to adjust itself to the gloom. Though I could see no sign of Bruno, I thought that I could discern the dull, scraping sound of someone—or some*thing*—moving backstage.

At length, I cleared my throat and—speaking at a volume sufficiently loud to be heard throughout the cavernous auditorium—addressed my unseen adversary thusly:

"Bruno! This is Mr. Poe! Speaking as one who has always considered you a friend, I implore you to lay down your weapon and surrender at once. Should you do so, you may expect to receive a fair and impartial trial. In view of the appalling nature of your crimes—whose atrocity bespeaks a mind lost to reason—the jury may well be persuaded to acquit you on the grounds of mental instability. In that case, you will evade the harshest penalty of the law, and live out the term of your natural life confined to an asylum for the criminally insane. Surely, such a fate, however grim, is preferable to the one that awaits if you persist in your present course of action; for when the police arrive and see that you are offering armed resistance, they will not hesitate to respond with lethal force."

For several moments, I awaited a response to this appeal—but none was forthcoming. As I stood there, listening for any sound that might reveal Bruno's location, it suddenly occurred to me that the cunning young man might already have slipped out of the theater, using the backstage door. Even now, he might be effecting his escape from the museum—or, even more alarmingly, making his way back down to the basement to complete the bloody work that Barnum and I had interrupted!

Clearly, there was no time to lose. Keeping my body bent low, I hurried down the aisle. Arriving unmolested at the stage, I placed my hands upon it—vaulted up onto the proscenium—and hastened backstage.

A single gaslight burned on the wall. Several yards away stood the great, circular cage. Within it loomed the shadowy bulk of the monstrous *Necrophorus* beetle. Apart from an occasional twitching of its feelers, it remained absolutely motionless, as though it were patiently awaiting the feeding it would receive at the climax of that night's performance.

Not far from the cage stood a large, wooden clothing rack, upon which hung the many elaborate costumes used in the show. Assorted props were ranged along the wall. Among these items was a sheaf of formidable-looking spears, carried by the actors who represented the imperial guard of Atlantis.

I quickly hurried over—grabbed one of the spears—and, extending it before me, proceeded to advance slowly, around the cage, toward the rear door.

I had taken only a few steps when, with shocking abruptness, something hard was thrust against the back of my head, and a familiar voice behind me said: "Drop it, Mr. Poe. Now!"

That the object pressed to my skull was the barrel of a pistol there could be no doubt. I immediately opened my hands and let my own weapon clatter to the ground.

"Now, turn around slowly," my antagonist ordered. "And keep your hands up."

Doing as he commanded, I found myself face-to-face with Bruno, who had the muzzle of his dueling pistol leveled at my brow. How, I wondered, had he been able to approach me so stealthily, without making the slightest noise? The answer became immediately apparent; for—lowering my eyes—I saw that he was barefooted, having evidently removed his shoes before stealing up on me.

"Well, well," he said with a malevolent smile. "Guess you're not so smart after all, eh, Mr. Poe?"

Believing that help was on the way, I frantically cast about in my mind for ways to stall the deranged young man for as long as possible.

"Smart enough, at any rate, to have discovered your secret," I replied with assumed nonchalance. "Earlier, you appeared to be curious as to the means by which I arrived at my deduction. Would you care to hear my explanation?"

"Go ahead," he replied, keeping his weapon aimed at my head. "But make it quick."

"It was my interview with your mother that led me to solve the mystery."

"My mother!" gasped Bruno, his pallid complexion turning a bright, crimson hue. "How did you find out about *her?*"

"My purpose in traveling downtown this morning was precisely to investigate the mundane facts of your daily life. Let me hasten to add that I was motivated by a desire, not to pry into your personal affairs, but rather to obtain those small but colorful details that would enrich the official biography that Mr. Barnum had commissioned me to write."

"I was wondering what brought you into town this morning," Bruno muttered. "That sweet little piece of yours didn't say much about it—just that you were working on my book."

Ignoring the shockingly offensive way in which he had referred to Virginia, I continued thusly: "Having located your residence, I was much surprised to discover that—contrary to your own representations—your mother was very much alive. After making my introductions, I was invited inside your abode. Though it may be imprudent to say so, I would be lying if I did not confess that—even at that moment—I found certain aspects of your mother's behavior intensely disquieting, and I wondered to myself what effect such behavior might have on the sensitive moral constitution of a growing young boy. Still, I had no solid cause for suspicion. Several circumstances, however, quickly elicited within me a growing sense of alarm.

"On the bookshelf in your parlor, I spotted your well-worn edition of Thomas Crofton Tyler's *Traditional Faerie Legends of the English and Scottish Peasantry.* Sissy, of course, had told me on several occasions that, like herself, you had always been fascinated by the stories in that volume. One of these tales, as I had recently discovered, was 'The Girl

Without Hands'—a work that could hardly fail to have a powerful effect on the mind of an impressionable child. When I then discovered that your mother's name was identical to that of the flower mysteriously inserted into the mouths of the killer's mutilated victims, there began to glimmer, in the deepest chambers of my intellect, a faintly conception of the awful truth.

"It was not, however, until I observed the ring worn by your mother that my suspicions turned to absolute certainty. At first—though the ring looked strangely familiar to me—I could not recall where I might have seen it. And then I remembered—in the engraved reproduction of Mr. Gilbert Opdyke's portrait of Isabel Somers! Your mother, in short, was sporting the very piece of jewelry removed from the severed hand of one of the murder victims! When she went on to explain that she had received the ring as a gift from *you*—and at the very time of Miss Somers's death—whatever doubts I had been harboring about the killer's identity vanished in an instant.

"At that moment, other realizations came rushing in upon my consciousness. It dawned on me that the natural color of your mother's hair, still visible amidst the prevailing gray, was the precise shade of auburn as the tresses of the victims, as well as of my own darling wife. I also recalled that you had worked at Alexander Parmalee's establishment at the same time that Lemuel Thompson—the poor man executed for the slaying of Ellen Jennings—was employed there. Thus, it would have been exceptionally easy for you to plant the evidence that implicated him in the murder—as, it now appears, you did with Abel Tomblin.

"One mystery remained. Given your deformity, how could you have physically accomplished such gruesome killings? Even with your remarkable abilities, it seemed inconceivable that you could have perpetrated these fearful—these unspeakable—atrocities with your *feet*. The answer was not difficult to infer. Of all classes of *terata*, the absence of the upper limbs is the simplest to feign. I recalled your preference for loose-fitting shirts and jackets, beneath which you could have easily concealed your arms by holding them behind your back or pressing them tightly to your sides.

"As for your motive in committing such ghastly acts of violence, I could only surmise that your upbringing by a mother of such dubious, if not *dissolute,* character had left you with a profound detestation of womanhood that found unbridled expression in murder."

Throughout my explanation, Bruno had regarded me with a mixture of keen interest and grudging admiration. I saw at once, however, that I had overstepped the limits of discretion in my remarks about his mother. No sooner had the words issued from my lips than his countenance underwent a dramatic transformation. His complexion turned absolutely scarlet—his eyes blazed with fury—his features grew contorted with rage.

"Why, you lousy, stinking bastard!" he cried in a shaking voice. Bubbles of spittle formed at the corners of his mouth, endowing him with an unnerving resemblance to a rabid canine. "Keep your damned yap shut about my mother! I'd be nothing without her. She used to read me that story all the time when I was a kid—the one about the girl who got her hands chopped off. Told me the same would happen to me if I didn't behave. It spooked me so bad that I began wondering how I'd manage if I lost *my* hands. So I started teaching myself to do things with my feet. Practiced in secret, day and night. After a while, I got so good that I could do practically anything with them—eat, drink, comb my hair, use scissors. When my mother found out, she came up with an amazing idea. I could pass myself off as a freak, join a circus, make some good money. And it worked! Everything I have I owe to her! She made me what I am!"

All too true, thought I. The hopelessly dissipated female who raised you was indeed responsible for making you the creature you became. For while you were busily teaching yourself the skills that would allow you to pass as a *physical* freak, she was turning you into something infinitely more horrifying—a *moral* monstrosity!

"I think I've heard enough of your blabber," the young madman continued with a snarl. "It's time to say good-bye, Mr. Poe. Turn around!" Reaching out his free hand, he grabbed me roughly by the shoulder, spun me about, and thrust the barrel of his pistol between my shoulder-blades.

"Surely," I said, "you do not intend to execute me in so cowardly a fashion—by shooting me in the back."

"Who said anything about shooting?" he snorted.

This statement could not fail to perplex me, as I felt certain that the young maniac intended to kill me without further delay. My confusion, however, was exceedingly short-lived; for—using his weapon as a prod—Bruno directed me across the backstage area and commanded me to halt directly before the cage in which the gargantuan insect was housed.

Leaning his head over my right shoulder, he then placed his mouth close to my ear and, in a tone of diabolical pleasure, said: "Just look at the jaws on that thing. Big and sharp as scythes. And see how they're moving? He can't wait to tear into some food. Barnum likes to keep him hungry. Makes him go wild when they toss him those chickens at the end of the show. Guess he won't be too hungry for chicken tonight, though."

So horrific—so appalling—was the implication of this statement that I instantly felt the blood congeal in my veins.

"Now open that cage door and get inside," Bruno continued, cocking the pistol and raising it to the back of my skull.

"By no means shall I do your bidding," I declared, struggling with only partial success to keep my voice from quaking with terror and revulsion.

"Have it your way," came the mocking reply.

At that instant, I was stunned by a savage blow to the back of my head, administered by the butt of Bruno's pistol. My legs buckled—my vision grew cloudy—and I dropped to my knees. Though badly dazed, I retained a measure of awareness. I could hear Bruno reach over my shoulder—throw back the bolt—and swing the cage door open. All at once, I was seized by the collar of my jacket and savagely yanked onto my feet.

"Nice knowing you, Mr. Poe," sneered the madman. And so saying, he shoved me violently toward the opening between the iron bars.

That our ordinary physical capacities represent only a fraction of our latent powers becomes strikingly evident at moments of extreme crisis. Faced with the prospect of such a fearfully, such an *inconceivably,* hideous death, I reflexively thrust my hands upward and grabbed onto the horizontal bar that served as the lintel of the cage door. Bending my legs so that my feet were elevated from the ground, I then swung myself backward and, letting go of my grip, dropped back to the floor, bringing both of my boot heels smashing down upon the unshod right foot of my enemy. I could feel the delicate metatarsal bones crack as I landed with the full weight of my body upon his arch.

Emitting a deafening howl, Bruno staggered backward, while I spun around and lunged for his gun-hand. Grabbing him by the wrist, I attempted to wrestle the weapon out of his grasp. His face contorted with agony, the young fiend furiously struggled against me, attempting to level the muzzle at my head, even as I strove desperately to keep it pointed away from me. All at once, I shoved my right thumb through the trigger guard and squeezed down on Bruno's index finger, causing the pistol to discharge harmlessly into the air.

This latest thwarting of his murderous design aroused Bruno to a new pitch of fury. Tossing aside his now-useless weapon, he drew back his right fist and unleashed a vicious blow at my face. Though I evaded the full force of his punch by ducking to the left at the last moment, he caught me on the side of the head. As I had not yet fully recovered from being clubbed on the back of the head, this blow, however glancing, was enough to send me toppling to the ground. In the next instant, Bruno had pounced upon my prostrate body, his fingers pressed to my windpipe.

Frantically, I clutched at his hands, attempting to break his stranglehold. In my weakened condition, however, I was powerless to do so. My situation was desperate in the extreme. If I did not act within seconds, I would subside into unconsciousness. Calling upon a reserve of strength whose existence, until that instant, was utterly unknown to me, I reached both of my hands high above my head— clasped them tightly together—and brought them down, clublike, on the bridge of my assailant's nose, which broke with a sickening *crunch.*

He screamed and fell backward, landing directly outside the open door of the cage.

At that instant, the giant beetle—which had remained motionless during my fight with Bruno—suddenly stirred to life. With a great flurry of its barbed, many-jointed legs, it burst through the opening and—seizing Bruno's flailing right arm between its powerful jaws—sheared off the limb just above the elbow.

Never while I live shall I forget the agonized roar that issued from the young man's lips. As he writhed on the ground, clutching the ragged stump, I quickly scrambled to my feet. As I attempted to flee, however, my boot soles slipped on the blood spraying from his dreadful wound, and I went crashing back onto the floor.

The sound of my fall seemed to attract the attention of the monstrous beetle, which instantly lost interest in the mutilated young man and came scuttling toward me with a terrifying agility. Before I could get out of its way, the monster was upon me.

Mere words cannot convey the agony of terror I experienced at that moment. Only inches above my face loomed the inconceivably hideous maw of the giant beetle, its mouth parts glistening horribly, its curved, serrated mandibles moving with a sickening avidity.

In the extremity of my despair, I thrust my hands to either side of me, groping wildly about for a weapon. All at once, the fingers of my right hand closed on an object I recognized immediately as the spear with which I had armed myself earlier. Drawing it toward me, I angled it upward and—with a savage thrust—drove it through the abdomen of the monster. Greenish-yellow slime oozed down the shaft of the spear, suffusing my nostrils with a loathsome stench, as the mortally wounded insect gave a single, violent shiver and died.

As the full weight of the lifeless monster settled upon me, I struggled to extricate myself from its suffocating bulk. By this point, however, my strength was entirely spent. A hideous dizziness oppressed me—a swirling mist of inky blackness began to becloud my vision—my consciousness commenced to dim.

At that moment, as though from a great distance, a discordant hum of human voices reached my ears: shouts—screams—exclamations of shock and alarm. Even as my auditory powers failed, I vaguely discerned the sound of footsteps swarming down the aisles—leaping onto the proscenium—and pounding across the stage. All at once, I could feel the great, smothering burden being lifted from my chest. Through the fog of my rapidly dimming vision, I thought I perceived a crowd of anxious faces peering intently down at me: Barnum—Sissy—Constable Hayes—Gunther the Alligator Boy—and others I did not recognize.

Then darkness washed over me, and all conscious sensations were swallowed up in a swift, rushing descent into the blackness of utter oblivion.

CHAPTER THIRTY-FOUR

The severity of Bruno's injury ensured that he could not possibly survive. My own saviors—Barnum, Constable Hayes, and the rest, who had arrived in the very nick of time to free me from the smothering mass of the monstrous insect—did everything in their power to assist him, applying a makeshift tourniquet to the truncated remains of his arm in a desperate effort to stanch the uncontrolled hemorrhaging. The overwhelming bodily and mental shock he had sustained, however—combined with the fearful loss of blood—was more than the young man's slender frame could tolerate. Only minutes after I regained consciousness, he expired in a dreadful manner—eyes protruding, lips pulled back in a *rictus* of agony, skin drained to the ghastly whiteness of a leper.

Happily, the situation proved very different in the case of Willie Schnitzler, thanks in large measure to her prodigious bulk. Though Bruno had plunged his knife deep into her bosom, the sheer quantity of fat enveloping her vital organs served as a natural barrier against the weapon's lethal thrust. Her wound, though far from superficial, did not endanger her life; and—following a brief period of recuperation—she was able to resume her usual activities. Her recovery was a great source of satisfaction to Sissy and myself, who had come to regard her as nothing less than an exceedingly large and hirsute guardian angel.

The sensational nature of all that had transpired guaranteed that it would excite extraordinary interest in the press. And indeed, the newspapers seized upon the story with an avidity surpassing even that which they had displayed at the time of Abel Tomblin's slaying. Bruno—formerly depicted as a latter-day Theseus—was now portrayed as a monster whose crimes exceeded the enormities of Caligula. Those newspapers least sympathetic to Barnum—James Gordon Bennett's *Herald* in particular—reached new heights of sanctimony in their condemnation of the showman. Only an establishment as innately unwholesome as the American Museum—so Bennett claimed—could have served as a sanctuary for "the greatest fiend of the ages." That Bruno had formerly worked in the supposedly uplifting environment of Alexander Parmalee's Gotham Museum was a fact conveniently ignored by Barnum's detractors.

This frenzy of publicity might have been expected to delight the showman, who regarded even the most unfavorable attention as preferable to none at all. Indeed, I fully anticipated that he would exploit the situation by immediately mounting an exhibit of the "Armless Wonder's" life, crimes, and hideous death, with Bruno's taxidermically preserved, severed arm as its chief attraction. Contrary to my expectations, however, Barnum seemed eager to put the entire matter behind him. The affair had left him feeling uncharacteristically downcast—less, I gathered, because of its ghastly and tragic consequences than because of the way he himself had been duped by the cunning young fiend. To have fallen victim to such an egregious deception was a decided blow to Barnum's singular sense of pride in himself as "The Prince of Humbugs." The death of his prized giant beetle also contributed greatly to his dispirited mood.

I was not entirely surprised, therefore, when, several weeks following the climax of the affair, I read in the papers that Barnum had decided to take temporary leave of the country and embark on a tour of England and the Continent. He would be accompanied by a troupe of his most celebrated performers and curiosities, including Sammy Wainwright, Gunther the Alligator Boy, Crowley the Man-Horse, the Great O'Bannon, and Willie Schnitzler. The declared intention of the trip was to exhibit his attractions in the capitals of Europe— "to take the Old World by storm!" as the showman proclaimed to reporters. Clearly, the prospect of relieving countless foreign customers of their hard-earned shillings, kreuzers, guilders, and francs was just the sort of tonic Barnum required to restore his crestfallen spirits.

The showman's wish to disassociate himself entirely from Bruno's murderous career rendered my biography of the "Armless Wonder" instantly superfluous. Shortly before departing on his trip, however, Barnum sent me an envelope containing a brief note of gratitude, along with a very generous payment for my services. With my financial difficulties thus relieved (at least temporarily)—and with no writing assignment requiring my immediate attention—I was able to devote myself to projects of a more personal significance. I was especially interested in pursuing the idea I had conceived several weeks earlier—to wit, the composition of a short rhymed poem on the supremely lyrical topic of the death of a beautiful young woman. Before embarking on this undertaking, however, I first decided to apply myself to another, as-yet-uncompleted task.

I resolved to decode Isabel Somers's journal.

As the reader will recall, this diary had been written in a form of cryptography which, to the untutored eye, appeared hopelessly indecipherable. And yet, the solution—which I arrived at after only a very short analysis of the various characters—proved to be by no means difficult. The reader should bear in mind that the basis of the whole art of solution, as far as regards these matters, is found in the general principles of the formation of language itself, and thus is altogether independent of the particular laws which govern any cipher. The difficulty of reading a cryptographical puzzle, in short, is by no means always in accordance with the labor or ingenuity with which it has been constructed.

With these considerations in view, let us now turn our attention to the method by which I resolved the enigma. For purposes of demonstration, I shall employ, as a sample, the passage I had first perused in Barnum's office:

;48 9$*8: 5((6+8 I($9 + ;$&5:--5*& *$; 5 9$98*;
;$$)$$* !6; 6))$ I(634;I?00: 8!.8*)6+8 ;$ 06+8
;48 ~5: $*8 ~6)48) 6* ;46) -6,:.;48 ;4(88 4?*&(8&

~600 25(80:)88 98 ;4($?34 ;48 8*& $1 ;48 9$*;4.
;48 8*+80$.8 ~5) &806+8(8& 2: 46) 05-=8:, -($08:.
3(?8)$98 1800$~! 5 08;;8(~5) 8*-0$)8&, 8!.(8))6*3
;48 4$.8 ;45; + 5*& 6 95: $*8 &5: 28 (8-$*-608&.
~800, ~8)4500)88 52$?; ;45;!

My first step was to ascertain the predominant letters, as well as the least frequent. Counting all, I constructed a table, thus:

Of the character 8 there are 49.

;	"	25.
$	"	24.
4	"	20.
0	"	19.
5	"	17.
*	"	17.
)	"	17.
6	"	16.
(	"	14.
&	"	11.
:	"	11.
9	"	8.
-	"	7.
+	"	7.
1	"	5.
?	"	5.
2	"	4.
/	"	3.
3	"	3.
!	"	2.

Now, in English, the letter that most frequently occurs is *e*. Indeed, it predominates so remarkably that an individual sentence of any length is rarely seen in which it is not the prevailing character. Here, then, I had in the very beginning the groundwork for something more than a mere guess. As the predominant character in the code was 8, I commenced by assuming it was the *e* of the natural alphabet.

Now, of all words in the language, "the" is the most usual. I therefore searched for repetitions of any three characters in the same order of collocation, the last of them being 8—my assumption being that such repetitions would most probably represent the word 'the.' On inspection, I found no less than seven such arrangements, the characters being ;48. Under the supposition that 8 represented *e*, I therefore deduced that the semicolon represented *t* and that 4 represented *h*. Thus a great step had been taken.

Having arrived at a single word, I was able to establish a vastly important point—that is to say, several commencements and terminations of other words. Let us refer, for example, to the third instance in which the combination ;48 occurs. We know that the semicolon immediately ensuing is the commencement of a word, and, of the five characters succeeding this 'the,' we are cognizant of no less than four. I therefore set these characters down by the letters I knew them to represent, leaving a space for the unknown—

th ee.

Going through the alphabet, I arrived at the word "three" as the sole possible reading. I thus gained another letter, *r*, represented by (.

Looking beyond these words, for a short distance, I again saw the combination ;48 and employed it by way of *termination* to what immediately preceded. I thus had this arrangement:

;4($?34 the.

Inserting the natural letters, where known, it read thus:

thr$?3h the.

I then substituted dots in place of the unknown characters:

thr . . . h the.

Immediately the word "through" made itself evident, thus providing me with three new letters, *o*, *u*, and *g*, represented by $, ?, and 3.

Already, I had no less than six of the most important letters represented. There is no need to proceed with further details of the solution. As I had anticipated, Miss Somers's cipher—for all its *apparent* complexity—proved to be the most rudimentary species of cryptography.

If the simplicity of her code came as no surprise to me, however, the *content* of her journal proved nothing less than shocking. The reader will get some sense of the startling nature of its disclosures when the sample passage is translated fully. Here is what it said:

> The money arrived from V today—and not a moment too soon. It is so frightfully expensive to live the way one wishes in this city. The three hundred will barely see me through the end of the month. The envelope was delivered by his lackey, Croley. Gruesome fellow. A letter was enclosed, expressing the hope that V and I may one day be reconciled. Well, we shall see about that.

As I continued to peruse the now-deciphered journal, I discovered at last the entire truth regarding the poor, doomed woman and her relationship to Morris Vanderhorn. That truth was so vastly different from everything I had imagined or surmised as to render me positively thunderstruck with amazement.

Isabel Somers, contrary to my earlier conjectures, had not been Vanderhorn's mistress.

She was his *daughter!*

What I learned was this: Isabel Somers had been the product of an illicit liaison, occurring some twenty years earlier, between a pretty young housemaid residing in upstate New York and Vanderhorn, who was then employed as an itinerant peddler of whiskey. Her mother having died in childbirth, Isabel was taken into the home of compassionate neighbors, who raised her as one of their own offspring.

It was not until she reached her majority that Isabel learned from her adopted parents that she was not their natural child. At that time, they presented her with a small, cedar chest containing a cache of mementos belonging to the woman who had borne her. Among these items, Isabel discovered a diary that revealed the identity of her natural father.

Shortly thereafter, Isabel herself—who had evidently inherited her mother's wayward propensities—had become pregnant by a heartless young cad, who soon absconded to the west. Fleeing her hometown in shame, she made her way to New York City, intending to procure assistance from the man she now knew to be her father—Morris Vanderhorn—who, by this point, had achieved inordinate wealth and (through his marriage) social position.

No sooner had she arrived in Manhattan than she appeared at Vanderhorn's mansion and demanded a private audience with him. If Isabel Somers had inherited her mother's recklessly ardent (if not wanton) nature, she appears to have received from her male progenitor a capacity for audacious, ruthless, and utterly self-interested behavior. She threatened to expose the sordid secret of his past, unless he supplied her with continuing financial support. In view of the hard-won respectability he had struggled for years to achieve among the city's elite class, Vanderhorn could not risk such a scandal. He acceded to her demands. He appears to have had another motive, as well. Far from being outraged at such flagrant extortion, he could not help but feel a fatherly admiration for the unscrupulous young woman, who embodied so much of his own nature. Indeed, he appears to have made several efforts to achieve some sort of personal reconciliation with his new-found daughter.

It was not long after she was set up in her new living quarters that Isabel Somers gave birth. As though in retribution for her sins, the creature that emerged from her womb was so hideous in appearance that the attending midwife swooned at her first glimpse of it. Its head was of an immense size and completely overgrown with coarse black hair, as shaggy as the fur of a North American *Ursus horribilis*. Its clawlike hands were so deformed as to hardly retain a human shape, resembling the talons of goshawk or gyrfalcon; while its dark, pupilless eyes were as large and unstaring as a barn owl's. Its thick-lipped mouth bristled with gnashing, yellow teeth. From the instant of its birth, it displayed an appetite so unbounded that no amount of sustenance could slake it. It never slept, keeping up a weird, inhuman keening day and night.

For a young woman who thought of little else but her own pleasure, the idea of being burdened with such a creature was intolerable. And yet, she could not bring herself to do away with the child, as countless others in similar circumstances have done from time immemorial (the dreadful practice of infanticide being as old as the species). It is true that, for a brief period, she thought of delivering the infant into the lethal care of a "baby-farmer"—one of those unutterably depraved females who, for a fee, take in unwanted newborns, only to let them perish miserably of neglect. In the end, however, she could not be a party to the destruction of her child. Within her bosom there beat a heart that, however obdurate, still retained a measure of maternal feeling.

At length, she arrived at a novel solution. Having paid several visits to Barnum's museum, she knew that the showman prized his human oddities above all his other performers. Believing that her monstrous offspring would find a welcome home at the museum, she abandoned it late one night at the entrance to the building. Her assumption proved correct. Within a short time, the grotesquely malformed infant—brazenly advertised by Barnum as a genuine "changeling"—had become one of his main attractions.

To ensure that her child was well cared for, the young woman went so far as to approach one of the showman's own employees and surreptitiously hire him to watch over the infant and tend to its importunate needs. This, of course, was Abel Tomblin. She also made occasional trips to the Hall of Oddities to see her child. It was during one of these visits that she evidently attracted the baleful attention of the demoniacal Bruno.

How Isabel Somers's brutal death affected Morris Vanderhorn will never be known. Certainly, when Barnum and I had interviewed him at his mansion shortly following the tragedy, he had evinced no emotional response whatsoever to the murder. In any event, he did not long outlive his daughter, having perished soon thereafter at the hands of his perfidious wife and her hunchbacked paramour—who, at the time of this writing, remain at large.

EPILOGUE

U nconstrained by any further obligations to Barnum, I was at last able to focus my energies on the project I had so long deferred, and at length produced a work whose publication, in the pages of the New York *Mirror*, created nothing less than a sensation. I refer, of course, to my intensely lyrical poem, "The Raven." Its appearance was greeted with unprecedented popular and critical acclaim, the *Philadelphia Inquirer* declaring it a "sublime, *shivery* masterpiece," while *The Gentleman's Magazine* confidently claimed that "it may well defy competition in the whole circle of contemporary verse writings."

As the most discerning reviewers recognized, its unique poetic force derived from the striking originality, not merely of its conception, but of its construction, which relied (to put the matter in the simplest possible terms) on a metrical scheme of octameter acatalectic, alternating with heptameter catalectic repeated in the refrain of the fifth verse, and terminating with tetrameter catalectic. To assert (however immodestly) that nothing even remotely approaching this combination has ever been attempted in the history of Western literature is only to state the obvious.

If my poem elicited a wildly enthusiastic response from reviewers, its effect on the general reading public was nothing short of *electric*. Within weeks of its publication, the mournful cry of "Nevermore" was on the lips of literate people all across the nation. It seemed as if the entire population had committed the poem to memory. Tributes—in the form of fond, parodic imitations—appeared everywhere: in periodicals, commercial advertisements, theatrical skits, political lampoons. Actors declaimed it from the stage, and professional elocutionists added it to their repertoires, making it a staple of the American lecture circuit. Before long, it had even been incorporated in several standard schoolbooks, becoming an immediate classroom favorite. After years of struggle, public neglect, and professional disappointment, I had risen to the ranks of the poetic immortals—borne aloft on the inky wings of my grim, ungainly, ghastly, gaunt and ominous bird of yore!

Under ordinary circumstances, this period of unqualified professional and popular success would have been among the most satisfying of my life. My pleasure, however, was severely diminished by my intense concern for Sissy, whose own mortality weighed heavily on my mind. The shock she had suffered at the hands of the demoniacal Bruno had dealt a dreadful blow to her always-precarious health. For weeks following the tumultuous climax of the affair, she took to her bed, reduced to a state of such excessive debility that, at moments, I despaired of her recovery. Her illness wrought a fearful alteration in her appearance. Her dark eyes blazed with a too-too glorious effulgence. Her pale complexion became of the transparent waxen hue of the grave, and the blue veins upon her lofty forehead swelled and sank impetuously with the tides of the most gentle emotion.

Day and night, our devoted Muddy waited upon her, cooling her feverish brow with moist compresses—plying her with spoonfuls of nutritious *consommé*—and, in general ministering to her every physical need. At length, our prayers appeared to be answered. By slow degrees, Sissy's strength returned. The ghastly pallor receded from her cheeks, replaced by a more natural coloration. After the passage of nearly a month, she was able to rise from her sickbed and resume a more normal existence. Even so, I anxiously scanned her visage each morning, to assure myself that the grim angel, Azrael—whose hovering presence had cast such a fearful shadow over my beloved—had truly been banished from her vicinity!

On a brilliant fall morning during the first week of November, Sissy expressed a wish to take a stroll through the countryside. I greatly rejoiced to hear this request, taking it as an exceedingly favorable sign of my dear wife's steady improvement. Accordingly, we packed a small picnic lunch and—bidding farewell to Muddy (who had declined an invitation to accompany us on our jaunt)—set off across the meadow in a westerly direction.

It was a day of singular beauty, the trees ablaze with a glorious array of autumnal hues. Hand in hand, we rambled at a leisurely pace. The crisp, fragrant air was infinitely more bracing than any medicinal tonic, infusing our souls with an exhilarating sense of vitality and pleasure.

At length, we arrived at the banks of the exquisite little brook where, months earlier, the germ had first been planted that would eventuate in the composition of my now-celebrated poem, "The Raven." Settling ourselves under the same towering tree beneath which I had rested on that memorable occasion, we undid the bundle containing our food and enjoyed our modest, if intensely satisfying, repast.

We remained at the enchanting spot for somewhat more than an hour, chatting merrily and drinking in the splendor of the setting. At length—the sun disappearing beneath a few vaporous clouds—we rose and headed homeward.

Muddy was waiting for us in the parlor, wearing a look of barely suppressed excitement, as though she were concealing a surprise. After asking about our ramble—and assuring herself that her daughter had not overtaxed herself—the good woman reached into the pocket of her apron and extracted an envelope.

"It was delivered while you were gone," she declared, handing it to me.

"Why, it is from Barnum!" I said, closely scrutinizing the writing. "It has been mailed from England."

"Oh, goody!" Sissy exclaimed, clapping her hands excitedly as she settled onto the sofa beside Muddy. "I can't wait to hear it!"

Lowering myself onto the chair by the fireplace, I tore open the envelope and proceeded to peruse the letter.

"What does he say?" Sissy eagerly inquired.

"To date, his trip appears to be nothing short of triumphant," I replied. "According to his account, he has not only managed to secure a personal audience with Queen Victoria but has, by some undisclosed means, succeeded in obtaining the original gown she wore at her coronation. He has also acquired numerous other rarities, including the actual boot removed from the amputated leg of Lord Uxbridge during the Battle of Waterloo. All of these items will be put on exhibit at his museum immediately upon his return from Europe.

"And listen to this," I exclaimed as I continued to scan the letter. "Willie Schnitzler and the Great O'Bannon have gotten married!"

At this unexpected news, both Muddy and Sissy emitted simultaneous cries of delighted surprise.

"Apparently," I continued, "they have been in love for some time. Moreover," I said, reading further, "they are planning on having a child!"

"Oh my," Muddy said with a giggle. "Can you imagine what that baby will look like?"

Raising my eyes from the letter, I said: "Rest assured, dear Muddy that, should such a happy eventuality occur, you—along with the rest of the world—will have ample opportunity to view the infant; for there can be little doubt that our good friend, Mr. Barnum, will waste no time in displaying the little prodigy to the public."

"Well," Sissy observed, "I just hope that Willie and Mr. O'Bannon are as happy as we are, Eddie."

"They certainly appear well-suited to each other," I replied. "It is doubtful, however, that any other couple could ever achieve the transcendent bliss that heaven has vouchsafed to us, dearest Sissy."

"Oh, Eddie," she replied, "how you talk."

Then she smiled, causing my heart—not like a grim ungainly fowl but rather like a glorious bird of the genus *Falco peregrinus*—to take wing and soar.